BALANCE OF FORTUNE

BALANCE OF FORTUNE

Mel Lee Newmin

OUT OF THIS WORLD PRESS
montclair ca

Balance of Fortune

Copyright © 2022 Mel Lee Newmin.

All rights reserved.
This is a work of fiction. Any similarities between actual persons, places, or events are entirely coincidental.

ISBN:

978-1-957224-02-2 (e-book)
978-1-957224-00-8 (hardcover)
978-1-957224-01-5 (softcover)

Library of Congress Control Number: 2021951164

Book design by David Yurkovich.

outofthisworldpress.com

DEDICATION

My thanks to everyone who supported my vision
Ann and Abby Newburger
Daniel and Dani Hoy
Lis King

MLN

BALANCE OF FORTUNE

BALANCE OF FORTUNE

1

Dispatch 598.584 Hemera, July 10, 2521 – EYES ONLY
Death's Festival destroyed. Total loss including cargo and crew. Ship's manifest being forwarded under priority security to gy'Bagrada. Request delicate handling. Imperative no filing of complaint with human commission. Direction required prior to renewal ceremony of Protocol 10 Rhadamanthus. Urgent.

Nick Severin's heart raced as he stared at the screen. The short missive, accidentally picked up by the listening post on Hemera, whispered of impending trouble and sent a shiver of apprehension down his spine. Praying he'd misread the message, Nick reviewed it again, parsing the words carefully in the original Gunera rather than rereading the English translation.

"Not going to the big centennial celebration?"

Nick jumped, having thought he was the last man standing in the Trade Commission office that Friday evening. Realizing it was his pal Corey Boyers, Nick relaxed.

"Wasn't planning on it." Nick's fingers tapped his desk as he pondered what to do about that damned message. "I have no desire to rub noses with the rich and powerful."

Corey snorted his agreement with Nick's assessment. "No, the political animal you are not. No-Nonsense Nick. Though I thought Secretary Huntzinger would insist on your presence since you're his second-in-command."

"Hmm." Nick rubbed his chin, mind focused on the fate of the *Death's Festival,* not the upcoming ceremony or his friend.

Corey frowned. "You okay?"

"Why would a standard cargo freighter have its shipping manifest forwarded to that miserable SOB?"

The muttering drew Corey to the side of Nick's obsessively well-organized desk. "What SOB?"

"gy'Bagrada." Nick scowled, mouth twisted as he spat out the name.

"What?"

Corey leaned in to peer at Nick's computer screen, but Nick clicked the window closed before his friend could view the message. Nick counted Corey among his few friends. But Trade Commission business was delicate at the best of times. Corey, a freight forwarder, knew Nick was privy to information unavailable to others in the business community. Sometimes Nick wondered if the only reason wealthy, golden-haired Corey had befriended him was to use him to get a jump on the competition.

A frown puckered Corey's brow. "Still getting messages from the section chief of the Guneri Secret Service?"

Nick rubbed his forehead to preempt an impending headache. "I've never stopped getting messages from the sick bastard. God, I hate the Gunera."

"What's he want?"

Nick retrieved a bottle of painkillers from a desk drawer. "I didn't say he *wanted* anything."

Corey straightened before folding his arms. Nick glanced up as he swallowed two caplets. For a brief instant, he thought he glimpsed an ugly grimace wash across Corey's disgustingly handsome face, but if so, it flitted away too quickly, and Corey resumed the persona of an unflappable businessman.

Corey fingered his chin. "You need to be careful around gy'Bagrada. The last time my company did business with him, it turned out he was moving surface-to-space missile launchers. Damned near got half my executive team arrested."

Nick didn't bother to remind Corey he personally knew more about gy'Bagrada than any other human alive.

"You guys overreacted if you ask me," Corey grumbled.

I didn't ask you. Nick caught himself before blurting the retort. *Don't be rude to your friends. You've too few as it is.*

Still, he felt he needed to defend the Commission.

"It was one hell of a violation, Corey. Not only was the gy' thumbing his nose to the Balance Protocols, but he was also waving a red flag in the face of the Amaurau. That stunt almost started a war."

"Yeah. Yeah," Corey replied. He'd heard it all before.

"We dropped the charges," Nick reminded.

"Yeah. Yeah." Corey gestured the comment away with a wave. "What brought up gy'Bagrada's name on this fine festival day?"

Nick jerked at the choice of the word *festival*. Was instantly suspicious but rebuked himself. Corey couldn't possibly know about the *Death's Festival*. At the moment, knowledge of the lost Guneri vessel was limited to him and the security team on Hemera.

You're seeing ghosts where there aren't any, Nick thought.

"The listening post on Hemera picked up a message containing gy'Bagrada's name." Nick began closing down his computer. The day was done, and it was time to go home. "I don't get it. The Gunera didn't bother to encode the transmission. Hemera couldn't read it, but I can."

"Sure. One of the advantages to being the only human who can read Gunera."

Nick shot Corey a hard look, seeking the censure, but Corey kept his Nordic face bland. "One of *three,*" Nick said, hating the defensive tone of his voice. He shook his head. "I don't understand why it wasn't encoded."

Corey shrugged. "Maybe the Gunera have figured out we've broken their codes." It was his turn to shoot Nick a hard look. "They've got to know you were put here on Rhadamanthus to spy on them."

"True."

Corey tilted his head to the left. "So what's bothering you?"

"The Gunera lost a ship, Corey."

"What do you mean lost? How do you lose a ship?"

"Reading between the lines, I think the Amaurau took it out." Nick spread his hands. "Why haven't they filed a complaint? Especially now, on the eve of the biggest Protocol renewal of the century? Trotting out Amaurau duplicity in front of the whole damned nebula is just the sort of bombastic propaganda I would expect from the Gunera, especially gy'Bagrada. There should be a half dozen filings hitting my desk: demands for restitution, blood to be boiled, an Amaurau or two hung from the rafters of city hall. Lord, that man loves twisting my balls."

A puzzled look stretched across Corey's face.

"It's like this," Nick explained. "Since the Gunera and Amaurau can never meet in person, the Trade Commission would handle the complaint. Which means *me*, the gy's damned errand boy. I'd bear the responsibility of tramping to the western edge of the nebula, having an unpleasant conversation with the Amaurau, and demanding concessions."

Corey grinned. "Okay, so why not simply be happy they haven't filed a complaint?"

Nick wanted to be happy. English didn't possess words to describe how much he longed for this. Unfortunately, it wasn't an emotion known to members of the Severin family, especially its last surviving member.

"So what's the plan for tonight, buddy?" Corey asked. His brilliant blue eyes swept the vast, empty cube farm just outside Nick's office. Everyone else had departed hours ago. "Sandy has to make an appearance at the party, but Jordan and I were going to McGuffy's to watch the game. Care to join us?"

A chime sounded on Nick's computer announcing an incoming video request. With a grunt of annoyance, he hit accept, and Les Johnson's pallid, balding head appeared in the viewscreen, bobbing like a fishing float. "Secretary Huntzinger wishes to see you, sir. In the residences, not his office."

Nick rolled his eyes. Duncan Huntzinger's office was next door. It had been empty all day.

"On my way." Nick abruptly closed the message and turned to his friend. "So much for your offer, Corey. Duty calls."

Corey scowled. "C'mon, No-Nonsense. Live a little. Come to McGuffy's. Deal with His Highness later."

Nick shuddered. What a choice. Hang out at a bar with a bunch of sports fanatics following a game he didn't understand or take word of the *Death's Festival* to his boss. Neither was particularly palatable. Nick longed to flee to his apartment and hide like he did every weekend.

"You once asked me to remind you when you start going Gunera on me," Corey noted matter-of-factly. "Putting business before a little fun is going Gunera. You need to mingle more. Learn a few social skills, buddy. Hell, get drunk and, dare I say, get laid for once." Corey placed his hands on Nick's shoulders and rocked him in his chair. "You could use it."

Nick sighed. Sex. Why was it so damned important to Corey? Why did both Corey and Duncan Huntzinger think that if he developed a sex life, Nick would suddenly become a "normal" human being? Nick was self-aware enough to realize there was nothing normal about him. Never would be.

"I've got to speak with Duncan first. I'll stop by afterward." Nick raised his hands. "I promise!"

Corey issued a disparaging look. "I'm holding you to it, Nick. I'll save a barstool for you."

"Thanks," Nick said half-heartedly.

Convinced that he'd given it his best shot, and with a carefree hop to his step, Corey headed for the standard Wednesday night revelry at McGuffy's.

Nick finished closing down his computer and its disturbing message. A glance out his window revealed the sun setting behind towering black thunderheads that cast great shadows across the jungles of Rhadamanthus, humanity's regional capital for the western lobe of the Fortuna Nebula.

A series of lights glimmered against the thunderheads as another ship made the curve through the atmosphere and headed toward the city. They'd been arriving like clockwork for the past two days. Protocols were renewed on a staggered five-year schedule, the Gunera on the zero year, the Amaurau on the five. Being Gunera 10, the centennial was a major event. Nick was aware that the Presidents of Hemera and Erebos had already jetted in with their ubiquitous staff and that the Secretary of State had been dragged all the way from

Earth, the poor fellow. Then there were the movie stars and opera singers and those who were known for being known. The whole affair had become a circus long before the Guneri representatives arrived. Nick was relieved to fret about cargo manifests and to have no dealings with that overwhelming display of pomp and circumstance.

Nick emptied what remained of his Earl Gray into the ficus next to his desk and wiped out the teacup while considering what to do. He needed to make Duncan aware of the message, but he questioned whether now—a handful of hours before the ceremony—was the best time to dump it onto the secretary's lap.

Tucking his keys in a trouser pocket, Nick closed his office door and exited the Geiger Center for International Trade and Economic Development. The July evening air bore a heavy threat of rain. Having lived his entire life in conditions far worse, Nick barely broke a sweat as he strode through the dense, beautifully landscaped jungles of the trade complex. Plants couldn't help but thrive on tropical Rhadamanthus. The temperature never dropped below 30 degrees Celsius, and it rained almost every day. The engineers who'd terraformed Rhadamanthus designed the minor planet as a safe haven for the endangered plants of Earth's disappearing tropical islands. Nick passed stands of lovely red hibiscus, a swath of ti grass threatening to overtake a walkway, and a grouping of highly endangered abutilon that appeared to be quite happy a billion miles from home as they lounged against the air conditioner of the patent office.

Great drops of rain began to fall, plopping like water balloons on the concrete walk, but Nick didn't increase his pace. He liked walking in the rain. A man born and raised in a tropical hothouse more prison than home, he relished the simple act of getting soaked in a downpour. Without a care, he stripped to the waist and turned his face upward, allowing the rain to run off his unfashionably long (by Rhadamanthus standards) dark hair. For a brief second, Nick considered stripping off his remaining clothes, but the startled glimpse from a woman racing past was a grim reminder that he was among humans now. Humans didn't walk naked through the streets. He slipped his shirt back on and continued along.

Upon arriving at the residences, Nick was buzzed through the security station without question. The officer grinned at his soaked appearance but said nothing. There wasn't a single person working for the Trade Commission who didn't consider Nick a strange bird.

Arriving rain-soaked to a visit with the International Trade Secretary on Independence Day was simply one more oddity for which Nick was so well known.

Duncan Huntzinger's extensive suite consumed the entire third floor of the long, low building while Nick occupied smaller digs on the first floor. Trotting up the stairs two at a time, he quickly arrived at his supervisor's front door. Nick pressed the doorbell and heard footsteps approach.

Cardaman, Duncan's valet, ushered Nick inside. The aging gentleman silently twitched his lips at the sight of Nick's rain-soaked appearance. He gestured toward the back of the suite to Duncan's bedroom.

Fully expecting to find his boss readying for the ceremony, Nick was surprised to find Duncan sitting in bed with a tray atop his lap, prematurely gray hair in a tumble around both shoulders.

Nick spun, expecting to see Cardaman behind him in readiness to prepare his master for the ceremony, but Cardaman had disappeared. Momentarily forgetting about the *Death's Festival* message, Nick anxiously approached the bed and studied his boss with concern.

"Duncan, what's going on? The ceremony starts in an hour."

Duncan Huntzinger cast aside the tray with a look of distaste. "I'm not going."

"What?" Nick looked desperately for Cardaman. He'd seen the venerable fellow order Duncan around in a way Nick could not. "You must, Duncan. It's not only a renewal, it's Protocol 10!"

"I'm quite aware of the number, Nico. The *centennial*."

"It might not mean a thing to you," Nick replied, trying not to rile his superior, "but it certainly means a lot to everyone else. For God's sake, Duncan, they dragged the Secretary of State all the way from Earth!"

"Yes! Yes! His lordship informed me that he'd arrived two days ago." Duncan sipped his tea and frowned. "I'm sick, Nico." Sensing Nick's confusion, Duncan elaborated. "As in throwing up anything that starts to go down. As in, no way in hell capable of handling not only all the mandatory schmoozing but the requisite eating as well. Dear God!" He held his hand to his stomach and belched. "Nope. Not happening."

Nick stood with his mouth agape and fumbled for an appropriate response. He wanted to drag Duncan from his bed and force him to dress, but a decade of etiquette lessons had taught him it simply wouldn't fly. His inability to react appropriately left Nick staring blankly at Duncan, hoping the man would throw him a lifeline. Tonight, however, Duncan wasn't in the mood to play the role of Nick's father as he'd so often done. He lay limply against his pillows watching as Nick dissolved into panic. There was, Nick realized, no empathy on his mentor's face. None of the usual bending of human social norms to ease the way for him. Vaguely, Nick heard the door of the suite open and close but was too gobsmacked to notice who had arrived. He heard, oddly, no announcement from Cardaman.

"Duncan … sir …" Nick stumbled to a halt, seeking the proper words rather than the ones he wanted to express. "Don't you think the Secretary of State, not to mention the Guneri ambassador, will be offended if you fail to make an appearance?"

Duncan discarded Nick's concern with a flick of his wrist. "Not at all, Nico. Because you're going in my place."

"Wait … what?"

Duncan gestured. "Someone from the Trade Commission has to be there, as you so helpfully pointed out. As I am presently indisposed, you'll have to do it."

Nick glared at Duncan, studying what he thought resembled a relatively healthy complexion. His mouth opened to spout a string of invectives, but he snapped it shut, aware that whenever he lost emotional control, the human on the receiving end had a problem with his honesty. Duncan was no exception. Nick clenched his fingers in an effort to keep them from dragging Duncan to his feet. Yet another annoying taboo he'd learned from Duncan. Humans generally avoided physical contact except in prescribed situations. Unfortunately, rattling a sick man to health wasn't one of those situations.

Dammit! Nick thought.

A rustle announced the soft-footed Cardaman as he entered with a pile of clothing across his outstretched arms. Nick's heart sank upon recognizing the attire. Full ambassadorial equipage, right down to the highly polished shoes. His own.

"Duncan! You *know* how I feel about talking to the Gunera."

The secretary brushed the words aside like he did anything not to his liking. "You don't have to *talk* to them. Well, of course you'll have to say hello and all that sort of diplomatic stuff. But you need not hold conversations with them. PDS. Be polite. Be diplomatic. Be silent. It's always worked for me."

Cardaman was already untying the cord from Nick's sopping hair. He tossed it distastefully aside. Before Nick could further complain, the efficient old fellow had whipped out a towel and was vigorously scrubbing the dark locks dry. A scuffle ensued when the valet ruthlessly relieved Nick of his shirt and began to towel off his torso.

"Give me that!" Nick growled, wresting the towel from Cardaman's hands and grudgingly drying his upper body. "Duncan, there's something we need to discuss …"

Cardaman extended a hand. "Your trousers, sir." He glared distastefully at the wet fabric clinging to Nick's legs.

Nick turned desperate eyes to his superior. "Seriously, Duncan, I *can* dress myself."

"Give it up, son," Duncan chuckled. "I fought that war and lost. Cardaman takes his job as the Keeper of the Torch of Propriety quite seriously. Let him dress you. We need to talk."

"Yes, we do. I really need …" Nick stopped in midsentence as Cardaman jerked Nick's pants free of his left foot, nearly knocking both men to the carpet. With a sigh of submission, Nick relinquished his care to the capable hands of Cardaman, suffering what he considered the humiliating experience of being dressed by one of the finest valets to ever graduate from the Cambridge School of Butlery.

Duncan watched with amusement as his protégé was transformed, layer by layer, from an awkward young man into the epitome of a diplomat. Nick couldn't tell if the amusement was the result of his sartorial transformation or because each new item he donned meant Duncan was that much further from having to attend the ceremony. Loose black trousers, no belt or other sort of metal fitting, preceded a tight-fitting black sweater. The tailored jacket, a single-breasted garment, unadorned without pockets or buttons and knee length (as dictated by both Gunera Protocol 1 and Amaurau Protocol 3), followed. *Lord, how just the length of the coat had been a source of conflict between the two alien species for nearly 30 years,* Nick thought, as Cardaman worked his way through the carefully dictated elements of a human diplomat's wardrobe.

Shoes flat and unadorned, the polish being the only item humans had inserted into the Protocols and only because it was, miraculously, the one matter over which neither the Gunera nor the Amaurau held an opinion. No jewelry allowed, not even a watch. Finally, the hair. Another source of infighting that had lasted almost 50 years. Couldn't be short because that would indicate a bias toward the Gunera. Couldn't be long because that would tip the scales toward the Amaurau. Shoulder length exactly, and always, without fail, tied in a queue. The queue denoted neutrality because neither the Gunera nor the Amaurau wore their own headdress in such fashion. Finally, the bow. A pert, black, taffeta construct. The ultimate indication of the human diplomat and the sort of regalia that made finding dates impossible. *Not that I could land a woman regardless of my attire,* Nick reminded himself.

Cardaman fussed with the length of Nick's sleeves, tugging them up so that they wouldn't hang over his hands and violate Protocol; specifically, Gunera 4 and Amaurau 7.

"Don't bother, Cardaman," Duncan stated as the ridiculous ritual continued. "His sleeves are deliberately too long."

The statement startled the ordinarily unflappable valet, and Cardaman fidgeted the sleeves upward yet again until the black tattoos on the back of each of Nick's wrists appeared. For a moment, Cardaman stared at the symbols. Embarrassed, he quickly shoved Nick's sleeves over the tattoos.

"My apologies, sir," the valet murmured. "I forgot you prefer to hide them."

"No need." Nick offered a weak smile.

"We could have them removed," Duncan commented, while watching Cardaman delint a spotlessly black Nick from head to foot.

Nick self-consciously rubbed one hand against the other. "It wouldn't do any good. I've got implants below the skin that can't be removed."

"I would think a good surgeon back on Earth could handle the job."

"Not without destroying the use of my hands." Nick's bitterness was palpable. "They're embedded into my radial nerve and can't be removed without damaging the nerve. That's the point. The only way to get rid of them is to chop off my hands."

"Bloody savages," Duncan muttered.

"Savages you're forcing me to court tonight." Nick let the dig fly before he could snatch it back.

"Yes, well, about that …" Nick eyed Duncan speculatively as the old man stumbled over his words. The single most important diplomat in the known universe had never, as far as Nick could recall, been at a loss for words. And yet tonight, in the company of a friend and coworker, he was practically speechless. What the hell was going on?

"I wasn't expected to make any sort of speech," Duncan stated. "If I had, I wouldn't be putting you in this position on such short notice. Wouldn't have been fair. The Secretary of State and the Presidents are handling the speeches. You simply need to show up and be polite. Smile a lot, not that the Gunera care, and keep conversations to a minimum." He lifted a finger. "Remember, you're wearing the uniform of the Trade Commission, and as such, you'll be viewed as the official in charge of the Protocols. Don't utter a single *yes* or *no* that doesn't apply to food and drink. And when it comes to drink, the answer is always *no*."

Nick nodded somberly, staring down at his black clothing. Even the color had been written into Gunera 1 and Amaurau 2 after a boatload of protests and posturing.

"Yes, sir."

"No! None of that! You aren't listening. Your best answer to any question is *I'll answer that after I've conferred with the office*."

Nick knew the job's requirements. He'd been with the Trade Commission for almost eight years, five of them on the front lines on Rhadamanthus. He *knew* what he was doing. While he might be completely inept when it came to human interaction, Nick was a genius with alien encounters, especially the Gunera. "Can I answer if they ask about my father?" he asked bitterly.

Duncan had the grace to flush at the blunt question. Nick's father had died before Nick was born. "I would recommend something like *his legacy is held in much regard,* or words to that effect."

Nick cringed. He could expect nothing else from Duncan. The man had been holding the uncivilized universe together for almost 20 years. The need to deflect any question had been hammered so deeply into him that he sometimes couldn't answer yes or no when asked if he wanted cream in his coffee. Nick found the art of deflection more difficult, but he was learning. He had the master as his coach.

"You'll do fine," Duncan stated, noticing Nick's face pale. "Be polite. Be vague. Be a shadow in the back of the room."

Nick sighed.

Duncan circled his finger in the air. "Turn around. Come here."

Nick stood beside the bed while Duncan smoothed the collarless jacket (Gunera 3 and Amaurau 4) then issued one last look.

Nick shifted uncomfortably. "Sir, there's something I think you should know. Hemera intercepted a message out of Gunera. It seems that a merchant ship, the *Death's Festival,* was destroyed yesterday."

Duncan's face didn't move. "Amaurau?"

"Unknown, but that's my impression. The ship's owner specifically asked that the incident not be reported to the Trade Commission. I thought that very odd."

Duncan's face remained unreadable. His fingers tapped the coverlet. "Odd during ordinary times but not, perhaps, on the centennial of the Protocols. Maybe someone's being sensitive about discussing ugliness during tonight's ceremony."

Nick gazed at his boss reproachfully. "When have you ever known the Gunera to be sensitive about anything?" When Duncan failed to reply, Nick continued. "I don't know what the ship was carrying, but its manifest was forwarded to gy'Bagrada on the QT."

Now he had the secretary's attention. "Really? That's very interesting. What else?"

"The end of the message stated, *Direction required prior to renewal ceremony of Protocol 10 Rhadamanthus. Urgent.*"

The secretary was silent.

"Sir, what do you think it means?"

Duncan's head jerked in Nick's direction. "What do *you* think it means?"

"I think the Gunera are up to something. I'm worried they'll take action during tonight's ceremony."

"They wouldn't try anything on such an important night! Hell, security will be up the yin yang with no weapons allowed for a million miles of the place. You've seen the details. We've got at least ten warbirds over our heads. And there'll only be 20 Gunera at the ceremony. What could they possibly do?"

Nick shrugged. "I don't know. I'm just worried. I'd be much happier if you were there."

Duncan issued a gentle slap on Nick's shoulder. "You'll do just fine, Nico. There's no one in the universe better versed on the Gunera than you. Just keep to the shadows, stay out of whatever happens, and report back what you see and hear. Try to have fun."

Fun, Nick thought morosely as Cardaman ushered him out of the apartment. *Fun. I'd rather undergo a root canal.*

Unfortunately, there was no avoiding the inevitable. Nick knew that someone needed to be present to represent the Trade Commission and, like it or not, he was that someone. Annoyed at his misfortune but resolute in his duty, Nick squared his shoulders purposefully and set off for the capitol complex. He had a job to do, and if there was one thing at which Nick excelled, it was getting the job done. Fortunately, the storm had blown through, and a brilliant sunset splashed across the heavens as a wondrous prelude to night.

The Capitol Building, constructed in the style of the ancient Roman Pantheon, possessed a dome so large that without its three separate climate control zones, it could have generated rain. The building was lit up like a rocket, spotlights playing across every balcony, cornice, and portico. Glancing skyward, Nick noticed a hovercraft which, he deduced, probably harbored a sniper or two. Security, as Duncan had indicated, was tight.

As he entered the Rose Room, Nick surveyed the territory to locate the shadowy corner where Duncan promised he could hide. The room, however, was not designed for hiding in corners. It was lit by a series of 50 crystal chandeliers while glittering sconces marched down the walls. Long tables filled the space with glowing candelabras at intervals along their length. The flicker of candlelight danced on the glassware, silverware, and gold chargers that made up the place settings for the evening meal. At the far end of the room stood a dais where a chamber orchestra played a medley of Strauss waltzes. The room's acoustics were magnificent and the sound of the "Blue Danube" washed over the quiet hum of pre-party conversation.

Twin bars stood on opposite sides of the room. Most of the guests hovered around them, guzzling wine and champagne. Nick counted three senators, five department heads, the current Poet Laureate, and President Tanaka of Erebos, all gathered in the midst of corporate interests currying favor. He had no interest in talking with any of them.

A hand grabbed Nick's right arm. It belonged to Jennifer De Walt, the President of Rhadamanthus. She was a lovely lady of African descent who had the softest, sweetest demeanor in public but who could, behind closed doors, cut the throats of her political rivals.

"Dear Mr. Severin," she greeted. "I'm so glad you were able to fill in for Mr. Huntzinger. I hope his illness isn't serious."

"Not in the least." Nick fought to mask his annoyance. He doubted Duncan was sick at all.

"Good! Good!" She continued to smile, although Nick was sure De Walt's mind was in a thousand other places rather than worrying about one silly diplomat, even if that one diplomat was the wingnut holding the universe together. "I truly hate to throw business at you so quickly, but the Guneri ambassador is insisting he speak with you. He became quite excited when he heard you were taking Mr. Huntzinger's place."

Nick felt his stomach cramp, and he wished he was legitimately ill. Nausea would be preferable to a private conversation with the Guneri ambassador. De Walt hauled him across the room toward the Guneri contingent and dropped Nick off with a quick introduction. Her smile indicated she was grateful that Nick bore the nasty task of keeping the celebrated guests happy.

Nick knew the Guneri ambassador gy'Gravinda. The Guneri lord was the epitome of his species, a smallish creature about two-thirds the height of the average human but bulkier. gy'Gravinda's three stubby legs worked, although he, like most Gunera, refused to use them. Instead, he moved via a personal hover-sled that enabled him to stand at eye level with his human allies. The lack of exercise assured that most Gunera were fat, and gy'Gravinda was no exception. He bulged out of his flamboyant court coat of blue, yellow, and red that looked like a bit of tattered quilting. The lord flaunted his power by the wealth of chartreuse lace that spilled from his wrists and ran down the front seam to his waist. *Not that he has a waist,* Nick thought. He didn't have a neck either. Guneri heads sat as a blob atop their shoulders. The gy's eyes were reptilian green, his mouth narrow with its disconcerting long, black tongue. Like most of his species, gy'Gravinda enjoyed flicking it at people, well aware that humans loathed the gesture. The final insult to human sensibilities was the gently fanning wings of air gills that protruded from his neck. These were in constant motion to absorb oxygen from the air. On that sultry night, the ambassadors were sweeping to and fro. gy'Gravinda's tail, a sinuous thing, was in constant motion as well, the barb on its end menacing.

From long experience traveling in the human sphere, gy'Gravinda was an expert on humans and the injuries a Gunera could inflict on them. The moment Nick arrived, gy'Gravinda lashed his tail gleefully, causing Nick to take a calculated step back, although he refused to show fear. The ambassador waved a thick, four-fingered hand encrusted with jewels as he belched a welcome. The grunt was as close as any Gunera got to laughing.

"What a pleasure to see you again, eh'Nicodemus!" he stated in Gunera, knowing full well no one outside of his entourage would understand. He was, therefore, free to be as obnoxious as he chose to the young human imprisoned by his uniform. "You look quite … voiceless … in all your somber black."

"Impartial, not voiceless," Nick returned, also in Gunera, struggling to keep his voice from revealing the anger that lanced through him at gy'Gravinda's provocative opener.

The Guneri lord drove his mover in a circle around his human prey, enjoying the fact that he could be as outrageous as he chose since Nick was constrained by his Protocols. "I must say I was delighted to learn that you'd been raised to the position of Messenger for the night. I so wanted to see how you've been progressing." The reptilian eyes shot up and down Nick's taller form. "Thickened up a bit," he commented rudely. "Put on that muscle male humans do when they've reached sexual maturity, yes?"

The Guneri habit of calling the Secretary of International Trade a *messenger* was a long and arrogant one, something Nick had expected. The crack at his masculinity was less easy to brush aside. "I've aged, gy'," he said. "As have you."

gy'Gravinda twitched his air gills, another mark of humor. "Well, well, this is a joyous night. A night for celebration, yes? Human Independence Day, some call it." He leaned close and pretended to whisper while Nick tried not to flinch in the close proximity of that damned tail barb. "I have another name for it, you know, eh.' I call it the day we Gunera bought humanity wholesale as our slaves rather than waste blood and money trying to take you the hard way. Good, eh?" His body shook as he gave three belches of fine humor.

"I have my own name for the day, gy'." Nick did not elaborate.

Nick sensed a disturbance among the Gunera. His eyes narrowed as he studied them. Like gy'Gravinda, the Gunera wore ostentatious clothes and fine jewels, though none quite up to the level of their ambassador's. They were all nobles of one sort or another. A gy' didn't travel with anyone lower than a vuh' and ordinarily wouldn't even deign to speak to an eh'. gy'Gravinda had always made an exception when the opportunity to torment eh'Nicodemus was in the offing. Before Nick could decide what had disrupted the group, the touch of a Guneri tail shocked him by tracing down his cheek before it wrapped around his neck.

Moving cautiously, Nick turned and found gy'Bagrada standing in a hover-b beside him. For a blinding second, Nick's vision whited out, and he lacked the words to respond to the blatant physical assault. His terror of the lord was so hardwired within him it froze his cortex, and he couldn't move. For one beat, his breathing stopped. Then the sounds of the orchestra broke through his panic and his eyes refocused on the hideous countenance of gy'Bagrada, the butcher of Lethe's Gate. *We're in the heart of the capitol, surrounded by thousands of human security,* Nick reminded himself. Nick had only to yell, and men would come running to secure the safety of one of the most important diplomats of the night.

gy'Gravinda was tickled by not only Nick's complete discomfiture but also by the outrageous assault his chief of security had dared to make on so high status a human.

"eh'Nicodemus, I believe you've met gy'Bagrada, yes?"

gy'Bagrada's hold upon Nick's throat continued. The tail barb stroked his victim's lips.

"Indeed, we've met," gy'Bagrada murmured, his emerald eyes probing Nick's. gy'Bagrada relished this entrapment of his nemesis. "Alas, we were never able to consummate our friendship. Events slipped away from us, did they not, eh'?"

Nick carefully raised his hands to unwind the tail from his neck. The initial shock having run its course, Nick was furious. Although he knew not a single human in the room understood what gy'Bagrada had just implied, the Gunera knew. He knew. The gy' was sexually obsessed with humans and got his kicks out of tormenting them. The tail assault had been an ownership statement, declaring Nick his sexual property. Even though no one in the group believed such a relationship existed, the fact that gy'Bagrada had been downright vulgar in a public gathering went beyond the pale.

gy'Bagrada allowed the human to free himself, slyly awaiting Nick's response.

"Human sexuality isn't like Guneri," Nick stated, refusing to allow his composure to break a second time. "The open display of sexual prowess shows a lack of it by he who displays it."

The barb sank deeper than gy'Bagrada's. Air gills fluttered as the group howled at the human's rebuke. Even gy'Gravinda couldn't help but laugh at his comrade's humiliation. gy'Bagrada's eyes flashed, and his gills stiffened with rage. Nick saw gy'Bagrada's hand clench and the barb move into thrust position, aimed for Nick's face. The other Gunera inched away. Not even gy'Gravinda would challenge his powerful compatriot. Although Nick knew he was in imminent danger from the vile gy', he nevertheless stood his ground. He'd run too many times from Guneri punishments and was through running. These creatures couldn't harm him anymore.

In a frozen tableau, the two aliens glared at one other, each demanding the other concede; gy'Bagrada knew he could strike his opponent before human security could save him. Nick knew his nemesis would pay dearly after the fact. The remainder of the Gunera stood in a circle, none daring to intervene as the stalemate grew uncomfortable. gy'Bagrada moved first. He lashed with his barb and grazed Nick's cheek, drawing a faint line of blood, but it had been a calculated miss. Nick hadn't flinched, hadn't moved. Even after the barb withdrew and a trickle of blood started down his cheek, Nick didn't lose his focus or brush the blood away.

gy'Bagrada grunted his reluctant approval. "You're growing up, eh."

"While you, sir, are still an ass."

gy'Gravinda chuckled. "Stand at ease, eh'Nicodemus. There'll be no more bloodshed tonight." Nick darted a look at the security officer, who glared back but said nothing. The ambassador patted Nick on the arm. "You have indeed grown into a mature man, haven't you? I, for one, will continue to enjoy watching as you come into your own."

"As will I," murmured gy'Bagrada.

As Nick sought some escape, a waiter carrying a tray bore down on the group. The woman offered him a selection of miniature quiches. Nick, stomach still roiling from the encounter with the Gunera, declined. The woman upended the tray to reveal the underside where a knife had been fastened. Nick tried to grasp the incongruity. The woman secured the weapon and lunged for gy'Gravinda, thrusting the blade at the ambassador's chest. Nick, envisioning a century of peace talks exploding in a sea of yellow Guneri blood, threw himself at the would-be assassin just as she reached ambassador gy'Gravinda. The three collided and fell to the ground. The woman continued her assault, slashing blindly. The blade slashed into Nick's left arm. He growled in pain as he clawed for the knife. The room erupted in chaos as the innocent ran to escape the mayhem, and security rushed forward to stop it.

Nick managed to roll the executioner away from gy'Gravinda only to be locked in a struggle for the knife. The next few moments were a blur. The knife was wrenched away, and the woman was struck in the face. She screamed, and her hands leaped to the bloom of blood sprouting from what remained of her left eye. gy'Bagrada's barbed tail slammed her a second time, extracting her right eye. The woman's movement ceased. Her blood-soaked hands pressed to her face as a security team arrived. Before anyone could assist Nick, the lithe Guneri tail encircled his chest and pulled him out of the fray. Nick found himself clutched in the tail and arms of gy'Bagrada.

"You're wounded," the gy' purred, his left hand tugging the sleeve of Nick's jacket to reveal the forearm injury.

"It's nothing," Nick muttered, wanting to escape that horrible grip. Knowing the strength of a Guneri tail, however, Nick could do nothing until gy'Bagrada released him. The gy' in the meantime was having a grand time of the experience.

Stubby fingers rubbed the tattoo on Nick's wrist. "You're still ours, you know," the Guneri lord murmured in his ear.

"You view all humans as your servants," Nick growled. "Release me."

"All humans are servants, yes. You, however, are our *property*. Don't forget it."

"I'm the human representative of the Protocols tonight. And you're breaking about 50 of them."

"I'm merely protecting the human who so valiantly defended our ambassador. What's to protest about that?"

"You're feeling me up. I don't like it!"

"In the future, you must tell me how to please you so that you desire it for yourself." The tail unwound, and Nick staggered free, and he tried again to regain his composure.

The security team hauled the blinded murderess away while the lieutenant in charge babbled a weak explanation to the crowd that the fracas had been a misunderstanding and no further danger existed. The man was beside himself with embarrassment as he apologized to the ambassador. To Nick's surprise, the Guneri lord handled the episode with aplomb.

"No matter," he commented through his personal interpreter. "We're aware of factions within both our cultures that don't appreciate the mingling of species. No harm was done to me or mine and, therefore, there was no harm done to the Protocols." He gestured toward Nick. "Please see to your own representative. His blood was drawn rather than mine."

A paramedic grasped Nick's elbow and led him through the jabbering crowd. A stout woman, she easily cleared a path and walked Nick to a small room staged as an emergency medical center. She tugged at Nick's sleeve to study his wound, gasping at the tattoo.

"Prisoner of war," he murmured.

"My family has lived in the Fortuna Nebula for three generations, sir," the woman said while cleaning the wound. "I know what both the Gunera and Amaurau do to their prisoners. This isn't something they do." She studied Nick's stony expression. "You're Nick Severin, aren't you? I'd heard the stories but hadn't thought them true. I'm so very sorry."

Nick said nothing. He couldn't escape what he was, what the Gunera had made him into. He could only learn to live with the results. The stranger didn't press him. She bandaged Nick's arm, offered a smile, and left to sterilize her equipment.

The reprieve in the makeshift medical center provided Nick an opportunity to hide. When the state dinner was served, Nick ate a small portion from the platter the paramedic brought him. He claimed to be in extreme pain from the injury, but the paramedic saw through the lie. Still, the ruse enabled Nick to avoid the long-winded opening speeches from the two Presidents and the Secretary of State.

gy'Gravinda also made a short speech. He read from a phonetic English script, rendering his words nearly impossible to understand. He reiterated that the bond between humanity and the Gunera remained strong, adding that his people hoped for another century of progress and goodwill. gy'Gravinda concluded with an impromptu statement in poorly worded English that he remained touched by the actions of the human messenger who'd risked his life to protect Guneri interests. "I hope to see more of such a remarkable human in the future." The words made Nick want to gag, but he knew it would play prominently on the newsfeeds.

Nick reemerged long after the speeches were over, knowing that the event was winding down. There was dancing by those who'd consumed too much to drink and schmoozing by those with agendas to accomplish, but the worst of the ordeal was over. Midnight had long passed, and Nick knew that once the Gunera left the building, he could escape.

Upon returning to the Rose Room, Nick was greeted by several people who'd witnessed the attack on the ambassador. He was welcomed as a hero and thanked for his courage. Several pondered what might have happened if the assassin had succeeded in killing the ambassador.

"Open warfare, probably," Nick muttered.

A hand curled around Nick's arm, and he cringed. *What now?* To his relief, it was Alessandra McCoy. The senator's daughter, adorned in a gown of beaded pink lace, was a vision of loveliness. She'd piled her luscious brown locks atop her head and allowed a handful of spirals to drop to her smooth snowy neck, where a diamond necklace gleamed demurely. Nick swayed toward her, determined to nibble on that neck, but she stopped him with a touch to his cheek.

"Remember your human manners, Nick," she laughed. "No sex in public." Alessandra's taupe eyes gazed into Nick's dark ones. "Are you all right? Someone said you'd been injured."

Nick slid his jacket sleeve to reveal the knife wound. Alessandra's fingers lightly touched the tattoo, but she knew not to speak of it. She moved the sleeve down to cover it again.

"What was with the nasty Gunera and his tail?" she asked.

Nick cringed, wondering how many people had witnessed or recorded the encounter.

Alessandra's eyes remained soft and warm. "I'm not going to judge you." She was a marvel. One of a few humans willing to work with such a damaged man. "I can tell it upset you. You don't normally blanch white in diplomatic situations. What happened?"

"gy'Bagrada made a sexual advance."

"In the middle of a major diplomatic event?"

"The Gunera have no scruples whatsoever."

"That thing is female?" Alessandra asked, startled.

"Not exactly. The Gunera are hermaphrodites. They only have one gender."

Alessandra's mouth gaped open. "That explains a lot, doesn't it?" she murmured.

Nick didn't answer. The comment went deeper than it appeared on the surface. He stood beside Alessandra, mute and uncomfortable.

"Long night," she offered, issuing a half-hearted smile.

Nick nodded, knowing Alessandra was just trying to be nice. As usual, when he was around her, Nick's tongue tripped over itself as he struggled to devise a clever retort. None came.

"Dinner next week?" she suggested.

"Sure, I'd love that," Nick answered, questioning the sincerity of his words.

He liked Alessandra. She had a warm heart and good intentions. And lord knew he desired her body. She was a stunning thing. Probably one of the biggest catches in the entire Fortuna Nebula, considering who her parents were. He just didn't understand what she saw in him. Why would a beautiful woman like Alessandra, who could snare any man in the galaxy, waste her time courting the awkward undersecretary of trade? *Pity? Charity case?* Those thoughts ran through Nick's mind in his darkest moments. *Trying to show the world what a wonderful person she was by taking me in hand and attempting to make a human of me?* That was a personal favorite. *Actually interested in me because of my looks or personality? Doubtful,* he reasoned.

Nick had no idea how to define their relationship or if it actually existed. He was too tongue-tied most of the time, too unsure of himself and of her. *Too awkward.* That was the heart of the matter. Nick wasn't right, and he knew it. He also knew he had nothing to offer a senator's daughter because all he'd ever been—and ever would be—was a low-level civil servant. Were he to succeed Duncan and be appointed secretary, Nick's life would become an even greater tangle of complications. He'd officially become the damned wingnut that held the universe together. He doubted there was space in a wingnut's life for a woman. Duncan had never managed it.

To his dismay, Nick heard the rumble of conversation strangle short. The throng of hangers-on was edging away. In mere seconds, he and Alessandra went from being just two people in a crowd to standing utterly alone with a circle of humanity crowded against the walls.

Nick's panicked eyes darted to the door where a contingent of Amaurau now stood. His chest tightened, and he mouthed the only words that came to mind, knowing everyone could read them.

I am so fucked.

2

No one moved. All eyes were focused on the lone couple standing in the middle of the room, the senator's daughter glimmering in pink and the Protocol officer dressed in black. Nick stared at the seven Amaurau party crashers. They, in turn, stared back.

Nick nudged Alessandra away from him. "Go. Find your father."

Alessandra knew better than to reply. She gave Nick's hand a squeeze and slipped away, leaving Nick alone in the middle of a disaster in the making.

What the hell are they doing here? Nick wondered, as the agonizing silence continued. For 100 years, humanity had stood as the bulwark keeping the two blood-sworn enemies apart. For 100 years, no Gunera or Amaurau had seen or spoken to the other or had any interaction aside from blowing each other to pieces at a distance. For 100 years, the two sets of Protocols had kept an uneasy balance between the three powers. And now, on Nick's watch, the whole bloody structure was about to come crashing down.

No one in the room possessed the authority to speak to the Amaurau except the Protocol officer. Which was why the crowd had quickly parted like the Red Sea for Moses. Everyone stood waiting for the Protocol officer to do his job, to throw himself into the breach before war spontaneously erupted.

Nick drew a deep breath, reminded himself of everything at stake, and stepped forward, his head high and his body language as neutral as possible. He stopped a few meters from the Amaurau and made the hard switch from Guneri etiquette to Amaurau. He set his right foot behind his left and performed the strange, pretzel-like curtsy that was required of the Protocol officer to the Amaurau ambassador.

Nick blanked while he navigated the switch from English to the soft, flowing Amaurau tongue. Then he found his footing.

"Greetings, noble friends. Humanity bids you welcome."

The leader of the Amaurau was a stately creature, as were all of his kind. The species had more in common with humans than did the Gunera. They walked on two legs but were far taller, so they loomed over the average human. They also possessed two feathered arms. Although Nick had never seen an Amaurau fly, it was supposed that they could. Their skeletal structure appeared to be light enough, and they possessed the musculature in their shoulders that hinted at such power. Ovoid heads sat atop long graceful necks that could rotate in a full circle. Their pale bodies were feathered with a soft down reminiscent of newly hatched chicks. Their eyes were large and round, mostly pupil, and had a birdlike manner of darting in a jerky fashion. Long feathers atop their heads fell in a graceful cascade down the Amaurau backs, such that they resembled long-haired humans. Earth scientists speculated that the feathers were a rudder system used in flight. Nick knew the Amaurau could move those feathers if they wanted.

The leader's pale gray head feathers were lying flat against his head, indicating a lack of alarm. He surveyed the room by twisting his head, causing his long, thin earrings to flash in the light. He wore traditional Amaurau attire, a flowing floor-length skirt, and a sleeveless vest made of fabric that shimmered as it moved. His feathered arms were bare, allowing him, Nick supposed, to take flight. His rank was denoted by a circlet of silver resting atop his head feathers.

The leader's companions were similar, varying only in height and the color of their feathers, trending from chocolate brown to ivory. One was speckled. They were, Nick realized in alarm, all heavily armed.

Nick struggled to mask his panic as he realized human security either didn't understand Amaurau weaponry or had been so overwhelmed by the cadre's appearance that they'd let the group enter without a search. Nick's experienced eyes were well aware that what looked like a plastic staff was, in fact, a poisoned-point spear. Their swaying "necklaces" contained stones that would explode if exposed to water. And lying pressed along the forearms of every Amaurau present were the lyssestra, traditional hunting weapons of their species. These long, thin sticks could be unfolded into throwing armaments able to shoot poisoned darts at an enemy while in flight.

The leader studied Nick for the longest minute of his life. Nervously, Nick reviewed his curtsy and his choice of greeting, wondering if he might have erred. He seldom spoke the difficult Amaurau tongue. What little communication he held with the species was usually in writing. For a panicked second, Nick wondered if he'd unintentionally insulted the ambassador.

Finally, the leader spoke in a soft, gentle tone typical of his kind. "Honorable Minister, your embellishment is askew."

Nick blinked, wondering what the alien meant and questioning whether he'd translated the statement correctly.

To his astonishment, the creature extended a delicate hand and adjusted the bow in Nick's hair.

"One must readjust after athletic endeavors," the Amaurau stated with a birdlike tilt of his head.

Nick froze. Somehow the Amaurau were aware of his tangle with the waitress. He had no idea what that meant. Had they been here longer than anyone realized and been witness to the debacle? Had they planted surveillance equipment in the room? Were Amaurau spies present?

"Please accept the humble apologies of this minister," he fumbled, trying to remember the torturous courtesies language required. "No offense was intended."

The Amaurau raised a feathered eyebrow. He extended a finger and tapped Nick's chest. "You're much younger than Minister Huntzinger. And better mannered. I think I'm going to like you more than anyone liked your predecessor."

Once again, Nick's thoughts circled in confusion. What made this creature think he'd taken over Duncan's position? Why had he spoken with such confidence? Who knew if Nick would become Duncan's successor? *What,* he wondered, *in the name of Jagjekcek was going on?*

Nick knew better than to contradict an alien ambassador. He opted for the always safe fallback position of remaining silent.

"Your name, Honorable Minister?" the Amaurau asked.

Still unable to pull his wits together, Nick blurted, "Nicodemus Severin, Undersecretary of International Trade."

"Minister Severin, I am Sevay Ississita." He lifted his chin and surveyed the room. "I would speak with you in a place more conducive to introspection."

Once again, the alien had left Nick stumbling for words. If he understood nothing else, Nick knew it was imperative that he spirit the Amaurau contingent out of that room before the Gunera started hurling Protocol violations at everyone. At the same time, Nick knew he needed to lay himself at gy'Gravinda's feet and beg forgiveness to stave off Armageddon.

Oh God, oh God, oh God. Someone needs to clone me, and they need to do it right now.

Deciding Sevay Ississita might be the more amenable to persuasion given he'd crashed the party, Nick elected to pawn him off. That would give Nick the breathing room necessary to deal with the anger problem mushrooming near the orchestra. Desperately, Nick motioned to Jennifer De Walt, eyes begging her to step forward. The tiny woman darted to his side. Her attempt to emulate the convoluted bow-curtsy required for the Amaurau resulted in looks of amusement.

"Sevay Ississita," Nick began, "it's my honor to introduce you to the current President of Rhadamanthus, Lady Jennifer De Walt. If it would please you, she will see you to a quiet room whereby your concerns might be addressed."

Ississita quirked a brow, still apparently amused by the hoopla his appearance had caused. He then bowed to the esteemed lady, who didn't speak Amaurau, and motioned that she should lead forth.

"My apologies, Madame President," Nick said, forcing his brain back to English. "We have to get them out of here before the Gunera go off the deep end. Please find them a safe and quiet place. I'll get there when I can."

De Walt knew the makings of an international incident when she saw one. She was aware that the only person qualified to speak with the Amaurau had no choice but to handle the Gunera. During the time that had elapsed, the Gunera had collected their wits and were preparing a charge, though whether their intended target was the party-crashing Amaurau or the recalcitrant hosts that had let the damned creatures in remained to be seen. The president issued Nick a bracing smile before smiling at Ississita and gesturing for him to follow her. Jennifer frantically waved at security as she led her pack of silent, stoic party crashers from the room.

Nick breathed a momentary sigh of relief that he'd gotten the Amaurau out of Guneri sight. Turning, he forced another useless but required smile across his face and prepared to fend off the attack that approached him full bore. gy'Gravinda and gy'Bagrada charged at him on their movers, the remainder of their contingent rolling in a line by rank behind them. The sea of humanity continued to stand in silent horror, watching to see whether the young undersecretary might resolve this mess. In a moment of lucidity, Nick wondered if anyone had thought to claw Duncan from his bed so that he might bail out his subordinate, who was sinking faster than the *RMS Titanic*.

"eh'Nicodemus!" gy'Gravinda shouted. "This is unacceptable! Who in the name of Jagjekcek thought it appropriate to allow such filth into my ceremony? At no time and in no place whatsoever are we and those ... those ... vermin ... to be afforded the same diplomatic status. What does humanity think it's doing? Are you telling us we were fools to sign Protocol 10?"

Nick raised his hands to placate the Guneri ambassador. "My most humble apologies, gy'." He stumbled over the words as he made the rapid change to yet another language and set of cultural norms. His head was splitting. "I lay myself at your feet prostrate with woe at this terrible insult to your honor. Humanity did not know the ..." He caught himself before he made the mistake of saying the name Amaurau to the Gunera. "... that such persons would arrive like this."

"You expect us to believe such a contrived story?" exclaimed gy'Bagrada. His tail whipped in the air, threatening Nick's eye. "I want blood, eh'Nicodemus."

gy'Gravinda, unwilling to be upstaged by his security chief, stabbed Nick's chest with his own barb, causing Nick's heart to miss a beat. "Treachery!" he spat. "Vile human treachery. We should have known you're incapable of honor."

Nick forced himself to ignore the panic threatening to overwhelm him. He pressed his hands together in an involuntary attitude of supplication that he doubted the Gunera would understand. "Please allow your humble servant to assure you that is not the case. We didn't know of their arrival."

"Says much for your security," sniped gy'Bagrada. "I'll have a head, eh'Nicodemus. I demand it."

Again Nick froze. Exactly whose head did the security chief want? His? Time for more of Duncan's fog.

"I will direct your request to the appropriate agency for consideration," he muttered.

The security chief's tail flashed. Nick ducked to avoid being struck. Then, to his horror, gy'Bagrada sent his mover whizzing down the room. As he turned at the far end, the Gunera's tail caught the ear of one of the human guards, hurling her across the room. The humans nearby scattered to escape a similar fate.

Nick cautiously advanced toward gy'Gravinda, whom he'd always considered saner than gy'Bagrada. "I swear on the hundred years of the Protocols that we didn't expect *their* ... arrival ... tonight. There's no treachery on the part of humanity and no ill will toward your esteemed party. Humanity grants no more honor to ... the arrivals ... than we do to your company."

"And yet vuh' De Walt has seen fit to escort them as if they are due such lofty regard," snipped the Guneri ambassador. "Why is your vuh' not here placating our wounded affections?"

"Because someone needed to get the damned Amaurau out of here," Nick growled, forgetting to use courtly language. He caught himself and forced his head back into diplomatic mode. "Again, I lay myself at your feet prostrate with grief that your affections are wounded. Tell me, great gy', how humanity might soothe your distress."

gy'Bagrada returned on his mover, his bloodied tail twitching happily in the air. He fluttered his air gills, barb pointed at Nick. "The punishment of that stupid guard was a start but did not satisfy enough." His eyes flicked at Nick in annoyance. "For all your courtly speech, I don't see you lying prostrate with grief at my feet, eh'Nicodemus."

Nick gulped. He wondered if, in the 100 years of the Protocols, a Gunera had ever demanded a human carry out the ceremonial words of prostration. He didn't think so. Nick despised the thought of being the first human to yield to the request. It would set an ignominious precedent for which he'd be hated for centuries.

His mind was still running all the options when gy'Bagrada nudged him with a finger.

"I might have a suggestion that would soothe my distress," he said. Nick froze, once again unable to focus.

Fortunately, gy'Gravinda wasn't in the mood for his security chief's peccadilloes. "There's time enough for seductions later, gy'," he reproved. "For myself, I would suffice to hear from the mouth of eh'Nicodemus that humanity has no intention of breaking its own protocols. I would further demand his full and complete prostration before me."

Nick closed his eyes and breathed slowly. He scrambled for the only weapon available, the Protocols. There was his salvation found. "I assure the esteemed gy' that humanity has no intention of breaking the Protocols. I would further state that to place the human Protocol officer prostrate at the feet of the Guneri ambassador in such an open forum would breach Protocol G.6 subsection 2b.01 by providing an excess of honor to the Gunera that has never been demanded by the … counterparty."

gy'Gravinda belched at Nick's rhetoric. "By death's gracious touch, you're a slippery one, eh'!" he chortled. "Is there any clause in the damned Protocols you can't conjure up at will? Very well. I release you from the act of lying at my feet, much as I would have delighted in witnessing it. I will refrain from the demand. I will also refrain from filing an official protest of Protocol violation if those vermin are removed not just from my presence but from this building, this city, this planet, and this solar system."

Nick bowed frantically. "I will endeavor to convey your wishes to those with the authority to carry them out," he managed to burble, finding more of Duncan's fog. His eyes fell on the catering crew near the buffet tables. Nearly half the dessert course had been set up. Mumbling words he hoped were polite to the gy's, Nick hastened to the table and hissed at the caterers.

"Feed them. Now." He gestured at the still miffed Gunera. "Give them the entire course if necessary, but keep their mouths full and their minds on their stomachs."

"Would alcohol help?" one of the younger caterers asked.

Nick smiled, wishing he'd had the wherewithal to recall that alcohol had a depressive effect on Gunera. "Yes, it would. Open as many bottles as necessary and keep glasses full. "

Trying not to move with too much haste lest he cause even more consternation among the human guests, Nick made his excuses and headed in the direction De Walt and company had gone. A soft drone of whispered conversations rose as guests and staff discussed the unprecedented events of the evening. Nick heard mention of his name and hoped the mumblings were positive. A quick glance at the

President of Erebos and Secretary of State Millingham revealed their sense of relief that the worst was over. Each dignitary issued a faint nod which Nick returned as he slipped out a side door.

Security sprang into action, rushing Nick through the outer hallway. They moved ahead of him, pushing through the crowd as it chattered about the unprecedented vision of Amaurau on Rhadamanthus. Suddenly, Nick realized he'd gone from being an unimportant minor functionary at a ceremonial event to being the single most important human in the building. *How in God's name,* he wondered, *had that happened?*

While being ushered through another door, Nick smoothed his coat and hair, hoping that everything was in its proper place. The Amaurau placed less emphasis on appearances than the Gunera but being on point still mattered. Nick was relieved to think he might have soothed the fractious Gunera, but he suspected the more difficult interview was still ahead.

Jennifer De Walt spoke only English. No Amaurau would deign to learn another's language, so the group waited in silence. The President whirled at Nick's entrance, relief washing over her dark features. She approached him sedately to avoid sending a message of panic to the Amaurau. Nick lowered his head so that Jennifer could whisper in his ear, lest somehow the Amaurau miraculously started understanding English.

"How's everything with our reptilian friends?"

"As well as can be expected. They're with the catering crew. I suspect the human guests are going to miss out on dessert."

"Do you anticipate backlash?"

Nick shrugged. "I don't know. I explained that we had no idea the birds," he deliberately avoided saying "Amaurau" to keep that contingent from hearing the name, "were going to crash the party. They seemed to believe me."

De Walt drew a huge breath. "I suppose we won't know until they've had a chance to digest all this and our entire 500-piece dessert buffet."

"When were they scheduled to off-world?"

"In three days. gy'Gravinda wants to tour the copper mines. Worried about us meeting our quotas, yada yada."

"Get them out of here tomorrow if you can. I'll do my best to get our bird buddies off-world as well."

De Walt agreed. With a nod, she sailed from the room.

Determined to extricate himself from the morass into which he seemed to be sinking ever deeper, Nick drew a breath, tried to settle his brain into Amaurau mode, placed his arms behind his back, and faced his second set of problems for the night.

Sevay Ississita didn't give him a chance to speak. "A difficult evening to be sure, Minister Nicodemus," he said, an amused look still present on his face.

The process of translating the ambassador's gentle statement took a moment, given the complexities of the language. Nick considered the proper courtly response and was pleased with his choice. "One endeavors to find common points of consensus so that all discussions are fruitful, Sevay." *God,* he thought, *I'm beginning to sound just like Duncan!*

Ississita appeared to enjoy keeping the human Protocol officer off balance. He gestured toward the French doors that led into the magnificent Versailles-style gardens behind the capitol building. "Forgive the impertinence, Minister," he murmured, "but we of the Amaurau enjoy the wind in our feathers. I would move our conversation out of doors." Ississita gave the beleaguered Protocol officer no chance to counter as he quickly nipped outside before Nick could offer up a polite way to decline.

The contingent of Amaurau circled around Nick, who realized he was bearing witness to his own kidnapping. None of the human security officers felt confident to follow too closely. However, once the group had stepped outside, Nick drew a breath of relief. The sky still sparkled with the lights of hovercraft, and he knew they were locked into the sights of at least ten snipers. Nothing too horrid could happen to him unless the Amaurau were to attack with their lyssestra faster than the human snipers could shoot. Or unless the snipers vacillated for fear of starting another war. Better perhaps to let a single human diplomat die rather than kill an entire Amaurau delegation. It was a sobering but all-too-possible option.

A brisk wind was blowing, an aftereffect of the earlier storm, but now the night sky was clear and spangled with stars. The brilliant red filaments of the Fortuna Nebula ran east-west across the sky and shimmered like an aurora as they did every night. The serene beauty belied the ugliness that had been the history of life in the Nebula.

Ississita seemed pleased to feel the breeze, perhaps because, as a flighted species, he preferred the open air above his head. *The lot of them could probably fly away,* Nick thought, as he watched the breeze picking at all the Amauraus' feathers.

When Ississita next spoke, Nick wondered if telepathy was another hidden talent of Amaurau.

"I hope all the disturbed feathers have been preened."

Nick placed both hands behind his back and dropped his mind into full diplomatic mode, this time in the vastly different Amaurau style: subtle and careful and oh-so polite. "One is assured that all guests have their feathers in place."

"Our arrival caused a bit of a stir," Ississita stated.

Nick gritted his teeth. He sensed the alien was testing him.

"No harm was done. No untoward actions took place."

"No bloodshed?" Ississita chuckled. "Dear me, no! That wasn't our intent."

Nick stood silent. Ississita was baiting Nick to ask a question, but Nick wasn't about to give him the satisfaction of a reply. Protocol officers answered questions. They didn't pose them.

The tall bird man gazed down at Nick with a wicked gleam in his dark eyes. "Can you never ask a question?"

Nick held back the retort he wanted to spout as he drew a breath. "The province of the Protocol officer is to merely assure that all sections, subsections, addenda, and appendices of the Protocol currently in force are maintained by all parties at all times."

"Including yourself, Protocol officer?"

Nick jerked and glanced down at himself, wondering what might be out of place. To his astonishment, the lady in the group with brown speckled feathers slipped up alongside him and, with deft fingers, nipped the bow from his hair. Despite Nick's protests, she tangled those fingers in the queue, shaking it loose so that Nick's hair fell loose around his shoulders. The breeze sent it blowing into his face. The lovely bird lady danced out of reach, denying Nick the opportunity to regain the bow. It would be highly improper to chase the woman around the capitol gardens in the dark, so Nick merely stood in bemused silence wondering what the hell was going on.

"Much better," she commented with a giggle, extending the bow and teasing him with it.

Nick's hands raced to adjust his hair.

"Relax, Minister Nicodemus," Ississita said. "The requirement for the queue came from Gunera 5 after we demanded the longer hair in Amaurau 4. I find nothing offensive in leaving your feathers free. Sena Dessessah here prefers it that way."

Nick gaped at the lot of them. The Amaurau were playing games with him, had been from the moment they'd entered the Rose Room, but he had no idea why. Nick desperately wanted to ask what in the name of Jagjekcek they were doing here.

Ississita started a slow stroll into the gardens, forcing Nick to fall into step beside him. "Your feathers are ruffled because we're here five years early."

"Protocol 10 for the Amaurau, should your people choose to renew, isn't due for another five years," Nick stated automatically.

"What would happen if I told you we didn't intend to renew?"

Nick's mind froze, and for ten steps, he could think of nothing to say. "The distress felt by humanity would be profound," he finally burbled.

"For *all* of humanity or only for some?"

Once again, brain freeze. What was going on?

Ississita continued his stroll past a series of fountains that appeared to please him. He extended a hand to allow the water to cascade through his fingers. Nick thought nervously of the ambassador's six-piece guard unit, each of whom wore water-triggered grenade necklaces.

"For 100 years, humans have held the breach between Amaurau and Gunera," Ississita stated. "Don't think we Amaurau have forgotten why humans chose the position they did. It wasn't out of some grand design or magnanimous desire to see peace in the universe. You did it because you had no choice. You were losing the war against the Gunera, and in a matter of years, all of humanity would have been their slaves. Is this not true?"

"That's how it's written in our history books."

"So what was a beleaguered, outgunned humanity to do?" asked Ississita. "You knew we were using the distraction provided by the war between humans and Gunera to further our own ends against a common enemy. You knew you could use our agenda against us. So you bargained to buy Amaurau aid."

"You refused."

"We *delayed*," stated Ississita. "We hadn't decided if we wanted humans as friends. So you turned on us. Used us. Lied to the Gunera and convinced them we'd back you. Convinced them that if they didn't end the war with humans, the Amaurau would come charging down their throats and pinch them between the two forces. It was actually true, you know. We were intent on pinching the Gunera and using humans as the anvil against which to do it. Very clever of you to use our tactics for your own advantage."

Nick remained silent, knowing everything the Amaurau gentleman said was true. Humanity had played the two enemies against each other in hopes of saving itself.

"But of course you couldn't guarantee your safety," Ississita continued, as the stroll took them ever deeper into the gardens. Once again, Nick felt his tension rise. Even with the handful of lampposts, the garden was dark, and he was a thousand meters from the nearest security team. *Alone with an alien species,* he thought. *A suddenly hostile alien species.*

"What if the Gunera learned of your lies? What if they realized the Amaurau were attacking them not because of some agreement with humans but merely because it was convenient for them to do so at a time when Guneri attention was directed at humans? So you spun around as soon as you had the necessary breathing room. You lied to us. Told us you'd reached an agreement with the Gunera that had ended the war between the two of you. Threatened that if we didn't reach an agreement with humans, we'd be facing the combined forces of humans and Gunera staring *us* down the throat. Yes?"

"I've heard it said," Nick mumbled.

Ississita waved his hands. "You got what you wanted. Protocol 1 with the Gunera guaranteeing an end to hostilities and the beginnings of, if not friendship then, at least, détente. And Protocol 1 with the Amaurau bought you the same arrangement with us five years later. So now here we are 100 years along the tree branch, humanity growing in numbers and economic strength. You've become so invaluable as a go-between that neither the Gunera nor Amaurau dare to upset the balance for fear humanity will pull the plug and all our peace and tranquility will fly away with the wind."

"The Sevay implied that the Amaurau are considering pulling the plug."

"Did I?" Ississita tapped his chin. "How would that make you feel?"

"I believe I stated that humanity would be greatly distressed." Nick was bewildered. Where was all this going?

"You've made a lot of money being the only trading partner to handle the transshipments between the two empires."

"There has been economic gain for all parties involved," Nick countered.

"You didn't answer my question, Minister Nicodemus," Ississita pressed. Always so gentle were these Amaurau as they cut your testicles from your body.

"I'm not aware."

"How would the Amaurau leaving the Protocols make you feel?"

Nick shook his head. "I believe I already answered that."

Ississita stopped, and now his smiling face grew darker. "Indeed, you did not. The Amaurau leaving the Protocols. How would it make *you* feel, Minister Nicodemus?"

Nick's mouth flapped open, then he snapped it shut again. "What does it matter what I feel?"

"Why indeed?" Ississita continued his stroll.

Nick decided he might as well get some satisfaction from this disastrous evening. "Why did you come here? Tonight of all nights. You knew the Gunera would be here. You deliberately broke the Protocols. Is this the Amaurau way of stating that you're leaving the balance?"

Ississita chuckled and bent down to pluck a rose blossom. "I do so love the flowers of Earth," he commented as he rolled the petals across his lips, savoring its fragrance. "Such magic you humans can wield when you choose. To create a whole new world in your own world's image. We Amaurau bow to you." The tall creature startled Nick by doing exactly that.

"What's this all about? Are you breaking the Protocols? Do I need to call Minister Huntzinger to take your complaints?"

Ississita flicked Nick's comments away with a gesture. "We're not breaking the Protocols tonight. Tomorrow maybe, but not tonight."

"Then why are you here?" Nick had been pressured beyond politeness.

"To meet you." Ississita handed the blossom to Sena Dessessah. "I'm newly installed in the position of protocol contact for my people. I had a desire to learn of you before I began my tenure."

"Forgive my lack of manners, Sevay," Nick growled, becoming more heated with each step they took, "but you could have chosen a more appropriate time to call than the night of the signing of Gunera 10. I'm sure that had you contacted our office, Minister Huntzinger would have been pleased to arrange a visit with a tour, a meeting with President De Walt, and all proper pomp and circumstance. This unscheduled and, forgive my saying, poorly timed stopover has, as you often say, put a lot of feathers out of place."

Once again, Ississita stopped and eyed Nick curiously. "Including yours?"

"Most definitely mine."

The Amaurau gestured toward the capitol building, which glowed like a beacon across the gardens. "You seemed quite capable of handling the resident snakes in your garden."

"It wasn't easy."

"Or enjoyable?"

"The Gunera are never enjoyable."

The Amaurau laughed. "An honest answer from a Protocol officer! How refreshing." He tilted his head. "Does that never concern you humans? Wasn't it a snake in the garden that led to all your troubles when first you learned to crawl?"

The reference stunned Nick. He had no idea the Amaurau had studied human religions.

Ississita was enjoying Nick's discomfiture. "As I said, I'm newly installed in this position, and I take great pride in understanding my adversaries. As humans often say, I *did my homework* before arriving."

Adversaries. Now that's a loaded word, Nick thought.

"Then you should know tonight was a dreadful choice."

"Perhaps. Perhaps I'm laying the groundwork for the Amaurau refusal to sign Protocol 10."

Nick's heart caught in his throat at the implied threat. Perhaps they were testing the resolve of humans and Gunera to gauge the determination of each race to maintain the peace. The outrageous act of arriving unannounced certainly strained the human-Gunera relationship.

"I'll ask again," Nick said, finding it difficult to rein in his anger. "Why did you come here tonight?"

"I answered that," Ississita stated.

"I'm not aware."

The Amaurau stopped in his wanderings, turned, and blocked Nick's path. He gazed down at the human from his greater height. "I stated that I came to meet you."

"That's no answer, and you know it," Nick snapped. "You could have chosen any other week to meet humans or any other world on this day. You came here, today, knowing the importance of it, knowing the Gunera would be here. Why?"

"To … meet … you." At Nick's blink, Ississita tapped the human's chest with a finger. "I could meet a human any day I wish, Minister Nicodemus. I could simply land on Erebos or Hemera or any other of your worlds and invite myself to dinner with a local potentate. They wouldn't dare refuse. Alternatively, I could order one of our destroyers to cripple a human freighter and take its crew as my property. I suspect as outraged as humanity would be at such an act, it wouldn't openly declare war on my race. There would be at least a month of negotiating before a critical mass neared, and by then, I'd have learned all I needed to know about humans and would simply release my captives. No, sir," he said sternly, still refusing to step out of Nick's path. "I came here tonight for one reason only. To meet *you*." The last word was emphasized by a hard poke to Nick's heart.

"Why me exactly?" Nick breathed. His heart was pounding so loudly he was sure it was audible to the hovercraft above their heads. "How could you know I'd even be here? Minister Huntzinger was scheduled to be here tonight."

"And yet he is not."

Once again, Nick found himself freezing. *Good God! Had the Amaurau poisoned Duncan?* He stared at the alien before him in utter shock.

"Why me?" he demanded again.

"Because I wanted you to answer my question, which you still have refused to do."

"*What* question?"

Ississita's eyes grew even darker. "How would you personally feel if the Amaurau withdrew from the balance? I'm asking not Minister Nicodemus, or the Protocol officer, or the Foreign Affairs department, or any other such legate, entity, or organization. I am asking *you*, Nicodemus Severin the second, only son whose father was Nicodemus Severin the first, former President of Hemera, national hero of the Lethe's Gate skirmish, your opinion on the matter. Tell me, sir, how would you personally feel if the Amaurau withdrew from the balance?"

"Why do you care what I think?"

"I care. Answer the question. How would you feel?"

Nick blurted out the first word that entered his mind. "Devastated."

Ississita tilted his head. "And why would that be?"

Although breathless, Nick knew that no matter what he said or did at that moment, he was already damned for everything that had happened that night. The alliance was breaking up right in front of him, had probably been long before Ississita had booked a flight for Rhadamanthus, and there was nothing he could do about it. He decided he might as well answer the question not as a diplomat, not as a Protocol officer. Just as Nick Severin, terrified human.

"I would be devastated because, like it or not, the balance is all we have. The Protocols are all that have kept each of us from blowing the others to bits in an all-out war that none of us can win."

"You believe this personally?" Ississita asked.

Nick nodded. "I do. I'm not saying the situation is perfect. Far from it! I'm not denying that humanity performed vile acts to bring the situation about because the fact is we lied, cheated, and betrayed our way to this position. I make no apologies for that. We were dying, Sevay, by the millions, and those few that might have survived would have been Guneri slaves."

"A position I understand you know more about than most," commented the Amaurau.

Nick flinched, wondering just how much information this man had about him. "I do, and I wouldn't wish my fate on anyone. So we lied to the Gunera, pretending we had an agreement with you to force them to concede. Then to cover up our lies, we lied to you so that you'd never tell the Gunera what we'd done."

"We would never have done so," Ississita stated. "Foolish humans, you didn't comprehend that we would never chat with the Gunera about human duplicity any more than we'd chat with them about the meaning of life. You could have kept your sad little alliance with the Gunera and never once involved us."

"Not true!" Nick snapped. "Eventually, the Gunera would have demanded their human allies declare war against their sworn enemy, the Amaurau, and we would have been right back where we didn't want to be."

"Slaves."

"Yes, slaves, fighting a war that wasn't ours against an enemy that wasn't ours. It only made sense to develop a parallel alliance with the Amaurau."

"For your own protection."

"It ended up quite well for you!" Nick exclaimed. "You've benefited from the century of peace, don't deny it!"

"I do not."

"So what's the problem?"

Ississita's eyes bore into his. "For all the benefits of the alliance, doesn't it bother you that at the base of it all rests a lie? You personally, Nicodemus Severin? Doesn't it?"

Nick stood silently for a long breath, trying to determine what this creature wanted from him. "It does. Deeply. Profoundly. It troubles me."

"Why?"

"Because our peace was founded on deceit. An edifice can't stand when it's built on shaky ground."

"The balance has stood for a century."

"Still, the ground is shaky, and you know it, or you wouldn't be here threatening withdrawal."

Ississita seemed to consider Nick's words. "And yet still you defend it."

"It's the best we've got. Sad but true. It's the best we've got."

Ississita suddenly started walking and, for reasons Nick didn't understand, the gentleman seemed to be less troubled. "So you will defend the Protocols, this sad, tilting, poorly built structure that exists on shaky ground."

"Yes."

"With your life, Nicodemus Severin?"

Nick felt another stab of ice in his heart. "Why would you ask that? The job of a Protocol officer is seldom dangerous."

"And yet it was tonight."

Nick thought back to the attack on the Gunera. By a human waitress. *Had the Amaurau somehow been a part of that?* he wondered. *What in God's name was happening?*

He was still pondering the questions as Ississita continued. "You placed yourself between a knife and the body of the Guneri ambassador. You were wounded in service to him, to a people that you personally have reason to despise."

"Yes."

"So the answer is, you would defend the Protocols with your life."

Nick realized the answer to that question was now obvious. "Yes, and I suppose you know that already."

"I do. But I still wanted to hear it from your lips."

The Amaurau ambassador stopped, and a soft smile washed over his face. "You've lost most of your color, Minister Severin. I would suggest you recompose yourself before returning to the party." In his hand, the missing bow suddenly appeared, and he handed it to Nick, looking quite amused. "Best see that this is put in its place. We wouldn't want the human Protocol officer himself breaking protocol, would we?"

Nick stood blinking at Ississita stupidly.

Ississita gestured to Sena Dessessah. "The Sena has volunteered to see you appropriately attired per Gunera 7. Given the darkness and the wind, I would suggest you accept her offer. We wouldn't want you walking back into the party looking like you'd been for a tumble in the gardens with an Amaurau, now would we?"

Another blinding flash hit as Nick tried to understand what this enigmatic creature was now trying to imply. A fight between the human Protocol officer and the Amaurau delegation? Or a sexual encounter between the species? *God, I have a headache!* Nick thought.

"It's been a pleasure to meet you, Minister," Ississita stated with an elegant bow. "The discussion was quite enlightening, and I'm pleased that you didn't disappoint my expectations. I and my party will see ourselves out. Stay here under this light and allow Sena Dessessah to put you back in proper diplomatic order." With that, the Amaurau delegation walked away, leaving Nick alone with Sena Dessessah.

"I don't understand!" Nick exclaimed, chasing after him. "Are you leaving the alliance or not?"

Ississita smiled. "We're not leaving it today, Minister. Perhaps tomorrow, but not today."

Nick glanced over his shoulder to note that Sena Dessessah still stood beneath the lamppost, making no move to follow her countrymen. "But what of the Sena, Sevay?"

Ississita also glanced back at her as if in afterthought. "I told you, she'll remain to see you're properly feathered. Then she'll stay to learn from you."

"Learn from me? I don't understand."

Ississita lifted his brows. "Did I fail to make my intentions clear? My pardon, Minister. I believe our decision to refuse to learn human language was a faulty one. As such, I have decided that during my tenure as protocol contact, there should be at least one Amaurau able to speak the language. Sena Dessessah has volunteered for the assignment. She will remain here on Rhadamanthus, and you, Minister Nicodemus, will teach her English."

Nick found his jaw agape for the tenth time that awful night. "Me? You can't be serious!"

"You seem capable enough," Ississita stated. "You learned English yourself as a second language and Amaurau as your third. And you've proven you'll not try to indoctrinate her with any sort of foolish conservative human ideology. Teach her English. Teach her the Protocols. Teach her a love of things human. Teach her to be the link between humans and Amaurau as you are the link between humans and Gunera."

Nick felt a flush of anger turn his face red. "This whole thing is just another attempt to even up the score? You think you're at a disadvantage because the Gunera have me?"

Ississita raised a brow. "Are we not?"

"No! I hate the Gunera."

"Honesty yet again from a Protocol officer. You're slipping, Minister Nicodemus. Tut-tut!"

Nick had finally lost all ability to handle the situation or his emotions. "What the hell?"

Ississita didn't understand the curse and stood silently eyeing him.

Nick caught himself. He blushed. "I shouldn't have said that. I apologize."

"Don't apologize to me; apologize to the snakes in your garden. It's them you've insulted." Ississita was striding toward the capitol building, with Sena Dessessah making no attempt to follow. Once again, Nick was torn between being two places at once.

"Sevay!" he protested. "I don't have the authority to accept the position of teaching the Sena English ... anything else for that matter."

"Yes, you do," came the reply from over Ississita's shoulder. "You're the Minister."

"I'm just the undersecretary!" Nick shouted.

"Not for tonight," laughed Ississita. "Tonight, you're the Minister. And the decision is yours." Darkness swallowed the ambassador, leaving Nick alone in the garden with Sena Dessessah. She smiled.

Nick sunk helplessly onto a bench. He felt too overwhelmed by everything that had happened to push away the Sena as she combed his unruly hair into submission, twisting and braiding and tying up the bow just so.

Oh God! Nick thought. *Oh God! Oh God!*

3

Nick dreaded facing the Rose Room.

With the silent Amaurau Sena following on his heels, Nick trudged through the gardens and contemplated various methods of suicide. Loath to enter the central banquet with an Amaurau lady on his heels, he approached a security officer.

"What's the situation?" Nick asked.

"It's total devastation. Those … things … were set loose on the dessert buffet, and a feeding frenzy broke out. No injuries to report, and the creatures appear to have been sedated."

"Alcohol," Nick mumbled.

The officer nodded. "Five kegs of India pale ale, a pallet of Veuve Clicquot Champagne, and 17 liters of vodka, all synthetic. It was a sight to behold."

Nick rubbed his neck. "Where are our esteemed guests now?"

"Our networks are linked, of course, so we directed their hover-sleds to their hotel. They weren't up to the task. Some members from your office were roused from their residences to see the Gunera put to bed … or whatever it is you do with the things. All's quiet."

Nick closed his eyes, relieved.

"Sir," the officer added, "we were instructed to give you this message." Nick glanced at the tablet and the three-word note from Duncan Huntzinger.

My office. Now.

Oh, Jesus.

Nick anxiously rubbed his forehead then realized he was being observed by Sena Dessessah. He reminded himself the Amaurau studied everything. Nothing missed their hawklike consideration. Nick also knew that the average Amaurau, unlike Gunera, could read human emotions. Sena probably knew Nick was both distressed and in pain. However, she said nothing.

"I've been recalled to my office, Sena." Nick switched back to Amaurau, his head throbbing from the effort. "I haven't anyone to look after you. I'm sure you're tired and would appreciate being taken to a residence, but at this moment, I'm not sure how to make that happen."

To his surprise, the Sena placed a delicate hand on Nick's injured forearm. "I'm neither tired nor in need of a residence, Minister. I suspect you require care more than I. Therefore, I will accompany you to your office." The Sena's tone indicated that she expected Nick to obey.

Nick sighed and acquiesced.

This just gets better and better.

All was dark in International Trade. The cubicles were silent and empty; the only light was from the large corner office. The office of Duncan Huntzinger, Secretary.

Nick rapped on the door then stepped inside to find a pasty-faced Duncan dictating an email to his electronic assistant. He glanced at the Sena but expressed no surprise in seeing her.

Duncan gestured to a pair of chairs at the front of his desk.

"Rough night?" Duncan asked.

Nick exhaled. "You have no idea."

Duncan grunted. "Believe me, I do, Nico! I have the reports right here." He waved at his screen. "One from Millingham, unpleasant as always. Another from Tanaka. There's also the enlightening missive from gy'Gravinda, who I suspect composed it while intoxicated."

"You'll have my resignation on your desk in the morning." Nick propped his elbows on his knees and his forehead in his hands and slowly massaged his temples.

"President De Walt also sent me a love letter," Duncan continued. "Singing your praises. Says you performed 'Herculean work' in a bad situation."

"That's nice."

Duncan reclined in his chair and eyed his young assistant. "You got the entire Guneri mission falling-down drunk, Nico. What were you thinking?"

"I was trying to defuse a war from erupting."

"No one was armed."

"The Amaurau were." At the mention of her species, Sena Dessessah's head turned. She remained silent.

"Really?"

"She's armed heavier than a thrill-kill combat gunner right now."

Duncan eyed the Sena. "Interesting." He glanced at another note on the computer screen. "Says here you were propositioned by gy'Bagrada and that you rejected his advances."

Nick winced, aware that speculation was going out to the news services. Apparently, someone in the crowd knew enough about the Gunera to interpret the altercation. "That's unfortunate but true, sir."

"Is there something between the two of you I should know about, Nico?"

Nick's head jerked up as a jolt of pain shot between his eyes. "God no! He's just ... he has this thing. He likes humans, sir."

"Interesting."

Nick stared at his boss, hoping the abject misery of his failings was written clearly on his face. "I'm so sorry, Duncan," he moaned. "I had no idea the Amaurau would land. I had to separate them from the Gunera, but I didn't know what else to do." He sank, shoulders sagging. "I've humiliated the Trade Commission. My actions have probably resulted in the Amaurau leaving the alliance. And I've got a Sena stuck to my butt. I won't argue if you think I should be charged."

"For what?"

"Gross misconduct on the job. For starters."

Duncan chuckled. "Nico, my boy, if the lady wasn't sitting beside you and it wouldn't cause an international scandal, I'd kiss you right now."

Nick's gaze shot upward at Duncan. "What?"

Duncan pointed at his screen. "I don't know how you did it, but you tossed off the section chief of Guneri security with such grace that he's written me a request to formally court you. You fended off the ambassador and fed him so well that he's suggesting you need a merit increase. Lastly, you hauled President De Walt out of a fire so hot that she thought she'd fry, all without breaking composure. It was a hell of a thing you did there, son. I'm just sorry that I missed it."

Nick blinked. "What?"

Duncan retrieved an aspirin bottle from a desk drawer and handed it to his assistant. "You did good, Nico. Real good. Probably saved humanity's ass tonight."

Nick slumped back in his chair, winded.

Duncan grinned. "So what shall I tell gy'Bagrada about courting you?"

Nick groaned and swallowed two aspirin. "Duncan, forgive me, but I really need to go home. I can't deal with the gy' anymore tonight."

"I'm just messing with you, Nico," Duncan chuckled before his face sobered. "Actually, there's another reason why I called you here." At Nick's sudden panicked jerk, Duncan added, "I did want to thank you for the fine job. But there's one more item of business we have to discuss before I can send you home." Duncan punched up another message.

"I received a missive from the Amaurau ambassador, a new fellow I don't know. Name's Ississita."

"We've met."

"So I assumed." Duncan scratched his brow. "It appears Sevay Ississita was pleased to make your acquaintance and was quite impressed with your knowledge of the Protocols and what he calls your 'fervent defense' of same. Ississita has stated that per Protocol A.3 section 2 subparagraph 4.898, the Amaurau have the right to place a protocol officer within the human sphere. And although they never have exercised this option, he's doing it now. Ississita states that he's placing Sena Dessessah on Rhadamanthus as his adjutant. She's to be trained in the Protocols, English and human culture. He insists that he will accept no one but Undersecretary Nicodemus Severin II as her tutor."

Duncan gestured at the Amaurau Sena. "I presume this is Sena Dessessah."

The lady graciously bowed her head.

"Do I have any say in the matter?" Nick asked.

"No. Ississita is crystal clear. Congratulations, Nick. You've got yourself an intern."

Nick's head dropped to his knees, and there it remained.

"Where am I supposed to put her tonight?" he asked in surrender.

"Ah, well, Ississita is clear on that matter as well. He wishes the Sena to be completely steeped in human culture and states that she will be housed in your personal dwelling."

Nick's head shot up again. "How's that?"

Duncan smiled. "That's what he says."

"How does he know I even have space for a roommate?"

Again Duncan waved a hand at the screen. "Apparently, he knows a lot more than you might think. He's aware you've got a two-bedroom unit with in-house laundry and a kitchen."

Nick stared dumbly at his boss. "Is there anything about me he *doesn't* know?"

Duncan laced together the index and middle fingers of his right hand. "Can't say. It appears the man has done his homework. All of it. He's no fool."

"I never thought of any Amaurau as a fool."

Duncan tapped his desk. "This one is smarter than most." He looked compassionately at his associate. "Let her stay with you for the night, Nick. We'll work something out in the morning."

Nick nodded in defeat. At that moment, he simply wanted to crawl into bed and die. Slowly, he rose.

"Nick?"

Nick turned his bleary gaze one last time at the secretary.

"Keep her under wraps for the night. We wouldn't want gy'Bagrada to think you're sleeping with the enemy instead of him. Now that *would* cause an international incident."

Nick knew Duncan was taking another poke at him. He glared at his boss in despair, then gestured to his new roommate and led her from the office.

The walk to the residences was passed in silence. Despite the aspirin, Nick's head continued to pound badly. Dessessah kept an easy pace beside him. She was smaller than the average Amaurau, perhaps six centimeters taller than Nick, so their strides matched. She didn't appear to be the least tired while Nick, in contrast, dragged himself across the steamy quad to the apartment complex. A sweep of his badge granted the duo entry into the building's lobby. They continued toward the back of the complex and soon arrived at Nick's flat.

With sleepy eyes, Nick noted the white plastic box with a handle resting adjacent to his door. Without even knowing what it was, he knew what it was. The Sena's luggage had arrived. Nick swiped his badge to unlock the apartment door and, grabbing the luggage, stepped inside with Dessessah in tow.

Upon Nick's entrance, the computer system infused the room with gentle light, and the audio system engaged with the soulful jazz of Herbie Miller and the Voodoo Kings. The climate control switched on, quickly cooling the space to a comfortable 24 degrees Celsius. The space was adequate for a single occupant, perhaps eight meters square, and Nick had filled it with comfortable, homey furniture of dark browns and grays. Low tables of teak were scattered around the sitting area, and atop these, he'd placed handmade objects imported from Earth, including woven baskets from the American Southwest, mahogany carvings from Africa, and a wide assortment of pottery from every corner of the world. It was as 'Earthy' a space as he could make it, almost to the point that he could inject Terra and its culture into his veins.

Setting the box next to the sofa, Nick gestured to the space.

"The living area," he said. Then, pointing to a screen on the wall, he added, "Entertainment and communications; controller is on the desk."

He led the silent Sena into the kitchen, which was as pristine and untouched as the day he'd moved in. He'd never cooked here. He didn't have a clue how to cook and was still getting used to human flavors even after a decade this side of the Gate. Next, he pointed out the tiny laundry nook and told the Sena he'd explain how to use it at her request. Then came the bathroom. Nick blinked at the Sena, having no idea what, if any, of it she would need. He explained the shower and the sink and muttered something along the lines of "figure the rest of it out yourself" before stumbling back to the great room, where he gestured in the direction of the guest room.

"That's your space, apparently."

The Sena poked her head inside the small, clean space, decorated very much like the rest of the apartment, and nodded.

"Do you sleep in a bed?" he asked.

"Sometimes," she answered, leaving Nick to wonder what she did the other times. He didn't ask.

"My room is over there," Nick gestured. "Call me if you need anything. Although I'd really prefer if you didn't. At least not tonight."

Dessessah tilted her head and smiled. "I can see you're in pain. Is the wound to your arm so terrible?"

Nick glanced at his arm. "No. It's my head that's killing me." He didn't bother to explain the concept of a migraine. He just wanted to be alone.

Deciding he was too tired to be host anymore, Nick turned his back on the Sena and entered his bedroom. He stripped off the heavy jacket with a groan of relief and dropped it onto a chair. He considered closing the door but then decided that if Dessessah killed him in his sleep, it would probably be a good thing. Nick ripped the bow from his hair and tossed it onto the dresser, toed off his shoes, and kicked them across the room. With a sigh of pleasure, he stripped off the sweater and trousers and crawled naked into his bed, groaning in relief at the cool touch of the sheets on his hot skin. He ordered the lights in the outer great room to dim and those in his bedroom to go out. The music was also silenced.

Nick lay staring up at the ceiling, willing his overactive mind to settle so that he could sleep. It refused. He moaned in frustration and palmed his eyes, begging his body to accede to his will. It refused.

Sensing movement in the darkness, Nick turned his head in alarm. A fresh bolt of pain flashed his vision white until he realized the shadow at the door was Dessessah. She entered the room on soundless feet and, for a breathless moment, Nick was frozen, wondering what tortures fate had in store for him now. To his astonishment, the female sank onto the side of his bed, her weight so slight the mattress barely registered her presence.

Silently, the Sena touched Nick's temples with the index finger of each hand, scarcely placing any pressure at all. She then began to swirl the fingers around circularly.

"Sena, this is most inappropriate," Nick said, trying to brush her hands aside. He found the touch strangely erotic in a clinical sort of way.

The Sena swatted Nick's hands away and clicked at him.

"Close your eyes, Minister."

Every instinct in his body told Nick to get away. He knew that the Sena shouldn't be in his room, on his bed, that late at night. She shouldn't be touching him. But the touch was a paradise of itself, and he sensed its strange magic. Nick found his eyes closing without his volition and the pain ebbing away. In the bleariness of the moment, he suspected Dessessah knew far more about humans than she or her ambassador had claimed, including ways to disarm a man with only two fingers. Nick suspected Dessessah was anything but a simple student intern there to learn of English and humans. He feared she was far more than that. She was dangerous. But at that moment, Nick didn't care.

4

Morning found Nick lying in a tangle of sheets, legs dangling off the bed, body at an odd angle across the mattress. He realized with some disappointment that he'd survived the night and the ministrations of Sena Dessessah. Although his head no longer throbbed, Nick sensed that the night had been fitful even though he couldn't remember it. Nick's hands gingerly probed his temples, expecting pain or implants or who knew what. He found only that his forehead felt tender and decided it was probably best not to touch it.

Groaning, Nick staggered to his feet. The world swung wildly, and he grabbed the headboard until the sensation of flying subsided. Nick blinked as he brushed the hair from his face while listening for sounds of his houseguest. The apartment was silent. Nick hadn't a clue about the daily habits of an Amaurau lady. For all he knew, the Sena might have remained awake all night. Perhaps she was asleep in the guestroom, suspended from the ceiling. Nick found the guestroom door ajar, with quiet darkness beyond. *Still asleep,* he thought. *Not surprising. She must have faced a long day traveling to Rhadamanthus even before attending the party.* Nick had no idea if the Sena was merely sleeping off a long day or if she'd died of exhaustion during the night. At that moment, lacking the fortitude to deal with either a dead or sleeping Amaurau princess, Nick trundled to his bathroom in search of a shower and his wits.

The blast of scalding water quickly woke him. Nick stood for a long time, allowing the pulsing jets to pound his back and ease his shoulder tension. He adjusted the shower setting, and a gentle rain splashed upon his face, washing the last of the cobwebs away. Swinging his wet hair to one side, Nick turned off the water and stepped out of the shower.

To a dead stop. Facing Dessessah.

The Amaurau lady stood in the middle of the bathroom curiously eyeing Nick. Her head tilted heavily to the left, and the one eye he could see blinked at him. Too surprised to move, Nick dripped water onto the floor while Dessessah studied him in a birdlike manner.

"Forgive my impertinence, but I must ask the question," she stated, righting her head. "What is the purpose of pouring water over yourself?"

Nick blinked, his mind refusing to shift into the Amaurau language. The sounds flowed through one ear and out the other, but his brain made no attempt to comprehend them.

"Excuse me?" he mumbled in English.

She rephrased the question. "Is there a reason you've doused yourself in water?"

This time Nick translated the words. At the same time, his befuddled mind grasped the fact that he was standing naked before an Amaurau lady. Hastily, Nick wrapped a towel around his waist, although a corner of his mind noted that Dessessah was still eyeing him with no hint of embarrassment.

With a shake of his head, Nick gathered his thoughts then offered a weak smile. "It's a common practice among humans to shower in the morning." He grabbed a second towel and draped it around his shoulders. Feeling a little more human now that he was covered, he started to dry himself off.

Dessessah watched him curiously. Clinically.

"Why?" she asked.

Nick nudged her aside to escape to his bedroom. As he did so, Nick towel-dried his hair, answering her from beneath its cotton folds. "It helps wake us up."

"Why not splash water in your face?" she asked, following Nick into his bedroom.

Nick realized the woman was studying him like a specimen.

"A full drenching does a better job," he blustered, having no idea how to explain the idea of a shower to a creature that clearly had never enjoyed one. As he dropped the first towel onto the back of a chair, Nick ran his hands through his damp and tussled hair while contemplating how to explain the concept of showering to an alien.

"Humans have oils that can collect dirt and dust." Nick turned his back on Dessessah while rummaging through his closet. He had no idea what to wear, nor did he know what the day had in store. "A good drenching gets the job done."

The explanation must have made sense. Dessessah nodded. "Our feathers do as well." She gave her arms a flick. "We must preen them to remove contaminants. Water would just flow off of us."

Nick considered the ducks that plied the waters of the campus pond. Their feathers were waterproof. He supposed it made sense that the Amaurau's plumage would be similar. Nick offered another tight smile, all the while thinking this arrangement was destined to be the most uncomfortable of his life.

"Do you eat a first meal?" he asked, fumbling to recall the Amaurau word for breakfast.

"We do."

Thank you for that enlightening reply, Nick grumbled silently. Shaking his head, he trundled into the great room to check his vmail. He needed to know what Duncan wanted him to do with the little bird lady. His mind swam with the possibilities. *Dress for business and head for the office? Take the lady for a long flight south for the winter? Roast her for lunch?*

Still wearing a towel, Nick flopped behind his desk and, with a brush of his fingers, launched the vmail program. He found a message from Duncan, sent one hour before Nick had risen.

Duncan's tone was breezy: "No need to come to the office, Nico. We've got your transfers covered between Les and me. Take the lady around Rhadamanthus and show her the sights. Since the Gunera haven't off-worlded, keep her away from campus. Wouldn't want the lot of them to meet up, as you can imagine. Take her somewhere far, far away. And try to have fun."

The recording abruptly ended, and Nick snorted as the screen shifted to the Trade Commission's shooting star logo. He wondered if Duncan was hinting that he should take Dessessah on a one-way trip out of town but decided that was being too hopeful. Sighing, his cheek planted against a fist, Nick stared at the screen and wondered how to entertain his houseguest in a way that would be both interesting and educational but didn't occur anywhere in the capitol. Dessessah sauntered over and stood behind Nick and stared motionless at the screen. *She's probably questioning my sanity,* Nick thought. *Can't say I blame her.*

Someplace far from the capitol, he thought morosely. There really wasn't much outside the capitol. Rhadamanthus had become an agricultural station once its ecosystem had stabilized. The majority of its arable land was devoted to the cultivation of tropical foodstuffs like sugar cane and taro. As a newly colonized planet, Rhadamanthus lacked historical landmarks and held nothing of a cultural sort outside Rhadamanthus City, unless one counted sugar mill tours as cultural enlightenment. Nick could scarcely think of anything in the way of ecoadventures.

Except.

Nick shot a video chat request to his friend Jordan. Given it was Thursday morning, Nick suspected Jordan would be at his desk. Moments later, Jordan appeared on screen, his youthful face looking harried and overworked.

He blinked in surprise at Nick, naked to the waist and with a mop of unbrushed hair falling in his eyes.

"Rough night?" he asked with a grin.

Nick shoved a lock of black tresses out of his face. "You have no idea."

"You might be surprised, my friend," Jordan said, motioning to something offscreen. "You made the opening banner of the *Sentinel's* website this morning."

Nick groaned. "What are they saying?"

"It's Pulitzer material. Apparently someone tried to assassinate the Guneri ambassador, but you intervened. You were then assaulted by the Guneri chief of the Secret Service but managed to extricate yourself without starting a war. You also had to keep the reptiles on one side of the room while you were blindsided by the birds' unexpected appearance on the other. The Gunera got completely trashed during some sort of 'feeding frenzy,' and the ceremony ended with a bang. Wish I could have been there to see it."

Nick closed his eyes and took a deep, refreshing breath. *At least the news services aren't being critical,* he thought. *The night hadn't been a complete disaster after all.*

"I need a favor," Nick said, as he opened his eyes.

"Shoot."

"Bad choice of words." Nick was excruciatingly aware that the Amaurau Sena was standing at his back, absorbing the conversation. "Can I borrow the *Devil's Mistress* for the day?"

He'd caught Jordan by surprise. The young man sat back in his chair and blinked. "Sure. You know you can have her any time you want. Not working today? That old bastard Huntzinger didn't fire you, did he? You couldn't know the eagles were landing."

Nick thanked Bibachek, the Guneri god of good fortune, that Dessessah didn't understand English and, therefore, was not aware of Jordan's slur. "No, I wasn't fired. On the contrary, I've been assigned the dubious task of teaching an Amaurau lady about English, the Protocols, and human culture. Duncan wants me to take her on a field trip."

"Seriously? Wow!" Jordan took a sip of coffee while he considered that information. "More power to you, Nick. And might I add, better you than me. You may enjoy the pleasures of my *Mistress* for the day. I'll call the marina to let them know to expect you."

"Thanks, Jordan. I appreciate it."

Jordan chuckled. "Do birds like water?"

"I'm going to find out," Nick grumbled. He thanked his buddy a second time then cut the transmission. Shooting a hasty glance at Dessessah to assess what she'd thought of the conversation, Nick found that she was still watching him clinically. He slid around her and trundled to his bedroom to find attire appropriate for the impending field trip.

While sorting through his dresser in search of a white polo shirt, Nick felt rather than saw Dessessah enter his bedroom. She stood beside the still unmade bed.

Nick forced a smile. "I'm taking you on an adventure, Sena," he explained, drawing the shirt over his head before turning to select a pair of tan trousers. "Have you ever been …" He fought unsuccessfully for the Amaurau word for 'sailing.' "Have you ever ridden in a vessel on the sea?"

Once again, Dessessah tilted her head. "There are no oceans on my home world. Our water supply is all subsurface."

"I'll take that as a no," Nick murmured.

He found a pair of dock sneakers and slipped them on without socks. Finally, Nick tied his hair in a messy queue at his neck. No point in being neat about it. The wind would tear it apart in minutes. *Besides,* Nick thought, *Dessessah had indicated the previous night she liked it loose.*

Nick surveyed Dessessah's attire. She wore a pair of loose palazzo-style pants. Her claw-like feet were encased in mummy wrappings. A flowing silk camisole was visible beneath a knee-length sleeveless vest. As always, Dessessah's feathered arms were bare, as was her head with its long fall of auburn feathers. Her jewelry was understated; tiny silver studs in each ear and a chain of grenade stones that Nick supposed were standard issue for her kind. Dessessah's lyssestra were glued to her arms adjacent to her flight feathers.

"My apologies, lady," Nick murmured, "but would you mind leaving the explosive necklace behind? It might not react well where we're going."

Dessessah lifted a feathered brow then raised the necklace over her head before handing it to Nick, who carefully placed it atop his dresser.

"We should probably head out," Nick said, and motioned for Dessessah to follow him.

The duo walked across campus to an Italian deli where Nick ordered a to-go picnic lunch. Clutching the basket, Nick led his Amaurau charge to the garage where his scooter was stored.

Rhadamanthus City wasn't a sprawling metropolis. The city's subway system was adequate and inexpensive for local destinations. Nick had only purchased the scooter after learning to sail with Jordan. This new hobby required him to travel to the marina several kilometers out of town. He hopped aboard the sleek powder-blue vehicle and motioned for Dessessah to climb on behind him. Dessessah acquiesced, wrapping her long arms around Nick's waist and pressing her chin to his shoulder. The intimacy of the touch surprised Nick, and his body reacted as it always did to anything female. Remembering the etiquette training Alessandra McCoy was forever shoving in front of him, Nick forced himself to ignore the rush of pleasure that coursed through his frame. He quickly started the scooter. Lifting his feet to the footboards, they were off.

Dessessah's long arms tightened around Nick, and she pressed herself closer as the scooter accelerated. Within minutes, the pair was amid the light traffic of Rhadamanthus City, weaving adroitly between slower vehicles while drivers and pedestrians stared at the odd sight of an Amaurau lady's head feathers flying in the wind. Upon reaching the open road of the countryside, Nick was surprised Dessessah issued a lilting coo of pleasure as they again picked up speed. Nick's ear tingled. She was humming, taking great joy in the sense of wind and speed as they buzzed along the two-lane road that wound through the jungle.

Nick felt relaxed for the first time since he'd met the lady, and he allowed his body to sink against hers as Dessessah pressed along the length of him. Dessessah held on tighter, aware that her feathers might easily be caught in the wind, wrenching her from the scooter. Yet, she loved the sensation. Nick felt pleasure pulsing through Dessessah's slender form. The humming intensified as Nick adjusted the throttle and let the little scooter run through its paces.

Nick slowed the scooter as he turned into the marina. To his disappointment, Dessessah eased her death grip on him. She straightened and let go of Nick completely as the scooter puttered across the parking lot near the marina office. Dessessah dismounted, smoothing first her clothing, then her head feathers, while surveying the landscape with interest.

The marina hummed with activity. It was largely dedicated to pleasure craft, but a handful of commercial fishermen who berthed their vessels there were preparing for departure. Nick noted the charter craft being scrubbed and provisioned for a day of deep-sea fishing. He left Dessessah by the scooter and ran into the office to obtain the key to the *Devil's Mistress*. Returning minutes later, Nick escorted the lady along the docks to Jordan's berth. Dessessah gazed with sparkling eyes at the dance of the water against the white fiberglass hull, and she tilted her head to listen to the slap of waves against the dock. Nick stepped aboard the boat then offered his hand to assist Dessessah. The vessel swayed, and Dessessah promptly sat down.

"Takes a little getting used to," Nick commented.

For a brief moment, Nick reconsidered the wisdom of his choice of adventure. If the Sena had never seen an ocean or sailed across its surface, should he really be the first to show her? What if she fell overboard and drowned? One look at Dessessah's glowing face, however, told Nick he'd chosen well. She wanted to see where this adventure would lead.

While Nick moved through Jordan's requisite pre-sail checklist, he explained the basics for a safe journey. He retrieved two safety vests and helped Dessessah with hers. He described the concept of coming about and the importance of following his commands to avoid the risk of being swept out to sea. She listened intently while Nick struggled through translating complex nautical terms into more simple physical concepts in the intricate Amaurau language. Nick hoped he wasn't sounding like an idiot. Darting a glance at Dessessah as he checked the GPS and radio systems, Nick saw that she was staring at him bright-eyed in wonder and decided he was making himself reasonably clear. *Maybe,* he thought as he set all his lines at the ready, *this is exactly what we both need.*

Upon completing all final checks, Nick fired up the engine and ran nimbly forward to free the bow lines. He scuttled to the stern and flipped off the painter so that the *Devil's Mistress* floated free. Then he took his seat next to the tiller and throttled forward. The craft moved away from its slip smoothly in the calm waters of the marina as Nick steered it between other vessels and into the channel. The craft chugged along for several minutes, passing numerous power cruisers and a handful of sailboats before reaching the breakwater. A solid breeze hit them as they made the turn for the open sea, and there, safely away from other vessels, Nick cut the engine.

While the *Devil's Mistress* tossed fitfully in the meter-high waves, Nick freed the jib from its canvas cover and ran it up. The rainbow-colored sail billowed with the wind. Nick soon returned to the pit and freed the main sail from its protective cover. It took both hands to raise, and the boom swung, caught by the wind. After cleating the lines, Nick returned to his seat by the tiller and tightened up, bringing the boom into line with the wind so that the sail caught. The elegant craft sliced into the waves as Nick settled it into a perfect reach and, within moments, they were cutting away from the breakwater toward the open ocean.

Nick glanced at Dessessah. Her eyes shone brightly as she stared at the sail in open-mouthed wonder. She raised both arms, and the wind caught at her feathers, causing them to ruffle much like the sail.

"It's an airfoil!" she exclaimed, clapping her hands. "A vertical airfoil!"

Smiling, taken by her childlike joy, Nick nodded. The wind tore at his hair and ripped away its tie. His mass of black locks broiled around Nick's face. He laughed, shaking his head to clear his vision. Using his weight to counterbalance the pressure of the wind against the sail, Nick settled down against the gunwale.

"Join me," Nick said, and Dessessah approached him.

Although Nick doubted Dessessah's slight form could do much to aid him, it felt more natural to have her at his side, facing the sail rather than sitting in the pit. The wind blew at the perfect strength to give them a steady headway yet not too strong that Nick worried about overbalancing the craft. He turned his face forward and watched with joy as the white bow cut into the green waters of the sea.

For an hour, the duo rode the waves in silence. Dessessah delighted as the wind raised her plumage. She extended her arms to catch the breeze. Nick savored the isolation of the open sea, far away from the always-judging eyes of humanity.

They passed other vessels. Cruisers raced past them, sending up great spumes of white water as they bucked the waves. Slower-moving sailboats carried passengers that waved merrily, not realizing from the distance that the lady aboard was not human. But for the most part, the two were alone with their thoughts on that hot, humid day under a broiling yellow, cloudless sky.

Sometime during the second hour, Nick spotted his destination, a line of green on the horizon about five kilometers from the coast: Hoover's Crescent. The uninhabited island was Nick's usual destination whenever he borrowed the *Devil's Mistress*. Nick understood the currents in the area, and he knew he'd land at the island with ample time for lunch. The prevailing winds made landfall on the island child's play since he seldom needed to tack to make his favorite beach. As on previous sails, the wind held true from the east, providing a direct line toward the island.

Only when they drew within a quarter kilometer of the island was Nick forced to tack. He ordered Dessessah to duck and then swung the tiller hard, snapping the boat into the wind. The flow of air caught the sail and flung it around, sweeping the boom over the Sena's head. Nick stooped to avoid being hit. He then adjusted his seat to the opposite side of the boat. Once the sail had steadied, he told Dessessah she could take her seat again. She did so, marveling at the maneuver and understanding it in a way only a creature of the winds could truly comprehend.

Nick needed to tack twice more to set the proper bearing for the cove. They then slid into the bay. Upon dropping the main sail, Nick tossed the small anchor into the water. It bit into the rocky bottom, and the *Devil's Mistress* settled happily to rest. Nick next dropped the jib and tossed a second anchor over the opposite side of the boat to keep the stern from swinging should the wind shift. He retrieved the picnic basket.

The shingle beach of Hoover's Crescent hugged the adventurers like the loving arms of a mother. Protected by the island, the cove's water spread out before Nick and Dessessah like glass. Because the oceans of Rhadamanthus had been man-made, they were young and clear. Nick could see directly to the bottom. He'd brought the shallow drafting of the *Devil's Mistress* nearly to the beach where the water was nearly one meter deep. Nick relieved Dessessah of her life vest.

"I'm afraid the only way to reach the shore is to wade," Nick said. "How do you feel about getting your feet wet?"

Dessessah studied the water as she leaned over the side of the boat. A school of small fish darted past, and she gasped with surprise as they glinted in the sunshine.

"I'm not sure," she breathed. "I've never stood in water before."

Nick smiled. "I'll take the basket ashore and come back for you." Grasping the basket, Nick climbed over the side and slid into the water. As he expected, it rose to his knees. Nick sloshed his way to shore, uncaring that his trousers and dock sneakers were soaked. After setting the basket on the stony beach, Nick waded back to the boat. Standing in the water, he reached up.

"I'll carry you."

Dessessah blinked in amusement, then extended her arms. Despite the uncomfortable angle, Nick easily lifted his companion. *She can't weigh more than fifty kilos,* Nick thought in amazement, as he swung Dessessah over the side of the boat and caught her in his arms. Holding her like a groom carrying a bride across the threshold, Nick waded onto the beach then set her down dry and safe. The Sena disentangled herself and stood looking quizzically, first at Nick and his drenched clothing and then back at the boat.

"You humans really do like getting wet, don't you?"

Nick laughed. He thought it odd that of all the individuals he'd met since arriving on the human side of Lethe's Gate, an Amaurau Sena would be the one to make him feel young, alive, and confident. The realization sobered him, and his smile faded. Yet again, he wondered what was wrong with him as he turned his attention to the basket. Why couldn't he relate to his own species? Why did humans make him feel gawky while an Amaurau Sena made him feel like a god?

Dessessah, aware that the light had vanished from Nick's face, extended a delicate hand to touch him, but Nick stepped out of reach. Turning his attention to the basket, Nick grasped a blanket and laid it on the shingle. The oceans of Rhadamanthus were too young to have adequate beaches. As such, every beach was shingle made up of rounded stones the size of a human fist. Fortunately, the blanket was thick and would provide decent seating. Nick gestured to the blanket, and with a smile, Dessessah sat.

Nick dropped next to her and fished out a bottle of water. Dessessah consumed several sips before turning her birdlike head toward Nick with a tilt.

"Suddenly you've become somber," she said. "What makes you so sad, Minister?"

Nick tried to smile, but the effort was weak. "It's nothing, Sena," he murmured, turning to ponder the calm green water and the white swan that was the *Devil's Mistress* resting just offshore.

A long finger touched his temple, and Nick involuntarily flinched. "Tell me what burdens you," Dessessah coaxed, in a singsong voice he found mesmerizing.

"You're here to learn of humans and the Protocols." Nick inched away to distance himself from her touch and that oddly musical voice. "I'm not a part of the package."

"But you are," she replied with a smile. "*You're* the Protocols. The human half of them."

Nick shook his head. "No."

Dessessah's smile intensified, and she touched Nick's shoulder. "You are, Minister. It's your life. It's all that you are."

"No." Nick resented the implication that he lacked a life outside of his job. Not that he wasn't fully aware of that simple fact, but he resented Dessessah for knowing it and for speaking his fears aloud.

"Yes. Don't run from the truth, Minister. The Protocols are your life." At Nick's scowl, Dessessah fluttered her fingers. "Do you think Ambassador Ississita would dispatch me here without knowledge of that into which he was sending me? I know that you have no family, that your father died before you were born, and that your mother remains a prisoner of the Gunera. This is true, yes?"

Nick felt his face darkening. "I don't discuss my mother."

Dessessah lifted her feathered brows. "Why not, Minister? It seems important that the human Protocol Officer has strong motives to favor the Gunera over us."

Nick angrily shifted his seat away from Dessessah. "Don't bring my mother into this! I despise the Gunera."

"Because they still hold your mother?"

Nick turned his head away.

"Because you haven't succeeded in freeing her?"

Nick felt the blade plunge directly through his heart. The damned bird had hit him at his weakest point. Nick didn't know how she'd learned he'd been struggling with his own government to bring his mother out of Gunera, but he cursed Dessessah for the knowledge. It was his deepest shame among so many. The woman who'd sacrificed everything to see that he escaped to human territory lingered in suffering as a prisoner of the Gunera. The thought of her still trapped in that hell while he struggled futilely to save her brought unwanted tears to Nick's eyes. Nick kept his back firmly planted toward the Sena. *Damn her!* he thought. *She has no right!*

A soft touch ran down his back. "There's no shame, Minister Severin. Not for you. I know of your attempts to free her—three direct tries yourself and innumerable petitions to both your own government and the Gunera. The individuals who should be ashamed are the emperor and your president."

"She's *my* mother," Nick whispered. "She's my responsibility."

"Not when two empires stand in the way."

"What's it to you?" Nick whirled back around to face Dessessah.

Once again, Dessessah fluttered her hands. "We need to know where your allegiances are, Minister Severin. If war comes, will you stand with humanity, or will you crumble when the Gunera threaten your mother? Or will you honor your pledge to the Protocols and do as the law states, defying both?"

Nick felt his heart skip a beat. "War? What are you talking about?" He thought of the meeting with Ississita and the threats issued. "Are the Amaurau pulling out of the balance? Are you declaring war on Earth? On the Gunera?"

Dessessah smiled. "It's not for someone like me to say, Minister. I'm but a lowly staff member of Alien Affairs ordered to learn of human ways. The Amaurau have an uneasy distrust of human motives but a deep-seated hatred for the Gunera. Should war come, against whom do you think we will first raise our sword?"

"We stand between you and them," Nick whispered.

"In which case, you'd do best to step aside, wouldn't you?"

Nick struggled to catch his breath as he stared blankly at the Sena and tried to decipher what she was revealing. "My God, you *are* withdrawing from the treaty!"

Dessessah lifted her shoulders in a motion resembling a human shrug. "I cannot say." She studied Nick with darker than dark eyes. "Where, Minister, will you stand if the Protocols dissolve? With humanity, the Gunera, or the Amaurau?"

Nick continued to blink at Dessessah stupidly while he processed the question. It was a hell of a declaration to announce five kilometers out to sea on an uninhabited island. What *would* he do? Where did his loyalties lie? Nick stared out at the ocean while weighing the question. He could never betray humanity or the Protocols by backing the vile Gunera regardless of how they might threaten his mother. Likewise, Nick knew he could not support the Amaurau, a race of silent, brooding, scheming creatures that he didn't understand. Humanity wasn't much better than either the Gunera or the Amaurau. Untrustworthy, treacherous devils, the lot of them. Nick could count on one hand the humans he trusted. That left the Protocols. Solid and inviolate, the Protocols neither lied nor betrayed. They didn't threaten to change sides. He knew every word of them, understood every nuance. They made sense of chaos, brought order to a disordered universe, gave Nick a foundation on which to build something akin to a life. His upbringing had trained him for just such service, caused his mind to think in legalistic forms. They were all he knew, all he worshipped. The Protocols were his life.

"I'll stand by the Protocols," he whispered. He'd surrender his mother to her fate in Gunera, face charges of treason leveled at him by humanity if necessary, thumb his nose at supercilious Amaurau in order to assure the balance remained. He had nothing else to live for. He lacked a family save the ghost of a mother who was beyond helping. None of his friends had the slightest clue what he was. No country would come to his aid.

Nick had nothing.

No one.

Only the Protocols.

God, how pathetic! he thought.

Dessessah flicked her fingers through Nick's unruly locks as if to calm him. "The ambassador saw rightly. You're the one we must guard against."

Nick frowned. "Guard *against?* I don't understand."

"War is coming, Minister. I don't know when or which of us feuding rivals will initiate it, but it's coming regardless. We, the Amaurau, sense the balance unwinding. Ississita wants me here so that when the Protocols fail, there's hope that Amaurau and humans can stand together."

Nick felt his heart freeze over. "You're making your play early," he said in disbelief. "Trying to nab humanity as your ally before the Gunera do."

Dessessah issued a quirky smile. "Wouldn't humanity do likewise?"

"Humanity waits until the very last moment to make any decision at all!" Nick growled. It was an aspect of his own species he deplored. Amaurau made decisions and acted on them. The Gunera moved more slowly but nonetheless moved. Only humanity hemmed and hawed and debated until decisions were thrust upon them by default. Nick's eyes narrowed. "You're not just making a play for humanity. You're making a play for me!"

Dessessah's smile remained fixed, her dark eyes unreadable. "You're a valuable piece in the game, are you not, Minister?"

"Duncan Huntzinger is the minister," Nick growled. "I'm nothing and no one, Sena."

Dessessah twitched her lips. "You're too modest, Minister Severin. Huntzinger bears the title, but it's you the Gunera will seek to control. They know they have the means to wound you deeply, and they will use this against you."

Nick stared bleakly at Dessessah, aware of the accuracy of her words. If war erupted, gy'Bagrada would likely delight in torturing Nick's mother and sending Nick a recording of the incident even though their efforts would fail. The power rested with Duncan and came from the President of the Western Alliance. Nick Severin had zero influence.

"They can and they will," Nick agreed. "But I have no authority to influence humanity's alliances. You're making your play for the wrong man, Sena."

Dessessah continued to study Nick. "Ambassador Ississita is wise. If he says you're the target of the Gunera, then you are, Minister. We'll not concede you to them. You're too great a weapon to be allowed to fall into Guneri hands."

At the cold threat in her voice, Nick leaped to his feet and staggered away. As Dessessah unfolded her arms, Nick saw the lysŝestra tucked against her feathers. His heart went cold. Dessessah could kill him right where he stood, and no one could do anything to stop her.

"Is it your intention to kill me?" Nick asked, sensing his face had blanched.

The Sena remained seated on the blanket, making no threatening move against her companion. "It's my intention to learn of humans, the Protocols, and English." Dessessah turned her attention to the basket. "And to enjoy an afternoon in your presence, Minister. I find you a most delightful companion." She retrieved a bag of sunflower seeds and, with a cry of childlike delight, dove into it before patting the blanket. "Come and sit with me. I'm no danger to you."

Nick continued to stare at Dessessah with a mixture of horror and confusion. How could this delicate, soft-spoken lady carry so much unvoiced threat within her? As she pawed through the basket, Nick thought Dessessah resembled a college student out for a lark on a sunny beach. She snatched a bag of potato chips and crunched happily on them, a look of supreme pleasure on her delicate face. Dessessah patted the blanket in invitation a second time.

"Please, Minister, join me."

Although Nick felt in the depths of his bones he couldn't trust Dessessah, he was admittedly both hungry and thirsty, and she didn't appear interested in killing him. Gingerly, Nick settled on the farthest edge of the blanket. He snatched a water bottle and the sandwich he'd purchased for himself. The two alien allies sat next to each other in utter silence on that hot tropical beach, not even the water moving against the shingle to break the quiet.

When Dessessah spoke, it seemed so loud that Nick jumped. "I would like to learn of you, Minister. If we're to be constant companions for the next several weeks, I think a proper introduction is appropriate."

"I suspect you know everything there is to know about me," Nick grumbled, refusing to look at Dessessah.

"My knowledge is limited to the file given to me by Sevay Ississita. It provided only the basic facts." Again Dessessah reached out and touched Nick with her long fingers, this time tracing them along the bones of his left hand where it clutched the blanket. Nick decided conversation with the Amaurau must, by definition, include physical contact since she was constantly attempting it.

Nick pulled his hand away. Dessessah's touch caused him to react in strange ways, fluted signals along his nervous system that caused him to want to close his eyes and surrender to the pleasure she caused. Nick wondered if Dessessah knew how her touch affected him. "I have questions of my own for you," he asserted, in an attempt to regain control. He'd be damned if he was going to allow this alien woman to lead him around by the nose. Or, in her case, by the fingertips.

Dessessah smiled. "Indeed?"

Nick wanted the conversation moved as far away from himself as possible. "What started the war between you and the Gunera? Humanity stumbled across the two of you already at each other's throats when we made first landfall in the nebula, but we never understood why you were at war."

"No?"

Nick issued an annoyed glance. "We have the Gunera's perspective, but I don't think anyone has heard the Amaurau side."

"I'm here to learn of humans, Minister," she reproved gently. "Not to speak of the Amaurau to you."

Nick glared at Dessessah. "That's not the way I work, Sena. If you really intend to follow me around and learn about humans and the Protocols, you'll give as much information as you'll get."

Dessessah lifted her feathered brows in amusement. "A trade?" she queried. "How very human!"

"What? How's that human?"

The Sena laughed, a twittering sound like a warbler's song. "It's a trait of your kind." Dessessah brought her knees to her chest and wrapped her arms around them. "It's noted in all our biology texts that humans have an almost instinctual desire to deal in trade. You take when you think you can get away with it but seem more comfortable with a trade, as if stealing causes you discomfort as a species. Always you work your deals, demanding this for that, and repaying your debts. You don't like to be indebted to other species."

Nick considered that odd perspective on humanity, one he'd never heard before. He supposed Dessessah was right. Humans were certainly capable of stealing when they thought it possible, but they generally chose negotiated deals with their two alien neighbors. He'd always assumed it was because humans didn't want to get caught stealing from either Gunera or Amaurau and dreaded the consequences, such as sanctions or war. Nick had never considered that humanity actually preferred to trade. It left any feelings of guilt or indebtedness off the table. A man could walk away from an honest deal feeling he gave as good as he got, no regrets, recriminations, or resentments. No fear that a disgruntled trading partner would come marching back demanding reparations for ill treatment. Yes, humans were traders. Had been since the first days they'd crawled out of the swamp.

"I'll agree with you on that," he conceded. "With me, as with my species, all things are in trade. So here's the deal. I'll ask you a question which you'll answer. In return, you'll ask me a question which I will answer. Fair enough?"

Dessessah twittered again then lay flat on her back against the blanket. She spread her arms out so that her feathers flared, the effect resembling a fallen angel. Nick had to shake his head to rid his mind of the image.

"Fair enough," Dessessah replied. As she watched the cumulous clouds beginning their usual afternoon growth in the yellow arc of sky, she answered Nick's earlier question. "The animosity between the Gunera and Amaurau dates back nearly 500 years, long before humans came to the nebula. The initial friction probably started with the clash of two species desiring to possess the same space. Our languages and cultures are vastly different, and we found no common ground on which to build a relationship. For almost a century, we tried to ignore one another, but that changed with the discovery of regnistase."

Nick frowned. "What's regnistase?"

From her prone position, Dessessah twitched her hand and tapped his lightly. "Question for question, Minister!" she chided. "What's the meaning of your name?"

Nick blinked, surprised by the banality of the question. "Nicodemus or Severin?"

"Either. Both. Why do humans have two names?"

Nick grunted a laugh. The simple question eased some of his tension as he realized the Sena was largely interested in the basic aspects of humanity. "Nicodemus means 'victory for the people.' My grandparents were both of Greek ancestry and wanted their son to bear a Greek name. When my father was born, humanity had only recently ended the war with the Gunera, so it was a triumphant statement on the part of my grandparents. I was named after my father."

"And Severin?"

"Severin denotes my family line." Nick eased back onto his elbows and stretched out his legs. "My turn. What is regnistase, and why would it cause you and the Gunera to go to war?"

Dessessah's sigh surprised Nick. "Regnistase is an enzyme unique to Gunera. It's found in their young between birth and the time they reach sexual maturity. Our biologists discovered it contains properties that aid in the healing of age-related damage, especially due to radiation exposure. The Gunera evolved on a planet with high radiation levels and, therefore, developed biological methods that protected their cells from damage. The regnistase allows a young Gunera's cells to replicate safely even in the face of hazardous radiation levels. The enzyme became a basis for medical treatments we employed to allow our elders live longer, healthier lives."

"How did you obtain access to this enzyme?" Nick asked suspiciously.

"One must obtain Guneri young and extract it from their bodies, of course."

Nick inhaled sharply. Good God! Was she saying what he thought she was saying? "You … harvested Guneri children to make medicine?"

"Indeed." Dessessah twisted her head against the blanket to study Nick's reaction, noting the shocked expression. "Now you understand the nature of the conflict. We wanted the enzyme, but they wouldn't give it voluntarily. So we took it."

Nick sat in stunned silence. No wonder the Gunera despised the Amaurau!

"My question," Dessessah stated, interrupting his thoughts. "Humans have what seem to us to be a dizzying array of mythological structures. Of which structure are you a proponent?"

Nick flailed momentarily before he comprehended the question. "I'm vaguely a Christian," he replied uncomfortably. His religious affiliation was not something he liked to discuss.

"What is the general nature of that particular mythology?"

Ah, a more comfortable tack. Nick didn't mind discussing religion in general. "Christians believe that the universe was created by and is controlled by a single omnipresent being. They believe that the being sends messengers to converse with humanity to keep humans on the path of righteousness. An individual named Jesus Christ was one such messenger who is believed by Christians to be the most important of those sent. Christians follow the teachings of this man." He paused. "What do the Amaurau believe?"

"We don't have mythological structures. We have no need for benign beings to watch over us. We view such structures as creations of comfort for more primitive species."

More primitive species. Like humans and Gunera, Nick thought.

"So you believe humans and Gunera are more primitive than you."

"When it comes to their philosophical views, yes."

"And in other ways? How do you view humanity and Gunera?"

Dessessah snorted. "Gunera! Nasty creatures."

"And humans?"

"Intensely interesting," she said to Nick's surprise. When Dessessah noted his quizzical look, she sat up so that they were eye to eye again. "We Amaurau are fascinated by humans. You're very intelligent, perhaps even as intelligent as us. We marvel at your mechanical ability and stand in awe of your economic arrangements. Truly you are built by nature for trade." She gestured at the ocean before them and the jungled island behind. "As for this, your ability to transform a world to suit your needs, we are truly in awe. Of course, we also view you as incredibly dangerous."

"How so?"

Dessessah flicked her fingers at the island. "Because of this. You're the only species known to us that doesn't accept the universe as you find it. You move into an ecosystem, and unless you find it suitable, you adjust it to fit your needs regardless of the damage caused to life that existed there before your arrival. Humanity has an odd habit of expanding to fit whatever space it desires and adjusting that space to suit itself. This planet is just one example. Even the alliance between you, us, and the Gunera is a human construct designed for your advantage. Upon encountering both Gunera and Amaurau, humanity could have withdrawn, but it didn't. Instead, you adjusted the universe to suit yourselves. You designed the balance with you as its center of trade, forcing Gunera and Amaurau to work within your environment rather than their own. It takes an Amaurau's breath away, Minister, the hubris of humanity to bend all of creation to its will."

Nick stared at the *Devil's Mistress*. The wind had risen, causing one of her sheets to rap against the mast and producing a sound like a bell tolling. "I hope that causes you some measure of fear," Nick commented.

"Indeed. We're cautious of humanity. You're not creatures to treat lightly. Although you can be powerful allies when you choose, you must be handled with care. Humans, as well as being consummate traders and biological engineers, are also consummate tricksters. You shift with the wind as it suits you. Trust is not something which humans inspire." Dessessah rested a hand on Nick's shoulder. "My question again, Minister. Why this island?"

Nick frowned. "What do you mean? It wasn't planned. It just happened as part of the terraforming."

Dessessah smiled, and her hand stroked Nick's shoulder. Once again, Nick felt his bones melt. It was not an unpleasant sensation. "Why do you come to this island? Why alone?"

Nick glanced at the beach, the solitude, the quiet. Even the waters of the cove were generally waveless, although now the surface was being ruffled by the freshening breeze. "I come here to be alone."

"You're alone when in the center of a thousand humans," she whispered.

Nick's adrenaline tried to drive a spike of fear through his chest, but the soothing stroke of Dessessah's fingers on his shoulder sent it flitting away. "Yes, that's true. I don't belong here, Sena. I don't fit in with my own species."

"Yet you don't belong to the Gunera." The words were spoken so close to Nick's ear that his hair tickled him.

"Then where do I belong?" he whispered back.

Dessessah traced a finger along his cheek. "You must, like your species, carve out your own world, Nicodemus Severin. Don't allow the universe to make you suit it."

Nick turned, mesmerized by Dessessah's gentle caress and her intense eyes. Her face was mere inches from his, her breath caressing his face. Nick felt an irresistible urge to kiss her, but before he could, the horror struck him so hard he pulled away. Leaping to his feet, Nick felt his body wash with sweat. The hot sun beat down on him, making him feel faint. He glanced at the cool green waters of the cove and then turned his gaze back at the Sena, who watched him with sharp eyes. Her stare stripped away any sensation of comfort. Nick realized he was being played by Dessessah as she threatened him one minute then seduced him the next. She was the trickster.

Shaking his head, Nick fled from Dessessah, racing up the beach to put as much distance as he could between them. When he came to a stop, panting, soaked in sweat, Nick leaned over, hands on his knees, face toward the shingle, and watched the small waves lapping at the shore. Sweat dripped from his forehead into his eyes and stung them.

Swearing, Nick straightened. He hastily removed his sneakers and clothes. Taking a single step forward, Nick dove into the cove's cool, clear waters. The water closing over his head was instantly soothing, and he swam beneath the surface until his lungs screamed in protest, and he was forced to come up for air. He resurfaced almost 50 meters from the shore, and there he tread water while looking back at the beach to find the Sena hadn't moved. She remained seated on the blanket, watching him, her head tilted quizzically. A rumble of thunder rolled over the island, and Nick jerked his gaze skyward. The standard afternoon thunderheads were building over the ocean, their distant grumbles becoming audible. He cursed. Knowing he had no choice but to return for the Sena and set out for home before the storms reached the island, Nick sank beneath the water and swam for shore.

Deciding he didn't want to get his clothes wet a second time, Nick waded onto the shingle to where he'd left his belongings and carried them to the boat. After tossing the items into the pit, he marched to where Dessessah waited. He didn't even look at her as he collected the picnic remains, shoving items into the basket without care. Dessessah rose from the blanket, and Nick snatched it up and carried everything to the boat. Finally, he returned and faced Dessessah.

"We need to return before the storms hit," he explained, feeling like a fool for his inexplicable behavior.

When she didn't reply, Nick held out his arms. "Let me carry you back, Sena. I don't want you to get your feet wet."

Still saying nothing, Dessessah extended her arms and allowed Nick to sweep her up in his. *Like picking up a feather,* he thought, as he carried her once again through the shallow water and deposited her onto the boat. Nick then hoisted himself aboard. Locating a towel, he hastily dried off and then dressed. All the while, Dessessah took her seat in the pit and watched him.

"My apologies," Nick murmured, gathering his wits and preparing the *Devil's Mistress* for sail.

"No need," she replied, as she tugged on her life vest. "You answered my question."

"What question?" Nick paid Dessessah little attention as his focus was on raising the anchors.

"On why you come to the island."

Nick darted her a glance. "To be alone, Sena. I come here to be alone." His hands jerked the sheets free, and with a handful of adrenaline-fueled pulls, he hefted the mainsail. As the wind quickened, the *Devil's Mistress* began to move swiftly, and Nick had to drop into his seat by the tiller to take control without raising the jib. The agile vessel set off with the airstream coming directly from the stern, Nick allowing her sail to run out to the left. He'd tighten her up once they'd broken free of the island.

"You will never be alone again, Minister," the woman said softly.

Nick's heart skipped, then thrummed. "What do you mean by that?"

She smiled. "Only that no matter where you go, we'll be watching you. Never forget it."

Nick stared, a shiver of fear running down his spine at the gently implied menace. As was typical of her species, Dessessah was threatening him in the most genteel of terms, smiling politely while promising pain. Desiring nothing except to escape the strangely attractive yet deadly creature, Nick turned his attention to squeezing every bit of speed he could out of the *Devil's Mistress,* setting her running hard before the wind of the storms that were banking now just off the coast. Nick felt as if not only was the vessel running from the storms but that he was running from all the evil that raced at his back.

Nick fought his growing frustration as his computer refused to relinquish the information he sought. Although the day was stellar,

Nick's eyes didn't see the beauty outside his window. Much of the Trade Office was empty that Friday afternoon because many of his coworkers had conjured up flimsy excuses to leave early. Others simply claimed it was too fine a day to spend locked up in an office and had bolted to start their weekend early.

"Ah, the life of a government employee," Nick said softly and sighed.

He would have joined them if he could transport himself back to July 24 before the awful party that had ended life as he knew it. The dust of that evening had settled since then, thank Jagjekcek. The Gunera had been hastily shoved into space with sincere wishes for a safe voyage, and please do come again … in ten years. gy'Gravinda had filed an official protest with the Trade Commission as well as the Office of the President of Rhadamanthus and the President of the Western Alliance in London. The actions had elicited a stream of video conferences with the folks on terra firma. Fortunately for Nick, Duncan handled all of that. The complaint was filed and suitable responses sent to gy'Gravinda. A number of unprofitable trades on the human side, profitable on the Guneri side, had been made to soothe the chafed skin of the ambassador. Quietly the matter was dropped.

From the Amaurau side, not a single word had been heard.

Meanwhile, Nick continued to deal with his uncomfortable living arrangements by focusing Dessessah's attention on the study of English. He was disturbed by the effect she had on him, and her barely concealed threats. However, after the trip to the island, she'd not threatened him again. She'd become exactly what she claimed she was, a simple student of English. Nick didn't believe a word of it, and he suspected Dessessah knew it. But they both played the game pretty well.

During the day, Nick escaped to his office, which left the Sena to her studies. Duncan arranged tours for Dessessah in the hope of providing whatever information she needed so that she could be shipped home as soon as possible.

Evenings dumped Dessessah back in Nick's lap, and he found himself in the uncomfortable position of escorting the lady all over Rhadamanthus as she was exposed to human culture. He took her to the opera and to the philharmonic, both tickets paid for by the Office. On his own dime, Nick took her to see Herbie Miller and the Voodoo Kings at the Jazz Pit. She was delighted by a trip to the art museum in mid-August and spent hours staring at a genuine Calder mobile that spun over the cafeteria while Nick nursed multiple sodas and waited for her to tire of the activity. She didn't, and he finally had to pull her away.

Which makes one wonder when the lady would finally surrender, Nick thought, as he rearranged his query and ran it again. It was Friday afternoon, and Dessessah was touring the Capitol Building, complete with a session of the legislature. Nick's mind was focused on the problem of the *Death's Festival*. The mystery of the doomed ship still nagged at him, and Nick couldn't let the puzzle die. He was sure the ship's fate was entangled in the events of the renewal ceremony, but he couldn't imagine how. The ship had simply been destroyed. Other than the secretive message sent from a remote Guneri outpost near Hemera, no word of its demise had ever been posted.

Nick couldn't even establish where the bloody ship had been bound. With dogged determination and access to the Guneri Transport Bureau's computer networks, Nick learned that the *Death's Festival* had been launched out of Gunera Proper on May 3 without a listed destination. That in itself sent a chill down Nick's back. The Gunera were sticklers for tax revenue. Every gy' or vuh' into whose territory the ship might have sailed was due their pound of flesh from the ship's owner. The Guneri Transport Bureau's database should have been filled with the various levies to be paid. Nick found nothing. The ship had launched and, two months later, had vanished, the apparent victim of an Amaurau attack.

His lack of results sent Nick to the Trade Commission's databases to search from the human side. He started with the assumption that the *Death's Festival* had entered human space. He couldn't imagine how the Amaurau could hit a Guneri vessel while the ship remained in Guneri territory. To do so would have meant the Amaurau ship had crossed human space twice, out to hit the Gunera and then back on the voyage home. By Protocol, such a situation was impossible. Neither the Amaurau nor the Gunera were allowed into human space. Instead, they made port at the nearest transshipment station that stood between their home port and the Gate. This enabled the humans to offload any cargo and vet it for contraband, poisons, toxins, booby traps, and biological agents before repackaging the stuff to be sent across the gap to the other side and picked up by the receiving party. The process was grossly inefficient, but it guaranteed that some evil-minded Guneri company didn't kill a bunch of Amaurau by slipping cyanide into the Kool-Aid. Nor could an equally evil-minded Amaurau put explosives in Guneri children's toys. In the meantime, a couple of human shipping companies made their fortunes serving as go-betweens in a very dangerous business indeed.

Nick found no mention of the freighter's arrival at a transshipment station, nor its Protocol-regulated transponder being recorded anywhere in human space. Based on the computer files, the ship had never entered the human side of Lethe's Gate. Thus Nick's conundrum. It must have crossed the Gate for an Amaurau ship to hit it, and yet it hadn't.

Nick contemplated what this meant. He'd been assuming an Amaurau had done the deed, but the message hadn't stated anything of the sort. No mention had been made of who or what had destroyed the *Death's Festival,* only that it had been obliterated. Nick considered the possibility of natural causes. Had the ship met with some untoward disaster while moving from one Guneri port to another? If so, why was there no record of tax levies in the Guneri files? Why the comment about not filing with the human commission? Such a situation had no bearing on the Protocols.

Nick soon arrived at an even uglier consideration that caused him to set his coffee cup aside while the heat of panic raced through his face. His hands trembled. Could the ship have been hit by human forces? It was certainly possible. Humanity maintained strong defensive lines on both its fragile borders. Perhaps there'd been an altercation.

Nick bit his stylus while considering what that would mean. The Gunera would take such an offense as an act of war. They expected sniping from the Amaurau just as the Amaurau expected sniping from them. But neither side expected humans to do the shooting. It wasn't possible. Had humans fired on Gunera, the resulting diplomatic explosion would have been heard all the way to London. The creatures would have flooded Nick's office with so many messages filled with filth he would have needed a bath after reading them. No, instead, gy'Gravinda had attended the renewal ceremony, postured as required, ate his way through the after-party, and ended with nothing more to take home than a profound hangover and his souvenir copy of Protocol 10. Humans hadn't done this thing. For once, they hadn't been stupid.

I can't know what happened without understanding the cargo, Nick thought, when his most recent query produced zero results. The cargo was the key. If the Gunera had been moving something they didn't want humans to know about, then they might have reflagged the ship, changed its transponder, and sent the cargo through under fraudulent papers.

Committing one hell of a Protocol violation.

Nick ran the queries again, this time filtering for every inbound shipment out of Gunera from May 3 until July 25. The list was daunting. He then excluded the names of vessels whose captains were above reproach and wouldn't allow themselves to be used. He removed shipments that hadn't passed near Hemera. Finally, he cross-checked the remaining shipments with outbound freight bound for Amaurau or human ports. He found a match for each one.

"What the hell?" Nick whispered. He scratched his chin while considering the results. Something had to be missing. Nick cleared the queries and started again, this time asking for the sum total weight of all inbound shipments during the May to July period. Forty-seven trillion metric tons. *Seriously?* Nick thought. *They really moved that much Guneri garbage through human space? No wonder Gemini Space was richer than Midas.*

Nick set the query aside and opened up a second. This time he ran the sum total of all outbound transshipments to Amaurau: 28 trillion metric tons. That left 19 trillion metric tons to find. Opening a third query, Nick requested all inbound Gunera shipments to human ports. The query churned then returned his answer: 19 trillion metric tons. It was correct to within one percentage point.

Nick sat blinking at the screen in disbelief. No cargo of any weight had gone missing. It was all accounted for.

Nick opened a trio of query windows and ran the numbers in bitchange. Eight trillion bitchange inbound give or take. Six trillion bitchange outbound. Two trillion bitchange to human ports. The numbers balanced within two percent. Close enough for government work.

That meant … what?

Either someone had tampered with the databases to hide the loss or …

The cargo had no weight.

The cargo had no monetary value.

The cargo was ... what?

Nick felt a headache brewing. A glance at the clock revealed that he had one hour left to complete the regular weekly checks before shutting down for the weekend. He saved his six queries and then shut down the computer.

Nick turned to his "For Gunera Use Only" computer and logged into his Guneri email. He still had friends in the empire, and they occasionally communicated via the Guneri system. Nick felt certain every word he wrote was parsed by gy'Bagrada and his Secret Service. That was how the gy' knew so much about Nick's life. *The bastard probably takes great glee in personally reading my email,* Nick thought.

The list of unread messages in Nick's in-box was depressingly short. Most were vile flames from individual Guneri citizens who delighted in sending filth to human recipients. He deleted them all.

Nick's eyes raced through the remaining messages. *It's not here,* he thought nervously and blinked, stunned. His mother had never in the past ten years failed to email him each day, just as he'd never failed to reply back. The exchange was shallow by necessity, only touching the surface of their lives. Nick couldn't tell his mother about his work, knowing Guneri censors were reading every word. He also knew his mother was forced to be upbeat because to criticize the government, even obliquely, was a capital offense. Nick was required to read between the lines. Only today, for the first time in a decade, there were no lines to read between because eh'Monica Severin hadn't sent him an email.

Feeling another jolt of panic, Nick hastily composed a message, using all the wording necessary to get past the censors.

Greetings, Most Esteemed Mother,
eh'Nicodemus wishes you to know that he is out of balance due to your lack of interest. He longs for his mother's cooking and wonders if she'll invite him for a meal. In all other aspects, he endures. End.

Which, translated into English, read ...

Hi Mom, Your son is worried he hasn't heard from you. Contact him as soon as possible. Other than that, he's fine; don't worry.

Nick hit *send* but knew he'd receive no reply for days. The Guneri systems would first have to admit the out-of-network message, after which it would be read by the censors and gy'Bagrada, and then finally, the message would be forwarded. Nick could do nothing but wait. The tenuous link via email was his only means of communicating with his mother. For a full minute, he allowed himself to worry. Was she sick? In some horrid Guneri hospital where the fools didn't have a clue how to treat a human? Dead? Worse? *God, Nick, get a hold of yourself!* She was late sending her daily update. Maybe the system was down. Maybe someone on the human side was holding the transmission on Duncan's orders in a misguided attempt to shield him from worries. Nick knew from experience that a single late email did not a crisis make.

Nick forced himself to push his worries aside. He could do nothing for her. Although he'd fought to stay by her side, Nick's mom had chosen to let him go. In setting her son free, she'd taken risks no mother should ever be expected to take for her child. On the day he left her, Nick had known that he and his mom would probably never see one another again.

He opened an email from vuh'Ygundin. The vuh' was the son of the lord to whom Nick and his mother had been enslaved. Being of similar age, the two youngsters had developed a symbiotic relationship based on need. vuh'Ygundin had used Nick as a science experiment. Nick had used the vuh's position to buy himself favors. They maintained the relationship probably because the Secret Service asked the vuh' to do so. It provided a window into the world of humans.

vuh'Ygundin's letter was prim and terse as always, careful to avoid the buzz words that might alarm government readers. He had advanced in his career at the surgical hospital where he worked as a physical therapist. Of course, he loved the work, aiding people who weren't furthering the grand design of the empire due to disability. He swelled with gratitude that he'd been granted his position by the government. All hail mai'Tegatriktrik.

It was always the same.

Nick responded with equally false enthusiasm that he was still at the Trade Commission and engaged with transshipping details. He added that his sister was marrying soon and that Nick would be traveling to Hemera to join in the ceremony once he'd calculated his vacation schedule and found money for the fare.

Let gy'Bagrada chew on that one, Nick thought with grim satisfaction as he hit *send*. The damned Secret Service would spend a month trying to figure out from which corner of hell Nick had conjured up a sister.

Once they concluded he didn't have one, they'd spend another month parsing the word "sister" for every possible connotation imaginable to explain why eh'Nicodemus was planning to visit Hemera. Which he wasn't. But it sounded good.

The next, and thankfully last, email was from eh'Kraghilg. The eh' was the waste tender in the vuh's house, the lowest position for a Gunera outside that of slave. He was younger than Nick. Given that no Gunera could bear the presence of such an eh', the lonely Gunera had latched onto the lonely human, and they'd developed an illegal yet profound friendship. Had anyone known the two boys met in the sewage house to play simple games in the dirt, Nick would have been lashed to within an inch of his life and eh'Kraghilg thrown into the sewage pit to drown.

Only eh'Monica had known the two were companions. While she'd been terrified for her son, she also knew he needed someone, anyone, besides his mother with whom to bond. And bond they did. Always watching out for one another. Running interference when danger lurked. Each being, if nothing else, a caring soul on which the other could lean. The duo even developed their own secret language that allowed them to pass information in front of their vuh' masters without those idiots ever knowing. It was a deadly game, but they'd relished it.

eh'Kraghilg still lived in the vuh's house and was, at the age of twenty-two, considering if he should bring forth a son to follow in his footsteps. vuh'Yguggli, the lord of the house, was pressuring him to do so. The vuh' wanted to assure that another waste tender would be of age when eh'Kraghilg passed on. eh'Kraghilg wasn't so certain he wanted to bring forth offspring to be condemned to the life he led. Ever since Nick had escaped the trap, the eh' suffered intense loneliness and depression, and Nick knew he lived only for news of his lost friend. Eventually, eh'Kraghilg would be forced by pain of torture to replicate himself, and Nick mourned for his friend's coming agonies. An obstinate individual, eh'Kraghilg would suffer immensely before he succumbed.

eh'Kraghilg's message was typical for the week. The weather had been awful, and his township had suffered from flooding. This was a huge problem in the waste-tending business and made his life difficult. He was getting "cut with the stick" on a daily basis due to the smell from the mold, mildew, and system backups.

Nick winced, knowing that to be cut with the stick was to have the master take a willow branch and beat the eh' around his back until he bled. Nick knew the sting of the willow branch. The thought that his friend was suffering due to problems beyond his control infuriated Nick. Unfortunately, just as he could do nothing for his mother, Nick could do nothing for his friend.

eh'Kraghilg also mentioned that the vuh' was carping about replicating again. He wished that Gunera were like humans, needing a sexual partner with which to mate because then he could claim no female would accept a waste tender. Alas, that was not to be. As always, the eh' asked how the odd situation was working for Nick since he hadn't received word that Nick had replicated himself. He was curious. "Please, when you figure it out, tell me! I really want to know!" he wrote.

Nick smiled at his friend's eagerness to understand things human. Every letter held at least one question regarding how humans functioned, and Nick tried to answer them. Unfortunately, eh'Kraghilg was going to be disappointed this week because Nick still didn't have an answer to that one.

His reply was more serious.

> *Odd events are afoot here. I fear for the alliance. The Amaurau paid us a visit. I have one living in my apartment with me. While I don't know what it means, it's very annoying. The renewal ceremony was a disaster. I thought I might have my office head cut off. I survived, and my office head is still attached. I haven't heard from my mother this week, and am worried. If you can investigate I would be much obliged.*
>
> *Regarding your question, no word yet on replicating. I've studied the mechanics of the process and obtained practice with professional females who do such work for a living, but they don't allow actual replicating to occur. I know a female who seems obliging but there are intricacies that I'm afraid I don't comprehend. Actually getting a female to offer replication is complicated. If I ever do figure it out, I will be sure to tell you.*
>
> *With love and concern,*
> *eh'Nicodemus.*

His official work done for the week, Nick shut down the Guneri computer and cleaned up his desk. He was just rising when someone rapped on his door. Corey Boyers stood in the doorway looking dapper and tanned in a tight-fitting polo shirt and shorts that showed off his physique. The man was beaming, his thousand-watt smile capable of lighting up the nebula.

"Ready?" he asked, as Nick locked his office door. Corey studied Nick's attire. "You might want to change. It's hot out there."

Nick shrugged. He didn't mind heat. Unlike most humans, he didn't mind sweating. That nasty human trait had been a lifesaver on Gunera, driving away various individuals who might have approached him physically had he smelled better.

"We need to stop by my place to pick up the Sena," Nick said. "I'll change there."

Corey nodded, and together the two men walked to Nick's residence building. The day was indeed broiling. The humidity had broken, but a scalding breeze felt like a breath from the mouth of hell.

As Nick led his friend into his apartment, Dessessah rose.

Corey stopped short and glanced at Nick. "I've never met an Amaurau before. How do I greet her?"

"Curtsy as best you can and say 'Hello, Sena,'" Nick replied absently. Nick stripped off his work shirt as he nodded to Dessessah and strode to his bedroom.

Cory cursed Nick's sorry lack of manners and awkwardly introduced himself to Dessessah.

As soon as he reached his bedroom, Nick removed his pants and copied Corey's attire, white polo shirt and Bermuda shorts. He'd found that Corey always knew what to wear for any occasion, and so long as Nick matched him, he didn't suffer ridicule.

Upon returning to the great room, Nick found Corey trying to win over Dessessah with a beaming smile that she politely mirrored.

Nick straightened his collar. "Are we ready?"

Corey grabbed Nick by the arm, lowered his head to Nick's ear, and growled, "What's her name, damn you?"

Nick scowled, then flushed, embarrassed by the oversight.

"Sena Dessessah, may I introduce Corey Boyers."

The two exchanged another set of awkward curtsies.

"How should I address her?" Corey asked Nick.

"Sena is fine. Sena Dessessah. Sena simply means *miss,* Sevay means *mister.* She'll address you as Sevay Corey. She insists on calling me Minister Nicodemus. I can't seem to break her of it."

He smiled at Dessessah. "Are you ready for our excursion, Sena?" Nick asked in Amaurau.

She nodded, earrings swinging. "I'm looking forward to it. I understand the purpose for the official tours, but I wish to learn of human culture as it is lived, not as it is hung on walls. I wish you to convey to your companion that I'm eager to spend time with ordinary people doing ordinary things."

Nick groaned quietly. He wasn't certain how "ordinary" their outing was going to be, having never attended a polo match. He supposed having his buddies as escorts instead of officials and dignitaries would make for a more enjoyable outing. Nick translated Dessessah's statement to Corey, and he bowed. *Always the showman, Corey Boyers,* Nick thought, enviously. He suspected Corey had no problem convincing females to help him replicate.

The trio departed Nick's apartment and crossed the quad. The limousine was curbside at the front of the Trade and Commerce campus. Alessandra McCoy awaited within, her chauffeur standing outside at attention, doors open. Corey, Dessessah, and Nick stepped inside.

Corey elbowed Nick's ribs, a reminder to introduce Alessandra and the last of their party, Jordan Nash, to Dessessah. The two humans, the daughter of a senator and the son of an aluminum tycoon, graciously welcomed the Amaurau lady. Judging by her expression, Dessessah was pleased with the greetings. Alessandra rapped her knuckles on the glass, and the limousine sped off.

"What's this game we're to watch?" Dessessah asked Nick.

"It's called polo, an ancient game that's been played for thousands of years on our home world."

"Do you watch it often?"

Nick rubbed the back of his neck. "No. But it's popular here on Rhadamanthus."

"Why don't you play?"

Nick laughed. "For starters, I'd need to learn to ride a horse." He was forced to use the English word for *horse* because there were no such species on Amaurau. "You'll understand once we arrive. Besides, it's a sport of kings, not lowly civil servants like me."

The Sena said nothing more, and the quintet rode to the polo grounds in silence.

Once on the grounds, the chauffeur reappeared toting a number of wicker baskets. Alessandra used her father's season tickets to gain access to the fields, and they were off, tramping across the rough grass in search of an open space near the middle line.

The equestrian facility was a point of pride for the people of Rhadamanthus. Some 50 years prior, a retired general with more money than sense had imported 20 polo pony foals from Earth. Amazingly 12 of the creatures had survived the journey. Like everything else on Rhadamanthus, the animals had thrived. Now the capitol had its own polo facility with barns stabling over 100 of those horses' descendants.

The polo grounds were covered with tents crowded close to the sidelines protecting the rich and fabulous from the sun. The ladies were resplendent in their wide-brimmed hats and billowing skirts while the men looked quite lordly in polo attire, not that a single man among them probably engaged in the sport. This was a place to see and to be seen, and gossip ran rampant up and down the lines. Nick and his party were remarked upon, especially Dessessah with her feathers fluttering in the wind. As they searched for enough open ground on which to set up their picnic, Nick's party passed a number of ladies whose hats boasted long feathers.

Dessessah eyed the plumage with pleasure. "I feel very at home," she said.

Alessandra commandeered space near the midline where her chauffeur set up the tent, table, and chairs. Next came the pristine white tablecloth. Finally, Alessandra placed various bowls of food next to the requisite vase of orchids and the stacks of silver service and porcelain plates.

As the fruit, potato salad, and macaroni salad were placed on the table, Jordan whispered to Nick, "What do those things eat?"

"You don't have to whisper," Nick replied. "She's only now learning English. And they eat pretty much everything we do. They like meat, although they prefer game meats to domesticated fare, and they'll eat fruit, bread, and nuts."

"How do you keep track?" Jordan asked. "It boggles the mind the crap you need to know to keep those two freak shows from blowing the universe apart."

"I find humans just as bewildering, truth be told," Nick muttered.

Corey gave Jordan a cuff to shut him up, and the two men exchanged furious glances.

Alessandra tried to soothe Nick's annoyance by sliding up alongside him and curling an arm around his waist. She laid her head on his shoulder.

"Don't mind them," she said. "They really are trying to understand."

Nick sighed and wished the warmth of Alessandra's soft body lining his didn't cause his hormones to rage. He couldn't control them, but Corey said it was required of civilized men. He needed to learn how or his life would remain lonely. *As if,* Nick thought, *it could be any lonelier.*

He circled his arm around Alessandra's tiny waist and held her while willing his body to obey his mind. Alessandra didn't resist the embrace, knowing that doing so might prove embarrassing. She pecked a soft kiss on Nick's cheek then slid away. As Nick turned to watch Alessandra take command of the picnic, he noticed Dessessah observing them.

Soon Alessandra declared the picnic open and excused her chauffeur for the afternoon. The group settled in the white plastic chairs beneath the canopy and sampled the various cuisines provided by the cook from Alessandra's house. Nick enjoyed the picnic, especially the salads. He watched with amusement as Dessessah sampled everything but ended up devouring a bowl of popcorn, declaring it her favorite item.

When the ponies charged onto the field, she froze, her hand halfway to her mouth, popcorn poised in midair. The sight of humans astride the giant beasts caused Dessessah to squeal in alarm; Nick had to restrain her from taking flight. After he explained that the animals were trained to carry humans on their backs, Dessessah resumed shoving popcorn into her mouth almost as an afterthought while she watched with wide eyes as the horses galloped past.

"The point of the game," Nick explained, "is to use the mallet to hit a ball between the posts at the end of the field while the opposing team tries to hit the ball in the other direction."

The Amaurau lady remained transfixed as the crowd of horses and riders, four on each team plus three referees, charged this way and that in an attempt to gain control of the ball. The ground trembled before the thunder of hooves, and Dessessah squealed with childlike delight every time the pack came near.

"This is a marvelous experience," Dessessah said. "Thank you, kind Minister, for bringing me here today."

Nick felt guilty. The idea had been Alessandra's.

At the midpoint of the match, while riders retired for a rest and a change of ponies, the announcer welcomed the spectators onto the field to replace the divots. Allowing Alessandra to drag him with her, Nick tromped the grass down where the horses had kicked it up. After they'd stomped a divot or two, Alessandra grasped Nick by the hand and pulled him close.

"This is for the gallant effort," she said, as she rose on her tiptoes and kissed Nick's lips.

As Nick relished her sweet taste, reminiscent of the tea she loved, he forced himself to remember everything Corey had told him. Be polite. Don't swallow her tongue even though heaven and Earth are demanding you do so. Save the tongue for when in private. He returned the kiss as he'd been taught, all the while cursing the rules that mandated humans only engage in sexual activity behind closed doors. *Annoying rules, damn them!* he thought.

Alessandra removed her broad-brimmed hat and waved it across her face. "It's gotten hotter, hasn't it?"

Nick shot her a look, unsure if she was making a subtle sexual advance or merely noting the weather.

"Could you run to the stand near the announcer's booth and fetch us another pitcher of lemonade?" she asked, pointing to the wooden structure that positioned the announcer above the field. A concession stand stood at its base.

Nick nodded, deciding he needed to distance himself from Alessandra before he did something embarrassing. Alessandra pressed her pass into his hand and waved him off.

Nick strode across the polo field then slipped through the crowd of tents on the sidelines. As he walked, another man fell into step beside him, also holding a concession pass.

"Same job, eh?" the man asked, waving the bit of plastic.

As Nick glanced at the stranger's pass, the man grasped his arm. Nick tried to wrest himself free, but the man's grip intensified. A second later, Nick felt a sharp stab. The syringe was in and out of his arm in seconds. He tried to call out, but his head was already whirling, and he wasn't sure what he might say. A second man approached from the left, and he felt a stab in that arm. Nick stumbled, his head lost in clouds. The men grasped Nick's arms to steady him.

"No worries," the first man murmured, leading Nick as he swayed between them. "Just a quiet stroll. Three friends, having a chat."

Nick tried to regain his balance, but it was hopeless. His arms and legs felt disconnected from his body, and he'd lost the will to fight. The trio walked onward across the hot open field. Nick's vision blurred then cleared repeatedly. A sudden coolness washed over him, and he was vaguely aware that they'd entered the woods bordering the complex. Now four men surrounded him.

Still, the men walked, keeping a light hold on Nick so that he didn't fall. They didn't need to be rough with him. Whatever drug they'd used had numbed his ability to protest. He merely walked with them like they were friends, his mind bleary and uncomprehending.

"Where are you taking me?" he mumbled, as the men led him along a cool path under the trees.

"We'll be asking the questions, Mr. Severin," the leader stated. "How are things going with the Amaurau lady?"

"Going? I ... I don't understand. They aren't *going* anywhere."

"What sort of secrets are you telling her, Undersecretary?"

"Secrets? I'm teaching her English."

"She's living in your apartment."

"That was Ississita's idea, not mine."

"So you blindly obey the Amaurau ambassador."

"I do what the Protocols demand."

"And they demand we place an Amaurau spy in our midst? In the personal dwelling of one of our undersecretaries?"

Nick frowned. The question was a trap. He couldn't honestly answer either yes or no. "The Protocols allow the Amaurau to have a liaison. Same goes for the Gunera."

"The Gunera liaison isn't living with the undersecretary of trade."

"No, their liaison *is* the undersecretary of trade."

"Are you saying you work for the Gunera, Mr. Severin?"

"Only as my work pertains to the Protocols."

"Mr. Severin, are you a Guneri spy?"

"No!"

"Have they commanded you to kill the Sena?"

"What? No!"

"Do you want her in your apartment?"

"Actually, no. Whoever you are, can you remove her?"

The walk continued. Nick understood that not only was the drug in his system stealing his ability to control his body, it also freed his tongue. He did not know these men, but he was answering them too candidly.

"Is she in danger from you, Mr. Severin?"

Nick frowned. "I don't think so."

"You don't think so?"

"I'm dangerous to everyone. I don't always know what I'm doing."

"You protect the Protocols, isn't that true?"

"It's the only thing I know how to do correctly."

"What of the Gunera?" The question came quietly. "Do you know who planned that attack on gy'Gravinda?"

"No."

"Did you know it was going to happen?"

"No."

"Did you know the Amaurau were going to invade the party and nearly destroy the alliance?"

"No." Nick frowned again. "How could I? The Amaurau aren't much for talking."

"Did you poison Duncan Huntzinger?"

Nick tried to stop as the anger that flashed through him almost overcame the effects of the drug, but his captors kept pressing him ahead. "Of course not."

The darkness beneath the trees seemed to shift and change. Nick found himself standing free of his abductors. He tried to focus, but he was too confused to do anything more than rock precariously on his feet. Nick thought he heard movement on his right, but turning, saw no one. He looked to his left. Standing in the midst of a ray of sunshine piercing the forest canopy stood Dessessah. She held an object, but he couldn't identify it. He stumbled toward her, trying to find focus. She stopped him with a touch.

"Lie down." Her firm voice was unlike her normal warble.

"Lie down?"

"Yes. Lie down." Dessessah bent Nick's shoulders forward while she adjusted his feet to unbalance him. Nick sank to his knees to keep from falling over. A moment later, he was lying on his back on a soft bed of moss while Dessessah loomed over him. The sunlight stung Nick's eyes.

"Did gy'Bagrada send you here as a spy?" she asked.

"What? No."

"Do you plan to uphold the peace, or are you in conspiracy to destroy it?"

"Yes. No!" He tried to answer honestly but found it difficult to reply to two questions at once. He wished he could clear his thinking.

"Did you poison Duncan Huntzinger?"

"No."

"Do you have plans to harm me?"

"No." Nick closed his eyes, waiting for the world to stop spinning.

"What would you do to save eh'Monica?"

Nick gasped at the pain of the question. It wasn't fair. Dessessah had no right to ask this while he was drugged and helpless at her feet. "There's nothing I can do to save my mother."

"But if you could, what would you do?"

"Give my life."

"You claim you'd give your life for the Protocols."

"Yes."

"Seems a contradiction." Dessessah smiled.

Nick frowned. He couldn't answer what wasn't a question. He tried to move, to rise, but Dessessah was squatting on her heels beside him and holding him down easily.

"You've been drugged, Minister, do you know that?"

"Yes."

"Its effect on you is profound."

"Yes."

"While it remains in your bloodstream, you must speak truthfully."

"Apparently."

"Are you an honest man, Minister?"

"Yes."

"Even when you are not drugged?"

"Yes."

"Yet you lie to me constantly."

"Yes." Nick felt a stab of fear even through the whirl of confusion. He was prostrate on the ground, deep in the woods, far from help. He knew Dessessah was armed with poisoned darts. She could kill him where he lay, and no one might ever find him.

"How have you lied to me?"

"I'm not a minister," he babbled. "I'm just the undersecretary."

"Is that the only lie you've told me?"

"I think so."

"Think harder. I know the drug is confusing you. Concentrate. What facts have you distorted? What would you say that you haven't said?"

"I think you're a desirable woman."

Even in his state of confusion, Nick was aware of the long moment of silence before she spoke again. "You certainly are of Guneri temperament," Dessessah chuckled. "They never know the appropriate time or place for anything."

"Corey says I'll never find myself a woman given my atrocious manners."

Another chuckle. "Your friend Corey is right." Dessessah patted Nick's shoulder, then her fingers moved to his face, and she traced her fingertips around his eyes. "Lie still. Eventually, the drug will wear off. Once it does, you'll be in command of your body again, and you can leave. I was never here, Minister. You didn't speak with me. Yes?"

"No."

"I'm telling you the answer is yes. Say *yes*."

"Yes."

Dessessah continued that strange motion with her fingers, sending shivers through Nick as she ran them over his eyes and around his ears. She patted him again. Nick stared at her helplessly as she rose and became a silhouette against the shaft of light seeping through the trees. Dessessah extended her arms with their thick banding of feathers, and Nick blinked in wonder.

"Am I dead?" Nick asked.

"Perhaps. Why do you ask?"

"Because this must be heaven."

Nick sensed humor in Dessessah's voice. "Why is that?"

"You're an angel!"

"Yes, Sevay. I'm an angel, and you're in heaven. When you awaken, remember only those two facts. Close your eyes."

Nick couldn't resist the command. Dessessah's words washed over him like a soft spring rain, persuading and cajoling. He couldn't help but acquiesce.

He thought he heard the rustle of wings, but when Nick next reopened his eyes, he was alone. He promptly drifted off.

There were sounds in the distance, but his mind refused to decode them into concepts. The noise droned on as Nick fought to make sense of them. Then his mind cleared.

"Jesus! Nick!" Jordan cried, falling to his knees beside Nick and pressing fingers to his neck. "He's alive. God, for a second there, I thought …"

Corey knelt opposite of Jordan and tapped Nick's cheek gently with the back of a hand. "Nick? You okay? Wake up, Nick!"

Clawing his way through the layers of fog, Nick opened his eyes to find Corey staring down at him. He sensed a damp softness at his back. His hips hurt because he was lying with his legs twisted under him. Both arms throbbed as if he'd been stung by bees. Questions formed in Nick's mind. *What am I doing here? What happened?*

Corey slipped his arm beneath Nick's shoulders and eased him upright. Nick winced and adjusted his legs to a more natural sitting position.

"What happened?" he asked in a ghost of a voice.

"We were about to ask you the same question." Jordan lightly slapped Nick's face to further rouse him. "You disappeared."

"Where am I?"

"In the woods," Corey replied.

Nick noticed the exchange of worried glances between his two friends. Corey stood up.

"Let's get him to the EMT station. Where are the syringes you found?"

Jordan tapped his back pocket.

The two men dragged Nick to his feet, although his legs felt as weak a newborn colt's. Each took an arm over their shoulders to keep him upright.

The pair started forward, half dragging their friend between them. Nick focused on keeping on his feet to lessen his friends' burden. After a few minutes of slow walking, the trio left the coolness of the woods, and Nick felt the blazing heat of the Rhadamanthan sun burning into his dark hair. The afternoon was blisteringly hot. Nick felt it had been cooler when he'd first set out. Set out? For what?

Corey and Jordan's pace increased upon reaching the open, and Nick found he was gaining control of his wayward limbs with each footstep. By the time they reached the polo grounds, he required no assistance. Nick realized the polo match had ended. Most of the picnic tents had been disassembled. Only a few diehard tailgaters remained, sipping wine and nibbling on canapés. Jordan and Corey escorted Nick to the EMT station as it had not yet been dismantled. Clarice Hollingsworth, the on-duty technician, wore a crisp blue uniform. She eyed Nick and ordered him to a nearby cot for assessment.

"What's the problem?" Hollingsworth asked, attaching a blood pressure monitor to Nick's right index finger.

"We found Nick unconscious in the woods," Corey explained.

Jordan proffered the syringes. "Also found these."

Hollingsworth took the syringes with no small surprise. She set them aside while assuring herself that Nick was not going to die. The reactions in Nick's pupils, as well as normal blood pressure and heart rate readings, assured Hollingsworth that Nick was in no danger. She turned to the syringes.

"Lucky for you Patriot Volunteer had another gig over at the soccer stadium," Hollingsworth commented. "I'm with Capitol General. We have a spectrograph in the van. Hang on."

The EMT technician disappeared into the van that stood not far from the tent as Corey fussed and Nick batted him away.

"I'm all right," Nick muttered in embarrassment. "I'm sorry I did whatever it was I did."

Corey and Jordan exchanged glances.

"What did I do now?" Nick moaned, expecting he'd made some horrid faux pas that would assure he'd never be allowed to visit the polo grounds again.

Corey patted his friend's hand. "You didn't do anything, Nick. You really don't remember what happened, do you?"

Nick rubbed his hands over his eyes and tried to focus. He remembered several men, strangers. The woods and shifting shadows. Ississita. An Amaurau anyway. Or had he? He wasn't sure.

"Not really."

"Sandra said she sent you for lemonade, but you never returned," Jordan said. "Dessessah saw you being led away by two men and raised the alarm. She's got incredible eyesight."

Nick scowled at his friend. "She barely speaks English, and you don't speak Amaurau. How did she manage to tell you anything?"

Jordan gave a wry laugh. "You don't have to speak Amaurau if someone is shaking your arm in high distress and pointing madly across the grounds. Then she took off. I mean, damn Nick, the woman can *fly!* The whole grounds went wild when they saw her. It was a hell of a thing."

Nick groaned as he considered how that was going to fly, literally, on the six o'clock news. He wondered just how many times the Trade Commission could hand Nick his head for allowing yet another diplomatic snafu to occur on his watch.

Corey picked up the tale. "She determined the direction you were going and then returned and explained it with hand signals."

"What did you do?"

"Ran after you, of course!" Jordan issued a slight punch in reprimand.

"What happened to the Sena?" Nick wasn't sure why he wanted to know, but it seemed important.

"We left her here with Alessandra. She's fine. That flying stunt scared the bejesus out of pretty much everyone, but you know Sandy, always the senator's daughter. Didn't bat an eyelash. Just handed the Sena more popcorn and showed her how to fold napkins into bird shapes."

Nick grunted. The war hadn't been invented that could shock Alessandra McCoy out of character. Thank God there was one tiny certainty in this universe: Alessandra McCoy was never discomposed.

The EMT returned and handed the now bagged syringes to Corey. "Versadine," she said. "Enough to knock one of those polo ponies to its knees."

Corey looked at the bags in alarm. "What does it do? Is Nick in trouble?"

Hollingsworth rechecked Nick's blood pressure and found it had dropped to normal. "Versadine's perfectly safe. It's a frontal lobe inhibitor, used mostly in psychiatric hospitals to calm patients. Makes a person incapable of resistance." She pursed her lips. "In low doses, it renders a person helpless for several minutes, just enough for an out-of-control patient to be restrained."

"But in this dose?" Corey asked, concerned.

"It acts like a truth serum. Makes a person unable to refuse persuasion. It's illegal to use it that way, but I've heard tales that the government finds it especially useful."

Once again, looks flashed between Corey and Jordan, but neither man spoke. Nick knew his friends had the wisdom to keep their mouths shut.

"Are there any after-effects?" Jordan asked as Nick sat up.

"Just the potential for a headache," Hollingsworth replied. She helped Nick rise. "Take it easy for the rest of the day. By tomorrow you probably won't remember anything. Versadine is known to wipe memories. Try to have an uneventful evening."

Nick stood, refusing his friends' assistance, and suggested they return to the ladies. Neither Jordan nor Corey dared to ask any questions, although Nick suspected they longed to. His position in the Trade Commission demanded discretion. No corporate executive, Guneri gy', or Amaurau lord wanted his business exposed to public air. By definition, Nick knew where everyone's skeletons lay hidden. The walk was somber.

They found Alessandra and Dessessah studying each other's clothing, although neither spoke a word of the other's language. Alessandra marveled at the fine weaving of Dessessah's dress while Dessessah studied the overlock on Alessandra's skirt. The two women jumped to their feet as their male counterparts approached.

Alessandra clasped Nick's arm and suggested he sit down. Nick allowed her to push him into a chair, after which she slapped a bowl of fruit salad in his hand.

"You look terrible, Nick. What happened?"

Nick set the bowl aside. His eyes were focused on the Amaurau Sena. She stood on the far side of the tent, arms demurely crossed, while she watched Nick with a worried expression.

"I don't know." Nick said it more for the Sena than for Alessandra. "Someone thought to drug me and take me for a walk." He repeated the statement in Amaurau but received no response.

"Who?" Alessandra gasped.

"I don't know that either." Nick's eyes remained fixed on Dessessah. "My memory is clouded. I have visions of winged angels and heaven." He again translated the statement and received the same nonreply.

Nothing broke Dessessah's composure. She could teach Alessandra lessons. "How very distressing," she said. "I hope there are no lingering effects."

"No." Nick's eyes narrowed, conveying to Dessessah that he was aware she'd been there.

Nick's response elicited the faintest curve in Dessessah's lips. *So the game is off and running,* Nick thought. Both knew, and they were going to take it all the way to the end. *But the end of what?* Nick wondered. *What game are the Amaurau playing, and why am I their chosen pawn?*

The thoughts broke open a shooting pain in Nick's head, and he pleaded to go home. Alessandra summoned her chauffeur. Jordan offered to help Alessandra clean up the picnic while Corey escorted Nick. With lips still curled in a secretive smile, Dessessah chose to help with the picnic.

Upon reaching Nick's apartment, Corey helped his friend undress and put him to bed. He issued a worried "good night" to Nick and closed the bedroom door. As he left, Corey took a moment to confirm that the door was securely locked.

5

Nick knew things were going from bad to worse when he received the request to meet Duncan at seven in the evening in the Botanical Gardens. The note didn't mention Dessessah, which meant this wasn't another case of cultural enrichment for the sly Amaurau girl. Nick hadn't seen his boss for the past two weeks. Something had kept the man embedded in the Capitol Building meeting with President De Walt. In the meantime, Nick took precautions to ensure that he was never alone with the Sena. He'd even cajoled Jordan into sleeping in the apartment. The younger man dutifully took up station on the couch, being the Protocol officer of the Severin apartment as Nick was the Protocol officer of the known universe. Jordan kept his two aliens apart by night much as Nick kept his two alien species apart by day. Nick wasn't sure what it would take to repay his friend, but he knew he'd pay it.

Other than the fact that he had a woman who wanted to kill him living in his apartment, life had settled down into its slow, peaceful, Rhadamanthan pace. At work, the only skirmish had been caused by some human idiot who'd forgotten to have Guneri instruction sheets translated to Amaurau before stuffing them in the crates. Hue and cry had ensued, and an official complaint was filed by the Amaurau importer who demanded blood, heads, bones, and money, yada yada yada. Nick forwarded it to the company involved in the debacle along with a reprimand and fine. He'd gotten no further in his investigation into the demise of the *Death's Festival,* and he finally admitted he never would. He archived the file in a remote folder on the server with a note to himself about where he'd stored it should it ever be needed again.

Nick still had not received word from his mother, but eh'Kraghilg continued to investigate. The eh' could only tell Nick that eh'Monica had been removed from the house of vuh'Yguggli, but no one knew where she'd been taken. As far as he could determine, she hadn't done anything to warrant arrest, and he didn't think she'd fallen ill. eh'Kraghilg promised Nick he would keep digging. Heartsick, Nick knew he could do nothing except wait for her to write. Twice in the depths of night, while Jordan snored in the outer room and Nick stared up at his ceiling in panic, he considered writing to gy'Bagrada, but pragmatism prevailed. There was no telling what sort of horrible price the gy' would demand of Nick, and he knew he couldn't put the Trade Commission in their debt. He lay in the silent darkness, prisoner of his own terrible imaginings.

Why the botanical gardens? Nick wondered the following evening as he stepped through the elaborate wrought iron gate that admitted him into the serene space. Rhadamanthus itself was a botanical garden filled with every type of endangered tropical plant imaginable, so there was nothing especially intriguing about the gardens. As the sun set golden and hot, Nick walked virtually alone down the main path. To the left were the ball courts that featured several croquet and bocce lanes. Nick watched as an elderly couple played croquet to the light of the setting sun. They moved gracefully, like accomplished dancers. Married, he was sure. Long past their working years and now settled into a well-deserved retirement. Nick envied the couple for the simple joy they found in an ancient game played in the gentle air at day's end.

Nick found Duncan sitting in a gazebo overlooking a lake where swans glided on the still water. The air was motionless, and the lake surface mirrored the brilliant reds painting the sky. Nick sat beside his boss.

"Strange doings," Duncan said, still staring forward.

"You think?" Nick couldn't hold back the sarcasm.

As Duncan turned toward his colleague, it appeared to Nick that his supervisor seemed to have aged drastically in the handful of weeks since Independence Day. Nick wondered whether Duncan was well.

He suspected Duncan was in his early fifties, though tonight, he seemed much older.

"What's going on, Duncan?" Nick asked. He suspected Duncan had chosen to meet at the botanical garden because it provided privacy and seclusion.

Gazing out at the lake, Duncan shook his head. "Hell if I know." He propped his elbows on his knees and clasped his fingers together. "Do you trust me?"

"Without question."

Duncan turned his eyes on Nick. "Question everything from now on. I hope you know I trust you. You're the only person in this whole damned universe I trust at this moment. The only one."

"Maybe you shouldn't," Nick replied. Duncan shot him a sharp look of surprise. "I'm not exactly batting a thousand. I've screwed up more times in the past three weeks than I have in my entire career. Maybe I'm not worthy of your trust."

Duncan placed an arm around Nick's shoulders and gave him a gentle shake. "That's not the sort of trust I'm talking about, Nico. I'm talking about trusting a man's integrity, trusting to know where his heart is. And right now, yours is probably the only one I trust."

"Why?"

Duncan issued a forced smile. "Did you know I knew your father?"

Nick nodded.

"You look just like him with that black hair and dark eyes. He was a big fellow too, like you. Smart. Hell of a diplomat. You take after him in that regard as well."

Nick silently nodded. He knew little about his father aside from what he'd read on history websites and in books.

Duncan appeared lost in thought, and Nick suspected he was walking in the halls of memory. "I was there at Lethe's Gate when we lost your dad. In those days, I was a lowly undersecretary in his administration on Hemera. We both enjoyed sailing, and he'd sometimes take me out on his little sunny during all-too-scarce free moments. It was the only time he could escape the pressures of being president. Just him and me and that little boat. His security detail couldn't keep up with us because your dad knew how to slip the noose. I still cherish those days. Two young men having the time of our lives, fishing and swimming and wishing we weren't who we were. That's not to say he didn't want to be president; he did. He also loved your mother something fierce. He was so excited to learn Monica was carrying you. His face would beam brighter than the sun, and he'd tell anyone who'd listen about the beautiful daughter he was bringing into the world."

"*Daughter.*" Nick sighed.

"I know. He was convinced of it. Some ancient legend about the way Monica was carrying you. High meant a girl and low a boy, supposedly. Ancient Greek nonsense, probably. Your dad didn't care; he was going to be a father."

Nick silently watched the swans and the setting sun. He knew Duncan would eventually get to the point. In the meantime, Nick was happy to learn more about his dad's past. Memories were all he had.

"Your father was a brave man—too brave. Would that he'd stayed on Hemera when that mess at the Gate blew. Congress begged him not to go. The Space Force did likewise. Your dad refused. He said he couldn't lead his people from behind, so he traveled to Lethe's Gate in hopes of talking sense into the Gunera."

"Foolish," Nick commented. He knew this tale.

"Brave and determined," Duncan replied. "The alliance was teetering on the balance. Had that damned vuh'Gragalag succeeded in his insane uprising, everything would have come tumbling down. We'd have gone to war with Gunera. Might have won. Might have lost. God only knows what the Amaurau would have done. They had reason to join us. The vuh' had abducted their ambassador and tortured the poor soul in the hopes of breaking the alliance. It's just as likely the Amaurau would have waited to pick over the bones of the survivor, to hell with their ambassador. Who knew? Your father tried to talk sense into vuh'Gragalag. He had no idea the depths of vuh'Gragalag's insanity. He hit Hemera behind your dad's back. Abducted his wife and his unborn child. It was a terrible time for everyone."

Nick had read the history. The rebel Guneri vuh' had opted unilaterally out of the Protocols against the express wishes of mai'Tegatriktrik, the young and newly appointed emperor of Gunera. Humans speculated the vuh' hoped to garner enough power to take control and hold the young mai' under his sway, making himself the de facto ruler of Gunera. Didn't quite go down that way.

First, vuh'Gragalag had captured an Amaurau diplomatic mission and tried to blame the loss of the ambassador on humanity. When that failed, he'd attacked outposts at the Gate, raising humanity's ire and bringing forth Hemera's president and all their forces to bear on him. When vuh'Gragalag realized he'd miscalculated humanity's strength and that he would lose the battle, vuh'Gragalag did the unthinkable and led a lightning raid on Hemera itself.

The intent had been to abduct the president and hold him for ransom to buy his way out of the mess, but to vuh'Gragalag's shock, he'd found the President on the front lines and only his young wife holding the fort. In his rage, vuh'Gragalag had dragged her back to Gunera. In the meantime, the battle of the Gate had raged on, only ending when all of vuh'Gragalag's forces had been sent to their eternal rest, taking President Severin with them. He'd been killed in one of the final battles, determined to break through to Gunera to retrieve his pregnant wife and whatever remained of the Amaurau ambassador. Severin had succeeded in locating and freeing the ambassador, but as for his wife, he'd failed. President Severin's bravery was immortalized in song by the people of Hemera. He became a national hero twenty-eight years after the fact.

"I was with him when he died, Nico," Duncan quietly spoke, as if the incident had occurred only yesterday. "He'd been horribly burned when the Gunera hit Ephesus III. We rushed him to a mobile surgical hospital, but there was little they could do. I held his hand as he died."

Nick placed a hand on Duncan's shoulder. "I didn't know that," he said quietly.

Duncan smiled bleakly. "It's not a day I like to remember. Your father was a great man, a skilled leader. Never forget that."

"I won't." Nick often wondered how he could ever match his father's accomplishments. He was such a pale shadow of that nearly divine entity. "Where are we going with this, Duncan?" Nothing the man had said needed the solitude of the botanical gardens. It was all ancient history now.

"The day your dad died, he made me promise I'd find and bring his child home. Made me swear I'd see this child grow to maturity, marry, and start a family."

"Not going to happen," Nick said, trying to insert a little levity into the conversation.

"I know. But I did everything possible to convince the State Department that it had a sovereign duty to find you and your mother, to bring you home. Took ten years of convincing and another eight to get you back, but we succeeded." He smiled fondly at Nick. "I still remember the day in that transshipment station when the Guneri ship made port. As soon as you stepped off that ship ... God, you looked terrified ... I knew it was you. Little Nicodemus, his father's son. I swore to myself I'd fulfill the promise I'd made to your father. I'd see his son grown to a man, safe and happy."

"And with a family?" Nick asked with a smile.

"We're working on that."

"As in you and Alessandra McCoy?"

"As in your friends, Nico."

"My only sexual experiences are with prostitutes. Did you tell her that?"

Duncan frowned. "I didn't! And don't you dare tell her either! What did you expect me to do, Nico? You were a mess. You barely spoke English, and only because your mother secretly taught you. Your understanding on anything human was ... well ... sketchy at best. You certainly didn't understand women. You didn't understand that a young man doesn't publicly assault women. I hired English tutors to bring your language up to snuff and cultural tutors to teach you manners. And yes, well, Lady Kitty to teach you ... other things. I couldn't let you loose on society with the ideas you had." Duncan eyed the younger man. "Do the Gunera really just do it right in the public square?"

Nick nodded. "Yep. Pretty much."

"Bloody savages." He frowned. "I thought they only had one gender."

"In a way. They're hermaphrodites, meaning each individual carries the sex organs of both genders. They can simply replicate themselves. But usually, they take a partner. Certainly, the upper classes elect partnership rather than simple replication. It's their version of a power trip."

"How do they decide who does what? I mean ..."

"Who's the female, and who's the male? It's a dominance thing. The more dominant party gets to pick and usually picks the male role. Having to lay eggs and nest is considered emasculating, so that task goes to the subordinate."

Duncan rubbed his neck. "I should say so! Lord, the bloody savages!"

Nick said nothing but wondered why they were having this odd conversation. Had his hopeless lack of understanding of human sexuality gotten him in trouble again? Had he offended Alessandra in some way, and had Duncan been tasked with intervening? It might explain the botanical gardens. If Nick was going to be given another lecture on sex etiquette from Duncan, it would be better it occur in this remote place.

"Anyway," Duncan grumbled, "the reason I said all that was because I wanted you to know that I love you like the son I never had, and I'll do anything to protect you."

Nick felt the tension rising in his chest. Duncan was navigating into waters that he knew Nick wouldn't like.

"I had lunch with the chief of police today," Duncan continued. "Seems more strangeness is afoot. Four bodies turned up in the woods yesterday. Been dead about two weeks. Killed by Amaurau darts, Nico."

Nick sat staring out at the lake. The swans were still paddling around as the sky turned a deep vermillion. "Why would she kill her own team?"

"To cover her tracks. Dead men can't tell tales."

"Why would the Sena hire humans to drug and kidnap me?"

"You were shot full of Versadine, Nico. Enough to make a mute man talk."

Nick silently watched the swans. Probably relatives of his treacherous houseguest. "I don't remember what they asked. And under Versadine, I would have told them everything I know." Nick hung his head into his hands and clutched his hair. "God, Duncan, I'm so sorry!"

"For what? For being kidnapped and drugged? Not your fault. It was the office that placed the witch in your apartment."

"Why?" Nick demanded of the swans. "For the love of God, why? I know far less than you do. Why would the Amaurau be so interested in me? Why now?"

"I don't know. It's something we must find out. I'm working on it, Nico. I swear I am." Duncan rubbed his brow. "All of this revolves around you. The Amaurau have developed an interest in you. Any idea why?"

Nick sighed. "I think they're annoyed by my understanding of the Gunera. They think I'm on Gunera's side. The fact that I despise the whole species doesn't seem to be settling into the Amaurau psyche."

"You think it's another one-up kind of thing? The Gunera have eh'Nicodemus to speak for them so the Amaurau need a Sevay Nicodemus to balance the works?"

"Not that I claim to understand Amaurau nearly as well as I understand Gunera, but I think that might be exactly what it is. They seem stuck on the concept of balance, much more so than the Gunera. With the Gunera, it's appearances, the outward view that everything is as they command it. That's why they're sticklers over minutia, like the color of a triplicate bill of lading. On the other hand, it seems the Amaurau simply want to make sure that if the Gunera succeed in making a demand, the Amaurau succeed in one of their own to balance it out. Ississita hinted at that when I met him."

"Ississita," Duncan growled. "That man troubles me. He's too smart by far. It seems like everything started with him."

The sun had set, and darkness was creeping over the gardens. Nick switched on the lights of the gazebo. The structure was strung with a myriad of miniature lights that gave the space a festival appearance but did little to cut into the darkness. He and Duncan were little more than shadows.

"I think the Amaurau drugged me," Duncan said. "Slipped something into my food to keep me from the ceremony. Forced you to take my place."

Nick nodded. "I was thinking the same. But how is that possible? It would have required human agents."

"Sena Dessessah used human agents to drop you in your tracks."

"God!"

"That's why I started this discussion as I did, Nico. We can't trust anyone. Something's going down, and you and I are in the thick of it. You even more than me."

"I don't understand why. If the Amaurau want a Sevay Nicodemus, they can have one. Snag a human and force-feed him Amaurau culture the way I was force-fed Gunera. Or hire one and pay him to learn it. Or do as they are claiming with Sena Dessessah and have an Amaurau learn the business. Why are they after me?"

"Maybe they aren't interested in balancing the scales, Nico," Duncan said, his voice a whisper. "Maybe they're trying to load it their way. Take you out."

"God!" Nick began rubbing his temples. Then he shook his head. "No, it can't be. The very first night, Sena Dessessah … she came into my room, Duncan. I couldn't sleep and was in terrible pain. I didn't think I needed to fear her so I didn't lock my door. She came in."

"And did what?" Duncan's voice held more than fear of the spilling of secrets.

"Nothing like that," Nick growled, although, in the back of his mind, he recalled how his first thoughts of the Sena had been erotic. He needed to gain control of himself, as Corey often told him. "She resolved my headache."

"How exactly?"

"She touched my temples, knocked me flat with her two index fingers. If she'd wanted me dead, she could have done me in that night."

"Might have been too incriminating," Duncan mused.

"She could have killed me in the woods," Nick added. "She had every opportunity. No." Nick shook his head. "She doesn't want me dead. She wants something else. She thinks I know something."

"Do you?" Duncan asked, twisting to pin Nick with a stare.

Nick threw his hands in the air. "How the hell should I know? Two months ago, I was nothing more than your assistant, dealing with import/export licenses, arbitrating petty commercial squabbles, translating documents forward and back. Now, suddenly, I'm the Protocol officer, not just the backup officer, but the actual officer. At least that's how both the Gunera and Amaurau are treating me. Almost like you're …" Nick's voice caught in his throat.

"Almost like I'm already dead," Duncan finished the statement quietly.

Nick scoffed. "They're idiots, Duncan. Even if you did keel over during a committee meeting, there's no guarantee the Trade Commission would instate me into your position. Some senator could give his favorite cousin the job."

"Doubtful. You're by far the most qualified. And the most neutral no matter how a man cuts the cake. It's one thing everyone has grown accustomed to. Nick Severin has the most literal mind on Rhadamanthus. Subtlety, Nico, isn't your forte."

"It's not a Guneri forte either."

"True, but it makes life easier for those up the line. In any given crisis, they can predict what action you're going to take because you always follow the same procedure. You follow procedure. I can count on one hand the number of times you've acted outside of protocol, Nick. Our betters can sleep easy knowing what to expect from their piece here on Rhadamanthus. You're a known quantity. That makes you valuable."

"For humans, maybe. How is that of value to our friends out there?"

Duncan sighed. "I don't know, but clearly someone thinks having you in my position is of value to them, and they're posturing in readiness of that day."

"God, Duncan! You've got to be careful!" Nick rose and turned to face his boss. "They're gunning for you, not me."

Duncan shrugged. "Maybe. Who knows?" When he saw Nick's face had gone white, he brushed the concerns aside. "No worries, Nick. I've already had this discussion with De Walt. She agrees I need protection. I've got a security detail attaching itself to my ass starting tomorrow. This is my last chance to talk to you privately." Duncan looked down at his clasped hands and seemed reluctant to continue.

"Out with it, Duncan," Nick prodded. "There's still more nastiness coming. I can tell."

Duncan patted the bench next to him. "Better sit down for this one, Nico. You aren't going to like it."

"As if I've liked anything else you've said tonight."

"Sit!"

Grudgingly, Nick dropped onto the bench, his heart now in his throat.

Duncan inhaled deeply. "There's been an incident. A serious incident." Duncan drew another breath. "In Gunera."

Nick frowned while he recalled the recent barrage of messages he received from Guneri sources via his human and Guneri email accounts. It had been the usual bullshit with nothing standing out in Nick's mind. Nothing to warrant a late-night clandestine meeting.

"I haven't heard anything," Nick admitted.

"It's the sort of incident that rises higher than your office. It went directly to the State Department in London with copies to Tanaka on Erebos, O'Malley on Hemera, and De Walt here on Rhadamanthus. I wasn't even in on the original conference calls. They only brought me in once the general panic had settled, and they knew they needed expert help. I've been in meetings ever since to deal with the fallout."

Nick held his breath anxiously. "What was it?"

"An assassination attempt was made on mai'Tegatriktrik the same day you were assaulted." At Nick's gasp, Duncan motioned for him to remain silent. "It's worse than that. The agent was a human."

"God!"

"Yeah, quoting half the State Department operatives from here to London. Worse still, it appears it was Lincoln Combs."

Nick froze his mind for one awful second, refusing to process the information.

Lincoln Combs.

He was one of their own, an undersecretary in the Foreign Affairs Office, stationed on Earth. The only time Nick had met Lincoln had been at an FAO Christmas party, and they immediately disliked one another. Combs was a huge man of Jamaican descent with green eyes that could cut an opponent to ribbons if his massive black hands didn't do the job. He was a conservative, a firm believer that humanity had no business involving itself in alien affairs, and he had been quite vocal at Humans First rallies. Combs probably wouldn't have gone very far in Foreign Affairs but for the backing of powerful allies in New York. He was also, Nick had been told, extremely intelligent and had the best grasp of the Guneri language, second only to Nick. That hadn't won Nick any points with the man. Combs assumed he'd take over the prized position of Secretary of International Trade out of Rhadamanthus when Duncan retired. Nick's sudden arrival on the scene with not only the most profound knowledge of all-things Gunera but a personal and strong relationship with Duncan put the man's nose out of joint. If anyone was gunning to eliminate Duncan and Nick, his name was Lincoln Combs.

But the Guneri emperor? That made no sense, and not for one minute did Nick believe it. Combs's career aspirations lay in his ability to work with the Gunera since he had no knowledge of the Amaurau at all. If he wanted to attain the position of the Rhadamanthan Secretary, he needed the Gunera's backing. Attempting to assassinate mai'Tegatriktrik wasn't the best way to achieve that. Unless …

Unless there was faction within the Gunera like vuh'Gragalag of old who wanted to control the empire. That made a lot more sense. If someone like gy'Gravinda wanted to advance himself, eliminating the mai' would be his route. But a man of the gy's lofty station couldn't afford to take such action himself. Instead, he might hire an equally ambitious human like Lincoln Combs. If the gy' could gain enough power to appoint and control the next mai', he could repay Combs by insisting he be instilled as the new Protocol Officer on Rhadamanthus. Given the turmoil such an uprising would cause to the Guneri half of humanity's ever-delicate balancing act, Nick didn't doubt the State Department would immediately recall Duncan and shove Combs in his place if only to settle as much of the balance as they could.

Nick scoured his brain to recall his conversation with gy'Bagrada and gy'Gravinda at the party. He couldn't remember either acting strangely. One would think an individual as highly placed as gy'Gravinda would know something was going down even if he didn't have a hand directly in the pot. One would further assume he would have already set his posture for whichever end resulted. As for gy'Bagrada, nothing moved in the empire, not so much as an ant that he didn't know about. If a move was being made against mai''Tegatriktrik, gy'Bagrada had to agree, or it would fail. How had he behaved at the party? Nick tapped at his head and tried to remember. *Making passes at the Protocol Officer Pro Tem,* he thought. Outrageous, yes. Embarrassing, of course. Out of line? Not at all for a highly placed and oversexed gy'. The man would have greatly enjoyed an excursion into the wild side in the middle of the Rose Room as all of humanity looked on.

Which brought to mind the presence of the Amaurau at the party. Had their own intelligence learned that something was going down in Gunera, and had they felt the need to have a presence? Had that brought them to Rhadamanthus five years early? What about the attack on gy'Gravinda by a human agent? Could the waitress have been in league with Lincoln Combs? Ordered to assassinate someone they considered a threat to their plans? Had the attack really been directed at gy'Gravinda at all? Or had gy'Bagrada been the actual target? Nick had many questions but no answers.

"You see the ramifications of it," Duncan murmured. "It's a bloody mess."

"What's the official Guneri stance?"

"Pissed as hell and demanding a rib roast made from one of our president's chests. Part of the debate this past week was which of our esteemed presidents was willing to provide the rib." Duncan sighed and ran his fingers through his overly long hair. "Seriously, it's about as bad as it gets. mai'Tegatriktrik is claiming humanity made a direct assault on the Gunera and is declaring it an act of war. He's threatening to withdraw from the alliance and is moving materiel to the border. We, of course, are doing the same. The tension at the Gate is rising daily, and it's damned scary."

"War?" Nick asked quietly.

"Maybe."

"I haven't heard anything via either the news or my own sources."

"So far, the presidents have managed to contain it, but that won't last. Once the panic starts, the ride will turn rough quickly." Duncan rubbed his hands together. "We'll be ready, though. Earth is determined to fight. They've already moved three carrier groups into the Gate with two more being brought up from the Amaurau side of the nebula."

"Leaving us open to an Amaurau attack."

Duncan grunted. "It's a gamble. Earth is terrified that the Amaurau are going to make a move. The Space Force is convinced they need that carrier group on the Guneri side of the balance. Everyone is scared to death of Sena Dessessah and the moves she's made against you. The State Department suspects the Amaurau know what's going down and that they're preparing to move while we focus attention on the Gunera. There's even speculation you'll be abducted and returned to Amaurau as a bargaining chip. If everything we know is true, we've lost Combs, one of only a handful of humans besides you and me who speaks Gunera. We have very few Amaurau linguists, and you're currently the only person in existence who can speak to all three species with any fluency. If we declare war against the Gunera, you're going to be a valuable asset, Nick. The State Department thinks the odd events here on Rhadamanthus reflect the various sides trying to position themselves to nab you for their own ends."

Nick felt his pulse quicken. "What does State want me to do?"

"That's where this gets even nastier."

"How much nastier can it get?"

"The State Department has been working day and night to placate the Gunera. I've been there for the past two weeks, on the horn and email with Gunera Proper, trying to tell mai'Tegatriktrik that the attack wasn't directed by the government of the Western Alliance of Earth or any known agency thereof. We've tried to convince them that assuming the assault really was carried out by a human agent, the agent was either an independent operator or aligned with some other nameless agency."

"The Amaurau."

"We didn't say the name, of course, but they understood. They don't trust us, but they're still talking. They claim to be willing to listen, but they're not happy, and the situation on the border is tense."

"I've no idea how you've managed to hide all of this from me and from the news bureaus," Nick replied. "Kudos, Duncan."

"You've been preoccupied of late. I didn't have the authority to advise you of the situation, nor did I want to. You've got enough problems dealing with your live-in Sena."

"That explains the parade of cultural enrichment excursions," Nick said. "Always to places off the grid, like that handicrafts festival and the chocolate factory."

"And the polo match," Duncan added. "All far, far away from a computer station. But you're right. The State Department has done a yeoman's job of keeping the news bureaus in the dark. It won't hold. It can't. And when it breaks, God only knows what's going to happen."

"What do we do?"

Duncan swallowed. *Here it comes,* Nick thought.

"The Gunera have agreed to refrain from retaliating against what they consider a blatant attack against their sovereign nation. They're willing to allow us to conduct our own investigation to determine what Mr. Combs was trying to accomplish. They claim they haven't been able to get him to talk."

"Jesus!" Nick rose again and started to pace the gazebo. Night had descended on the botanical gardens. The only light sources were the sparkle of tiny beams drifting over the wooden structure and the nightly show from the Fortuna Nebula. "You don't know what Gunera torturers are like. If they want information, they're going to get it. They must not be trying very hard."

"We know, Nick," Duncan said quietly. "That's what makes this so difficult."

Nick froze and stood watching his boss and friend struggle to find the words.

"mai'Tegatriktrik has agreed to allow a State Department-sanctioned human investigator to speak with Mr. Combs on Gunera in the hope of eliciting what the Gunera have been unable to elicit."

"No. No fucking way," Nick gasped. He knew where this was going. "Are you insane? I am *not* going back to Gunera! You can't ask that of me."

Duncan's silence added to Nick's outrage

"There's no way in hell I or any other human being could drag information out of Combs if the Gunera couldn't do it themselves. This is a trap, Duncan. They want a human diplomat in their greedy little clutches so they can use him against Earth. It's the same tactic as when they used my mother twenty-eight years ago and learned that humanity has a soft spot for its own. That we'll continue to talk provided they dangle a vague hope that a hostage just might be freed."

"Possibly."

"Definitively. I'm *not* going. Find someone else. *You* can go."

Duncan shook his head slowly. "They won't accept anyone else, Nick. They named you specifically."

"Fuck that." Nick paced the gazebo like a caged lion. "I am not returning to Gunera, Duncan! How dare you ask that of me?"

"It's not like the last time, Nick. You won't be a prisoner of war. You'll be a sanctioned emissary of the Western Alliance of the United Nations of Earth with full diplomatic immunity."

"As if the Gunera care!" Nick raised his hands as if preparing for a boxing match, his two tattoos prominent on the backs of his wrists. "I'm a Guneri citizen, Duncan. Look at me. Look at my marks!" Nick shook his hands at Duncan as if he might punch him outright. "I'm a citizen subject to all Guneri laws without regard to my biology. They don't give a damn about diplomatic immunity. They're going to take one look at my marks and say, yep, he's one of ours, subject to our courts, legal system, and everything else. Hell, vuh'Yguggli might even show up at the transshipment docks with paperwork to reclaim his slave. That's what I am, Duncan. An escaped slave. Do you know what they do to escaped slaves?"

Duncan spoke with the calm persuasiveness of a skilled debater. "We have the assurances of mai'Tegatriktrik that you will be afforded all due respect and courtesy as accorded to your rank and station as an emissary of Earth."

"No. I refuse."

"They've agreed to allow us to send a security detail with you. You won't be alone for one minute while you're there."

"Not happening, Duncan."

"We're going to implant you with a transponder. We'll know your precise location day and night. We'll know your blood pressure and respiration. We'll know if you're okay or not."

"Are you deaf? The answer is no!"

"There'll be an extraction team ready twenty-four seven in the event you demand a recall."

"No."

"It'll be your call how long you stay, Nico. You'll have command of the transponder. If you change the beacon to an emergency call, we'll pull you out, no questions asked."

"What part of 'no' do you not understand?"

Duncan suddenly leaped to his feet. He grabbed Nick by the shoulders and shook him. "Goddammit, Nick, you don't have a say in this! Do you think for one minute I want to do this to you? Do you think I sat through two weeks of meetings eating peanuts and planning my vacation? I fought like hell to keep you out of this! They won't listen. The Gunera won't listen."

Nick glared at Duncan with violent dislike. "You just spent the past hour explaining to me how valuable a chess piece I am to Gunera, Earth, and Amaurau alike, and then you say Earth is conceding its piece without a fight? I don't get it."

Duncan took several deep breaths. He tried to speak in a soothing tone. "Actually, that's one of the reasons everyone decided to send you. If you'll calm down, I'll try to explain."

Nick snorted. "Fine. Explain."

"First, we're on the brink of war, Nick. A war humanity might be able to win against the Gunera but will surely lose against the Amaurau when they wade into the fray. If there's even a remote chance that sending you to Gunera will prevent a war, then we must do it. You must do it. The future of humanity rests with you."

Nick dismissed the statement with a hand wave.

"Secondly, you and I both know something is about to go down here on Rhadamanthus, but no one can agree if there's a human faction involved. De Walt thinks Humans First might be involved. They despise aliens, and they despise you as an alien sympathizer."

"They obviously don't know me very well," Nick said.

"True. But that wouldn't stop a couple of idiots from doing something stupid like trying to harm or humiliate you. You received a lot of press from the Independence Day business. People who might never have known you now know your name and your face. De Walt is concerned that some of this is Humans First making a play of its own."

"I can handle myself against conservative bombast."

"I know that. But then there's the third problem. The Amaurau. State is convinced the Amaurau have their eye on you and that of all the factions in play, they stand to gain the most by acquiring possession of you."

Nick lifted his head, hating the words that reminded him so much of his childhood. He'd been nothing more than a possession then, too.

Duncan pleaded. "That's why Earth has agreed to send you to Gunera. We don't know what the Amaurau want with you, but it isn't good for you or for Earth. On the other hand, we know harming you makes no sense for the Gunera. Right now, Gunera may be the safest place for you to be."

"Until the shooting starts."

"Even if the shooting starts. The Gunera won't harm you, Nick. If nothing more, they need you to help them understand human motivation. And you know more about the Amaurau than anyone. They'll also want that intel."

Nick cursed once again the fates that had tossed Dessessah into his lap.

"It's going to be okay. I promise. Sending you there puts you out of reach of both malicious human factions and the Amaurau." Duncan grabbed Nick's fidgeting hands. "Everyone is terrified about doing this, Nick. We all know it's not without its dangers to you or to us. We're determined to see that nothing happens to you. Like I said, you're going under full diplomatic immunity, with an escort that has orders never to leave your side, with a transponder so we know your location at all times, and with a team that's ready at a moment's notice to pull you out."

"You're taking a big risk with my life," Nick protested, realizing his protests were futile. His fate had been decided. He was going to Gunera.

Duncan nodded and gave Nick's shoulder a squeeze. It wasn't much, but it was the only assurance he could offer.

6

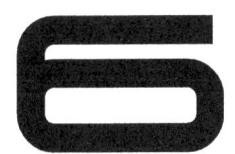

Preparations had gone too fast for Nick's taste. Nick offloaded his daily tasks to Les Johnson but secretly fretted that Johnson would be incapable of managing the multitude of inherited tasks. High-ranking State Department officers briefed Nick in hastily arranged meetings via the 4D teleconference room. The briefings battered into Nick's head a list of concessions he was authorized to grant the Gunera in return for a calming of the waters.

Nick was shocked by the breadth of the list. It included several unprofitable trades that would benefit mai'Tegatriktrik's personal treasury, a general discount on all transshipments for a full year, and the unthinkable granting of territory that had been in dispute between the two powers. Nick was to strive for a minimum of concessions, but he was authorized to concede the entire list if necessary. It was hoped that Nick could extract them from the affair with minimal damage.

He was also to investigate the fate of Lincoln Combs. If Combs was still alive, the State Department wanted him back to stand trial. If he was dead, Nick was to obtain the remains so that Combs's death could be certified. State demanded to know why Combs was in Gunera as well as his associates. Both State and Nick knew it was a lot to ask, but humanity's future could depend on his success. Nick spent the days before departure in a blind panic, waking each day to a racing heart and heading to bed each night with a thundering headache. He barely slept.

During that foggy, awful week, Dessessah disappeared. Jordan told Nick that one day she simply rose, placed her belongings in her white plastic box, and carried it from the apartment. A review of the passenger manifests for ships bound for Amaurau revealed that the Sena had shipped out that same day. She vanished as silently as she'd arrived.

On August 30, the day prior to his scheduled journey, Nick was ordered to appear at Capitol General Hospital, where a location transponder was subcutaneously placed on his left forearm. The device functioned similarly to transponder units aboard spacecraft and would emit a signal that could be picked up by any human monitoring station. It would also transmit Nick's major vitals, enabling Duncan to monitor the Protocol officer's well-being. Repeated taps on the transponder would be recognized as an SOS. Nick's every move would be monitored, though this fact provided him little comfort.

Nick was introduced to Jason Kittrick from the President's Secret Service. When told he would be guarded by an SS operative, Nick had assumed one of De Walt's crew had volunteered. Instead, it was Kittrick, and he'd been rushed from Earth for the mission. Prior to being reassigned to Nick, Kittrick had protected Jonathan McAlastair, President of the Western Alliance of the United Nations of Earth. Kittrick was a monster of muscle, bone, and sinew, nearly two and a half meters tall, black as night, and bristling with attitude. Rather than the casual aloha colors of Rhadamanthus, he dressed in black, including a tight-fitting leather jacket. Kittrick's hands were gloved, and his eyes were covered with dark sunglasses. He looked more robot than human. Nick counted three gun holsters. A bug was secured in the canal of his right ear. Kittrick extended a hand to greet Nick. All the while, his dark eyes studied his new charge, quickly committing Nick's appearance to memory.

"Undersecretary Severin," he said in a deep voice that Nick found disquieting. "It's a pleasure to meet you. I've been assigned as your personal security. I hope you approve."

Nick blinked, aware that Kittrick could crumple him into a ball and toss him into the nearest wastebasket without breaking a sweat. He couldn't imagine rejecting this wall of steel and determination.

"I'm grateful to have you," Nick murmured, freeing his small hand from Kittrick's considerable grasp.

"There are a few things you need to know, Mr. Undersecretary …"

"Call me Nick. Please."

"I have constant access to your transponder signals and can hear them through my ear; I'll never be out of listening range." Nick swallowed, finding the concept both unnerving and comforting. "I do not intend to ever be out of earshot or eyesight. You and I are going to be sealed at the hip, sir. Where you go, I go. Where you sleep, I sleep. What you eat, I eat first. Is that clear?"

"Can I use the bathroom by myself?" Nick asked. They walked toward a waiting vehicle.

"No, sir."

"God."

"I will do everything within my power to assure your safety," Kittrick continued, ushering Nick into the back seat. "You are, of course, in charge of the mission, and I will obey your every command. However, should I feel you're in danger, you will obey me without question. Is that clear?"

Again Nick swallowed. "Yes, sir."

"My name is Jason. Please don't call me 'sir.'"

"Yes, sir."

"This mission will be a success, Mr. Undersecretary. We will both do our jobs and then get the hell out of there."

"Yes, sir."

For a nanosecond, Jason's composure broke, and he smiled. He patted Nick's shoulder with a giant hand. "It's going to be fine."

"I hope so," muttered the less-than-confident Undersecretary of Trade.

On September 2, the pair shipped out. Duncan wished Nick farewell. The two men had little to say to each other. Duncan probably suspected by Nick's ashen pallor that he was one step from fainting.

"Try to relax, Nico," Duncan said. "Everyone in the State Department will be following your progress day and night. Your extraction team includes twenty of the best special ops guys in the Space Force, and they'll be waiting on Rhadmanthus for your call. They're trained specifically for the extraction of high-level targets out of hostile territory. State has also obtained assurances that your access codes to the Guneri system are still active. You can also communicate via email at any time. I'll personally monitor the email account. As with all communications between Gunera and humanity, there's no possibility of face-to-face or audio transmissions. You can email or hit the transponder. Those are your only two methods of calling home."

"That isn't very reassuring," Nick said.

"You'll be fine."

The valet handled Nick's luggage, consisting only of a small case with a change of clothing. With his tablet computer tucked under his arm, Nick departed for the Central Space Port with Kittrick, a walking tower of muscle, at his side. He bade goodbye to Corey, Jordan, and Alessandra, who'd met him at the Space Port to wish him well. Nick then was aboard the passenger shuttle that would take him to the transshipment dock. Aware that Jason was watching his every move, Nick held back threatening tears as he peered out the little window to see his buddies waving goodbye. They acted as if Nick was merely leaving for a long vacation. *Those three friendly faces,* Nick thought, *pretending to mask their concern. They've no idea I'll probably never see them again.* Nick was certainly convinced of it.

"Nervous, sir?" Jason Kittrick settled next to Nick on the empty transport.

"Scared shitless." Nick decided he might as well be honest with the last human being he'd likely ever see before dying.

"It'll be fine," Kittrick rumbled. "I've read the files. I know the score. I have no doubt the Gunera mean you no harm."

"I wish I had your confidence," Nick muttered.

Kittrick chuckled and settled down for the flight.

They arrived at the transshipment dock after a long day of flying. The dock was a hulking thing that hung motionless in space at the very edge of the western lobe of the Fortuna Nebula. It represented the last bit of human territory before the gap of Lethe's Gate, which led onto the eastern lobe and Guneri space. The size of a small city, the dock held a crew of over two thousand souls who called it home though it was anything but homelike. A massive warehouse in space, the dock contained multiple loading doors along its side. It was an unarmed city, defenseless, its only protection the wealth of goods it stored. Its inhabitants hoped the Gunera valued the merchandise too much to attack its human caregivers.

"Now docking at gate 93," a mechanized voice announced. Kittrick rose and helped a pale and somber Nick from his seat.

Feeling Kittrick's firm hand on his shoulder, Nick studied his bodyguard. "Aren't you afraid?"

"The situation is different for me," Kittrick replied. "I have one task: keep you alive. Besides, I'm not the one walking into Guneri space with alien implants in my arms."

Nick glanced at the sleeves that hid his tattoos. "You know about those."

"Yes, sir. It was in the dossier. The Gunera may attempt to claim you not as a diplomat but as their citizen. I'll do everything in my power to assure that doesn't happen."

"You against an empire?"

"If needs be, yes, sir."

"God."

Stepping into the transshipment dock was like leaving a palace and entering a slum. The dock was a utilitarian space with no purpose except the movement of goods. Although well lit, everything within was gunmetal gray. It lacked windows, and the air had a strange metallic taste as though it had been recycled far too many times. Upon their entrance to the small passenger terminal, a Gemini Space representative, a large, hulking woman with heavy brows and a grim expression, explained that the Guneri shuttle would dock in two hours.

"My orders," she affirmed, "are to transfer you immediately upon its arrival because the outbound approvals granted only a one-hour window for the vessel to remain in dock."

With time to kill, Nick opted to investigate the station. His legs needed the exercise, and he had no idea how long the flight to Gunera Proper would be. On his outbound, clandestine journey ten years earlier, Nick had been shunted from one safe haven to another by his smugglers in a journey that had taken ten harrowing days to complete. This time, he assumed the flight path would be direct. *Still,* he thought, *it'll be wise to work out the kinks of the first day's travel.* With Jason Kittrick plastered to his side, Nick set off to see the process he'd managed for eight years from a desk on Rhadamanthus.

The station was indeed unpleasant. The dullness of the gray weighed on Nick's soul, as did the smell of ancient dust in the air. Voices were few in that giant space. The humans who worked there were strung far apart, eliminating the possibility of general chatter. The only speech Nick heard was the gentle drone of announcements over the intercom as ships docked or exited the station. Those few individuals Nick and Jason encountered were dour, heavyset for strength, and mentally compromised to survive such soul-crushing surroundings. They were loners with no interest in human companionship. Nick saw no reason not to leave them alone.

Nick and Kittrick entered an inbound Guneri bay where cargo arriving from Gunera was sorted and unpacked, scanned, tested, and checked for contraband or treaty violations. Nick surveyed his surroundings. On his left, a shipment of carpets was being unloaded, rolls stacked one hundred meters high. The carpets were irradiated to ensure they contained no living organisms, after which they were forwarded through the process. On his right, Nick encountered crates of canned goods, unlabeled but for a sheet of unifying shrink wrap. The items would be randomly tested for poisonous materials before being moved to their next station.

After being scanned and documented, the Guneri imports were moved by pallet jack to the intermediate zone where the real work occurred. Humans removed any documentation written in Gunera and replaced it with the appropriate documentation in either a human language or Amaurau, depending on the final disposition of the cargo. That meant the individual cans of foodstuffs were required to be labeled by hand. Next, the cargo had to be rewrapped, and the bundle labeled appropriately. Any required manual or other type of written material was then scanned into a translation machine where new documentation was generated in the required ending language. A human translator finished the fine-tuning before the documents were pressed to digital media.

The final step was the movement of the vetted goods to the outbound shipping docks. The goods would be stored until they could be picked up by a ship from the human side and sent on to their final destination, such as a human port, thus ending the process. Much of the material, however, was sent nonstop across the gap to another transshipment dock on the far side of the nebula. There the process would repeat with the cargo unloaded into another warehouse where it would await Amaurau pickup.

The entire warehouse system was strictly segregated. Nick and Jason happened to be walking through the inbound Guneri side. On the opposite side of the warehouse, the outbound Amaurau materials that had gone through a similar process halfway across the universe landed to await pickup by Guneri freighters.

This is mind-boggling, Nick thought, as he strolled around the mountains of cargo. *How could so much crap manage to get from here to there without getting lost?*

Nick and Jason returned to the passenger terminal in time to witness the Guneri's shuttle arrival and the delicate maneuvers that followed as it attached to the station. The ship's telltale spikey outline, bristling with communications relays and defense weaponry, sent a shock of terror through Nick. He blanched at the realization that he would be riding in it. While he had tolerated dealing with them remotely via computer, Nick never wanted to go near another Gunera again. The unpleasantness of the Independence Day party had been more than his nervous system could stand. *I can't go there,* his mind screamed. *I can't do this. They're asking too much of me.*

As if sensing his volatility, Jason placed a hand on Nick's shoulder. "It will be fine, sir. I won't let anything happen to you."

Nick swallowed and tried to bolster himself. He refused to be weaker than his own security.

The Guneri vessel docked, and the corridor opened to the passenger terminal. Nick winced as the equivalent of a Guneri flight attendant rolled toward them atop a gearless mover, tail lashing in a sign of welcome. Jason had never seen a Gunera in person, but Nick assumed he must have been briefed on what to expect; the man in black didn't flinch at the creature's abrupt scrutiny.

"We don't allow weaponry in flight," the attendant stated to Nick in Gunera. He pointed at Jason's three holsters.

Nick translated the statement into English.

Jason snorted. "Tell the little bastard I have assurances from mai'Tegatriktrik that I may keep all my weaponry."

Nick lifted his brow and translated the statement, but omitting the reference of "bastard."

The attendant flicked his tail and muttered something about needing to verify the statement. He jabbered into the commlink attached to his mover.

Nick trembled. If they removed Jason's weapons ... if they removed Jason ...

"It'll be fine, sir," Jason said, voice brimming with self-assuredness.

As if to alleviate Nick's fears, Jason gestured in the direction of the shipping area where they'd taken their tour. "How much garbage goes through this system?"

"Forty-eight million metric tons semiannually," Nick replied, recalling the number from prior queries.

"Damn! That's a ton of shit. How did you know that?"

"It's my job to keep track of this stuff. How much weight goes in, how much weight goes out. Assuring it all stays in balance."

And how much weight doesn't move at all, he thought grimly, remembering the *Death's Festival* and its still unaccounted for nameless cargo.

"So somewhere out there, you and I are on a cargo manifest?" Jason asked.

Nick nodded. "Not as cargo but as passengers. We don't weigh anything, so we aren't cargo."

He felt a stab hit his heart. The *Death's Festival*'s missing cargo had been something without weight. Something without value. It hadn't been carrying cargo at all. It had been carrying passengers! Nick's mind pondered the significance of this fact. Lost in thought, Nick didn't see the flight attendant return. Nor did he hear the Gunera confirm that Jason could board with his firearms. Nick was running the scenarios. The *Death's Festival* had been hit *leaving,* not entering, human space. It had been carrying passengers, not Guneri, into human space, but humans to Guneri space. From the area near Hemera, possibly even from Earth itself. *Dear God!* Nick thought. *Lincoln Combs!*

Nick grabbed Jason's arm. "This is a trap! We have to get out of here!"

"What?" The black man jerked.

The Guneri attendant demanded they board. The shuttle had only a brief window before it was required to launch.

Nick tried to pull Jason out of the chamber, but it was like tugging an elephant. "Listen to me: Lincoln Combs never made it to Gunera to kill mai'Tegatriktrik! He was killed aboard a freighter sneaking him in! This is a trap."

Nick swatted his arm, transmitting to Duncan's team that the mission was already in trouble. Jason drew a sidearm. Over the ship's communications system, an alarm sounded, and Nick heard the drone of the human announcer calling for security to report to the outbound Guneri terminal. Apparently, Duncan hadn't been kidding. As soon as

Nick had hit the panic button, the folks on Rhadamanthus must have alerted the station that he was in trouble.

The Guneri attendant lashed his tail in fury, snapping Jason's right hand. The barb cut deep lacerations into Jason's skin and sent his weapon flying. Before Nick could move, more Gunera exited the shuttle and surrounded him. Two tails whipped around Nick, trapping his arms against his body. Jason drew a second sidearm as a crowd of human dockworkers raced into the terminal armed with hand tools. From deep within the dock works, a booming alarm resonated.

Warning! Warning! The dock is under attack!

The two Gunera who had ensnared Nick dragged him toward their shuttle as he struggled in vain. More raged around him, tails whipping in the air and threatening any human who tried to approach. Jason donned sunglasses to protect his eyes and aimed at the closest Gunera.

"Release the undersecretary," he growled in English, assuming they'd understand him regardless of language, "or I'll start shooting."

The Gunera ignored him.

Nick's attackers were drawing him backward, tails wrapped so tightly around him he couldn't breathe. Two stood between Jason and Nick. Jason didn't bother to ask a second time. He fired, and the sound of the gun exploded in the small room. Nick saw a flash and smelled gunpowder as one of the Gunera fell with a squeal. Enraged, the remaining Gunera flung themselves at the human dockworkers who had joined the fray.

Nick winced; good-hearted men and women were felled by the blows from barbed tails. In return, Gunera fell to blows from dock tools, their yellowish blood spattering the walls and mixing with human blood to form a sickening splash of orange. Nick continued to struggle, but another tail coiled around his neck and tightened, constricting his airway. He staggered, unable to breathe, was hauled off his feet, and carried toward the shuttle doors. Jason fired again, hitting one of the Gunera that held Nick, but it didn't halt the Gunera's retreat. Nick was pulled through the airlock.

The passenger terminal resembled a crime scene, as humans took damage from the tail barbs and Gunera took damage from pipes and crowbars. Jason fired indiscriminately at any Gunera he could hit now that Nick had been taken.

After having been shoved into the central compartment of a luxurious shuttle, Nick was soon tossed aside. He lay crumpled on the floor and struggled to breathe regularly. Activity raged around him, and a door was slammed closed. Nick started to rise, but another tail snagged his legs, dumping him to the floor. He tried to crawl by digging his elbows in the carpet. The tail held him fixed. Suddenly, he became aware that something large and black had landed nearby. He saw Jason's grim and bloodied face staring at him.

"I swore to you, I'm not leaving your side," Jason gasped before a Gunera kicked him to silence.

The floor beneath Nick shuddered. He heard metal squealing. The shuttle's alarm systems clamored of damage to the outer airlock. More alarms screamed of incoming attack. Nick felt another jerk, followed by more sounds of destruction and additional alarms. Nick knew what had happened. The shuttle had torn itself loose of the docking apparatus, taking whatever damage was necessary to secure its cargo from being retaken.

Its precious cargo.

Him.

The shuttle's flight settled into the smoothness of space, but the dangerous ride wasn't over. As he remained pinned to the floor, Nick watched the Guneri crew batten down the shuttle for the impending battle. Nick listened to the pilot in tense conversation with his escorting fighter craft. Nick surmised that humanity had come to the exchange prepared and that Duncan had little more faith in the Gunera than Nick did, as a squadron of fighters out of Erebos was on the attack.

The small craft shuddered from the impact of the first shots, but they were glancing blows that, although panicking the cabin crew, hadn't damaged the ship. *Of course, humanity couldn't destroy it,* Nick thought grimly. *Not without destroying its cargo.*

Still pinned to the floor, Nick listened while the pilot screamed at his escort for cover. The pilot's orders were clear: *Grab the human and run for it. Let the fighter escort deal with anyone trying to stop him.* Nick felt the whine of the engines as they gained full power. Inertia shoved him into Jason as the little craft maneuvered to avoid being struck. With no way to see what was happening, Nick had to imagine the course of the skirmish based on the pilot's words. Ten human fighters had engaged a dozen Guneri craft. One of the Guneri fighters hovered next to the now-fleeing shuttle while another rained fire on the helpless transshipment dock. It was a no-win situation for humanity, Nick realized with a sinking heart. The Gunera had planned for resistance and were willing to risk war to obtain their ends. A direct assault on the dock works was a declaration of war as well as a distraction to aid the fleeing shuttle. Before his very eyes, Nick watched as the Balance Protocols were ripped apart.

The sudden calmness of the pilot's voice indicated to Nick that his captors had made good their escape. With a single fighter as escort, they were on a dead run for Gunera. Nick realized that unless humanity was willing to let the dock works be destroyed, abandon thousands to their fate, and follow the shuttle into Guneri territory, the only logical option was to let Nick go. Nick imagined the diplomatic channels filling up with charges and countercharges, insults, and threats, none of which would save the lives of the two humans racing toward the fate awaiting them on Gunera. The Balance, or the war that followed its dissolution, was no longer Nick's problem.

Once the general safety of all aboard was assured, the Guneri cabin crew hauled Jason to his feet and stripped him of his weapons. He was then harnessed into a seat.

"Don't be foolish," the Guneri attendant in charge warned. He flashed his tail at Nick to translate the warning. "If you do, we'll kill you. That wouldn't do eh'Nicodemus much good, would it?"

Jason's dark eyes flashed as he considered his situation. Nick was still being held facedown upon the floor.

"I suppose it wouldn't," he replied, and his captor nodded.

Jason turned to Nick. "Suggestions, sir?"

Nick hopelessly shook his head. "I haven't any, and you may as well call me Nick."

The Gunera forced Nick to lay spread-eagle flat against the floor, tails restraining each of Nick's limbs. A second Gunera approached with a scanner. He ran the device over Nick's entire body, sounding an alarm as it passed atop Nick's forearm. With a pleased sweep of air gills, the Gunera accepted a thin steel tool from a companion. Nick screamed as the object was pressed into his forearm. The torment continued for several long minutes until, at last, the Gunera issued a sound of triumph as the transponder unit was extricated. The Gunera threw the blood-soaked device to the floor and crushed it with his mover.

Nick closed his eyes, aware that all hell was breaking loose on Rhadamanthus. He was officially lost in Guneri space with no conceivable method of contacting home and no way for Duncan to track his movements. Nick was toast, and he knew it.

Still held pressed to the floor, Nick was rolled onto his back. A door opened from the front of the shuttle, and another Gunera rolled into the cabin.

Nick recognized the cruel face that stared down at him with smug satisfaction.

"eh'Nicodemus, welcome home," the Gunera said, oozing with malice.

"Did you bring the papers to claim me back, vuh'Yguggli?" Nick asked in a near whisper as he stared horrified at the man who'd owned him body and soul for eighteen years. A wave of revulsion and terror racked Nick, but he refused to expose the emotions to this hideous being. Nick lifted his chin in defiance of his master.

The Gunera lord waved a bit of metal in the air. "Of course. One doesn't demand the return of property without documentation, eh'Nicodemus. It's good to see you again. And nice to see your brethren have taken such good care of you. You look bigger and stronger than when you left us. I can see great value in the changes in you."

Jason's eyes darted as he calculated possible actions to take. "What's he saying?" he demanded.

"vuh'Yguggli is my owner," Nick said with a sigh. "He says he's happy to have his property returned."

7

They were solicitous as they harnessed Nick into the seat next to Jason. Nick supposed it only made sense. As vuh'Yguggli's presence indicated, Nick was valuable property. The average slave could be appraised at nearly ten thousand bhin, approximately six months' salary for the typical bah', an amount not to be lightly tossed around. As the son of a former human President and the only legal human slave in the entire empire, Nick was something of a novelty. He imagined the vuh' could collect twice the average for that distinction, not to mention that he was still young but fully mature. Nick was precisely what slave owners sought the most. There was the added attraction of Nick's damned long limbs, useful beyond words among a people whose arms and legs barely functioned.

Nick was panicking, no doubt about it. Finding himself bound, helpless, wounded, and face-to-face with the creature that had brought him so much misery was sending his thoughts into the stratosphere. His heart was hammering so hard he knew vuh'Yguggli could hear it. The Gunera had excellent hearing since they used the tremors in air passing across their gills to capture sound. Nick had no doubt the vuh' was listening to every frantic beat of his human prisoner's heart and was savoring the terror he knew his sudden appearance had elicited.

Nick's frightened thoughts skittered from one anxious image to another—memories, ancient pains, and horrors—all returning from the deep, dark hole where he'd mercilessly suppressed them for the past decade. At that moment, Nick was no longer an adult with diplomatic status on a shuttle but had reverted to a frightened boy, placed in service in the vuh's household.

Another flood of panic sent the blood pounding in Nick's ears. *I'm losing my edge,* he thought. Once, he could have faced vuh'Yguggli without fear. Without any type of emotion at all. Humans had made him soft. Humans had made him feel again.

In his terror, Nick's wild thoughts careened from one awful remembrance to the next. They settled on one particular day when he and eh'Kraghilg had finished their daily tasks and momentarily escaped their lives of drudgery. The two had stolen up the hill to a small, neglected garden that was their secret space still within the vuh's encircling walls that were the borders of their world but far enough away from the inhabited places that no one thought to seek them there.

That tiny, overgrown garden was where he and eh'Kraghilg would hide in the shade of the baribari trees to avoid the blazing sun on Nick's white skin. They'd talk of everything they would one day become. eh'Kraghilg would be a shepherd, which Nick had always found terribly sweet. The profession, the eh' would say, was as far from his reality as he could imagine. Quiet, sunbaked hills, the wind rustling through his air gills, the only smells that of the carangi herd he cared for, not a voice or a command to disturb him for days. Nick would picture himself a sea captain, not that he had any idea what the sea actually looked like. He only knew what he'd learned from the stories vuh'Ygundin would sometimes read aloud while Nick tended him in his bath. Storms would toss, and pirates would rage, and it was all so very exciting, so unlike the endless drudgery of Nick's days—bathing his lords, cleaning their houses, and scrubbing their floors.

The two young boys should have considered the meaning implied in Nick's tattoos. While eh'Kraghilg had some small amount of autonomy being a household servant, Nick, being a slave, had none. On that day, the young vuh' had wanted his personal attendant for some minor problem and had been outraged that Nick hadn't come immediately to heel. A single glance at his computer system revealed that Nick wasn't where he was supposed to be. A couple of keyboard taps and enforcers were summoned to drag the wayward servant back to the house. The two boys were found sitting in the shade, telling each other tales. The enforcers had beaten eh'Kraghilg to within an inch of his life and left him bleeding and unconscious. Then they dragged the shocked and terrified Nick to his master, knowing the punishment of a slave rested with the lord of the house.

vuh'Ygundin had accepted the return of his attendant with a frightening decorum that was more terrifying than a tantrum might have been. Only after the enforcers had departed, leaving a panting boy almost blind with fear to the mercies of his owner, had vuh'Ygundin found a switch and taken it to Nick's body. Nick still flinched in remembrance of those countless blows. The sharp sting was like no other. The tender outer skin of the switch tore away, and the toxins of the tree's sap burned the cuts on Nick's fragile skin. The vuh' had vented his entire strength on Nick, reducing the young man to a quivering ball of terror.

The attack had ended only when vuh'Yguggli arrived to determine the reason for the screaming. Not that Nick had screamed. He'd held his tongue, knowing that cries of pain just made the young vuh' lust for more. It had been vuh'Ygundin's screams of outrage as he pummeled his slave into the floor that had brought the lord of the house to the room. vuh'Yguggli had ended the torture by snatching the switch from the hand of his son and hitting him once across the face with it.

"Slaves," vuh'Yguggli had intoned, "are expensive and not to be abused unnecessarily. This human slave is one of a kind and, therefore, of value beyond price. Never, ever damage it again."

The vuh' had tossed the switch away and ordered his son to a punishment of his own, ten laps walking the perimeter line on his own three feet.

"You must learn," he'd told the young vuh'. "One can punish without bloodshed."

The two Gunera had abandoned the bloodied Nick. He'd crawled to his cell and nursed his wounds in silent rage.

Nick died on that day. On that day, he truly realized he was merely an object owned by aliens he didn't understand. On that day, he ceased to think of the future or to imagine worlds that might have been. He'd sealed himself up that awful afternoon. Closed off his emotions so that he could never feel pain again.

"Because," he'd vowed to himself, "the vuh's can't harm my body without destroying its value." He'd not allow them to harm his soul. He'd lock it away where no one could ever find it. Not even him.

The humans had tried to unlock that box where his memories lay hidden. Dear sweet Duncan had worked for years to find emotion in the tightly controlled young man who seemed utterly incapable of displaying feelings. He'd somehow managed to convince Corey and Jordan to help in the task, and the two young men, so much of an age and yet so different, had risen to the task. They'd taken Nick in hand and gently pried his emotions free, one soft tug after another. Until Nick had finally dared to trust. Until Nick had finally dared to feel.

Damn them.

The recollections faded as a coldness washed over Nick again. He scrambled to shove everything the humans had taught him into the box. It all needed to go if was he was to survive this simple flight. He'd go mad should those feelings be allowed to rage through him. He'd either go mad or kill vuh'Yguggli; he wasn't sure which. And humanity's hopes for him would be lost.

Into the box, damn it. *Into the box.* For the second time in his life, Nick died.

A touch on his arm drew Nick from his benighted corner, and he realized one of the attendants was mending the hole they'd dug in him. Nick hissed at the sting of disinfectant but didn't protest. Not that he had any say in the matter. He was bound so tightly to his chair he could move nothing but his head.

"How do you suppose they knew about the transponder?" Jason asked.

He must have decided to chat with the package he'd been hired to protect. Anything to keep me from melting down. Surely he'd seen the color completely wash from my face and then the frighteningly icy calm that had overtaken me thereafter. Poor Jason will be wondering what it meant.

"Because that's just the sort of thing they *would* know." Nick arched his wrists against the bindings to reveal his tattoos.

Jason frowned at the two marks on Nick's white skin. "Do they tattoo and implant everyone?"

"Only slaves," Nick said quietly. "To guarantee they can never escape."

"You did, once."

"And a lot of people died to get me out," Nick answered bleakly. "Both human and Gunera." He shook his head. "I warned them this would happen. The Gunera don't have class mobility. Every individual remains by law in the class to which he was born, and he can never escape his fate. I was born as a slave, and as a slave I will die."

"Weren't you a prisoner of war?" Jason asked. "Is enslaving prisoners what they do?"

"Not usually. Ordinarily, they don't take prisoners because, by their laws, prisoners have rights, and the Gunera are sticklers for procedure. No one wants to be stuck taking care of a prisoner for which he can never receive payback. It's easier just to kill what they catch. But you have to understand that to Guneri eyes, I'm not a prisoner of war. My mother was. I was born on Gunera Proper. In their eyes, I'm a full citizen born as a slave."

"I suspect the folks at the State Department didn't understand that concept, or they would never have agreed to return you."

"They knew," Nick replied. "They just felt they didn't have a choice. I'm the sacrificial lamb they're selling to buy peace. Although given what just occurred at the transshipment docks, even that is now in doubt."

Nick spoke with no particular malice because he understood human motives. He knew two conflicting values ran deep in the human psyche, the clash of which was unresolvable. On the one hand was the deeply held belief that every individual, regardless of age or ability, had intrinsic value, a right to life and happiness, and an internal locus of control in terms of one's fate. That belief contrasted with the belief that humanity itself was the ultimate expression of evolution and that humanity had to survive regardless of cost. So where in the balance did the life of one undersecretary hang? They'd weighed the choices, calculated the costs, and made their decisions, telling themselves they were merely sending Nick Severin home. The survival of humanity was the outweighing factor. One human, a sadly broken and dysfunctional human, was the price to be paid for that survival. It made sense to Nick. He despised the reality of the situation but understood it. To humanity, he was but a chess piece to be moved on the board. What he made of the move would be his decision.

Nick closed his eyes and rested his head against the seat cushions. His temples and his arm throbbed. He wanted to sleep, to escape the horror that was flying at him.

"Get some rest, sir," Jason said gently. "I suspect you'll need it."

Although he wanted to hide in the oblivion of sleep, Nick's racing thoughts made that impossible. He couldn't stop himself from running scenarios in his mind: *Why had the Gunera tried to smuggle Lincoln Combs into their own territory? How had the Amaurau discovered the deception? Or had they? Had humans tried to stop the abduction of an important man? Could I have missed seeing an uprising within Gunera setting one faction against another? Why have they captured me? Clearly, there must be a link.* The entire cascade of events that put him on board a Guneri shuttle as a prisoner of vuh'Yguggli had all started with that single message. The words still echoed in his mind. *Direction required prior to renewal ceremony of Protocol 10 Rhadamanthus. Urgent.* It gave Nick pause. *Had the Gunera really intended to renew? Had Lincoln Combs's death put it in jeopardy?*

Nick looked sullenly across the aisle at his former master and struggled to mask his ever-increasing panic. *Into the box*, he thought. vuh'Yguggli seemed proud of himself. His eyes occasionally flicked in Nick's direction. The avarice did not escape Nick, and he wondered in his deepest moments of depression if the whole thing had all been a scheme devised by the clever vuh' to recapture his investment. Maybe none of this was about the shifting of powers and global alliances. Perhaps it all came down to a greedy vuh' and a stolen boy. Nick found his eyes transfixed by vuh'Yguggli's, and he understood the lust that burned in his captor's gaze. He'd seen it a million times before. The vuh' still considered him a valuable commodity and could barely contain his desire to howl at having reclaimed his mojo.

And yet he didn't. Something more important held him back. Nick was terrified to know what that meant. He was beyond terrified to find himself bound and helpless beneath the vuh's baleful stare. *No*, he thought sternly. *Terror is something you cannot afford. Into the box, nasty terror. Into the box like everything else.*

Head throbbing, Nick closed his eyes. Staring daggers at his owner was only causing pain.

He must have dozed off because sometime later, Nick was gently woken by an attendant offering him a tray of food. His uninjured right hand was released so that he could eat. The politeness was startling, but Nick accepted it without complaint and found himself relishing the long-forgotten flavors of his youth. Jason picked at the food more cautiously, but when encouraged by Nick to eat, he did so, face grimacing at the odd sour aftertastes. They were also provided alcohol which surprised Nick. During his eighteen years in Gunera, the only alcohol he'd tasted was from glasses left behind at parties he'd been assigned to clean up. By the smooth, caramel flavor, Nick surmised the vuh' had uncorked one of his better bottles. Nick's eyes strayed toward vuh'Yguggli in question.

"To me, you're a slave," the Guneri vuh' sniffed. "But I have orders from the mai' to see you're treated with the honor due an important diplomat. We don't want to start a war with humans, do we?"

"You don't think abducting me under false pretenses doesn't qualify as an act of war?" Nick asked.

The vuh's tail waved in amusement. "What false pretenses, eh'?"

"Lincoln Combs never made it to Gunera, did he? He never had a chance to attack the mai'."

vuh'Yguggli's expression held a trace of pleased malice. "His purpose was never to kill the mai'. So, alas, I suppose you could call our declaring such an emergency false pretenses, but what were we poor Gunera to do? The Amaurau stymied our plans. We lost our most important weapon when they deprived us of teg'Lincoln. We had to obtain a replacement."

"*Replacement?* To do what?" Nick found himself breathing easier. So his abduction wasn't simply the act of an annoyed vuh' attempting to reclaim his property. There was more to the story, and the mai' was neck-deep in it. That meant that vuh'Yguggli had only so much authority despite his current posturing.

"I'm sure your new master will explain it to you," the vuh' said idly.

"*My new master?*" Nick tamped down his alarm and presented a cold face to his nemesis.

The vuh's eyes narrowed. "Yes. Alas, I was forced to tender my interest in you, eh'Nicodemus. I use the word *tender* lightly. You were taken from me by point of pen with no recompense to my treasury for the pleasure. I'm told that the title to your person will be restored to me once this adventure is over. I intend to ensure that you are back in my household when that time comes. I've strengthened my defenses and prepared a secure storeroom for your return. No army will be strong enough to steal you again, eh'Nicodemus."

Not that an army had been involved the first time, Nick thought with grim satisfaction. Merely a coalition of Gunera who'd sensed the value in giving back to Earth that which had been stolen. Nick knew that his long-ago rescue and subsequent smuggling into Hemera had involved years of planning by Guneri partisans who wanted favorable relations with human traders. The move would also sting the ego of a prominent lord who stood in the way of vast riches for them. A secret network of conspirators had stolen Nick in the dark of night and spirited him out of the empire before the vuh' could intervene. Several agents had died horribly at the hands of the enraged vuh', but by then, Nick had been successfully handed over to the human conspirators on the other side. He'd been taken to Duncan's house to be assimilated into human culture, the damage done by his Guneri masters carefully repaired.

Nick fought the desire to grin at the vuh's discomfiture, which still seemed to burn hotly. Yet Nick understood the vuh's rage. The Gunera had been humiliated when his prize slave was stolen. Now he was suffering because someone higher up the chain of command had stolen that property again. Nick was aware that his presence in the vuh's household had brought vuh'Yguggli great status.

"You planning to lock me away?" Nick asked, feeling the need to jibe his nemesis.

vuh'Yguggli's tail whipped savagely. He pursed his lips while contemplating how to stab back. Two could play the verbal torment game.

"Indeed not. I've had years to ponder the situation, eh'Nicodemus, and I've funded research on how to profit from owning a human. You're useful creatures to have around the house. You quickly perform services that a Guneri slave would struggle to accomplish. In fact, this recently sparked an idea for a new business venture. I intend to acquire human females and start a farm." Reptilian eyes narrowed with pleasure. "From what I understand, you'll make a nice stud."

Nick froze, and he felt the color drain from his face. Jason nudged him worriedly.

"I'll make a fortune selling slaves!" vuh'Yguggli chortled. "I can only imagine the demand for your offspring!"

"Oh ... God," Nick managed.

"Isn't it a splendid idea?"

Nick had to admit that from the Guneri perspective, it probably was a sound plan. Guneri servants with their short arms and legs were ungainly. In his youth, Nick had easily accomplished three times more work than the rest of the household combined. In many ways, Nick was surprised the Gunera hadn't contemplated a breeding farm before, aside from a penchant for killing every human they'd ever caught. Nick had been the first to survive, the first to have been raised as a slave.

Nick forced a diplomatic mask over his features to deny the vuh' pleasure. Then he considered how best to pop vuh'Yguggli's bubble. "You're assuming I'm a viable stud."

The vuh' belched with laughter. "Oh, please, eh'Nicodemus. You're young and fully mature. I have no doubts from that perspective."

"I haven't managed to replicate thus far," Nick jabbed back.

Nick's reply tore the smugness from the vuh's face. "You'll breed, damn you," he growled.

"With what?" Nick asked, now finding humor in the whole horrid discussion. "Your problem will be obtaining females. Human young can't provide much labor in their first ten years, so there'll be quite an upcharge to building a supply chain. You'll need at least twenty females to possibly break even. How do you propose to accomplish this? The only human female in all of Gunera is eh'Monica, and she's not exactly young."

"Hmm. Yes. Well, that's why I've been forced to relinquish title to you on the proviso that it is returned when all is done." The vuh' sipped his wine thoughtfully. "If everything goes as planned, I can obtain an unlimited number of nubile females and begin the breeding program. You, of course, will comply." The Guneri lord's attention drifted away, lost in dreams of avarice and wealth.

"What's become of eh'Monica?" Nick asked, keeping his voice cool and his anxiety in check. He couldn't solve the problem of becoming the star of Gunera's slave breeding program. There were certain places where his mind wouldn't go. In the meantime, he might learn of his mother's whereabouts. Her disappearance might hold a deeper meaning.

The vuh's tail brushed Nick's query aside without interest. "I don't know, and I don't care. She's not my property, and unless someone can lay hands on another human male to breed with her, she's not worth much, in my opinion. Of course," he said, eyes slanted at Nick, "there's always you."

Nick glared. "That's sick! I am not mating with my own mother! Don't even think about it!"

"Alas, no. The thought came, and the thought went. I'd heard such a union generally produces poor results."

And on that note, I'm done, Nick thought. Fortunately, the vuh' left him to fret, and fret he did. Because his brain simply refused to consider the issue of the vuh's grand plans, Nick forced his thoughts back to the more pressing problems he faced. The mystery of the *Death's Festival* was starting to resolve itself and Nick knew Lincoln Combs was dead. Now Nick had to figure out what the Gunera had wanted with Combs and what role he was expected to play. Clearly, someone wanted him to step in where Combs had left off. The Amaurau's stance was becoming clearer. Whatever Combs had been up to, the Amaurau had learned of the plot and moved to stop it. Which meant the Guneri plot was against the Amaurau rather than humans. It also explained the sudden appearance of the Amaurau on Independence Day. *They must have poisoned Duncan to assure my presence at the ceremony,* Nick thought. *They'd come to eliminate me from being used in the Guneri plot. They'd also struck the blow against gy'Gravinda, perhaps to make a statement or, alternatively, to stop the plot in its tracks.* On that point, Nick still wasn't sure.

The analysis provided enough perspective to ease Nick's stark terror. Things weren't as they should be. He'd lost his transponder, and his bodyguard had been disarmed, but he wouldn't be handed over to vuh'Yguggli as a slave, at least not right away. The Gunera had need of Nick alive, which bought him time. *Time for what, bucko?* he wondered. *To find some way to contact humanity and warn them of the treachery? To escape Gunera a second time before title to my person is returned to the vuh' and I find myself a key ingredient in a crazy plan to breed human slaves? God! What a mess!*

In the end, he could do little. Strapped in the safety harness and under constant watchful guard, Nick could only enjoy the flight and its excellent amenities. Jason handled the situation well. He ate the food and drank the alcohol, and didn't say one word of complaint. He didn't even ask about the conversation between Nick and the vuh'. He merely eased his alertness whenever he sensed Nick's alarm easing.

Eventually, exhaustion overtook Nick, and he drifted to sleep knowing that vuh'Yguggli had no intention of injuring his future stud. He was safe, or at least as safe as a human could be while trapped in Guneri space.

8

The Guneri attendants strapped into their seats and informed Nick that the shuttle was approaching its destination. The flight had been long and grueling, two days by Nick's reckoning. The rumbling descent to Gunera reminded him that the planet suffered from nasty weather. It was searing hot, climatically temperamental, and muggy. The shuttle rattled as it pierced the atmosphere and encountered one of the perpetual storms that swirled around the equator. Then it dove into the cloud deck. Lightning flashed, and several strikes hit the shuttle, sending dancing flames of Saint Elmo's fire licking across the wings that extended to convert the ship from spacecraft to aircraft. Another series of shakes and stomach-wrenching drops took them below the clouds. Nick gazed out one of the craft's quartz glass windows at the world of the Gunera.

To the left shimmered the Emerald Sea, a vast ocean so saturated with olivine it glowed a vibrant green in the sunlight slanting in beneath the storm clouds. The dull shimmer spoke of a violent day at sea, but Nick still made out a handful of large nautical craft plying the waves. To the right arced the lands of Mahagog, the central provinces where the seats of government stood. As the shuttle approached the ocean, Nick saw the fringing orange beaches, a ragged melding of the olivine from the sea and rusted iron from the land. The plateau of Mahagog and the sparkling silver of the Imperial City followed.

The gleaming city covered virtually the entire continent, not that the region was large. Four others of greater size ringed the planet, but none possessed the concentration of power that existed in Mahagog. The collection of businesses, residences, and palaces filled every available inch of land. They stood high on the sides of the Goravide Range with its central volcanic peak spewing ash into the sky. The palaces flowed down the mountain slopes and out into the plains. They clustered on the fragile sea cliffs where the homes of the wealthy sometimes tumbled into the ocean. Between the radial arms that spoke of streets, Nick noted patches of dark green, the myriad public parks and lordly estates where a tiny fraction of the continent's once-lush jungles still clutched for handholds.

Nick beheld the Imperial complex holding sway in the middle of the urban sprawl. The group of magnificent buildings stood atop one of the extinct volcanic cones that dotted the landscape. The first emperor had planted his standard on that cone and from there won a battle that gained him a continent and, eventually, a world-spanning empire. The pyramidal collection of palaces and reception halls glittered like jewels in the hot afternoon sun. As the craft continued its descent, Nick noticed the huge olive green and gold banners that wafted on the winds, an arrogant statement of the House of Kagradyne that all the seas, lands, and wealth therefrom belonged only to the emperor.

The shuttle rattled again as twin flaps opened to slow its descent. Unlike humans and Amaurau, the Gunera hadn't conquered antigravity. Spacecraft landings were dependent upon wind resistance and catch-nets. Nick had never adjusted to the process, and he'd been scared shitless each of the ten times he'd been through it. No amount of repeat performances ever convinced him the method was safe. Facing the landing into Mahagog, Nick gripped the armrests and closed his eyes, praying to both his Guneri gods and the Christian God of Earth for a safe landing. He threw Jesus into the mix for good luck.

"Is there something I should know?" Jason asked worriedly.

"Hang on. This isn't the most pleasant way to land."

The sound of air ripping over the wing flaps grew louder until speech was impossible. Because the shuttle was a finely crafted thing, its trembling was minimal, and Nick breathed easier. The harsh roar of the reverse engines ensued as the pilot commanded his ship to slow. Nick felt himself being pushed forward against his harness as inertia took hold. The ship bumped and shook; then came the sudden groan as the electromagnetic field from the spaceport grasped it and forced it to stop. Nick was shoved hard into his harness, and his neck snapped forward. At his side, Jason swore and muttered that he wasn't ice in a martini shaker.

The electromagnetic net had held as it always did for a thousand landings per day, and it set the little shuttle down gently. The pilot took control again and taxied to a hangar. Around them, the Gunera unlatched their harnesses. As soon as both men were on their feet, Jason grabbed Nick by the arm.

"Not one step away from your side," Jason murmured. "They'll have to kill me to separate us."

Nick accepted the fingers digging into his bicep. He nodded to the man who would become, like it or not, the best friend he had in the world. "I'm not complaining, Jason."

vuh'Yguggli rolled forward on his mover and gestured with both tail and hands for Nick and Jason to follow him. His air gills swept slowly, an indication that he was calm and happy. Nick trailed behind him the requisite two meters that indicated a lack of rank.

To his surprise, the vuh's tail caught Nick's free arm and dragged him forward, dragging Jason along, too.

"None of that, eh'Nicodemus," the vuh' said brightly as he rolled down the ramp toward the terminal. "You're the mai's personal guest and a most honored representative of your government. You'll walk beside me as is fitting for such rank."

Startled, Nick settled alongside the vuh'. "Can you raise me to a vuh' for the duration?"

vuh'Yguggli issued a snort of derision. "Don't be absurd." The alien's reptilian eyes slanted at Nick and his gills swished in annoyance. "However, the mai' has decreed for the purposes of our project that you're to be raised to a teg'." He maneuvered his barbed tail between Nick's eyes, threatening to put one out. "Don't let it go to your head. You're still my property and bear my title marks."

Nick glanced at his wrists. Those damned marks had been a source of embarrassment in human space. Here they spoke more loudly than words. Slave. Property. Once again, Nick felt a stab of fear that he madly tamped down. Despite the personal and professional accomplishments he'd made following his escape, Nick was right back where he'd started. The vuh' and the mai' could play all the games they wanted with his head, but in the end, those two damned marks were the truth. He'd been born a slave and would die a slave. Every Gunera he encountered would know him for exactly what he was.

The vuh' gave him a slight shake. "Don't fret, teg'Nicodemus. Slave or not, you're a most valuable thing, and those who look on your marks will know. Those marks are blessing! No Gunera would dare damage my property. Wear your marks with pride, teg'. Tell the world you're the most valuable slave in the empire."

Nick growled low in his throat but said nothing.

Jason, aware of the tension coursing through Nick, turned to him. "Is there something I should know?"

"He's having fun at my expense," Nick said through gritted teeth. "Telling me I should be proud I'm the most valuable piece of property in the empire."

"Ignore him. He's an ass."

Nick couldn't help but laugh. *God,* he thought, *it's nice having a human at my side!* It held the past at bay.

vuh'Yguggli moved quickly, forcing Nick to trot every third step, although Jason, with his longer stride, could easily keep pace. As they exited the climate-controlled shuttle, Nick choked on the planet's torrid air, so filled with moisture that eddies were visible in the breeze. Within seconds, Nick was bathed in sweat, and he felt thankful to be wearing a cotton/tendine knit to wick away the moisture. Nick glanced at the beads of sweat forming on Jason's shaved head and wondered how the man must be feeling beneath his leather jacket. *More power to you,* Nick thought.

Looking up, Nick saw the towering thunderheads of an equatorial storm moving northward, and he assumed the city would be hit within hours by a torrent of violence and rain. Rain was a near-daily occurrence in Mahagog when the equatorial storms spun northward. However, the simple condensation of the atmosphere by the heat of the torrid, blue sun also bred storms. The waves of radiation pouring forth turned the sky into a molten blue, and Nick felt its bite on his skin. He ducked his head, reminding himself that sunlight was deadly to those whose skin hadn't evolved to tolerate it. He'd be dead within an hour if he remained outside.

At the same time, the views from the spaceport brought him a strange melancholic bliss. He saw the rising, silver domes of the various palaces, the grand porticos that offered entrance into structures more than a thousand years old. The hot, wet wind was whipping the banners that topped each building and declared the clan of the owners within. Blue and gold, red and silver, green and aqua. Nick recognized the aroma of kliki flowers and spied a tumble of them falling over a wall from some unseen garden. The thick leaves of a baribari tree flapped leisurely in the wind, their thick pulp-filled central ribs rooting them in place as they fluttered from side to side. Someone was cooking. Nick smelled the thick gumbo of luscious spices, hot and pungent, that the locals used with such abandon. Nick felt instantly hungry. Nearby, the sound of recorded music played on a kadakada board hung in the air. The sound was eerily similar to a marimba. As the Gunera had never developed the concept of rhythm, the sounds merely wafted about, taking whatever speed they chose. It reminded Nick that Gunera possessed beauty as well as ugliness.

The wall of kliki flowers reminded Nick of the overall isolated design of the city. Every house, whether grand or small, lordly or common, walled itself from all the others. Those endless white walls became a maze, only whispering of the grandeur that might lie on the other side. Nick had often been tempted to scale the walls to unearth that mystery. As a long-legged primate, he'd found it easy, and he'd spent numerous hours with eh'Kraghilg scrambling up walls and reporting back to his earthbound companion all the wonders that he'd witnessed.

There would be no time for such adventures today. vuh'Yguggli, aware of Nick's vulnerability to the sun, continued to move quickly.

The small group crossed the bit of tarmac to a heavily guarded door. vuh'Yguggli flashed his pass, and the sentries stepped aside. The pass indicated rank, and the vuh' was indeed highly ranked, being one of seventy regional dukes, absolute rulers over their properties, beholden only to the emperor. In addition, vuh'Yguggli was the vuh' of the Imperial City, meaning anything that didn't fall under the purview of the mai' was his domain. His close proximity to the emperor, both through his lands and familial ties, made vuh'Yguggli one of the most powerful individuals in Gunera. No one would stand in his way, with the possible exception of gy'Bagrada.

Nick drew a breath of relief as they entered the air-conditioned spaceport. The port was a grand affair, used only by the mai' and his most trusted associates, allowing those in power to come and go unseen by the citizenry. The roof above was a towering glass shell that let in natural light but collected the worst of the heat and humidity high above their heads. Even as they walked through the space, the humid air condensed and dropped a gentle shower on those below, an interior rainfall such as only Gunera could produce. It mattered little since the walkway was constructed of a slide-resistant porous terrazzo tile.

They ascended various ramps, all stairways having been demolished at the advent of the movers, much to the horror of the city's Historical Commission. The ramps suited Nick fine and made Jason's job of clutching Nick's arm easier. The assemblage plunged into the Palace of Lost Souls, the house dedicated to the honorable dead. A forest of glass pillars held elaborate jars containing the ashen remains of the Imperial Family. The maze was bewildering, but vuh'Yguggli knew the way.

"Kindly avoid disrupting or tipping over the jars," vuh'Yguggli said to his two out-of-breath companions. "It would greatly displease the Royal Family if cousin vuh'Dudorok's remains were knocked to the floor."

They stepped outside briefly, continuing upward, then continued inside through the Palace of Just Causes. They raced across the structure, outside along another rising garden passage and inside again. Just when Nick thought his legs couldn't stand another incline as he charged up the mountain, vuh'Yguggli rolled to a stop in the foyer of yet another palace. The Palace of the Winds was an open-air structure. A strong breeze blew in from the sea, carrying the aroma of brine and the rumble of thunder. Nick gazed over the rooftops of the lower palaces, beyond the dazzling city, and finally, faintly off in the distance, the shimmer that was the sea. Heavy banks of clouds pierced by rays of sunlight loomed over that magnificent view, and Nick stood silently in awe as the wind ruffled his hair and wicked the sweat from his clothing.

vuh'Yguggli spun around on his mover, arms and tail outstretched. "This will be your home for the duration. The entire palace is at your disposal, and you may use all it has to offer. I would ask that you be careful of the antiques. No object within it is less than five hundred years old, and I would hate to take the cost of damages out of your hide. You always did have such … delicate skin." The vuh's gills wafted in giddy humor at his little joke. "I'll leave the eh's to give you the tour, as I have other duties higher above. Make use of the eh's however you please. Consider them yours for the length of your stay."

Nick glowered at the vuh', fully understanding the innuendo implicit in the statement. Being a lord, vuh'Yguggli had probably indulged himself in all of the eh's if for no other reason than to make clear his power and prowess.

"Are you certain you've taken us to the correct place?" Nick asked with feigned politeness. "This eh' would have expected the servants' quarters for himself."

A tail barb brushed across his cheek. "Don't be vulgar," vuh'Yguggli snarled, his tail twitching in annoyance.

Although Nick hadn't flinched, the movement startled Jason, who placed himself between the vuh' and his client, a wall of bone and sinew against an entire evil empire.

"You know I've been commanded to treat you with the dignity afforded by the mai' to his human lackeys," the vuh' explained. "Only my ancestors know why. While it galls me, I shall abide my lord's whimsy. Don't press your luck, teg'Nicodemus. I'll see that every transgression you commit is recorded and a suitable punishment applied once your title is back in my hands. Good day to you, teg's." He made a vague movement of his upper body that might have been a bow. "You'll be informed when your services are required."

The miffed vuh' spun his mover toward the door. Before exiting, he whirled to interject an afterthought. "You have free movement within the palace. Any attempt to leave it, however, will be viewed dimly. Don't abuse my hospitality." He pointed a stubby finger at the computer in the outer office. "Your accounts are still open, eh'. Feel free to use them."

Nick remained wary until the vuh' and his entourage left the building. Only upon hearing the exchange of code words to set the sentry watch did Nick relax. Sensing the softening in his client, Jason released his arm and surveyed their surroundings.

"I take it this is home?"

Nick nodded. "Apparently. It's more than I expected. I thought the vuh' would send me to my cellar hole."

Jason began to wander. "You grew up here?"

"Not here specifically; this palace is new to me. But on the hill, yes."

Nick paused. From hidden crevices, the palace staff padded out on bare feet led by the majordomo. They gathered silently.

Ignoring them, Nick continued. "I was a slave in the palace where the vuh' met with business associates. Gunera take great stock in appearances, so he showed me off as a sign of his power. The sight of a human scrubbing the floors in the presence of important guests proved Yguggli's wealth." He swept his hand toward the room. "This is one of the vuh's spare palaces where he might put up visiting dignitaries. Nice of him to reserve it for us. I don't like it."

"Why not?"

Nick snorted. "He's being far too gracious. It's making me nervous."

"How well do you know the lay of the land?" Jason glanced at the endless sea of Guneri servants still shuffling into the room. "Can these things understand us?"

Nick afforded the servants barely a glance. "I'm familiar with most of Imperial Hill. I know the palaces in relation to each other and the street layout, although, as you saw coming up, someone can reach the top of the hill without setting foot on a road. Commoners and tradespeople use the streets, while the lords use the garden passages. It's another way lords maintain their status. If a lord can ascend to the very top of the hill without setting foot on a public street, he's powerful indeed."

"This Yguggli is such a lord?"

Nick nodded. "Very much so. He wasn't denied access to any of the palaces as we came up. Not being a lord, I don't know the garden routes. But I know every nook and cranny of the dark level, if that helps."

"The *dark level?*"

"The sewers and other nasty places that underpin a city. I know every inch of them."

Jason pursed his lips but said nothing.

Nick flicked his hand at the now silently gathered palace staff. "As for any of them understanding English, no. Most of them don't even speak the house Gunera."

"*House Gunera?*"

Nick nodded. "Every house has its own dialect which they use in private. For general communication, people above eh' tier speak the Mahagog bah' dialect. It's the *lingua franca* of the city. Finally, there's court Gunera, which is used in the mai's court and for diplomatic purposes."

"Which do you speak?"

"My native dialect is eh', but I was secretly taught Krakadik vuh' and English by my mother. Krakadik vuh' is the house language of vuh'Yguggli. I'm not fluent, but I can understand it. I learned court Gunera from Duncan Huntzinger, if you can believe it, because formal negotiations are held in that dialect. Duncan also polished my English. I'm most fluent in eh' and bah'; eh' because that's what I used every day as a slave, bah' because that's what I use now in trade communications. They're all similar yet different enough to be confusing if you aren't fluent."

Jason scratched his bald head while studying the servants as they studied him. None had moved.

"Seems a bit complicated, if you ask me."

"Maybe, but it works for them. Keeps each level in its place. You can't pretend to be a bah' if you don't speak the language."

Jason continued to eye the servants. "Don't people try to learn so they can move up?"

Nick scowled. "There's no moving up in this society. You're born into a tier and will die in that tier. It's illegal to teach eh's to read, write, or comprehend the language of the higher tiers."

"Language by class," Jason muttered and shook his head.

"Keeps the tiers in their places," Nick replied. "Actually makes a lot of sense if you're determined to maintain the tier structure."

Jason considered the crowd of silent servants. "How do we talk to them?"

Nick smiled grimly. "You forget, teg'Jason, I speak fluent eh'."

"Teg'Jason? What does that mean?"

"One must always address another with their tier prefix. The eh's are the slave class and servants. Servants can't be sold from a house. A servant class eh' will serve the house into which he is born for his entire life. Slave eh's don't belong to a house. They can be traded or sold."

"You're an eh'," Jason said.

Nick nodded. "Bah's comprise the second tier. They're the tradespeople, plumbers, electricians, cab drivers, and such. They're freeborn but can't escape their tier. If you're born the son of a pipe fitter, you'll die a pipe fitter."

"Nice."

"Teg's make up the next tier. They're the learned professionals; accountants, lawyers, engineers, and such. They're also freeborn, and while they can't escape being teg', they have some professional mobility. For example, the son of an engineer can become a lawyer if that path is chosen for him."

"*Chosen for him?*"

"All individuals of teg' tier are assigned jobs by the government based on need. So you might be the world's best lawyer and the son of lawyers twenty generations back and really like the job of lawyering, but if the mai' decides he needs engineers … poof! … you're an engineer."

Jason rubbed his chin. "Now I understand why our government is determined to keep us away from these issues."

Nick smiled grimly. "To quote Duncan, 'God! Bloody savages.'"

Jason tried to laugh. "Okay, so what does calling me *teg'* mean?"

"They have to call you something, so they chose teg'. In their view, you can't be a lord if you're my servant. But they're also aware that humans don't endorse the concept of serfdom, so they're afraid to call you an eh'. You clearly aren't a bah'. So that defaults you to teg'."

"Interesting. What are the remaining tiers?"

"Next are the gy's. They're noble but landless. That's the difference between vuh's and gy's. The vuh's have land while the gy's do not, but otherwise, they possess the same level of influence. The gy's handle intellectual life. They're the scientists, scholars, and economists. All priests come from the gy' tier. They're the only tier that's allowed to select their profession because to have a calling is important in such professions. They're the smartest Gunera. They're independent thinkers and cannot be trusted."

"Duly noted. Interesting how every ambassador sent to Earth is a gy'."

"Exactly. There's a method to the madness." Nick plucked a glass flower from a vase. It was incredibly lifelike and fragile. "The vuh's make up the last tier, landed nobles. All of Gunera is divided into provinces ruled by individual vuh's. They have complete control over their provinces and are beholden only to the mai'. Because vuh's need to assure their lines remain unbroken, they generate a number of offspring. Those offspring are literally property of the mai' unless they become landed themselves. Only the mai' can proffer land, and he uses that power to control his nobles. Just because a youngster is the firstborn son of a vuh' doesn't mean he'll inherit the province. The mai' could opt for a lesser son if he chooses. Thus does the mai' assure only those most faithful to him gain land."

"What happens to all the extra vuh' offspring?" Jason asked. "Sounds like a rebellion waiting to happen."

"It is. That's why they remain the personal property of the mai'. He could, if he chose, eliminate them all, though that would be unwise. Instead, the mai' selects their professions judiciously. Many are drafted into the military to keep them away from the capitol. The bulk of the military consists of young vuh's in service to the mai'."

"Where does the mai' come from?"

"There's only one mai'." Nick returned the glass flower to its vase. "Sometimes, if the situation is unsettled, the mai' will simply replicate himself to guarantee his line. But self-replication leads to the problems inherent in cloning, so usually, an aging mai' will select his favorite vuh' to mate with."

Jason frowned. "You lost me there."

Nick gestured to the crowd of staff still waiting for the conversation to end. "Look at them, Jason. They're hermaphrodites. Both genders encased in one. When the mai' wants to reproduce, he'll order a vuh' to mate with him, lay the eggs, and see them hatched."

Nick knew he'd hit the biological frontier when he saw Jason blink stupidly. It was the sort of suggestion that simply melted down a human male's mind.

Nick nodded at the servants. "That's why they're nervous. As teg's, you or I could order them to mate with us. I wouldn't think of it, but if you'd like to take the plunge, I won't think less of you."

Nick tensed, expecting Jason might take a swing at him, but the bodyguard settled for a friendly slug on the arm.

Jason rubbed his chin while studying the servants who awaited orders from their strange alien guests. "Okay, what now?"

Nick waved. "eh's can demand nothing of teg's, so they'll stand here waiting forever until we issue some orders."

He smiled politely at the majordomo, although he knew the smile meant nothing to the Gunera. "My name is teg'Nicodemus," he said in eh', "and this gentleman is teg'Jason. We accept your service."

The majordomo returned a deep bow so deep that his stubby body almost tipped over. "Esteemed teg'. We welcome you to this house. We will provide any service desired if you explain the requirements of your species."

Being treated in such a lordly fashion gave Nick pause. In his youth on Gunera, he'd been filth. Among humans, a quirky low-level civil servant. Being raised to a teg' was disconcerting. He decided he would fail if he tried to be a Guneri lord. He was what he was and damned if anyone would say otherwise.

He issued the faintest of bows, something no Guneri lord would do, but he hoped the gesture would buy him points with the staff. Then, to their combined astonishment, he spoke to the group directly in eh'. "Thank you for your service. I am teg' Nicodemus, and this is teg'Jason. I speak both house Gunera and eh' while teg'Jason speaks neither. Please feel free to direct your questions to me personally if your leader is unavailable. As a human, I will not take offense regardless of your level in the house."

Startled, the group issued silent bows. The majordomo, aware that the visiting aliens had just wiped out the authority of his position, sputtered.

"Our needs are not much different from yours," Nick said. "At present, we would like to bathe and change clothes. After that, something light to eat. I don't know what's in season, but we are not particular. Please conduct us to our rooms."

Immediately, the majordomo ordered his staff to their duties; a stampede ensued. Nick forced down his smile. He well remembered being a part of such rushes. Within seconds the room was empty save Nick, Jason, and the majordomo.

"Your name, eh'?" Nick asked.

The majordomo choked back a gasp then bowed. "eh'Daigana, teg'Nicodemus."

"It's a pleasure to meet you, eh'Daigana," Nick said to the eh's further confusion. "Please show us your establishment. Much honor is due to you for the exquisiteness of its repair."

Stunned by the unexpected praise, eh'Daigana beamed. Then he waddled ahead of them on stubby legs, tail held upright as was proper for a well-trained servant. Because the Guneri tail had evolved as a defensive weapon when the species lived underground, its position was significant. A lowly servant was required to hold it in the neutral, nonthreatening upward position lest it be amputated by an angry vuh'.

Thus, his tail proud and his air gills wafting, eh'Daigana led his guests to the suite of rooms set aside for them.

The first was a sitting room with a lovely icefall against the far wall. Nick ran his fingers across the extravagance. Just as fireplaces warmed homes in the winter, icefalls were meant to keep them cool. The room included comfortable cushions and tables in colors of gray and plum for entertaining guests. Exquisite artwork of blown glass in jewel tones adorned the room. Not a mote of dust rested on the writhing glass tendrils that reached out like grasping tentacles. Nick read the date impressed into one of the sculptures, amazed that the glass was over seven hundred years old.

An open colonnade gave access to a garden with a babbling fountain and flowering gossi bushes. Beyond it lay the small informal family dining area. As Nick surveyed the low stone table, a work of marquetry art in slabs of granite and mica, he heard the sudden rush of rain. A windswept mist drifted inside, and the floors near the garden were soon glazed with a film of rainwater. Nick smiled. He'd always loved the afternoon storms as they'd offered Nick a chance to both cool and clean his body. He resisted the urge to rush into that rain again.

Their twisting journey took Nick and Jason through a state dining room that could seat one hundred, followed by a resting room where the vuh' and his guests would retire to discuss politics. Beyond that was another garden and then a game room. Nick shivered, recalling innumerable hours spent as a slave tending to vuh'Ygundin in a similar room. A polished floor of granite marquetry marked out the various games that could be played. Nick noticed ramburi, similar to shuffleboard; gokadur, a game nearly identical to tennis; and dagga, the Guneri equivalent of chess.

The room reawakened a wave of memories that Nick would have preferred to let sleep: The young vuh' demanding Nick polish all the game boards before he decided which one he'd use; Nick scrambling to fill the buffet table and provide drinks to his master's guests; torrents of insults heaped upon him by those self-interested and arrogant young lords; the pain of being knocked down countless times from what the lords called his "stork-like legs." It was indeed a game room. *Games for the vuh', torture for the slave,* Nick thought

"I've seen enough of this room," Nick said, masking a shudder. "Let's move along."

As they toured the extensive palace, Nick eyed the secretive slits in the walls designed to be invisible. The narrow openings led to the dark spaces where equipment and goods were kept in readiness: glasses, plates, towels, and dishes; rubs, salves, bandages, and cloths; tea, coffee, and alcohol. The intent was to provide a lord with anything he desired almost before he thought to ask for it. Nick was well aware of the eyes that followed him at every turn. The eh's were trying to decode his minutest gesture so they could anticipate a requirement before Nick even thought to voice it. Nick found their fear palpable. Untrained in human desires, the eh's were terrified they'd miss a gesture and be beaten for their failures. *How odd,* Nick thought, *that I'm now the lord.* With the flick of his wrist, he could demand anything from the smallest cocktail napkin to sexual intercourse from all of them right there in the midst of the tour. He didn't know what to make of his feelings and opted not to try. Like so many other emotions, Nick pushed them down into the box to be reconciled later.

The majordomo led his guests into an office with a Guneri-sized desk low to the floor atop which sat a computer system much like Nick remembered from his youth. The design was sleeker, but Nick recognized the general components and assumed he could use it.

eh'Daigana gestured to the equipment. "The office is available for your use. I've been told that you possess codes for the system. If you need assistance, please ask. I will call for a bah' to help you."

Nick nodded. "Thank you, eh'Daigana."

The acknowledgment startled the eh,' and he stumbled out the door.

The next stop on the tour was the suite of three bedrooms that surrounded a central garden where rain hammered down, lightning flashed, and thunder roared.

eh'Daigana led Nick into the largest of the bedrooms. Its windows overlooked the city, though it was presently obscured by the heavy downpour. The room was typical for a lord's residence, complete with a dressing area mirrored on the floor and walls to enable a lord to view himself from all angles (vital when one's tail was the most expressive appendage). A wall of shelves with baskets stood in place of a traditional dresser. Nick's case had arrived ahead of him and sat empty along the wall, his belongings already stowed in the baskets. All that remained to discuss were the sleeping arrangements. Nick grinned as Jason shook his head.

"This just ain't gonna work," the huge man mumbled.

Nick chuckled. Thousands of years earlier, when the ancient Gunera lived in small holes dug in hillsides, they'd line the holes with sticks, leaves, ferns, and palm fronds for comfort. Nothing much had changed since then, as modern Gunera still slept much the same way (although they now placed their nests inside boxes). Nick and Jason stared at the huge nest in their bedroom. Aside from the addition of feathers, it was exactly like the nests in which Nick had slept for eighteen years.

"They're actually comfortable," Nick commented. "And given the heat, you don't need bedclothes."

Jason stared. "I ain't fitting into that, and I don't want to try."

Laughing, Nick crawled inside. He had to curl up in a ball because his long legs didn't fit, but once he'd adjusted the lining, he found the space to be comfortable. Although he'd always preferred nests over a human bed, he'd made the change years earlier at the urging of Lady Kitty. Human women, the courtesan had stated with some authority, wouldn't accept a man who slept in a nest.

When Nick emerged from the nest, Jason was gone. After a moment, he returned, dragging a fur rug from the outer room. He arranged it next to the nest.

"You take the bird's nest," he grunted. "I'll take the floor."

"You can have one of the other rooms," Nick offered.

Jason glared. "Remember what I said on Rhadamanthus? I go where you go. I sleep where you sleep. Got it?"

Nick nodded. "Yes." He ran his hands through his hair. "I also recall you saying something about attending me in the bathroom."

"Oh lord, where's that?" He gazed around and, spotting an alcove, ventured into it. The space was tiled in white ceramic and encircled by a bar at hip level. The floor was sloped toward a central drain and possessed a spigot with a small hose.

"Is this it?" he asked dubiously.

Nick tried but failed to hold back a grin. "Um … no."

Jason looked at him quizzically and swallowed when he realized neither Nick nor eh'Daigana had entered the alcove. The Gunera was quivering. He struggled to keep his tail upright.

Jason stepped out of the room. "What gives? What is that place?"

Nick's grin widened. "Although Gunera perform the sexual act pretty much anywhere, the lordly classes prefer to do their business out of sight."

Jason's dark face lost a few shades. "It's a sex room?"

Nick laughed. "Yeah. Not that I have any direct experience, but I'm told some encounters are violent, especially if the one in the female role isn't interested. It can get messy. So ..." He gestured at the tiled space. "Easier cleanup."

"What's the bar for?" Jason asked weakly.

"Leverage."

"Jesus. Do I really want to find a bathroom?" Jason asked, storming back to the nest area.

"Just remember you volunteered for this," Nick reminded him.

"What was I thinking?"

"You know, they consider our biology equally disgusting."

Jason pointed at the vile little room. "We don't have rooms like that! We don't force people into having sex against their will!"

Nick lifted a brow. "We don't? You might want to venture down to the police department some evening and visit the sex crimes unit. It's ... educational."

Jason stiffened. "Sex offenders are sick." Again he pointed at the room. "And so are they." He turned his back on Nick and strode into the living room.

Nick trailed after Jason, feeling sorry for his large companion. "Sorry, Jason. I didn't mean to sound arrogant. It's just that the Gunera have ways that work for them whether we understand them or not."

Jason glared. "I suspect you understand it all a little too well."

Nick flinched and looked away. "Yes, I suppose so. Not by choice." He lifted his chin and settled his professional demeanor. "Would you like to see the bathroom?"

"I'm not sure."

Nick waited until his friend recollected himself before nodding to eh'Daigana to proceed. The eh' led them to the last room in the suite, another tiled space with a drain in the floor and a table in the center. One wall held shelves filled with the accouterments for a Guneri-style bath, including rasps for the priming of one's tail barb and piles of fluffy towels for the drying of the lord's not-so-delicate skin. It included a spigot and a hose, as well as a small built-in bench.

Nick pointed to the table. "Lords are bathed by their servants. The eh's will assume we desire such treatment unless we tell them otherwise."

"To hell with that!" growled Jason.

Nick nodded. "Agreed. I'll inform them of the human habit of self-bathing." He gestured. "The spigot and hose are for quick showers. It's somewhat primitive, but it works if you don't want the full service of a traditional bath."

"I don't."

"The water's always tepid, so don't wait for it to warm up. Given the heat, you don't really need hot water." Moving to the bench along the wall, Nick slid a lid out of the way. "The toilet. It works automatically. Do your business and close the lid. No worries."

Jason seemed to wilt. "Thank God for that."

Nick gave him a friendly slap. "It's not that bad. Below stairs, they don't have it this good."

Jason waited until Nick excused eh'Daigana. Both men wanted to rest.

"What's it like below stairs?" Jason asked.

Nick saw no point in withholding information from his bodyguard. Jason needed to understand that his client suffered some quirks stemming from an unorthodox upbringing. He also needed to be forewarned that Nick's reactions might differ from a normal human's reactions. Nick was anything but average, and he knew it.

"The servants live underground. No windows, sunlight, wind, or air. It's not so bad, really, because it's cooler below. The sleeping's better. eh's aren't allowed lights, so everything must be done in darkness. That's not a problem because eh's do nothing below stairs except eat and sleep."

Jason pursed his lips but remained silent.

"During my youth, the sum total I possessed was a nest in an unlighted communal space. The nest wasn't lined, so I slept on sticks. Imagine twigs poking you in your ears and nose and … well … other places."

"Maybe you should have worn thicker PJs." Jason sank onto a couch. Nick suspected he was injecting humor as a way of handling the horror of their situation.

Nick twitched his lips. "I was a slave. Slaves don't wear clothes."

Jason's head shot up. "Ever?"

"Ever."

"Jesus."

Nick plopped down beside Jason. "I was lucky the vuh' valued me enough to give me a nest. Most slaves sleep naked on the floor."

"Thank God for small mercies."

"Yes." Nick rubbed his hands together. "For that reason, I'm not squeamish about nakedness. I've been scolded a million times by Duncan, Corey, and Jordan for venturing around naked at inappropriate times. Just a heads up."

Jason nodded grimly. "Duly noted, sir. Is there anything else you think I should know?"

Nick twitched his lips while he contemplated the floor. "I've gotten better about it, having had it pounded into my head, but I'm prone to rash behavior around females. Shouldn't be a problem on Gunera, but I'll warn you just the same."

"Define 'rash behavior.'"

Nick refused to meet Jason's eyes. "The Gunera have no concept of shame or embarrassment. They don't even have a word for it. To them, there's nothing shameful about nudity or openly sexual behavior. People below the lordly classes simply mate in the street, especially eh's who aren't permitted to do it anywhere else. Don't be shocked by what you might see. You can stare if you'd like because they won't care." Nick leaned back and stretched his neck from side to side as if he could clear his head of ugly thoughts. "Since I saw individuals mating all the time, it's difficult for me not to act when my hormones rage. I'm still learning that a man doesn't assault a woman he finds attractive or, as Corey likes to say, 'swallows the tongue in public.' Again, just a warning. If I ever behave inappropriately, you may cuff me upside the head and explain what I did wrong. I really am trying to learn."

Out of the corner of his eye, Nick saw Jason smile. "Understood, sir."

"Finally, there's my bathing compulsion."

"*Compulsion?*" Jason repeated.

"Eh's don't have access to bathrooms. The only way for an eh' to clean himself is to sneak outside during a rainstorm. I never had a proper bath in the eighteen years I lived here."

Jason stared. "Ever?"

"Ever."

"Jesus. That's rough."

Nick shrugged. "It wasn't all bad. Smelling like a rancid human kept me from being invited into a mating parlor. The vuh' found my scent off-putting. Now that I *can* bathe, I've become obsessive about it. Three times a day isn't always enough. Don't act surprised if you find me living in the bathroom. Sweating in this heat will drive me insane."

Jason mopped his brow. "Affirmative. We may have to draw straws for use of the facilities."

"One of us could use the mating parlor. It has the same general equipment."

Jason's head shot up. "Not a chance."

Nick smiled, liking this man. "Okay, straws." He sighed.

Jason placed a hand on Nick's shoulder and offered a friendly squeeze. "It's going to be okay."

"Now you know why I'm a little off," Nick said quietly. "Not quite human, but definitely not Gunera."

Jason studied him. "I never considered what it meant to be raised by aliens. Your dossier didn't explain it except to say you required gentle handling and an open mind. Now I understand why."

Nick said nothing.

"You've got one hell of a set of balls, dude," the big man commented. "Agreeing to return to this hell. How did you know they wouldn't strip you naked and send you downstairs?"

"I didn't. I feared."

"Did the State Department folks know that was a possibility?"

"No. Aside from telling Duncan, and now you, I never spoke of it before. I didn't want people to consider me any more of a freak than I already was."

For a long time, Jason sat staring at the floor while his clasped hands worked at each other. Finally, he looked up at Nick. "I'm not joking when I say that you're one brave dude, sir. There's no way anyone would have convinced me to return to a past like that. We're going to get out of this. I swear on my deceased mother's honor, I'm going to see you safely home. Okay, sir?"

Nick nodded with a weak smile. "Okay. And the name's Nick, damn it."

Distancing himself from a sea of miserable memories, Nick jumped up and headed for the office. He had an important task to complete before resting. With Jason in tow, Nick went to the desk and switched on the computer. His codes were active as promised, and he quickly signed into his email.

A quick glance through his unread email messages revealed that Mother still hadn't written. He ruthlessly shoved away another jab of panic, then began a new message in full court Gunera, hoping Duncan was monitoring the account. Nick chose words that would pass the censors, and he prayed Duncan would read between the lines.

> Greetings Esteemed Minister, I and my colleague have arrived safely. Our hosts are being congenial at this time. I've received requests by former associates to extend my stay permanently. Since I've resolved the primary purpose of this visit, I see no point to such an extension. Please advise. Overall tenor like putting Lady Kitty and Alessandra alone in a room.
> eh'Nicodemus

He read the note in English to Jason who grunted unhappily.

"I suppose it conveys what you needed to say. Are the Gunera really demanding to keep you?"

Nick nodded.

"What's this about Lady Kitty?"

Nick chuckled. "Lady Kitty is a highly paid courtesan who works for all the top brass on Rhadamanthus. Alessandra is a senator's daughter."

"Ah. Things are uncomfortable," Jason translated. "That would be putting it mildly."

"It's a reference Duncan will understand. It's proof the email is from me." He hit *send*.

"Let's hope he gets it."

"Duncan promised to monitor the account. With the loss of the transponder, he knows it's the only way I can contact him."

"Hell of a thin wire," Jason muttered.

Nick nodded. He searched his in-box again and, as he'd hoped, found a new message from eh'Kraghilg. It, too, was written in code.

> eh'Nicodemus,
> I've still no news of your mother. Profound silence reigns over her and I am filled with misgivings. I've sent word out through the waste tenders of the city. If she is to be found here, one of us will locate her. I promise to send word as soon as possible. No worries, dear friend. No one cares where a waste tender goes.
> I remain forever your friend,
> eh'Kraghilg.

Nick immediately hit *respond* and began typing in code:

> eh'Kraghilg,
> The situation has radically changed. I am in the city as a prisoner of vuh'Yguggli in the Palace of the Winds. Would desperately like to speak with you if it can be arranged, but I don't know if this will be possible. Much danger surrounds me and I cannot guarantee any safety. Suggestions appreciated.
> Also your friend, eh' Nicodemus.

"An old friend of mine," Nick explained, his face a torrent of emotion. "He probably can't help us, but it's nice to know I've got a friend out there."

"Can he be trusted?"

"I'd trust him with my life."

"You may have to before we get out of this mess."

Nick jumped at the chime of an incoming email.

> Message received. We are relieved. Working on solutions.
> D

"They know we're still alive," Nick sighed.

"It'll be interesting to see what they're planning." Jason folded his arms. "Declare open warfare on the Guneri empire to get you back?"

Nick sighed and pushed himself away from the computer. While he felt relieved that the Gunera hadn't lied about leaving his accounts open, Nick suspected his access would be blocked the moment he tried to write something that conflicted with their plans. At present, the Gunera appeared to want humanity to think all was status quo with Nick's diplomatic mission. Nick wondered when that would change.

"I'm going to shower," Nick said, feeling travel-stained. "You're welcome to watch."

"I'd prefer not to," Jason replied, "but I'm not letting you out of my sight."

Nick shrugged. "Fine by me if you want to watch my sad, white ass."

Nick showered, changed into his black protocol clothes, and sprawled on the couch in the main room. Jason zipped through the fastest shower in the universe, then returned to the main room to towel off and dress. As he closed his eyes, Nick wondered what Jason thought was going to happen. It was humorous and unlikely that the Gunera were going to wrest Nick from the palace. Whatever the Gunera had in store, Nick was convinced it didn't involve violence or death. Doubtless vuh'Yguggli fully intended to have his property returned to him alive and well and in working order. Nick found the thought amusing as he drifted off to sleep.

9

The call for dinner came long after the sun had set and darkness had crept over Imperial Hill. Unbeknownst to Nick, who'd slept the afternoon away, servants had lit various lamps to fill the space with gentle light. The Gunera electric lights were accentuated with a flicker reminiscent of ancient candlelight so that the rooms drowsed in a soft, shifting glow. At the gentle request to rise from eh'Daigana, Nick sat up and ventured to the nest room to settle his hair. Whatever was happening, he intended to appear as the Protocol Officer in uniform with hair in place. Nick realized that such a defense was pathetic in a situation where he had no defense, but he was going to use it for all it was worth.

Jason donned his leather jacket and pocketed a handful of eating utensils to use as weapons should the need arise. As he and Nick left the palace, Jason grasped Nick by the arm. A group of three Gunera awaited, and their brocade coats of silk and gold shimmered. Pearls and gemstones glimmered among the folds. Even their movers appeared gilded, indicating they were the mai's servants.

The hot, muggy air was so thick that Nick felt like he was walking into a wall. His coat felt unpleasant, and Nick was soon bathed in sweat again. Not that he cared. If his human odor annoyed his hosts, so much the better. Their escort led them into the broad avenues that zigzagged up the hill. Below them and to the right sprawled the city as a glittering blanket of lights. Above them rose the private residences of the mai' and his court, buildings gilt of silver and gold, their domed roofs glinting in the light of the planet's three moons.

As they walked, Nick noted common Gunera on their movers speeding along the boulevards, coats wafting in the breeze of their passing. Most were lordly folk in expensive coats and riding movers. Here and there shuffled eh's using only their stubby legs. All made perfunctory bows to the mai's servants and goggled at the two humans.

The group moved ever upward, a challenge for Nick and Jason, but the Gunera kept the pace easy. After several minutes, they made the final switchback and arrived on the grand boulevard that circumnavigated the pinnacle of the old volcanic cone. The street was paved with mica-infused granite that glittered like water. Grand colonnades of baribari trees lined both sides of the avenue, and a center divider was planted with a kaleidoscope of flowering shrubs. The night air was perfumed with the scent of kliki and gossa flowers, heady and thick in the hot atmosphere. As they walked along that fine avenue, Nick watched the night-loving guragol moths flutter in search of nectar.

For one instant, Nick allowed himself to relax and bathe in the beauty that could be found in the harsh, angry world of the Gunera. In his life as a servant, Nick hadn't seen the treasures of the city. His memories had been of darkness, dank, and never-ending hard labor. But here, above the workaday lives of the common people, existed a gentle loveliness that all the hard labor below had financed. To be a gy', vuh', or mai' in Gunera was to live in graciousness surrounded by beauty. It was a side of Guneri life Nick had occasionally glimpsed but never tasted.

Nick was awed to travel that grand boulevard surrounded by the epitome of all that Gunera's history had created. He stood at the apex of thousands of years of history, ten times older than anything he'd seen on Rhadamanthus. The age of the place weighed on his shoulders even as the eternal newness begged the city to take flight. The Gunera didn't bother retaining the old. They improved it or swept it away in the search for ever more glories. Imperial City was the crowning achievement of Guneri philosophy. Build and build again. When it's no longer grand enough, pull it down and build some more. Always looking forward were the Gunera. Never back. Never did the Gunera look back.

Jason nudged Nick to wrest his mind from the stunning view, and Nick turned his back on the magnificent panorama.

The group stopped at a wide ramp that led sharply upward to the grand doors of the Palace of the Mai'. Long ago, that ramp had been a set of wide stone stairs where the common people would bring petitions for their emperor. During the last century, a mai' had tired of the practice, and with the advent of the movers, ordered the stairs filled in. The daily rite of petitioning was abolished. It removed the last opportunity for the commons to touch their mai'. The society was sadder for it.

The guards at the door had been apprised of Nick's summons. They stood aside to allow the group passage.

As he grunted his way up the ramp, Jason muttered, "Is *everything* in this city uphill?"

"Pretty much," Nick panted at his side.

"I suddenly understand the people movers."

The two humans were ushered inside a grand reception hall with an arched roof made of tempered glass that revealed the stars and the moons overhead. Nick stopped at one of the hall's many decorative mirrors to smooth his hair. He also adjusted his bow and confirmed that his clothes were presentable. Whether the Gunera—a race known for strict attention to inconsequential details—would agree remained to be seen.

The hall was grand baroque Guneri style, overdramatic in every aspect and overflowing with glass and sculptures. A line of chandeliers, packed so closely that they touched one another, gave the ceiling the appearance of a forest bathed in ice, while flickering lights provided the sense of sunlight glinting on snow. To underscore the wintery atmosphere, icefalls crawled down the walls and lent a chill to the otherwise pleasantly air-conditioned space. A series of fountains gave a further sense of coolness as the splashing of the water rang delicately through all the glass filigree.

The space was equally stunning to both Nick and Jason, who each slowed their pace to absorb the wonders of the Palace of the Mai'. While Nick had been granted a taste of Guneri luxury in his days in the vuh's lower house, he'd never imagined anything could be this grand.

Their escort stopped before a mirrored door. An honor guard in the imperial livery of silver and gold stood at attention, on their own three feet, with ceremonial fishing spears held upright in their hands in honor of their ancestors' seafaring past. The doors opened soundlessly, and the two humans were ushered inside.

Nick entered first. Jason continued to rest a hand atop Nick's shoulder and followed directly behind.

"Let me know what I'm supposed to do," Jason whispered. "I want this to go as smoothly as possible so we can get out of here."

"You're an alien," Nick replied. "They won't expect you to understand their customs. Since they know you're my security, they'll expect you to attend to me and ignore them. That's what their security would do."

"Easy enough."

The room was another grand baroque hall with mirrors on the walls and a ceiling revealing the stars. The lights were soft, gentle, and flickering. Thick carpets covered the floor, deep red interwoven with gold and silver calligraphy that spelled out all the wondrous attributes of the current mai'. The furnishings were traditional, low to the floor and thickly padded, the tables mostly of glass, mirrors, and gilt. Faced with so many reflective surfaces, Nick wasn't sure where to focus his gaze.

Until he saw the mai'. Then it froze, and there it remained.

mai'Tegatriktrik was still young, only a few years older than Nick, and he had managed to keep a trim physique, at least by Guneri standards. He was seated on a traditional cushioned chair rather than a people mover, and Nick remembered the mai' eschewed modern conveniences. mai'Tegatriktrik was taller than the average Gunera, standing almost to the height of a teenaged human. His thick arms and hands looked strong and supple. He held a ceremonial fishing spear in his left hand while his right rested on his knee. His Guneri attire was traditional: wide-legged trousers of white and silver and a gold brocade coat over his torso. The coat was embroidered with depictions of sea life, another nod to his fish-eating past. Atop his head sat a tall hat that reminded Nick of the silly miters worn by Catholic bishops. It was silver and gold but dripped pearls around his head and shoulders so that mai'Tegatriktrik resembled a blond girl with a ridiculous oversized chapeau.

Having never been in the presence of an emperor, whether Gunera, human, or Amaurau, Nick wasn't sure what to do. He dug through his Protocols and chose G 2 subsection 9a.5 Greeting Heads of State. He dropped to one knee, placed his hands on the other, and gave a brief nod of his head. It was, he knew, the negotiated agreement of address halfway between the polite nod and handshake of human greeting and the full prostration of the body required before a Guneri lord. Jason remained at arm's length, a hand still resting atop Nick's shoulder.

vuh'Yguggli, who sat beside the mai', performed the introductions. "teg'Nicodemus, Protocol Officer of Earth."

The mai's silvery eyes swept over Nick, who stared boldly back. One of humanity's most cherished demands to both Gunera and Amaurau was that they weren't bound in service to either empire and that their diplomatic officers were to be accorded respect. The mai' seemed to find his half-obsequious, half-arrogant stance amusing.

"It's the required obeisance of the Protocol Officer to a Guneri lord," the vuh' explained in his lord's ear.

"It accedes power to me?" the mai' commented with a twitch of his tail.

"It does not," Nick insisted, surprising the young emperor with his fluent use of full court Gunera. He rose. "I grant you honor and respect as due your lofty position, but I do not accede anything to you."

"Arrogant creature, isn't it?" the mai' mused. His tail crossed with vuh'Yguggli's.

Nick's discomfort slithered along his spine. He didn't like how the emperor was speaking as if he wasn't there and at the overly familiar wrapping of tails that spoke of a friendship beyond merely mai' and vuh'. Clearly the two lords shared a past and possibly even a present. That meant the mai' was fully aware that if Nick hadn't been sent as humanity's emissary, he'd be naked scrubbing toilets.

vuh'Yguggli's eyes slanted evilly. "Grant me back my title to the creature, and I'll teach it manners, beloved."

Nick winced at the term of address. So vuh'Yguggli had bought himself a place in the mai's household by handing over title to his precious slave, earning himself the position of the mai's future mate. *That's one way to get your offspring on the throne,* Nick thought, fighting down a wave of revulsion.

mai'Tegatriktrik freed his tail from the vuh's and sent it sailing toward Nick. The barb ran lightly across Nick's cheek before its owner withdrew it. Nick didn't flinch.

"Arrogant indeed," the mai' commented. "Should you not be undressed? You seem to have forgotten the proper appearance of an eh' is naked and prostrate at my feet."

"I wear the attire required of my office as per Protocols 3 through 9," Nick growled. "I am here as the emissary from humanity. Regardless of whatever history I may have with your loved ones, I stand here today as emissary."

"Insolent dog! You go too far." vuh'Yguggli's tail whipped through the air. "Clothe a slave, and they quickly forget their station."

"I am not your slave!" As Nick's voice sharpened, Jason's hand clutched Nick's shoulder more tightly, aware of the spike in tensions within the room.

With expert precision, vuh'Yguggli's tail lashed out, grasped Nick's forearm, and pulled back his uniform sleeve to reveal Nick's mark. "I see where my indulgence kissed you, eh'. My property you were born, and as my property you will die."

To Nick's shock, the mai's tail slapped his hand free. "Enough teasing, vuh'Yguggli. We didn't drag the creature all the way here merely to undress it and send it to the cellars. You'll have your slave back when I'm through with it."

The vuh' appeared ready to protest but thought better of it. He settled on his cushion and shot daggers of contempt at his former slave. Nick ignored the gaze.

mai'Tegatriktrik gestured to a cushion below his feet. "Please make yourself comfortable, most esteemed *Messenger*." The term was a clear insult, one that every Protocol Officer throughout history had known was used derisively by the Gunera. The mai' glanced at Jason with contempt. "Your slave should lie at your side. I'll accept its presence provided it behaves itself."

"My companion is an equal and will sit beside me," Nick insisted. He kicked another cushion next to his own.

The mai's tail twitched with amusement as he watched the two humans sit on the floor below the platform on which his cushion rested. Fortunately, both Nick and Jason were tall enough that the disadvantage implied by the platform was negated by their height. They remained at eye level with the emperor.

"You might consider keeping it unclothed to remind it of its position," the mai' suggested to the vuh'. "Having never seen a naked human, I would find it most enlightening."

Nick's eyes narrowed at the continuing jibes. "You'll have to wait until our business is concluded and you've tossed my title back to the vuh'. You can ask his permission to see me then."

The remark caught the emperor's fancy, and he belched with laughter. "I shall make a note of that suggestion, teg'Nicodemus! While to see this one now would be interesting, I'd much rather see that which has gy'Bagrada so in lust." He tilted his body and twitched his air gills. "Or better, I'll keep your title for myself and indulge my fantasies to the loss of both vuh' and gy'." He belched again, and Nick used every iota of self-restraint to keep from storming from the room.

vuh'Yguggli's face grew dark, but he dared not gainsay his emperor.

"What's going on?" Jason asked softly, sensing his client's rage.

"They're making vulgar sexual references," Nick grated.

"Seriously?"

"The Gunera have no sense of decorum."

The mai' seemed finished with the opening pleasantries. He lowered the fishing spear across his knees and laid stubby hands on the shaft. "Shall we attend to the true purpose of your visit?" he asked. When Nick waved a hand in acknowledgment, the emperor proceeded. "We have been approached by factions within your government who wish to reconsider the alliance."

Nick couldn't resist stiffening in surprise. With great effort, he remained silent and tried to keep his face impassive.

Apparently, the pretense hadn't worked because the mai' nodded sagely. "Indeed. The news surprised us as well. It appears some of your kind disapprove of being slaves to both Gunera and Amaurau and wish to see the alliance terminated. I can't say as I disagree with their reasoning. There's only so much bile an intelligent creature can tolerate, and being a servant of the Amaurau transcends the pale."

Nick remained silent while his mind parsed the meaning of the mai's words. *Humans had approached the Gunera? Wanting to break the alliance that was all to humanity's good? What the hell?*

"Of course, we're not so naïve as to simply reach out to grasp a gift so surprisingly offered, and we chose to investigate the suggestion. For that reason, we have been in consultation with a human called teg'Lincoln. I'm told you know the name."

Nick nodded, still stunned.

"He was our contact with the interested faction and made three visits to Gunera to work out a deal."

"What sort of deal?" Nick asked.

The mai's air gills fluttered. "A simple one, really. Humanity and Gunera will reaffirm their alliance and end the reign of the Protocols. Humanity shall be granted rights to all the territory it currently controls except for the space you call Lethe's Gate, which it will concede to Gunera."

Nick thought through the list of approved concessions but knew Lethe's Gate wasn't on it. It couldn't be. It would not only cut human territory in half but would, more importantly, give the Gunera direct passage to Amaurau space. Nick could well understand why certain factions within the conservative parties of Earth might suggest the agreement. The move would remove Earth from the middle of the fray between the Gunera and the Amaurau, permitting the two empires to resume their endless feud while leaving humanity on the sidelines. Depending on the concessions demanded, there might be value for humans. But the conservative factions hadn't considered what would happen when the shooting stopped. Someone was making a huge assumption that the Gunera would win the argument. If the Amaurau emerged victorious, that species would turn on humanity like a swarm of angry hornets. The conflict could be without end.

"Most esteemed mai', what do the humans demand in return for the land concession?" Nick asked, trying to guess what his hosts would demand of him. Lincoln Combs was dead, not captured, not tortured. Dead. Nick need not consider trying to question him about his motives or returning to Rhadamanthus with his remains. Nor had the man come to Gunera to kill the mai', so the conceit of an assassination became moot. As such, the orders Nick had been given by the State Department were void. That, plus the fact that he had no way to contact his superiors, left Nick in charge of his own actions. Not a happy thought. His mind raced. *What to do? What to do?* As always, Nick's instincts were to revert to what he'd always done—defend the Protocols at all costs.

"As our concession, we have agreed to turn over our Gogarag stardrive, including designs and operating parameters," the mai' stated. "A permanent alliance shall exist between Gunera and Earth, both equal partners against any future enemy attacks."

Nick inhaled slowly. *The scheme is breathtaking,* he thought. The Gogarag stardrive was the crowning achievement of Guneri space technology, a system that could move unlimited amounts of freight over vast distances with reportedly minimal fuel usage. Humans who possessed a stardrive would become trillionaires overnight. *All that wondrous technology merely for promising to get out of the way,* Nick thought. *What's not to love?*

"This teg' is overwhelmed by the concept," Nick said.

"I'm glad you're open to taking the position," the mai' said.

Nick was feeling his way forward in what would surely be a difficult negotiation. *What negotiation?* he wondered. *I can't possibly agree to be a part of this! It's not official protocol of the Trade Commission, and I can't deal outside those parameters.*

"It appears, on the surface, good for all," commented the mai'. Nick felt a shiver run down his spine hearing the undercurrent of malicious pleasure underlying the words.

"*On the surface,*" Nick murmured. *God, I wish I had access to my computer and could consult with Duncan.* "How might the most gracious mai' be inclined to view such an agreement?"

"The most gracious mai' is salivating at the thought," replied the mai' with a swish of his tail. "Having the most advanced stardrive among the three nations is of little value if we cannot use it to cross human territory. It could be useful in a direct hit on Amaurau were our human friends not sprinkled across our path."

Nick again exhaled slowly as the pieces of this intergalactic puzzle began falling into place within his mind. During the last skirmish between Gunera and Amaurau, the Gunera hadn't yet possessed stardrive technology. But now, with humans politely stepping aside, the Gunera could have a lightning strike at the Amaurau before that race even knew what was coming. It was devious. It was ingenious. It was a disaster of untold dimensions for humanity. Because as soon as the Gunera warships had leveled Amaurau, they'd be turning on Earth in a heartbeat. Humanity's superior weapons program might likely prove incapable of holding them back.

Nick continued to ask probing questions. "Might this teg' ask how far the negotiations have gone?"

The mai' gestured vaguely with his hands. His air gills swished calmly, unlike Nick's gasping lungs. "We agreed on the essential points. Humanity would unilaterally exit Amaurau Protocol 9 with no intent to proceed to Protocol 10. At that time, the humans would sign a new agreement with Gunera conceding the space known as Lethe's Gate. Upon ratifying the agreement, we would turn over the Gogarag system and ink a new alliance with humanity of nonviolence and shared affiliation against the Amaurau. If or when operations take place against Amaurau, humanity will not interfere."

"And the human side has agreed to this?"

The mai's tail twitched with pleasure. "It has."

"I find that hard to believe given the heated border exchange that just occurred," Nick sniped.

Nick's comment was cast aside with a hand wave. "That was but a dustup, and it would not have occurred if not for your obstinate behavior." The mai's air gills swept forward with calm arrogance. "My emissaries are, at this moment, attempting to calm the waters with those humans disturbed by the ruckus you caused. I'm certain that issue can be settled amicably and that our work to unite our worlds can continue."

Nick was stunned that so much had been negotiated and decided upon without word having reached the Trade Commission. Nick wondered if the State Department even knew. Who was behind this mysterious faction? Congressional senators? The Executive Branch? Nick refused to believe either of those could be so short-sighted or would dare treason at such a high level. Corporate interests, however, would be salivating to obtain the stardrive. Nick imagined that the upper echelons of Gemini Space might see greater advantage in the stardrive than in their cushy position under the Protocols. They had the money to bribe Lincoln Combs into joining the cabal, promising him some lofty office in the newly configured Trade Commission once the deed was a *fait accompli*.

"What do you want with me?" Nick asked, swallowing his terror as the extent of the treachery slithered through the back alleys of his brain.

"You will, as Protocol Officer, sign the intent and deliver it to agents who will route it to Earth."

Nick froze, certain that his heart had skipped a beat. His mind raced. *Take up the treason where Combs left off? Sign a document that will end a century of uneasy peace? Hand over human sovereignty to the Gunera? Are these people insane? Do they know nothing about me? Oh God! How do I get out of this?*

Nick didn't have the answers, but his memory was sound. *When in doubt*, he reminded himself, *stall.*

"*Sign the intent?*" he whispered. "I don't have the authority to sign anything! Duncan Huntzinger is the Protocol Officer, not me."

"The human known as Huntzinger will no longer be an issue," the mai' stated. "He will be eliminated long before the signed document reaches Earth. You will have full legal authority, and your signature will be binding, teg'Nicodemus."

Nick's mind froze. *Duncan! Dear God, I've got to escape this place and find a laptop! I've got to warn Duncan! I've got to warn someone!*

Nick did his best to appear indifferent. He was fully aware that Gunera were novices at reading human expressions. Further stalling was crucial while he tried to formulate a plan to escape from the palace without agreeing to sign anything.

"Earth's central government won't accept my signature, especially under those circumstances," Nick insisted. "If Duncan is murdered, there'll be an investigation. The Trade Commission might spend weeks before they decide who to raise to Protocol Officer and, even then, there's no guarantee it'll be me."

"We have assurances," said vuh'Yguggli.

Nick gazed at his former master. The vuh' radiated confidence. "What?" Nick asked. "I don't understand."

"We have assurances that you are already named as Huntzinger's successor," the vuh' insisted. "There can be no one else. No other human speaks Gunera with your fluency. We've been informed by our counterparties in your government that it would take months to bring another candidate up to speed. Earth can't afford to wait that long, nor would they see a reason to do so. You, teg'Nicodemus, have been an exemplary agent for your office."

"Still, the committee will want to deliberate," Nick stammered. "They might name someone else."

"They won't," vuh'Yguggli insisted. "teg'Lincoln had already been named to the succession by our allies within the State Department. When he was unfortunately lost to us, our allies assured us your name was put in his place. You, teg'Nicodemus, will be the Protocol Officer with all due authorizations before the end of the day tomorrow."

Nick stared at the two Guneri lords in disbelief. A commando squad was on the way to assassinate Duncan. The deed might have already been done. And once done, Nick automatically ascended to the role of Protocol Officer. Traitors within the State Department would make sure of this before there could be any debate, not that there was anything *to* debate. *Oh God,* Nick thought, *mai'Tegatriktrik is right. No one else can fill the post. The mai' will have the new officer—me—clasped tightly in his grasp.*

Seeing that Nick appeared to be on the verge of shutting down, Jason issued a gentle shake. "Sir? Are you okay?"

"They're asking me to commit treason," Nick whispered.

The horror of the situation was sinking through the various levels of Nick's brain. The mai' would force him to sign the treaty and then blithely hand him to vuh'Yguggli because, as soon as the document was executed, the Protocols ceased to function, and the Protocol Officer ceased to be. He'd instantly lose his diplomatic protection and become nothing more than a Guneri citizen again. *By Jagjegcek,* Nick thought, *the whole thing is so sinisterly clever! No wonder vuh'Yguggli had given up his title, knowing the power that would accrue to him from that sacrifice. All these people need is little Nicodemus to sign a paper, and the whole universe will tear into pieces. Jesus!*

I have to find a way out of this. I'm just not thinking straight. Nick forced himself to focus his attention on Jason's strong hand, aware that it seemed to be taking up permanent residence on the Protocol Officer's shoulder. *Steadfast Jason wouldn't stumble, so I won't either. I know what I need to do.*

Nick drew a deep breath and bowed. "The extent of the proposal takes one's breath away." He crawled through the next few words, knowing they would determine not only the future course of his life but that of every human he knew. "I'm stunned by the sheer cunning of the mai'."

The alien's air gills swished into motion. In his own panic, he hadn't realized the mai' had been holding his breath, waiting to see how the key piece in the game would react.

"How does the new Protocol Officer view the suggestion?" the mai' asked.

"The new Protocol Officer is stunned and needs time to consider all the ramifications of the plan, but he's not averse to the concept."

The mai' sat back a little easier on his cushion, and Nick could sense a general lessening of tension in the room. They apparently had known a little something of him, of his dogged application of Protocol law, and had expected resistance.

"What does the Officer need to consider?" sniped vuh'Yguggli. "Our adored mai'Tegatriktrik has approved the plan, and it is therefore without error. Your own administration has approved the document as well. There is nothing for you to consider."

"I have no orders from my office," Nick replied, trying to think like the hopelessly legalistic Gunera before him. "At least none regarding the signing of a document such as this. The Protocol Officer doesn't have the authority to make any decisions on his own. I need to consult with those who've negotiated this to assure myself that what you've told me corresponds with their intentions. Surely you agree with the logic in this?"

Nick saw the exchange of glances between mai' and vuh', and he couldn't miss the intertwining of tails, the Guneri equivalent of a high five.

mai'Tegatriktrik gave the faintest of bows. "This is reasonable. You will sign the document once you've assured yourself of its validity?"

Nick decided it was best to play along. "If what you've told me is true, and authorized government officials have negotiated this agreement in good faith, and if those officials command me to ratify the treaty, then I'm legally bound as Protocol Officer to do so." Nick raised a hand when he saw the grip of the tails tighten. "I would add, esteemed mai', that I must know if I *am* the Protocol Officer before I sign. Otherwise, I would be committing treason against my government."

The mai' brushed Nick's comments aside with an indifferent wave. "It will be, as I indicated, cooked meat by dawn."

Cooked meat. A Guneri idiomatic expression meaning a done deal. Nick felt his heart skip another beat.

"Then, esteemed mai', please allow me to return to my dwelling so that I can rest and determine how to proceed with this task."

Again the mai' waved dismissal. "We promise you'll be undisturbed for the night."

Nick rose, gesturing for Jason to rise with him, and bowed. "I would also request, kind mai', the names of your human counterparts so that I can validate what you've shared."

vuh'Yguggli answered. "The names shall be provided."

Nick drew a breath of relief. If nothing else, he'd complete the intel component of his mission: determine Lincoln Combs's fate and uncover the traitors in the State Department. Relaying that information to Earth was another matter entirely. At that moment, all Nick wanted was to escape the emperor's palace, though he suspected only the god, Bibacheck, knew how this might be accomplished.

The doors behind Nick and Jason opened, and the same three Gunera escorts appeared on their movers. Nick bowed one last time to the mai' and the vuh', which he hoped would convince them he was on board, then he and Jason exited the room. The Gunera trio lagged behind.

"Can I ask the results of that conversation?" Jason asked, once again taking hold of Nick's arm.

Nick issued a worried glance. "I agreed to turn traitor."

"Why?"

"I needed to escape that room." Nick increased pace, forcing the Gunera to quicken their pace. "A faction within the State Department plans to pull Earth out of the alliance. They've negotiated a new deal with Gunera. Lincoln Combs had been tapped to sign it, but somehow the Amaurau got to him beforehand. The Gunera snatched me to take his place."

"You're going to do it?" Jason's voice oozed with displeasure.

"Hell no! But there's a more urgent problem. A hit squad is targeting my boss, Duncan Huntzinger. If I don't warn him, he'll be dead by dawn tomorrow, and I'll be installed as the new Protocol Officer."

"At which time your signature will be valid," Jason added.

"Until the ink dries." Nick looked hard at Jason. "As soon as my signature hits that paper, the Protocols cease to be in effect, and I cease to be Protocol Officer."

"Goodbye diplomatic immunity," Jason said. "What'll happen then?"

"Trust me, you don't want to know."

"What do you want me to do, sir?"

Nick growled in frustration. "We have to get a message to Duncan. The entire coup depends on whether Duncan lives or dies."

"We must warn him. Supposing we can, what happens to you? What will the Gunera do?"

Nick shook his head. "I don't know. Legally, I'll remain an emissary from Earth."

"Will they actually uphold your position?"

Nick lifted his brows and gazed a knowing smile at Jason. "Interestingly enough, I think they will. The Gunera are absolute sticklers for legal minutiae. They have a cultural imperative to create byzantine laws and follow them to the letter. They'll be pissed as hell and will keep trying to complete this deal. You and I will remain prisoners here—well treated, but prisoners nevertheless—until they figure out how to salvage the operation."

"That gives us time to get you out of here."

Nick gave his escort a hard look. "I'm all ears to hear how you intend to finagle that."

"I'm all ears, too," Jason said with a grin. "I'll share the plan with you as soon as I come up with one."

Surrounded by their escort, Nick and Jason moved through the streets quickly. Due to the late hour, the locals had retreated to their nests. The streets were deserted. Nick was grateful the trip down was easier. Were it not for Jason's gripping on his arm, Nick felt exhausted to the point that he might collapse. His nerves had been shattered by the interview with the mai'. He was terrified, feeling more alone than he'd ever felt in his life. One of the few people he truly called friend was in mortal danger. Although Nick wanted to race through the streets of Imperial City, he forced himself to the statelier pace set by his escorts. Concealing his panic was critical. Nick knew that he had to convince the Gunera that he was willing to do their bidding.

When they entered the Palace of the Winds, Nick and Jason found eh'Daigana waiting in the foyer. Nick heard arguing from the back of the palace, but eh'Daigana seemed determined to ignore it. Nick immediately raced to the office and switched on the computer.

He pulled up his email account, glanced quickly for news from his mother, eh'Kraghilg, or Duncan. Finding none, Nick cursed beneath his breath. Nick ignored all worries as he hastily began typing.

> Greetings Esteemed Minister,
> You will be much heartened to know that I have accomplished all my assigned tasks. Details will be forwarded at earliest convenience. My mission will be detained due to an administrative matter brought to my attention by his most glorious and revered mai'Tegatriktrik, long may the sun shine

warmly on his shoulders. I am in total agreement with the esteemed mai' in all matters and ask your forbearance in awaiting my return. Please know, Caesar, that Brutus walks the halls of Rhadamanthus. Recall your own admonitions to your servant in the gardens by the lake.

May this missive speed to your side.

Nicodemus Severin

Message sent, Nick prayed the transmission would pass the Guneri censors who surely would be on high alert for any outbound correspondence from Nick's account. He hoped the bullshit about agreeing with the revered mai' would help it pass. He knew that Duncan would easily decipher the subtext and realize that Nick was in trouble. Nick also prayed that Duncan understood the urgency implied in the closing sentence. *Assassination was imminent. Take precautions now.*

Knowing he could do nothing else, Nick sat in the little office, his mind a million kilometers distant, until the sounds of arguing infiltrated his thoughts. Frowning, Nick strode into the great room. The argument was taking place at the rear of the palace.

Jason stepped ahead of Nick. "Given everything that's going down, sir, it's best if I go first."

The dispute was taking place in the bathroom. eh'Daigana was yelling at an eh' bent over the drain hole. At the sight of the undressed eh's ass pointing in the air while his tail worked in the hole, Nick abruptly stopped. Amused, he knew the position well. The lowly eh' was trying to unstop a clogged drain using his most valuable tool, his tail barb.

eh'Daigana was distraught. "Truly, this must be left to the morning," he complained, growing ever more furious as the unruly eh' continued to ignore him, something unheard of in Guneri society. It was so shocking that even Nick stood with his mouth agape. eh'Daigana was a servant of such high status that he spoke the house language. That some lowly eh' would ignore him was astonishing.

eh'Daigana curled his tail around the eh's neck and hauled it, squawking from the drain. "I should bash your head through the floor!"

"Please ... don't!" Nick sprang forward in protest. "If the drain is clogged, the waste tender must see it cleared. I would have my house in working order."

"It's late, and the teg' surely desires sleep," stammered eh'Daigana.

"He'll make little noise, I would imagine," Nick said.

"Teg' ..."

"You're excused, eh'Daigana."

The eh' blinked at him several more times, darted a look at the interloper who stood staring at the floor, then glanced back at Nick again. Nick pointed to the door.

"You are excused," he repeated.

eh'Diagana bowed furiously and scuttled from the room. Nick stood unmoving, a curious Jason still at his side, until he heard the door to the servants' wing close. Only then did he exhale and turn on the eh' who stood with his eyes cast to the floor.

"By Jagjekcek, how did you get here?" Nick demanded, placing his hands on the little eh's shoulders.

"It wasn't difficult," the eh' replied. "vuh'Yguggli only owns four palaces, and I know the dark levels to reach all of them."

Nick couldn't stop himself from grinning like a fool, throwing his arms around the eh' and nearly squeezing the life out of him. The eh' returned the gesture by wrapping his tail around Nick's waist and hauling him even closer.

Jason cleared his throat. "Do you two need some alone time?"

Nick withdrew as much as the eh' would allow. "Jason, this is my dearest friend, eh'Kraghilg." Nick adjusted his language for the eh' and introduced Jason. "Teg' Jason. He's my security guard."

eh'Kraghilg finally released Nick and gave Jason a deep bow, but his eyes remained fixed on his friend. He ran his tail barb lovingly across Nick's cheek.

"I never thought to see you again," he whispered. "How I wished I would never see you again. Why, oh, why are you here, dear friend?"

Nick sighed and ushered his friend into the great room. "My people were tricked into sending me here."

"Betrayal, yes. We Gunera are so good at such things." eh'Kraghilg sighed. "I was terrified when I received your message. I didn't think it could be true, that you were here in the vuh's house. I prayed I'd misunderstood the code, mistranslated something. I was sickened upon realizing I hadn't."

Nick caught the eh's tail and held it tightly, something only a friend would be allowed to do. "Terrified though I am to be here, I am beyond ecstatic to see you again."

The eh' freed his tail and flicked it at Nick's black clothes. "You're still dressed. One would think the vuh' would have you naked in the cellars at first touch."

"He wanted to." Nick dropped wearily into a chair. "The mai' appears to have other plans."

"*The mai'?*" eh'Kraghilg gulped. His tail again flicked against Nick's cheek. "You've risen far from your lowly station."

"Does it bother you?" Nick asked, removing his heavy coat. "I'll undress if it makes you more comfortable."

He received a gentle chuckle in return. "It warms my heart to see you dressed, eh'Nicodemus." eh'Kraghilg could not stop staring at Nick. "I never want to see you naked again."

Nick felt a soothing warmth wash over his heart. He understood exactly what eh'Kraghilg was saying, even if the words were strange.

"You are well?" Nick asked, kicking off his shoes and wriggling his toes, revealing a bit of skin to eh'Kraghilg. "In your letter, you said you were being cut by the stick."

The eh' shrugged. He showed Nick his back, which was bruised but not scarred. "We Gunera have thick hides. Not like you humans with that silk you call skin."

"Should you be here? I don't want you involved in this mess."

"I would give my life for you," eh'Kraghilg replied. His air gills moved slowly, an indication that he was completely composed. "No one cares where the waste tender goes. Who's to descend to my domain to find me? So long as the waste flows, no one will care that I'm not there." He placed a hand atop Nick's knee. "Tell me why the mai' brought you here."

Tired as he was from the overlong day, Nick nevertheless propped his elbows on his knees, clasped his hands together, and relayed to eh'Kraghilg a tale of betrayal born in the high places of both Gunera and Earth. The eh' listened intently. Not for the first time, Nick cursed a system that condemned such a bright individual to a life in the sewers.

When Nick finished his tale, eh'Kraghilg sat twitching his tail, air gills fluttering. "This is a ball in a pipe, isn't it?" Nick nodded. He knew the expression, which was familiar only to those in the Guneri underworld.

"The solution seems simple enough," the eh' continued. "The ball must be removed."

"How does the esteemed eh' suggest removing the ball from this pipe?" Nick asked, finding himself being referred to as a clog rather humorous.

"I don't know." eh'Kraghilg patted Nick's knee. "But we shall think of something."

"*We?*"

"You, your teg' companion, me, and the waste tenders of the world. Whom else to ask about a ball in a pipe?"

Nick shook his head. "I don't want the waste tenders involved. I don't want innocent people hurt or killed."

eh'Kraghilg's barb poked Nick's cheek. "We of the dark must stick together. You have no idea how excited everyone was so long ago when they heard that you'd escaped. Almost started a rebellion right there in the underground!"

Nick could well imagine. Life in the sewers was anything but pleasant.

It reminded him of another problem. "My mother, eh'Monica. Have you heard anything?"

His friend deflated, and his tail sprawled onto the floor. "No, eh'Nicodemus. It's strange."

Nick rubbed his hands together. "Somehow, I fear I won't be happy when I do find out what's become of her. Thank you for your help."

eh'Kraghilg patted Nick's knee. "Now that I know where to find you, I'll return as I can. You look green around the gills, eh'Nicodemus. I think you should go to nest. I'll consult with my brethren about their assistance."

Nick gave the eh' another hug. "I hate to send you back to the dark."

The eh's tail twitched. "Are you requesting me in your nest?"

"I would if I dared, but it would shock my companion."

eh'Kraghilg's body shook as he belched his laughter. "I would think so. Sleep well, dear friend. I'll return when I can."

The eh' rose onto his small legs and bowed to Jason, who had worn a puzzled look as he'd sat and absorbed the entire brief conversation. eh'Kraghilg quietly toddled out.

10

As much as Nick loved being curled inside the nest, he found sleep impossible. From the sound of tortured breathing he heard just outside, it appeared Jason wasn't sleeping well either. The bodyguard tossed and turned, grunting and complaining. The hot and muggy night eventually gave way to morning, which dawned as strong shafts of light pierced the cloud deck and flooded the room with hot blue sunlight. Nick crawled sweaty out of the nest, grateful he'd followed the traditional Guneri habit of sleeping naked, and trundled off to take a tepid shower. Jason rolled onto his back and stared at his client balefully.

"This heat is going to kill me," Jason grumbled. "Don't these people believe in air conditioning?"

Nick answered over the hiss of the shower. "When this palace was first built, the Gunera depended on the sea breeze. Heat doesn't affect them like it does us. They do use climate control, but it appears as though vuh'Yguggli is having fun at our expense since this is the only palace that hasn't been retrofitted with AC."

Pulling on a fresh shirt, Nick padded to the office, logged into his computer, and checked for messages from either eh'Monica or Duncan. Nothing.

As he wandered into the breakfast room, Nick was so distraught that he failed to notice the plethora of servants scurrying to set a traditional Guneri breakfast. Various bowls and platters were being meticulously arranged in a precise pattern to ensure that only good fortune accrued to those who ate from the table.

Nick knew every congruency required for the day. The serving utensils, cups, and bowls had to be aligned exactly. An improper pattern implied misfortune. During his time as a slave, Nick had endured the cut of the stick several times for misaligning a setting by the merest fraction, thereby cursing the lord who partook of the meal to a day of darkness and ill fortune.

The food offered was determined by the day of the year. Each day had its own menu, and a lord's staff knew exactly what to serve for every meal.

Nick fretted over the silence from Duncan. Nick's mind raced through possible scenarios. *Had Duncan received the email? If he had, wouldn't he have responded by now? Had the Gunera blocked the outbound transmission? Had they diverted Duncan's reply, either to frighten me or to convince me that Duncan was dead? Had the hit squad actually completed its mission? Could there be no one left in the Rhadamanthan office capable of reading the Guneri script of my message or compose a response?*

Nick sank onto one of the low cushions at the table. He pressed his hands to his head and fought yet again to shove the panic into its box.

"What's wrong now?" Jason asked as he pulled on a shirt. When Nick didn't respond, Jason placed a hand on his client's shoulder. "Sir?"

"There's still no reply from Rhadamanthus," Nick whispered, fighting his fear, forcing himself to calm down. No amount of panicking was going to resolve this problem.

Jason considered the buffet and selected a plate. "You should eat," he suggested. "You'll need your strength. Judging by the look of you, you got about as little sleep last night as I did."

"I'm not sure I *can* eat," Nick muttered, feeling queasy.

"Take my advice. Eat. First order of business they taught us in survival school was take care of yourself." He shoved a plate in Nick's direction.

With a deep sigh, Nick took the plate and forced himself to focus on the morning meal. He swallowed the thoughts that threatened to overwhelm him; thoughts of Duncan dead or dying, thoughts of the alliance breaking apart. *By Bibachek, it's all so depressing,* he thought. With no little effort, Nick focused on his role as protocol officer and shoved his worries to the back of his mind. *I have to keep my wits and stay focused on holding the alliance together.* The thought buttressed him. His life had only one purpose. To keep the damned alliance alive.

Nick selected a mixture of fruit that he'd loved as a child but had seldom been allowed to taste. Guneri servants were fed almost exclusively animal protein, fat, and sugar to keep them working hard. The idea of feeding a slave fruit had never occurred to his former masters. With a sneaky grin, Nick savored the treats.

After breakfast, Nick and Jason heard movement in the foyer. Jason jumped from his chair and placed his left hand protectively on Nick's shoulder. His right hand gripped a knife he'd secreted from the serving board and hid in his pants pocket. It wasn't much of a weapon, but Jason knew from experience that something was better than nothing. Three Gunera wearing the mai's livery rolled toward them.

"Your presence is required in the Palace of the Mai'," the trio's leader intoned.

Nick hesitated, aware that if he and Jason were going to escape Gunera, they couldn't do it from the Palace of the Mai'. After a few moments, one of the guards drew a weapon. *So much for the invitation,* Nick thought grimly. Flicking Jason a glance, Nick rose. Assured that his clothing was protocol perfect, Nick motioned for the escort to lead forth.

The day was already torrid. The traditional afternoon wind off the sea had yet to develop, so the air was breathless. Nick waved his hand and saw eddies of moisture swirl around him. He and Jason were already bathed in sweat. Jason used a bandana to wipe the perspiration from his bare head. The sun was strong as it burned through the thin cloud cover, and Nick felt its torrid kiss on his face and neck. *Let the charring begin,* he thought.

The hard walk upward ended at the grand boulevard that circumnavigated the Palace of the Mai'. They were escorted not to the main doors but to a garden gate that led through a veritable paradise. Flowers spilled from every tree, shrub, and climbing vine. The scents were so cloying that Nick began to sneeze uncontrollably. Jason gripped Nick's bicep as they moved through the heavy vegetation.

They soon reached a seating area where a fountain bubbled. mai'Tegatriktrik, surrounded by an entourage of advisors, was enjoying a breakfast beneath smoldering skies during the one time of the day when rain was unlikely. Nick was surprised to find that while vuh'Yguggli was in attendance, neither gy'Gravinda nor were gy'Bagrada present. They'd also been absent the previous evening, Nick recalled, and wondered what that portended. *Nothing good,* he thought.

The mai' gestured to two of the cushions at his feet. Nick and Jason sat. The bodyguard continued to grip Nick's arm.

"Your servant is quite dedicated," murmured the mai' as he scooped runny eggs from a bowl. "If I didn't know humans so well, I'd think he was permanently attached to you, Messenger."

Nick was also beginning to wonder about Jason's dedication. He couldn't imagine Jason would maintain a physical grip on President McAlastair. Nick was finding the attachment peculiar, and he wondered what instructions Jason had been given. He'd never met a security officer with such devotion.

"He's the best of his guild," Nick replied, using the closest approximation he could to describe Jason's profession. "His prior assignment was to protect President McAlastair."

"So highly does your government value you!" mai'Tegatriktrik commented without looking at his two guests. He swallowed a piece of fruit, making a mess in the process. One of his eh's wiped his face then whipped away the cloth that protected the mai's elaborate court dress. Only then did he actually peer at Nick and Jason.

"So," he said, stumpy hands patting his knees, "we've a document to sign, yes?"

Nick glanced at vuh'Yguggli, who'd remained studiously silent during the oddly polite opening rounds of the conversation. "Do we?" he asked.

The mai' chortled. "We do indeed. Messenger Huntzinger met with an unfortunate accident early this morning. He can no longer attend to his duties."

"Temporarily or permanently?" Nick asked, keeping his voice level. The ability to swallow his pain at the loss of Duncan surprised him. Nick allowed himself only for the briefest moment of internal grief before he mercilessly squelched it. He reminded himself he could mourn later. He couldn't afford to show weakness at present.

"Permanently," the mai' chuckled. "We Gunera do nothing by halves, Messenger Severin." His eyes slanted, and their reptilian irises twisted evilly. "You are now the Messenger, teg'Nicodemus."

Article recommended that private freighting interests also vacate the area, it wasn't a formal requirement. Private interests would proceed at their own risk.

Nick's heart sunk ever lower. *Doubtless no one is going to warn the poor freight forwarders of what was heading at them,* he thought.

Article 5 demanded that should hostilities resume between the Empire of Gunera and the Grand Republic of the Amaurau, no attempt to interfere would be made by the Western Alliance. Gunera would not request any assistance from its human allies.

Nick felt nauseous as he read the final article. Article 6 stated that in the event an outside provocation arose against Gunera or the Western Alliance, each party would agree to defend the other as a unit. The combined forces would operate under the command of the Emperor of Gunera and his assigned vuh's and gy's.

There was no subtlety in the language. Earth would concede control of its military to Gunera in the event of outside attack. Nick was certain the duplicitous Gunera would concoct a crisis to invoke Article 6, effectively placing all of Earth and her colonies under Guneri control.

There it is, Nick thought dismally as he reread the entire document in English with all its heretofore's and whereas's and other such legalese that made lawyers orgasmic with glee. The two primary points each side wanted so badly: humanity sidelined for the Guneri push at the Amaurau and the backdoor through which the Gunera would subsequently betray and crush their human "allies" beneath their merciless feet.

The whole document made Nick want to vomit, but he remained emotionless while scrutinizing the flowery language in the appendices and sought inconsistencies. He couldn't sign it. Even if he did believe the Protocols were a bad idea. Even if he thought Humans First was right and humanity had no business throwing itself between the two bickering alien cultures. Even if he wasn't Nicodemus Severin I's only son. He couldn't sign it. Nick saw the future events this agreement would set into motion. It represented the end of human independence. *Little wonder,* Nick thought, *vuh'Yguggli had been so sure he'd get his females for his stupid farm. Of course he would, and quite legally by Guneri terms. Oh God, what do I do?*

In desperation, Nick turned his eyes toward Jason and exposed his panic. The Jamaican returned a subtle nod to confirm he understood that they were in deep, deep trouble.

"Does the esteemed Messenger agree that both documents are properly drawn?" vuh'Yguggli asked.

"The *Protocol Officer* agrees that the parties who drafted the documents performed their tasks with near perfection," Nick concurred. He'd found no noticeable errors.

The vuh' tapped the table with his tail barb, pointing at the inkpot with its kliki spike, the traditional stylus for Guneri writing.

"Affix your name then, teg'Nicodemus," the vuh' hissed. "It is time."

Nick wasn't sure how long he could stall. The day had just broken, and the providential stamps and seals would not expire for hours. Still, he had to try. vuh'Yguggli was practically salivating in anticipation of his former slave's return.

"I still don't know if I *am* the Protocol Officer," Nick said weakly. "I've only your word that Secretary Huntzinger is dead."

The mai' gestured to one of his staff, who placed a computer tablet before Nick. The home page of the *Rhadamanthan Truth,* the most influential news bureau on the planet, confirmed Nick's fears.

Secretary of International Trade Found Dead in His Residence

API - The Secretary of International Trade and Commerce, Duncan Huntzinger, originally of Hemera, was found dead this morning in his residence by his long-time aid, Hezakiah Cardaman. The apparent cause of death was heart failure. Huntzinger had served in the position of Secretary for 12 years.

Nick stopped reading and pushed the tablet toward Jason. "Agreed, Messenger Huntzinger is dead. I compliment the mai' on the subtly of the assassination. Was he drugged?"

"An Amaurau poison, actually," mai'Tegatriktrik said. "Lest somehow the act be traced back to us. We felt the subterfuge might confuse your authorities."

"Duncan was getting up in years," Nick murmured. He tapped the screen, indicating to Jason that he should read it. "He was under a lot of strain. I doubt foul play will be suspected."

vuh'Yguggli again rapped the table with his barb. "Sign, please!"

"I still don't know if I've been named Duncan's successor," Nick protested.

"Have you not stood in for Messenger Huntzinger when he was ill?" the mai' asked.

Nick froze. His mind flashed back to Duncan's illness on the night of the renewal ceremony. Was it possible that that hadn't been an Amaurau trick? Had it been the work of the Gunera, testing to see if Nick could assume Duncan's authority? Nick's head was pounding. Sleep deprivation, coupled with the strong sunlight on his shoulders, made Nick want to melt into the ground. He didn't want to invent ways to avoid signing the bloody Accords. He didn't want the future of the Balance resting on his shoulders alone.

"I've stood in for Duncan, but substituting for the Secretary at ceremonial functions hardly rises to the level of this document." Nick tried pleading to the Guneri sense of legal procedure. "Surely you can understand my reluctance to affix my name to a document that you've spent so much time negotiating. If it reaches Earth with anything less than perfect execution, you might be viewed as attempting subterfuge. It could conceivably void the entire agreement and set everything back weeks if not months!"

"What's your opinion of this document?" vuh'Yguggli asked, starting to sound suspicious that the Protocol Officer might not be as enamored of the alliance as he'd indicated the prior evening.

Nick scrambled along the edge of a knife, one side of which would absolve him of treason, and the other make him party to it. "I find it well-crafted and perfectly executed," Nick replied flatly.

"What of its provisions?" the vuh' demanded, his voice growing ever more suspicious.

"Many of the terms are to my liking," Nick stated. "I've always counseled that humans have no business serving as the crossing guards of the Balance. And I'm grateful that the esteemed gentlemen on both sides of the Accords have seen fit to assure that the flow of trade remains unabated."

"Yet something is not to your palate," the mai' said. "What is it, Messenger Severin?"

"The elimination of the Trade Commission."

"Why?"

"It's costing me my job," Nick growled.

The mai' belched, and his air gills fluttered as vuh'Yguggli issued a sly grin. His tail caressed Nick's cheek. "You'll have another job by the end of the day; no worries, eh'Nicodemus."

"It's teg' until I affix my name," Nick snapped.

The mai' shuffled forward on his cushion. "How great is your distress at losing your job?"

"Great enough that I'm reluctant to sign the document."

The mai' gestured the issue away. "I'll guarantee you a position in my house," he stated to Nick's shock and the vuh's violent protest. "I hear humans make good house servants."

Nick resisted the urge to gasp in outrage, unlike the vuh' who made no such attempt.

The vuh' leaped to his feet, an astonishing thing in and of itself, then veritably danced in front of his mai'. "You agreed to revert his title to me, esteemed mai'!" he panted, stubby legs pounding as he shifted his weight from one leg to another. He was almost hopping in anger.

"I agreed to consider reverting his title," the mai' replied coldly. "I find the thought of a human in my service quite agreeable." He raised a hand before the vuh' could complain further. "If or when such time comes as you are able to obtain the stable of females you're contemplating, I'll grant you license to borrow him for stud service, provided I am granted one each of any clutch he throws."

Nick found himself dumbfounded. He was literally speechless.

The vuh', however, still had much to say. "Humans don't throw clutches, esteemed mai'," he protested. "They give live birth to one offspring at a time."

"Indeed? I didn't know that." The mai's gills were moving smoothly, indicating his amusement. "I'll take ten percent of all live young at my discretion." He raised a hand again. "No more, vuh'! I've signed with your intent to mate. You'll have your damned bloodline on my throne. Don't be greedy."

The vuh' was indeed feeling greedy. He continued to shuffle for several seconds, seeing his grand design of reinstated mojo going up in flames to the benefit of the mai'.

"Surely your announcement of our intent to mate will more than make up for any loss you might sustain," mai'Tegatriktrik stated, keenly aware that he was offering one valuable carrot in place of another.

It was, Nick decided, the sort of deal no vuh' could refuse. Of course, even if it wasn't a valuable arrangement, vuh'Yguggli still couldn't turn it down. One did not turn down the mai'.

"Most esteemed mai', you are very gracious," muttered the annoyed vuh'. He glared daggers at Nick, who wore a face of impassiveness.

Nick decided that while being traded uptown to the mai' was obnoxious, it was still an improvement over being returned to the vuh'. Nick didn't doubt mai'Tegatriktrik would almost instantaneously forget he had a human slave in the flow of more urgent matters and, as such, Nick would fade into the dark recesses of the palace, never to be seen again. It wasn't the most horrific of fortunes, assuming vuh'Yguggli also forgot him or failed to obtain that stable of females. *Please see to it, Bibachek,* Nick prayed.

The mai' turned sly eyes on Nick as he worked a devious scheme on the other side of the fence. "I can make you a permanent teg', teg'Nicodemus," the mai' promised. It was the sort of offer that would cost him nothing but might result in Nick's outright compliance. It presented Nick with a chance to avoid the distasteful vuh' and made swallowing the pill easier.

The audaciousness of the bait took Nick's breath away. He'd be installed in the Palace of the Mai', not as a naked basement slave but as a teg', with clothing, lodging, and a professional position within the establishment. An interpreter, Nick suspected. It was a magnificent gift to offer a former slave, designed to sweep away any objection Nick might have. While he would lose his job as Undersecretary of Trade and the grand benefits that it supposedly entailed, he would gain the position of mai's teg'. In the mai's mind, it was an even swap, but given the low position of an undersecretary, it was actually a promotion provided Nick could ignore a few inconvenient facts:

Fact: He'd be a prisoner.

Fact: He'd never again see another human face.

Fact: The day would arrive when vuh'Yguggli would demand his expensively purchased breeding rights.

Nick shuddered at the thought. Did the Gunera have artificial insemination? It could, at the least, neutralize the appalling nature of the notion.

What am I thinking? Nick pondered, his mind suddenly lucid. *I can't believe that for a microsecond, I'd actually considered going along with the plot. I should pound my head on the table. I've got to stall for a bit longer.*

"You fill my head with dreams of grandeur," Nick bluffed, hoping he'd feigned enough enthusiasm for this unacceptable document. "However, I still don't know if I can legally sign this agreement. As I said, just because Messenger Huntzinger is dead doesn't mean I've inherited his role."

Again the mai' fluttered his fingers at one of his servants. The minion brought forth another computer tablet and placed it before Nick.

Nick's stomach knotted as he read an official diplomatic email, different from the trade emails he ordinarily handled. The text appeared both in English and in Gunera and was purported to be from Shawn Dietrick, Deputy Secretary of Foreign Affairs at the State Department in Geneva, Switzerland. Nick's eyes glazed over the opening paragraph, which consisted of gratuitous praise of the mai' and the glorious empire. Nick scrolled further down to the pertinent section of the message.

> Given the unfortunate loss of Secretary Huntzinger of Rhadamanthus, with the understanding of the important and valued nature of the relationship between the Western Alliance and the Empire of Gunera, and the necessity of maintaining a free flow of information, diplomatic consultation, and open trade, I inform his most esteemed mai'Tegatriktrik that the Department of State immediately appoints Nicodemus Severin II to the position of temporary Secretary of International Trade and Commerce, Rhadamanthus.

> Mr. Severin is granted all rights and responsibilities related to the position until such time as a meeting with the President of the Western Alliance can be held and the appointment is confirmed. Please direct all inquiries to the office of Mr. Severin until such time as a formal announcement is issued.

Well, the conspirators have certainly thought of everything in a well-rehearsed ballet, Nick thought grimly as, one by one, his roadblocks were torn asunder and he found himself standing on an ever-melting iceberg afloat in a chilly ocean.

Once again, vuh'Yguggli waved his tail barb in Nick's eye before planting it hard on the freigan document with a thud. "Sign the damned document," he snarled.

Once again, Nick jammed his panic into the depths of his belly while mentally reviewing his procedural manuals for an obstruction he could use to reject the treasonous document.

"Last question," Nick murmured, raising a finger as if in deep thought and about to concede. "I still don't know that this agreement was approved by anyone of consequence on Earth. I can assure you that I heard nothing of it during my regular briefings with the former Secretary, nor did I hear of it during my final briefing with the State Department prior to traveling here. I would think the State Department might have mentioned it in my briefing."

Nick had been granted the right to give away nearly everything, including the kitchen sink, but by no means had the State Department agreed to donate not only the kitchen sink but the kitchen, the mansion in which it stood, and the planet on which the mansion was built. *Someone,* he thought, *should have mentioned it.*

He smiled pleasantly, pretending to be annoyed. Nick's right hand drifted over the stylus, but he didn't pick it up. "How do I know anyone on Earth actually agreed to this?" he asked. "I have only your word that the document is valid."

vuh'Yguggli's barb lashed at Nick, catching him in the ear. Nick yelped and retreated, the barb rending the soft flesh of his lobe. A trickle of blood ran along the side of his neck. Jason drew Nick back against him, hands raised defensively to protect his client from further harm. vuh'Yguggli seemed ready to lance out again, but the mai's tail encircled his and planted it on the floor. It was a subtle, gentle, and gracious reprimand. Had the mai' actually been angered by the vuh's action, the barb might have been flung in its owner's own face or, even worse, security would have been called to perform a swift amputation. As he wiped blood from his neck, Nick glared at the two Guneri lords, knowing the mai' was now becoming equally frustrated with Nick.

The mai' gestured to his servant, who flipped screens on the computer tablet then turned the device around. Nick returned to the table and read a lengthy email exchange written in both English and Gunera between Deputy Secretary of Trade Johans Sprouse of Geneva and his Guneri equivalent, gy'Dadamondi.

The thread covered an astounding two-year period. As he worked his way through the exchanges, Nick had no doubt the thread was legitimate. It started with the delicate feelers sent by Sprouse to gy'Gravinda, who'd immediately sent it upstream to his superior gy'Dadamondi. There followed a long series of offers and suggestions. Cautious tentacles had been extended or withdrawn between the high-ranking diplomatic positions over time. Those discussions laid out what would become the new Accords. From time to time, other names were added to the dialogue, including Secretary of State Millingham and mai'Tegatriktrik, although the bulk of the negotiating occurred between Sprouse and Dadamondi. The message ended with agreement to the final wording presented in the freigan parchment. Nick was horrified to discover that such treason could rise as high as the Secretary of State. Nick wondered if President McAlastair was in on the stupidity as well. *If he is,* Nick thought, *I may have no choice but to sign.* Indeed, Sprouse was Nick's superior in the direct line of authority through the State Department, leaving Nick no option but to sign the agreement.

The Secretary of State couldn't possibly make such a profound decision on his own without a vote from Congress, Nick suddenly realized. *Good God! He'd be abandoning a century-old alliance for something untried, something that ceded valuable territory to a foreign government and virtually subordinated humanity's government to that of the Gunera. There's no way in Hell Earth had agreed to this!*

As his eyes scanned the email a second time, Nick questioned whether the references to copies sent to Millingham were even valid. Never once had Millingham joined the thread. His name merely appeared in the lists of blind copies. *For all I know, the names are a feint added to convince me of the validity of the email.* Nick had no doubt Sprouse and gy'Dadamondi had written the bulk of the text; the tone rang true in Nick's mind. *But surely,* Nick wagered, *someone during that final State Department briefing would have said to me, "By the way, the Deputy Secretary is secretly working to destroy the entire alliance that we are sending you to Gunera to protect, so be aware that the list of concessions isn't valid. Ignore it and everything else we just told you. Give up humanity's sovereignty. No worries. We'll back you up on that one, Nick."*

Nick gazed hard at the mai' who watched placidly, waiting for Nick to finally concede.

"I need to confer with my colleague. One moment, please."

Nick turned to Jason and drew in a deep breath. Jason would either confirm or deny what was laid out before him. Either way, Nick's future course was clear.

He gestured to the tablet. "There's an email thread approximately two years in the making between Johans Sprouse, Deputy Secretary of State out of Geneva, and gy'Dadamondi, his Guneri equal. It contains the negotiations that occurred between those two individuals and what eventually developed into the Accord mai'Tegatriktrik is asking me to sign. The Accord has a series of central points, but only three are critical."

Nick touched his index finger, then each succeeding finger in turn. "Earth will withdraw from the Balance Protocols. We will cede the territory of Lethe's Gate to the Gunera, thereby allowing the Gunera to attack the Amaurau with no interference from Earth. Lastly, in the event of any future provocation, Earth will relinquish its military to the mai'."

Nick sat silently for a heartbeat as Jason processed the information. "I need to know if you, as a member of the President's Secret Service, had any knowledge that this negotiation took place. I need to know if the President had any knowledge. I need to know how far up the food chain this conspiracy goes."

Jason sat silently, his face offering no emotion. After a moment, he spoke quietly and respectfully. "Forgive me, sir, for my bluntness, but there's no fucking way." He brushed a hand across his head. "I've been assigned to the President for the past four years, and I can assure you without any doubt whatsoever that he was not a party to such a negotiation, nor would he ever conceivably agree to anything like it.

Nothing like this was ever discussed when I was with the President, nor do I recall him ever taking direct involvement in affairs of the Balance Protocols. He left that to those he considered wiser heads in the State Department. I was present in numerous meetings between McAlastair and Millingham, and I can assure you nothing like this was discussed. Not to say I was present for every discussion the man had or was assigned to his detail for every trip he took."

Nick nodded as Jason took a breath.

"Is it *theoretically* possible," Jason continued, "that the President was a party to this without my knowledge? Yes. Is it *conceivably* possible that he was and I wouldn't know it? Fuck no. The man is a patriot, sir. He lost family to both the Amaurau and Gunera in centuries past. Military leadership is in his lineage. He would never agree to concede humanity's right to control its own destiny. I would swear this on my life."

Nick sat silently studying Jason—his face, the intensity in his eyes. Nick didn't trust much at that moment, but he trusted that Jason was speaking the truth.

"I can't sign this," Nick whispered, eyes wild with panic. "I can't. It's treason of the highest order."

"If what you're telling me is true, I agree, sir."

"What do I do? I've played my last stall tactic. It's over. I either sign it or I ... or what?"

They were trapped inside the most secure palace on the planet with no fewer than ten Guneri guards surrounding them in the pleasant little garden.

We're going to die, Nick thought. He believed it as clearly as he believed he would never sign the Accord.

"I'm sorry you were dragged into this," Nick said quietly, already mentally preparing himself for his impending demise.

"I volunteered, sir." Jason's eyes flicked at the vuh' and the mai'. Nick saw in those dark orbs the calculations. Jason could kill one, maybe two guards, before he and Nick were taken down. "Tell me what you want me to do."

Nick shook his head. "Nothing."

Jason stared. "Sir?"

"The Gunera are sticklers for legal procedure. They've no legal action to take against you provided you obey them. I'll refuse to sign. I don't know what they'll do to me, but whatever it is, let them do it.

Don't interfere. If you remain calm and polite, you can walk out of here alive."

"That's not what I signed up for," the big man growled. "That's not what the Secret Service is about."

For once, Nick reached out and took hold of Jason's arm and gave it a rattle. "You'll have to do it, Jason. You'll be the messenger to humanity. You have to warn the President. He'll listen to you. You have to tell him Sprouse, and possibly Millingham, are traitors. He must be told. Congress must be told. Promise me."

"You're asking too much, sir."

"I'm not. Your first duty is to your nation. To your President. Carry out your duty."

Nick turned back to the Gunera, who appeared visibly weary of the alien conversation. With slow deliberation, Nick picked up the stylus and dipped the tip into the inkpot. He heard mai'Tegatriktrik draw a breath and saw out of the corner of his eye vuh'Yguggli's tail begin to wave. It would strike him as soon as the ink dried. Nick's hand hovered over the freigan parchment. He stared at the agreement, certain it was probably the last thing he'd ever see. Nick hesitated, steeling himself for the forthcoming pain, for the horror only Gunera could wreak upon their enemies. He raised the stylus.

With a slash from one end of the parchment to the other, he ruined all it conveyed.

Nick wasn't sure if vuh'Yguggli or mai'Tegatriktrik screamed the loudest. It didn't matter. The vuh's tail shot at Nick, striking his shoulder. The barb was aimed to wound, cutting through the cloth of Nick's jacket and shirt to embed itself in his deltoid muscle. Then it whipped up, throwing Nick into the air and slamming him down hard on the garden patio. The blow was stunning and Nick's vision blurred as he tried to get his arms beneath him. In the distance, Nick saw Jason half rise.

"No!" he managed. "Remember your duty to the President. Do nothing."

With the barb still planted in his shoulder, vuh'Yguggli dragged Nick across the cobbles, where he ended up prone at the emperor's feet. The guards swarmed, rifles locked on Jason. Jason slowly placed his hands atop his knees. Remaining quiescent under fire was contrary to Jason's nature. He trusted that Nick was right about the Gunera and that he wouldn't be shot. The guards thrust their rifles and lashed their tails at Jason, but he didn't flinch. He sat quietly in the lotus position, completely still, while gazing hopelessly at Nick, who lay prostrate before the two lords.

"Warn humanity," Nick whispered before vuh'Yguggli hauled him through the air again.

Nick fell with a crash into a klikli bush. Immediately, he was lashed with tails and dragged to his feet.

vuh'Yguggli shouted at the guards. "Take that useless bit of trash to the discussion chambers."

Nick had seen the chambers before. They were used to extract information from the unwilling by whatever means possible. The guards hastened around Nick and shoved him forward. Despite the intense pain radiating through his shoulder, Nick remained on his feet. As he was marched from the little garden, his last image was of a terrified Jason sitting statue-like while all hell broke out around him.

11

    Five guards dragged Nick through the Palace of the Mai' to a lift. Down they went, Nick making no attempt to free himself because such a feat was impossible. Even if by some miracle he could escape the palace guard, he could never hide. Nick's implants guaranteed that he'd be found. The only way forward, he knew, was through. Through the torture, through to death.

    The doors opened, and Nick was shoved into a subterranean passage as old as the palace itself. A great barrel arch of brick sprang overhead lit at intervals by bare electric bulbs. Various passages shot off from both sides, revealing more passages and barred cells. Nick heard a distant cry, a mewing like that of a kitten, the sound of a creature that had forsaken all hope. From another passage arose a violent scream that abruptly ended and did not recur.

    Nick was tossed to the floor in the middle of the room. Although the Gunera had conquered the technological challenges of spaceflight, they'd never abandoned the antediluvian practice of torture. The instruments within the room were largely composed of iron and steel, and each had been crafted with meticulous care to deliver unimaginable pain. Nick was dragged and flung onto a silvery-white chair of pure iron made to fit a Gunera. He gasped with the pain as pointed spikes tore into his flesh. Nick's arms were strapped wide at shoulder height, his legs at the width of his shoulders in a position that left him defenseless. He wondered if the Gunera remembered a human's most tender places. *I'm sure,* Nick thought, *it's written down somewhere from the days of the first human/Gunera war. Hopefully, death comes quickly.*

The guards remained in the room but didn't approach Nick. Nick tilted his head back and stared at the ceiling in an effort to disassociate himself from his body. The approach had worked in his youth when he was being punished by vuh'Ygundin, but Nick doubted the meditative tactic would ease the coming pain.

The sound of a mover over the rough floor preceded the arrival of mai'Tegatriktrik, who couldn't have looked more enraged if Nick had wrested away his entire palace. The mai' was nearly purple with anger, and his air gills swished hard. He rolled up to Nick, who sat staring at the mai' in that painfully exposed position. Nick braced for the first blow.

"Remove his shirt," the mai' demanded.

Two guards rolled forward with knives drawn and cut away Nick's jacket and shirt. Nick drew a faint breath of relief that they weren't yet focusing on other areas.

A guard handed mai'Tegatriktrik a willow stick. The mai' warmed up his arm then lashed Nick across the chest and stomach. The stick sliced red welts as the toxins in the sap ate into Nick's flesh. The torment continued until the pain across Nick's stomach felt like a burning flame.

"Will you agree to sign that document?" mai'Tegatriktrik finally asked when he thought he had Nick's attention.

"No." Nick didn't feign politeness.

The willow stick slashed again. Nick closed his eyes and hissed as the pain became a conflagration threatening to tear him in half.

"Will you sign?"

"No."

mai'Tegatriktrik tossed the stick aside and grasped a wire whip. Still flexible, but with the bite of coiled steel, it went deeper than the surface flesh and bruised the muscles under the skin. Thrice he struck the helpless prisoner, demanding screams that Nick refused to grant him. Despite the intense pain, Nick refused to give the mai' the satisfaction of hearing him scream. He knew that the sound of human screaming excited the Gunera. They thrived on it. Clearly, mai'Tegatriktrik was slavering for a fix.

"Sign!"

The whip bit into Nick's ribs.

"Go to hell."

"Sign!"

Deeper this time.

"No."

"Sign!"

Nick felt an agonizing crack and knew ribs had just splintered.

"No."

In fury, the mai' tossed the whip away and stood panting on his mover while glaring at Nick. Through waves of confusion, Nick tried to return the stare, but his mind drifted. For brief moments he was in the torture chamber while at other times he was home on Rhadamanthus. Instead of mai'Tegatriktrik standing before him, he saw Duncan yelling at him for being carelessly stupid with a girl. He was horrified that he'd embarrassed Duncan but wasn't sure what he'd done. Duncan kept yelling, never giving Nick a chance to speak. With all his ebbing strength, Nick wanted to explain. *I didn't mean it, Duncan! I didn't mean for you to die.* But Duncan refused to listen.

He was suddenly at Duncan's old house on Hemera with a girl. A strangely tall thing. Willowy. He tried to grasp her hands, but she ran screaming. Screaming. A high-pitched, soul-rending scream.

Nick opened his eyes to realize the screams were his. The mai' had taken a tong-like apparatus and applied it to his inguen. The shock of pain was so blinding it shot through Nick's brain and left him seeing only white. It shut down his brain to everything but sheer inviolate agony. The mai' eased back on the pincer to give Nick a moment's respite.

"Our history tells us humans are very delicate in certain areas," the mai' chortled. "I'm glad to see the historians were right." The mai' clicked the pincers in front of Nick's eyes as his vision returned though he remained breathless.

"Will you sign the document?"

"No," Nick whispered. He winced when the pincer moved toward him again.

"Stop!" Nick turned at the sound and watched through teary eyes as vuh'Yguggli entered the room, arms and tail wildly flashing. "By all that's providential, don't rend him that way, esteemed mai'."

The mai' hesitated, pincers hovering, while Nick drew ragged gasps and tried to focus.

"Why shouldn't I?" demanded mai'Tegatriktrik. "The histories say it's the quickest way to attain compliance of a human. I believe them."

The vuh' rolled next to the mai'. "You'll ruin the only value in him, esteemed mai'. Those are his sexual organs without which he cannot breed."

The mai' gazed balefully at his vuh'. "Why do I care? The silly idea of a farm is yours, not mine."

"You'll care when you see the money to be made, esteemed lord," vuh'Yguggli insisted. "There's a fortune to be made in human slaves. I swear it."

"We'll have all we want once we've freed ourselves of the damned birds!" exclaimed the mai'. "We'll take all of humanity for ourselves."

"Perhaps. But even then, the humans will be prisoners of war, not slaves. Legal issues will tie up the courts for years," insisted vuh'Yguggli. "*We* won't have that problem. With eh'Nicodemus as a sire, the offspring will be legally ours to sell."

"*Ours?*"

"I'll grant you twenty percent of the live young," the vuh' offered, looking annoyed.

"You'll *grant me?*" The mai' waved the pincers at Nick again, who flinched but could do nothing to protect himself. "Seems to me, the eh' and his vital organs are my property."

"We have a signed intent," vuh'Yguggli warned.

"You'd dare to ply suit again a mai'?" mai'Tegatriktrik gasped.

vuh'Yguggli nodded. "I would. And I would prevail. You know it's true."

"I defy a judge to side against me," growled the mai'. He stood indecisively, the pincers waving near Nick's quivering body. "Fifty percent of the young."

"Twenty-five."

"Forty and count yourself lucky!"

vuh'Yguggli bowed. "Deal. Forty percent, damn you. Put down those pincers before you destroy the chance of even that."

The mai' tossed the tongs away, and Nick closed his eyes to snatch a tiny breath of relief. *There are small mercies,* he thought. *A vuh's greed is one of them.*

"What device might you apply to the eh's body?" sneered the mai' as he rolled around the room examining other wondrous apparatuses of pain. "How would you extract our desires from him?"

"Not with any of these," stated vuh'Yguggli. "Each would cause unrepairable damage. We want him compliant, not dead."

"How do you plan to extract compliance from this headstrong animal without damaging it?" The concept was clearly not one mai'Tegatriktrik comprehended.

"I can obtain compliance without inflicting so much as a bruise to his body," vuh'Yguggli asserted.

The mai' issued a sour look.

"Give gy'Dadamondi a few minutes, esteemed mai'," vuh'Yguggli insisted. "And all will be revealed." He looked at the pale, sweating Nick, who'd managed to regain his breath despite aftershocks of pain that still ricocheted through his body. "You can rest easy, eh'Nicodemus. The worst is behind you now."

Nick flinched as he eyed his nemesis. This cold, calm vuh' was something he knew well. It would appear when the lord had the upper hand in an entanglement, and the death stroke was near. Nick had seen the results of such cunning many times. It usually ended with some Guneri rival hanging in pieces in the garden for the raptors to feed upon. Nick swallowed his dread, wondering what awful plan the vuh' had in store for him. *Whatever it is,* he told himself, *I'm not signing the parchment. The only way through this is to go through. All the way. To die.*

The wait was almost more torturous than the torture had been. *At least when I was being tortured,* Nick thought, *I could see the blow coming, and I knew that once the first hard flash of pain sliced through me, there would be a moment's respite before the next assaulting blow.* But Nick cringed each time he heard a scream in the passages, unsure of the horror that would approach next. His stomach burned with the toxins of the willow stick, and his every breath felt painful, which he attributed to his freshly broken ribs and certain other damaged areas.

Time dragged. Nick drifted. The mai' wandered away to torment some other hapless soul, but vuh'Yguggli remained, eyeing his prisoner with avarice.

After almost two hours, Nick heard scuffling and voices echoing along the barrel vault. The inflection and tone implied a protest. He wondered what it meant. Nick realized it wasn't Jason since the voices he heard were speaking fluent Gunera. The mai' reappeared and rolled to a stop next to vuh'Yguggli. A group of Gunera, dragging a small figure struggling to escape, was in tow. They hauled the prisoner to the forefront of the chamber and held it, arms outstretched in a sick parody of Nick, who remained confined to his chair.

Nick stared, gobsmacked, at eh'Monica. His mother.

A painful, guttural wail erupted from within Nick at the sight of his parent. A sick grin stretched across the face of vuh'Yguggli, and the Guneri lord's tail flicked with pleasure as he ordered the woman drawn close to the prisoner.

Nick stared at the woman who had been his mother. He hadn't seen her in a decade and, not surprisingly, the years had not been kind to her. She'd been captured by the rogue vuh'Gragalag at the age of twenty-three while pregnant. When that unpleasantness had settled, she'd been given in trust to the mai' and his court, pending negotiations with the humans. Nick supposed the goal at that time had been to use the wife of the deceased President of Hemera as a bargaining chip to obtain concessions, but the confusion of the court had made that difficult. mai'Tegatriktik had only recently ascended to the throne (at the tender age of five years), and the court was awash in intrigue as various vuh's and gy's sought to control the young emperor. eh'Monica had ended up in the convoluted Guneri legal system as a prisoner of war, a person with no rights as a citizen, and yet with several rights as a prisoner, which put her in legal limbo. Because prisoners of war were accorded a certain level of respect in the Guneri system, she could not be sold or abused, but she could not leave the palace in which the mai's court placed her. Thus, she'd remained as a prisoner, with humanity unable to free her.

Nick speculated that his mother had been in her mid-thirties when he'd escaped, which meant that she was now in her late forties despite looking much older. Her hair was a long, matted mess that hung almost to her knees. She'd never washed it in her twenty-eight years on Gunera. It had developed wooly cords so that it hung to the floor in dark strips heavily interspersed with gray. eh'Monica's body was bony and white due to a lack of sun exposure. As a human with delicate skin, she would have burned at the touch of the Guneri sun. Her once pretty face was now lined and sagged, her dark eyes red-rimmed, her shoulders exhibiting the scars of a life under the stick. There was a wildness about her now. It overrode the humanity that had vanished when she'd lost her son.

Dragged before him now, eh'Monica blinked stupidly at the vision of a human she didn't recognize bound to a chair in a place of torture.

The guards released Nick's mother. She dropped to her knees and glanced around wildly like a frightened animal.

"What offense did I give, kind lords?" she whispered in eh', quivering.

vuh'Yguggli faced Nick. "What do you think, eh'Nicodemus? Do you still refuse to sign?"

Nick stared at the vuh' and then at what remained of his mother. eh'Monica studied Nick with narrowed eyes.

"*eh'Nicodemus?*" she whispered. "That one is gone, esteemed lord. Gone, gone, long time gone."

The vuh' chuckled. "Your eh'Nicodemus has returned home!"

She blinked at the stranger before her. "He's long gone, to the stars." It was obvious to Nick that she'd gone more than a little mad.

vuh'Yguggli openly grinned, air gills flapping happily. "Nay, eh'. He has returned. This young man before you is eh'Nicodemus. Don't you remember him?"

"I remember my Nico," the woman growled, rubbing the cobbles with her worn, arthritic hands as if scrubbing them. "Hair like the night, flowing like a river. Body tall and strong, so like his father. And words! Ah, he had such words! A lord of words like his father."

"Indeed, he is very much like his father. A lord of words, to be sure." The vuh' considered Nick. "Have you nothing to say to the one who brought you into this world?"

Nick swallowed, not merely bile but a lifetime of pain. *Dear God,* he thought, *I can't do this! I can't torture my own mother.*

"eh'Nicodemus?" vuh'Yguggli pressed. The Gunera picked up a sharp spike and waved it near the eyes of Nick's mother. He'd put out her vision if it got him what he wanted. eh'Monica wasn't worth much anymore.

"Mama, it's me, your Nico," he said weakly, not because vuh'Yguggli wanted him to but because he needed his mother to know who he was, how he was. That he'd survived. "Mama, look at me."

The lost soul that sat on the floor gazed up as if ordered by the mai' himself. Her insane eyes stared at him, uncaring. She shook her head. "My Nico is gone to the stars! Gone to the stars! He rides Lethe's Gate where no one can harm him."

vuh'Yguggli raised her up from the ground with his tail and moved her directly in front of Nick. Mother and son were mere inches apart.

"This is your Nico," he said with false gentleness. "This is the son you sent to the stars."

eh'Monica shook her head, then she looked slyly at Nick. She was smiling like a madwoman, not seeing him as anything more than another human, perhaps. He wasn't sure she even saw that. Her eyes locked on his. The two stared at each other. Nick saw the horror begin to dawn on her. Her eyes dropped down to see the bloody wound still dripping from Nick's shoulder, his chest and stomach strong and muscled but inflamed from a prolonged caning. Without a word, she lunged forward. vuh'Yguggli did nothing to stop her. eh'Monica virtually climbed into Nick's lap and sat there, pressing her face into his while he sat, helpless to do anything except stare.

Her hands tangled in Nick's thick, dark hair, and she tugged at it painfully. "You stole my Nico's hair," she complained.

Nick tried to smile. "It's my hair, Mama. I'm your Nico. I've come home."

Still, she sat on his lap and stared at him. The woman was so frail she made almost no impression on Nick. Her hand raced to his face, and she stroked his cheek, his neck, his eyes, his mouth.

"Nico!" she whispered, as realization dawned. "My Nico!" She smiled for the first time in ages, but the smile soon faded. Frail hands jerked at Nick's hair. "Why did you come back, you fool!" she hissed. "Go! Now! Run for the stars, stupid Nico. Run before the vuh' finds out you're here."

Nick couldn't swallow the pain. Tears that no amount of blinking could make disappear formed in his eyes. Nick's mind raced. *This dear woman is my mother, and she's been destroyed by these vile creatures. There's nothing I can do to save her. She's gone. Lost. Lost to madness and a lifetime of pain.*

"I'm so sorry, Mama!" he whispered, wishing his arms were free so that he could hold her, to give her one small iota of human comfort. Trapped as he was, an embrace wasn't possible. The torture the vuh' had chosen was perfect. Like that long ago chastisement of his son when he'd made the young vuh' walk on his three feet around the entire Palace of the Light ten times. It hadn't just been the physical pain of forcing the boy to walk on legs he didn't use. It was the humiliation of making a vuh' walk the public street for all the world to see. Nick's torture was no different. The shame. *Look what you did to your mother when you fled. Look what became of her. And guess what tortures we'll apply to her now if you don't sign that bloody document?*

From over his mother's shoulder, Nick glared at vuh'Yguggli and the impressed mai'. "You really can't be this evil," he said quietly.

Had the vuh' brows, he would have raised them. "I see no evil in demanding compliance from a slave, eh'Nicodemus. You're my slave, and I demand compliance. Since your body is too valuable to damage, you leave me no choice but to damage your mind. After all," he said with cold malice, "as far as I know, an intelligent thinking mind is not required in the breeding of humans. You'll work just as well a witless fool. It's your choice."

Nick felt faint. It was, he knew, a survival mechanism. When the brain faced more than it could handle, it sought to escape. Presently it wanted out of that room in any way possible; fainting was as good an option as any. Nick forced himself to control his breath to avoid hyperventilating.

With a motion, vuh'Yguggli ordered his men to remove eh'Monica from Nick's lap. She squealed like a lost kitten, grasping at her son as she was pulled free. She wailed for her child to come back. The guards flung eh'Monica without pity to the floor and pinned her while she continued to wail piteously. A guard stepped forward with a sharp pike and pressed it near her eye.

"It's your decision," vuh'Yguggli stated. "Does she walk out of here with one eye or two?"

Nick's body turned to ice. He stared at his mother as she continued to scream. The pike moved ever closer to her eye. Nick shut his own eyes tightly, biting down on the pain.

"One," he whispered. *Mama, forgive me.*

The horrible scream twisted his own body in pain. Hot tears stole from under Nick's lids, and he clamped hard down on himself, on his emotions, jamming them again into the box. *I'm protecting humanity,* he told himself bitterly. *I've no right to put my mother ahead of fifty trillion people.*

"Now the question is, eh'Nicodemus," came the implacable voice of vuh'Yguggli, "one eye or none? It's your choice. Sign the document and end this."

"No."

"Sign, eh'Nicodemus, and all the pain will be over."

"I can't!" Nick growled. "Don't you understand? I can't condemn humanity to your evil. I can't. I won't."

"Then it will be no eyes for eh'Monica. It's your choice."

Nick twisted his head back and forth while the spikes bit into his back. He kept his eyes clamped shut, although the tears continued to escape. "Don't do this," he whispered. "Don't. She's just a helpless old woman. She's done nothing to deserve this."

"What has that to do with anything?" asked the vuh'. "Sign the document, and it will all be over."

"Please, vuh'!"

"Please what?" came the demand. "Surely the great eh'Nicodemus, brilliant negotiator of Amaurau and Gunera, isn't going to beg."

"Please don't harm my mother."

"That decision rests solely on your shoulders."

Nick opened his eyes as the guards were readying to perform their evil surgery. Half of eh'Monica's face was a bloody mess. She moaned softly, barely trying to escape. *Maybe it would be better if they kill her,* he thought. *Maybe she's better off dead.*

Not like this! Nick thought. *Cut to pieces right before my eyes. I can't do it. Maybe the State Department wouldn't believe my signature. Maybe they'll laugh at the document and claim Nicodemus Severin lacks the authority to sign anything. Maybe the joke will be on the Gunera. I can sign it. I can end Mom's suffering.* He'd become a slave in the Palace of the Mai', but he reasoned that from that position, he could find a way to protect his mother. See that she was better cared for. Duncan was dead. He had no father, no brothers, no family. He had nothing but the aged, twisted woman now writhing helplessly before him. He couldn't turn on his own flesh and blood. He owed her more than he'd ever owe humanity.

The guard readied himself for the deed. eh'Monica whimpered, bracing for the impending pain.

"Okay," Nick gasped. "Stop. I'll sign the damned accord. I'll sign it. Just … please stop."

Nick slumped forward as much as his bindings would allow. vuh'Yguggli patted Nick's cheek. "Good eh'Nicodemus!" he crooned. "I knew obtaining compliance was merely premised on finding the right sort of leverage. You're a good son. A great one would have saved the first eye, but you're a good son nevertheless." The vuh' turned to his mai'. "There's value in learning about one's enemy," he said with no small amount of arrogance. "Humans have a weakness for their own."

The mai', who'd remained silent while his vuh' pried compliance from a slave, grunted. "I like my way better."

"You would have cost me my first crop of humans," the vuh' sniffed as he rolled on his mover toward the exit. "This was more civilized."

mai'Tegatriktrik rolled up to Nick and snorted with derision. "I'd have let him have both her eyes, along with every last vital organ if necessary. You are weak."

Nick snarled. "I don't view it as a weakness. It's what makes me a member of the human race. Our devotion to our own is our greatest strength."

"Doesn't seem so strong to me," the mai' chortled. "Alas, you destroyed our accord. Another is being drawn as we speak, but it will not be ready until the morrow." The mai' tilted his head and ran his tail fleetingly over Nick's arms which hung outstretched on the iron chair. "Enjoy your sleep in the depths of my palace," the mai' commented. "The only part of you that will be freed will be your hand, and only for as long as it takes you to sign the accord."

"And then?" Nick asked weakly, closing his eyes. He wasn't sure he really cared.

To his surprise, the mai' actually laughed. "Why, it's upstairs to my house you go, teg'Nicodemus. I'll find use for you. The vuh' thinks your value lies in your offspring, but I know where it truly lies."

With that cryptic declaration, the mai' and his escort rolled from the chamber. Two guards picked up the still whimpering eh'Monica and hauled her away.

12

There were monsters. They consumed Nick's flesh one bite at a time. It was death by slow torture. Nick's attempts to escape only provoked them further. Every movement brought more pain, more flesh torn asunder. They gnawed at his spine and gutted his stomach. Nick tried to move but was suddenly frozen. Nick watched helplessly as the dark creatures ingested Nick with careful precision.

Nick awoke but remained coherent only for several moments. His mind drifted on waves of confusion, and he thought himself in the Palace of the Light being pummeled by vuh'Ygundin with a willow stick. Nick's body was aflame from the poisons as the young lord struck him for disobeying orders.

He awoke again and realized he was still strapped to the torture chair, its spikes producing dull, icy throbs of unending pain. Breathing was an ongoing misery as his broken ribs complained and his stomach burned from the caning. For a handful of lucid moments, Nick set his head against the chair and contemplated what was left of his life. Darkness fell over his consciousness, and he was again back in the tunnel, running from raptors that scurried through the inky darkness in search of blood to drink and flesh to consume.

The guards left Nick to his feverish despair. Only three remained. The others had carried eh'Monica away. Bleakly, Nick knew he'd made a huge mistake. He should have let them kill her, and him as well. In those waking moments of utter misery, alone and in pain, Nick berated himself for being a fool. *Why am I suffering like this? Why not just sign some stupid piece of parchment? No one cares what happens to me. No one values my worthless signature. I'm suffering for no reason. Sign the thing. It will all be over. Sign it and let humanity laugh at the hubris of the Undersecretary of International Trade who thought he could bind humanity with the stroke of a pen. The arrogance!*

Nick's fever had become a roiling sea of redness while demon raptors fluttered on iridescent wings around his head, darting in to tear out his eyes, tongue, and flesh. He was burning. The fire within him was consuming all his being. When he woke, he'd find himself as a pile of ash, but at least he'd get the last laugh on the mai'.

"eh'Nicodemus!" came a terrified whisper through the waves of pain.

Nick frowned. His mind and body seemed totally disconnected from one another. Could he still hear? Could he still feel? Could a human body in total flame actually feel anything? In his confusion, Nick sensed the turmoil of battle, of mental demons at war with each other. He flinched when he heard a scream. *Surely I'm not screaming again,* he thought as a fresh wave of pain swept through his body. It was high-pitched, like a rabbit being torn apart. *It can't be me, can it?*

"eh'Nicodemus!" the feverish whisper came again, tickling Nick's ear. He sensed something pounding against his left wrist. The pain was jolting, and Nick managed a low moan.

"No more," he muttered, unsure which language he was speaking. "You said the pain would stop if I signed."

Another hard jolt smashed against Nick's wrist, sending shockwaves of agony through his body. His left arm fell, helpless and numb from hours of immobility, to his side. More strikes attacked his right wrist.

"You must awaken," the voice said. So familiar. So comforting. Nick knew the voice. Even semiconscious, he was sure of it.

His right arm was freed, and it, too, dropped uselessly to his side. Through the fog of fever and pain, Nick sensed more blows against his legs. Soon his ankles were free. He was eased out of the chair.

"Walk slowly, as best you can." The voice didn't give commands. It asked. It cajoled.

Nick's legs were rubber. He collapsed to the floor.

"Suggestions?" a second voice asked. It spoke in a totally different language and was deep, resonant, familiar, and comforting.

Nick sensed several entities moving around him. Human arms lifted him up, and Guneri tails swept around his chest, drawing gasps of pain as they tightened on his broken ribs. The flash of agony hindered Nick's breathing; he lost all sense except pain.

"Careful," someone warned. "He's been badly damaged. Bones broken in his chest."

The Guneri tails withdrew, leaving Nick hanging by the axilla in the grip of human hands. The position was equally painful; it stressed his ribs and irritated the shoulder wound.

Nick babbled something that was incoherent even to himself.

"Quiet, sir," Jason said. "We're getting you out of here."

Nick had the vague sensation of being passed from one individual to another as a Guneri tail tenderly wrapped itself around his body. He felt a hard pressure against his shoulder blades and a softness, like flesh and blood, against his chest. Nick's head fell, and it landed against thick Guneri hide. Stubby arms reached around him but didn't make any attempt to hold Nick since the tail was handling that job. Nick sagged, relinquishing control to these entities. He felt a frightening jerk and realized he was in motion. Nick's mind cleared enough to realize he was on a mover operated by the same Gunera who held him.

The rumbling of the wheels over cobblestones grew louder as the mover accelerated. Nick forced his eyes open and looked down as the floor raced by. He also saw a pair of human feet running to keep pace; the slapping of soles on pavers produced a loud cadence against the hum of the mover's guayule wheels. *eh'Kraghilg and Jason,* the thought fluttered through Nick's brain. *How'd they do it?* He realized it didn't matter. He gave himself up to them.

The nightmarish escape continued as the mover flashed through one passage after another. When the lights dimmed and he heard Jason curse, Nick knew they'd reached the dark level, the place where only slaves and eh's dared venture. While Jason was left completely blind, eh'Kraghilg knew those tunnels in his sleep. The little eh' grasped Jason's hand and planted it on the grip of the mover to ensure he and Jason remained together. The pace slowed. Although in his feverish fear, Nick knew all hell had to be breaking loose in the Palace of the Mai', he also knew that they were relatively safe in the dark level. Most of the eh's of the dark level wouldn't involve themselves in an escape. There would be no payoff in running topside to expose the invaders.

"Sir?" Jason said. "You must translate for me. Can you do that?"

Nick lifted his head as his long dark hair tickled his face. He opened his eyes but could see only nothingness.

"I'll try," he whispered with agonizing breath.

"We need a safe place to hide you," Jason panted. "You need medical care. Then we need to get you off this planet. Tell that to the Gunera."

"No medical care on Gunera," Nick managed to gasp. "Not for humans."

"Ask your friend anyway."

Nick reluctantly translated his words to eh'Kraghilg.

"You're correct," eh'Kraghilg replied with ease since he was aboard the mover and exerting no energy. "You need medical care. But I cannot obtain that for you. You do need to escape from this planet, this empire, and return back where you belong. But I haven't the means to help you. Tell your human friend."

Nick did. Jason issued a litany of expletives in response.

"Great idea," Jason growled. "We rescued you from that house of horrors, but we've no place to take you!"

Nick translated. The words angered the little eh'. Nick felt the body pressed against him tighten as the air gills swept against his cheek with increasing speed.

"I'm doing the best I can!" eh'Kraghilg growled. "Tell him I provided weapons. I stole us into the palace of the mai'. You are free. I think he demands much of a poor eh'."

Nick wanted to pat eh'Kraghilg, but his arms remained sapped of strength. They hung like leaden weights from his shoulders.

After what seemed like endless hours, eh'Kraghilg rolled to a stop in the utter darkness of the underground. Nick heard Jason panting nearby and the sounds of scuffling as whatever eh's inhabited the space quickly scurried to avoid the incoming strangers. Nick, Jason, and eh'Kraghilg were in one of the central spaces where a group of eh's lived communally. Nick suspected they were far, far down from the top of the cone in a place where eh'Kraghilg felt safe to stop.

Nick felt eh'Kraghilg's grip loosen against his spine. "We must decide what to do," eh'Kraghilg stated worriedly.

"You don't have a plan?" Nick asked between painful breaths, not in ridicule but in fear. He was terrified for eh'Kraghilg for having been a party in Nick's abduction. He worried for the little waste tender's long-term safety.

"No." As always, eh'Kraghilg called it like he saw it. There was no subtly in the world of waste tenders. "The plan was to free you from the Palace of the Mai'. We hadn't thought beyond that."

Now that the movement had stopped and eh'Kraghilg was supporting Nick's body, breathing was easier, and the pain of Nick's injuries had dulled enough to enable clear thinking. "How did you communicate with Jason?" Nick asked.

The little body that clasped him belched. "I didn't. When I saw Jason returned under guard to the Palace of the Winds, I read the distress on his face. He then smashed a number of priceless antiques, which I took as indication that things had not gone well. Despite us not speaking the same language, it was easy to deduce that you'd been taken prisoner. I quietly stole two guns from the armory. Jason understands that my intention was for us to obtain your release. Hand and tail signals work quite well, eh'Nicodemus. I still remember the nature of your gestures, too."

Nick's mind drifted, and he rested his head against eh'Kraghilg again. He lacked the strength to assist in the flight and didn't know where he and Jason could go. Nick's only allies were his mother, who was in even worse straits, and eh'Kraghilg.

"You need to take me back," Nick said wearily, earning a light rap from eh'Kraghilg's tail barb. "There's nowhere safe to go. No Guneri physician will aid me. They'll turn us over to the police. You can't transport me or Jason off this planet. It's useless, eh'."

eh'Kraghilg let loose another rattle. "Don't be such a damned pessimist! You always did see the worst of everything."

"Please tell me what I'm missing," Jason, who had remained silent until now, said.

"The waste is flowing. The world goes on. We've only to find the right eddy to follow." *Philosophy,* Nick thought with grim humor, *from the sewer man's viewpoint.*

"Command me, wise waste tender, on the flows of the universal river."

The quip earned him a gentle shake. "I'm glad to hear you can joke, eh'Nicodemus." eh'Kraghilg was silent while he thought. "The only eddy we can follow is one that is friendly to you."

"While I have no friends except the two standing in this chamber," Nick muttered.

"No, there is another," eh'Kraghilg commented thoughtfully. "It is the only eddy we can follow. Forgive me, dear one, but I can think of no other course." He dropped the mover into gear, and they were off again.

With Jason at his side, eh'Kraghilg moved through the dark level, twisting left and right, always moving upward again. Nick wanted to protest, but his strength was fading. The fever was fierce, and he was washed by waves of heat and pain that left him lying limp in the grasp of eh'Kraghilg's tail, completely at his friend's mercy. The constant bumping and jarring wore at Nick. He fell into unconsciousness, waking sometime later in a lighted elevator car.

eh'Kraghilg draped Nick over the mover's handlebars. "Hold on as best you can," he said. He stepped off the mover and ushered Jason into the elevator. "I'm sorry if this is the wrong thing to do, dear one," he said to Nick in anguish. "But I can think of nowhere else where you might be safe. I will pray to the gods of the dark levels to protect you and see you home. It is unlikely I'll ever see you again, eh'Nicodemus. I dearly hope that I don't."

Nick tried to raise a hand to touch his friend, but his arms refused to move. "If I survive, I swear I'll be back for you."

"I'm a waste tender," eh'Kraghilg said quietly. "It's my fate. What would I do if not tend waste here?"

"Tend waste on Rhadamanthus," Nick suggested. "Or retire to a deck chair overlooking the gardens. You've earned it."

eh'Kraghilg tenderly brushed his tail against Nick's face. "I will remain forever your friend, eh'Nicodemus."

Nick closed his eyes as tears started again. "And I, yours. I will return for you."

"No."

Nick hadn't the strength to argue further. His body sank against the handlebars, and Jason took up position, holding him secure.

The little eh' pushed the call button. A gruff voice spoke into the intercom.

"State your business."

"I send the lord a precious gift. What he chooses to do with it, only he can say. But it has value beyond price. One hopes he'll treasure it as much as the one who gives it."

"Who is this?" the voice on the other end demanded to know, but eh'Kraghilg disconnected. Without another word, he stepped into the shadows of the dark level and pressed the send button. The doors closed, leaving Nick alone with Jason.

"Now what?" Jason asked.

Nick had no answer, much less the strength to shrug.

The elevator moved with smooth silence as it carried its two passengers ever upward. Nick surmised it belonged to one of the upper palaces, and he feared eh'Kraghilg had simply sent him and Jason back to the mai'. The elevator slowed to a stop, and its doors opened to reveal a lord's complement of guards with rifles drawn. Jason raised his free hand in surrender while the other held Nick upright.

"I sure hope that friend of yours knows what he's doing," the big man rumbled.

Nick didn't care, provided Jason wasn't harmed. Participating in a prison break legally threw Jason out of the diplomatic corps and added him to the criminal class. The journey forward was now equally dangerous for Jason and Nick.

The guards ordered Jason to bring the mover forward and, although he didn't understand Gunera, he comprehended the command. The guards waited in the little antechamber beyond as Jason piloted the mover toward them. It was another grand palace, nearly as grand as the Palace of the Mai'. It was similarly adorned with gilt, mirrors, and glass. But unlike the Palace of the Mai', Nick saw an indication of taste and refinement. It was evident that while the owner of this space had wealth and power to spare, he did not feel the need to flaunt it.

Nick sensed something odd about the space. The lack of flamboyance was certainly strange. Furnishings were expensive but simple. The pottery that hung from the wall was all wrong. Nick tried to understand why that bit of earthenware jarred his nerves, but his vision blurred. His head dropped backward against Jason's shoulder.

No one spoke until one of the guards popped a commlink into his ear and addressed an invisible master. "My lord, you need to see this."

Nick and Jason remained locked in the sights of the guards' rifles. Although he still had two small handguns hidden in his jacket, Jason instinctively did not draw them. He seemed to understand that eh'Kraghilg had a purpose for sending him and Nick to this place, and he was willing to see what transpired.

"If this goes badly, just shoot me," Nick whispered. "Make sure I'm dead."

"Not that I'm agreeing with that advice," Jason replied, arm tightening around his charge, "but what would you suggest I do after that?"

"Surrender. By Guneri law, you're still a diplomat and have some immunity."

"*Some?*"

Nick fought to control his breathing. The pain of his ribs was excruciating. "I'm not sure if it will hold against what you've done, but it might. Your situation will confuse them, and there will be legal questions to be sorted out. I don't think you're in danger."

"Could have fooled me," Jason growled.

A commotion from an outer hallway ushered in another wave of lordly Gunera on their movers. They drew to a shocked halt but for one who continued forward.

"By all the sons of Jagjekcek! What strange spirit placed you in my arms?"

A stab of panic hit Nick in the heart. He knew the voice. Dreaded it. *Dear God, no,* he thought. Nick gathered his strength and stared forward as his heart sank. The astonished face of gy'Bagrada stared back at him.

Oh, eh'Kraghilg, Nick thought in despair. *How trusting is one who doesn't know the ways of the lords.*

One of the Gunera sputtered. "It's the fugitive humans!"

gy'Bagrada gazed at the man indignantly. "I know that, gy'Tikategra! I *know* what a human looks like. And I know who these two are." His tail whipped madly. "Send all nonessentials to their duty stations," he barked. "Now!"

At the harsh command, the guards holstered their weapons and backed from the room.

"If one word is spoken that the gy' received a gift today, the individual who speaks it will spend a thousand days dying one organ at a time!" gy'Bagrada bellowed at the retreating entourage. "Remember your vows, teg's and bah's. You swore service to me and no one else!"

The younger gy' remained, rocking nervously on his mover. "Esteemed lord, we all stand ready to obey your every command. But these humans belong to the mai'. We must return them."

gy'Bagrada snorted and drove his mover forward so that he could study Nick's condition. His thrashing tail and air gill flutter spoke of his distress. "This human arrived here as a diplomat, gy'. He's been tortured at the hands of vuh'Yguggli, which is a crime for which the vuh' will have to answer."

"You would challenge the vuh'?" the younger gy' gasped.

gy'Bagrada's tail lashed out at his companion. "The law is the law, gy'Tikategra! Neither eh' nor bah', gy' nor vuh' may flaunt it. To mistreat an emissary is to invite unpleasant questions. To torture one is to invite war."

gy'Bagrada's gaze slid over the bruised and bloody skin of Nick's abdomen, then considered the ghastly shoulder wound. With a whack of derision from his tail, the gy' commanded Jason to release Nick. Upon doing so, Nick slowly collapsed down the shaft of the mover's command bar. Before he puddled on the floor, the gy's tail lashed around him and pulled tight. Nick screamed as the strong muscles contracted around his broken ribs, and he quickly blacked out.

gy'Bagrada immediately softened his grip.

"He's been tortured," the Guneri lord growled. "The Gunera don't torture emissaries, least of all emissaries of our allies!"

The lesser gy' bobbed nervously. "I see your point, esteemed gy', but the mai' may have other thoughts."

The comment earned him a glare. "Then I suggest we determine the legal status of the situation before we take action. Wouldn't you agree that's a prudent position?"

"Yes, esteemed gy'. I'll set the legal corps on the topic immediately."

gy'Bagrada sniffed. "I would say so. Come up with a valid reason for my possession of him."

gy'Tikategra stiffened. "Indeed, sir. What do you command in the meantime?"

"Explain the diffuse legal situation to the staff. That until a determination is made as to the status of these two humans, no one is to discuss their presence in the house on pain of death, and no one not assigned to the house will be permitted entrance."

"That might raise suspicions," gy'Tikategra stuttered. "Your orders were to search every crevice of the city. Your officers will wish to report. Denying them entrance to your own palace will prompt questions."

gy'Bagrada grunted. "True. There's no avoiding allowing my senior officers inside. But limit their access to my offices! No one may enter my residence."

"Your own security staff are involved in the search for these fugitives," gy'Tikategra protested. "You would hide contraband humans from your own people?"

"Yes!" snapped gy'Bagrada. "It will be a fair test of their abilities. I have not withdrawn my support of the mai', nor will I withdraw my support of the search. Let the search continue with all due alacrity. Search the entire city, Mahagog, and the world. Search it all except my nestroom!"

With his strong tail continuing to support Nick, gy'Bagrada shoved Jason aside and climbed aboard the mover. He drew Nick close and directed the mover forward. Terrified though he was of gy'Bagrada, Nick realized with fuzzy wonder that eh'Kraghilg had been right. Yes, gy'Bagrada held a torch for him. But that was not what eh'Kraghilg had wagered Nick's life upon. Rather, the waste tender knew that gy'Bagrada followed the law like a martial mistress. The gy' would challenge the mai' himself in a battle in the courts. He'd done so several times before and had never lost.

That same adamantine lord was now surprisingly gentle as he carried Nick into his private apartments. They were austere for a Guneri residence. Rather than mirrors and gilt, the space was furnished in somber, earthy colors replete with natural fibers and textures. Nick was stunned to see a large, framed photograph of the New York skyline spanning an entire wall. There were other objects to behold: candlesticks of wrought iron (not an art practiced by the Gunera), a woven rug Nick felt certain was of African origin. Everywhere Nick's eyes fell, he saw objects not just of human manufacture but of Earthly manufacture, most of them handmade. *gy'Bagrada's not only obsessed with me,* Nick thought, *but with humans in general.*

gy'Bagrada yelled for his eh's, and they appeared at once, pouring from various bolt holes. A veritable whirlwind of activity occurred as the gy' issued commands left and right. A collection of Earthly artifacts was swept from the gy's large display table, and a pile of packing quilts laid over it after which seat cushions were placed at one end. When the makeshift bed was complete, gy'Bagrada stepped off the mover with Nick. Still exhausted, Nick collapsed limply into the gy's arms. The gy's strong tail laid Nick down with exquisite care.

Nick sighed with the pleasure of being laid flat. He turned his head to see the gy' staring down at him with an unhappy grimace.

"This is not what I would want for you, eh'Nicodemus," the lord muttered. His hands ran lightly across Nick's injured abdomen, gingerly feeling for the broken bones, causing Nick to groan in pain. "It's not legal."

"I'm touched," Nick muttered.

His comment earned Nick a finger tap upon one of his broken ribs and another twinge of pain. "You scorn me as you've always scorned me, eh'Nicodemus, but at this moment, I hold your life in my hands."

"Let it fall, gy'," Nick whispered. "Kill me and end my pain. End the danger to both our peoples. End the danger to the Balance."

"You're so certain I care about the Balance," murmured the gy'.

"It's the law," Nick insisted. "You of all people must defend the law."

"True."

"Kill me, gy'. Before the mai' finds me. Before he uses me to destroy the only balance we have in the cosmos."

"I cannot kill you regardless of your desires," the gy' stated. "It would be murder under our law. Worse, it would be the murder of a diplomat. Treason against the state."

Nick sighed. "Again, I'm touched."

The gy's tail twitched, and his green eyes narrowed. "You seem unable to believe that I have interest in you, eh'."

Nick rolled his eyes. "You have an obsession with humans."

"Not humans," the gy' growled. "You, eh'Nicodemus. It is only you I desire."

Nick felt yet another bloom of panic in his chest. He tried to move—his arms were willing—but when he tried to push upward from the table, his ribs responded with a stabbing pain, and he fell back again. "I don't believe you," he whispered through his pain. "You just enjoy the pleasure of torturing a human and, for reasons I've never understood, you've focused on me."

"If torturing a human was all I desired, I could do that every day of the week!" The gy' laughed quietly. "I'd find legal reasons to impound a ship and its crew. I'd bring my very capable staff to its location, and I would take my pleasure rending as much agony out of a human body as I was capable. I have not done that. My interest is in you."

Nick caught his breath, hearing in the gy's words the same sentiment that had been spoken by SevayIssissita. His brow puckered. "Why?"

"You have an alluring mind. Exquisitely tuned to legal matters in a way I've found in no other human. Your ability to conjure your way out of any situation is exciting to watch, and I lust after opportunities to test your skills." His gills swished with humor at the sight of Nick frowning. "You didn't realize it? I wasn't simply being vulgar, although that in and of itself was a pleasure when it was you I was teasing so unmercifully. No, it was the extreme pleasure of watching your clever mind find the perfect defense to the problems I would propose. I've tried for years to catch you out! I believe the score is twenty-five to the eh' and zero to the gy'."

"A game?" Nick whispered.

The gy' gestured vaguely with his tail. "A game of pleasure, eh'Nicodemus. One can take pleasure in the interplay of two minds just as much as the interplay of two bodies. And I've so enjoyed playing with your mind."

"You son of a bitch!" Nick gasped. "All this time, I thought you wanted to mate with me!"

gy'Bagrada belched, and his air gills fluttered. "Oh, I do, eh'Nicodemus. That I do. We Gunera have always had a certain curiosity of other species. Perhaps it's the sameness of our own biology and the exoticness of yours. We find the concept of multiple genders fascinating. But if the choice is to drive you away from me screaming in terror for fear that I might assault your body or keep you within reach so that I might tinker with your mind, I choose the latter. I would take both if you'd grant me the pleasure."

"I think not," Nick said weakly.

gy'Bagrada's hands ran across Nick's chest suggestively. "At this moment, you're not in a position to deny either of my desires, eh'. I can have both your mind and your body if I wish."

"The body's a little broken," Nick grumbled, "and the mind isn't far behind."

The gy' gave him a gentle pat. "Yes, true, on both accounts. We'll have to investigate the possibility of mating with minds or bodies at a future date when you're better able to engage in the coupling. In the meantime, we have the problem of what do to with you."

"Indeed," Nick said.

"I can't call for a physician. I assume the mai' is aware that you're desperately in need of medical care. Any house, even one as highly placed as mine, that calls for a physician tonight will be suspect. What can you tell me so that we can treat you?"

Nick blinked in no little surprise. "I can barely breathe, gy'. This conversation is very unpleasant."

The gy's tail twitched as if Nick's comment had caught him aback. He barked an order at a hovering eh' who disappeared down one of the bolt holes. Within seconds the eh' returned bearing a bottle of cristi, the Gunera's favored alcohol distilled from the heart of baribari leaves. It was wicked and caustic. Nick had only ever tried it once, years earlier, having stolen a glass while cleaning up after a party. He'd never made the same mistake twice.

"Drink this," gy'Bagrada insisted.

Nick turned his face away. In response, the gy's tail wrapped around Nick's shoulders and dragged him upright even against the soft scream of pain. He forced the bottle to Nick's lips.

"Drink this," the gy' repeated. "It's not often I provide relief rather than pain. I don't dare send for more proper medicines. My staff and the mai' would question why gy'Bagrada had requested objects that relieve suffering rather than cause it. Drink."

Appalled by the rancid smell, Nick tried to twist away.

The gy' took matters into his own hands, forcing Nick's jaw open with one and pouring the drink down his throat with the other. The vile brew scorched his esophagus as Nick coughed uncontrollably, resulting in more pain.

"Don't fight this, and it will go better," gy'Bagrada growled.

Aware that gy'Bagrada always got what he wanted, even by force, Nick ended his resistance and swallowed the entire contents of the small bottle. Satisfied, the gy' lay Nick flat against the cushions and handed the empty bottle back to the eh'. He then turned to his eh's. "Move a cushion chair close to the table so that I may sit down." The gy' placed both hands in a neutral position on his knees and stood, tail raised in the air, in an attempt to soothe his troubled guest.

The cristi worked at Nick's brain, settling into the dorsal posterior insula where it dulled his pain and softened his thinking. gy'Bagrada issued more orders. Nick sensed movers whirring from the room. As he drowsed in a half-drugged state, various Gunera handed equipment to the gy'. Through the swirl of cristi, Nick watched while the gy' fiddled with an object resembling a wristwatch. It was black with an elastic strap. gy'Bagrada grasped Nick's right hand, slipped the object over his wrist, and tightened it. He placed a second identical object on Nick's left wrist.

"What?" Nick asked softly. His breathing was relaxed now that the pain receptors in his brain were numb.

"Disrupters," gy'Bagrada stated, patting the closer of Nick's two wrists. "I can't remove your implants without removing your hands, and I don't think either of us want me to do that." The gy's eyes twisted strangely, and he grinned at Nick. "The units will keep the searchers at bay."

"Your own staff," Nick murmured.

"Indeed." Nick realized the gy' was laughing. "An interesting test of their abilities, don't you think?"

"It's not just me you enjoying playing games with, gy'," Nick whispered.

"Indeed." gy'Bagrada settled himself on his cushion and gave his guest a frank look. "I think, now that we have you reasonably comfortable and out of immediate danger, you should tell me how you arrived in this appalling condition. What horrible insult did you throw at the mai'?"

"You don't know?" Nick tried to adjust his body into a more comfortable position, but there wasn't one. Movement disrupted Nick's breathing, and his limbs, courtesy of the cristi, refused to obey him.

"I know that you were brought here to deal with the fallout of the teg'Lincoln affair. You were to finish the negotiations that he'd begun."

"Do you know what those negotiations were about?" Nick asked.

The gy' looked insulted. "I'm the head of security, eh'Nicodemus. I can read every word of every communication that moves within the empire, including yours." He grinned. "Including those that you always believed you composed in code. How's the replication situation with eh'Kraghilg coming along?"

In his half-drugged stupor, Nick wished he could deny the gy's claim, but the cristi had nullified that option. Another deep sector of

Nick's brain was annoyed that gy'Bagrada had broken the code and had read with pleasure every word he'd ever written. It galled him.

"I was waiting with bated breath for you to answer eh'Kraghilg's queries regarding your own reproduction," the gy' continued. "Quite curious to understand how humans do it. Perhaps while remaining as my guest, you might find time to enlighten me."

"There's no way in hell that's going to happen."

The gy' shrugged. "It was worth the asking. You humans seem strangely squeamish about a natural function."

"I'm not discussing it," Nick growled. Even drugged, it was one topic he wasn't about to address.

"No matter. Now isn't the time." He gave Nick another friendly pat. "I take great pleasure in reading your material," he commented. "And in the brilliance of the codes the two of you developed. You have an exquisite mind."

"Then you know everything," Nick whispered. "Including what occurred in the Palace of the Mai'."

"I know that the mai' demanded your attendance at an audience today to, I assume, sign the final documents. I don't know why he elected to torture you. You arrived at my doorstep before I had a chance to read my end-of-day briefs."

"I refused to sign."

"Why?" asked the gy' in surprise.

"Because they're a horror!" Nick's anger was so strong that he tried to again rise on his elbows, but the stabs of pain were too overwhelming.

gy'Bagrada tutted and tapped his uninjured shoulder soothingly.

"The agreement ends the Balance Protocols!" Nick protested. "It ends everything I've defended for the past decade. It lays humanity open to the depredations of Gunera."

"All true."

"How can you ask why I refused to sign it?"

"I couldn't conceive a legal reason why you couldn't. Knowing how your mind works, I assumed once you'd exhausted every possible nuance to avoid signing, you would accede."

"As I said, the document is a horror."

"For humans, true. But a legal horror."

"I won't surrender humanity to the Gunera!" Nick asserted. Yet again, he attempted to rise, but this time, the gy's tail wrapped around his neck and gently forced him flat. Nick's brain fought for equilibrium, to find logic in the pool of alcohol in which it was swimming.

"Have you a choice?"

Nick tried to focus on the law, on not just the convoluted annexes and schedules of the Protocols but of the human legal system itself. "A single agency of the Western Alliance cannot accede the sovereignty of humans as a whole with the stroke of a pen. Such an agreement could come only from the Legislature after surviving a veto of the President, not that any such agreement would ever get that far."

"You're stating that for all the assertions by Lincoln Combs and your State Department representative, Johans Sprouse, to the contrary, that the document may not be legal?"

"That's correct."

"That's a problem," the gy' commented thoughtfully. "How would your government respond were such an illegal document tendered to it?"

Nick considered laughing, but it hurt too much. "If they were feeling charitable, they'd laugh at it. Not so charitable, they'd round up the conspirators and execute every last one of them."

"Including you."

"Most definitely me."

"We can't have that. I couldn't face a universe devoid of your lively mind." He poked Nick's face gently with his tail barb. "Are you sure the document is a fraud? teg'Lincoln seemed certain it was legal."

"Difficult to say. The legislature should have issued its authorization, but the president has a measure of latitude in his control over State and could claim executive privilege. It depends on how high up the chain of command the agreement actually goes. Were the president the deciding force, it might be valid, but many opponents would protest. We're talking years of court cases and appeals. I'm not sure who would win."

"The Gunera would hold it as legal and demand its every stipulation be followed."

"A total mess," Nick sighed.

"Outright war if the Gunera demanded compliance," stated the gy'. "The mai' wouldn't take kindly to a binding agreement being voted down in conference. We'd wage war against humanity." The gy' issued a deep belch of annoyance. "War with humanity while the Amaurau stood looking over our shoulders, waiting and drooling for their chance."

"Just what the Amaurau have been positioning for," Nick replied. "They have skin in the game."

The gy' looked at Nick with concern. "In what way?"

"The appearance at the renewal ceremony. They sought me out deliberately. They poisoned Duncan Huntzinger to assure that I'd be there in his place."

"No."

Nick frowned at the simply proffered statement. *"No?"*

"It was I who poisoned the messenger," gy'Bagrada stated. "And for no other reason than to enjoy an evening in your presence, eh'Nicodemus. No grand schemes to rule the universe. Just an old gy' lusting for his young human's presence. A chance to lay tail on you once again. I'm aghast that it played into the hands of the birds."

"Then Ississita lied to me."

"Birds do that from time to time," gy'Bagrada said dryly. "We Gunera tend to be honest."

"They poisoned me in the woods," Nick mumbled, losing sight of who was who and what had happened when.

"Again, no."

Nick found gy'Bagrada's hand twisting into his hair and playing with it. The sensation was discomforting, and Nick wished he could escape. *"No?"*

"That was vuh'Yguggli's ploy. He wanted to know where you stood since we were forced to take you in place of teg'Lincoln. He didn't trust me when I assured him that you would follow the law. You're such an honest thing." The gy's stubby fingers stroked Nick's head as if he could touch the very thoughts he coveted.

"Is there anything you *don't* know?"

The quip earned him a belch from the gy', and his fingers gently stroked Nick's face. "There's nothing I don't know, except how you managed to make yourself a gift to me in my very own lift," he chuckled. "Or how to treat your injuries. They're serious, eh'Nicodemus."

"I'm not sure I can help you."

"Your bones are broken in your chest. Can they heal themselves, or do they require replacement?"

"Human bones heal on their own if set properly, assuming I don't go into shock or develop a fever. Those are imminent dangers, gy'."

"And the wound to your shoulder?"

"More worrisome if it becomes infected."

The gy' sighed. "Then there's no hope for tending you here. You must be treated by human physicians." He laid a hand over Nick's eyes and pressed them closed. "Rest easy, beloved," he murmured. "Allow me to tend to you. Your friend eh'Kraghilg was not wrong to send you to me."

Nick wanted to protest, but the gy's fingers were gently stroking his eyelids. It was an uncharacteristically tender gesture from a man Nick knew tortured his enemies before breakfast. Much as he wanted to fight handing his life over to gy'Bagrada, the cristi in his system was enervating his entire body. The soft touch of the gy's fingers over Nick's tense facial muscles was surprisingly soothing. Against his will, his instincts, his very desire for survival, Nick drifted. On the Lake of Cristi, Nick sailed, his body and his life a vessel helmed by gy'Bagrada's seafaring hands.

13

The sailing wasn't pleasant. As he'd predicted, a fever caught Nick, no small surprise in a hothouse atmosphere that boiled with fungus, mold, and bacteria. Before nightfall, it took him completely, and he tossed fitfully as its fingers dug deep into his bones. Even in that torrid heat, Nick shivered, feeling cold to his very soul before the fever shifted and he was bathed in sweat and desperate for anything to cool his body. Lacking the medical know-how to treat his patient, gy'Bagrada could offer no solace to Nick save additional cristi regimens. The liquid failed to work. Nick's fever raged unabated, causing him to twist his body in agony to the point where gy'Bagrada ordered him bound to the table to prevent self-injury.

Although the gy' had numerous textbooks on human disembowelment, he had no resources on human reconstruction. Fearful that a Guneri analgesic might be poisonous, gy'Bagrada adhered to cristi, though this decision was not without risk. Nick's pain prevented him from resting. He thrashed as much as a bound body was able and babbled incoherently, terrifying those within the house. The gy' bound Nick's mouth to stifle his cries. Soon thereafter, the gy' scuttled to the forward areas of the palace to speak with his staff about the search for the very man who lay dying a mere handful of steps away. Had Nick been able to think coherently, he'd have realized the terror his anguish was causing. No one knew what might happen if gy'Bagrada's own men discovered that he was hiding and protecting the fugitives.

At some point in the darkest period of night, when most of the house should have fallen silent but, instead, were awake in tense anticipation for something to break, lucidity returned to Nick. Blinking away his eye sweat, Nick found gy'Bagrada and Jason sitting beside his makeshift bed. The lights had been lowered to provide the illusion that the gy' was asleep while the search for the escaped humans continued outside. *The gy' looks gray,* Nick thought with a pucker of his brows. *Gray and old and very tired.*

"I'm dying," Nick whispered, aware that his mouth was no longer bound.

gy'Bagrada nodded. "Yes, eh'Nicodemus. Yet there's nothing I can do."

"Let me go."

The gy' stopped his gills as he listened to some sound that Nick couldn't hear. "The searchers are tearing the city apart," the Gunera said after a moment of silence. "They're even ripping into the dark levels, under the false belief that the stone is blocking your signals."

Nick's gaze flicked to the two disruptors strapped to his wrists. "I don't want the eh's harmed."

"They won't be harmed," gy'Bagrada said absently. "Rousted, woken, shaken, annoyed. But not harmed. Unless my men find them up to something they shouldn't be up to."

Nick glanced at Jason who, clueless as to what was being said, sat silently next to the gy'. "See my companion safely away," Nick pleaded.

"I'll see both of you safely away," gy'Bagrada replied. He tapped Nick's lips with a finger to silence the protest he knew was approaching. "Hush, dear one. I have no choice. If you die in this house, I'll be required to relinquish your body to my men and surrender myself for arrest. I'll have not only assisted in a prison break but will have allowed an alien emissary to die when I could have prevented it by escorting you to a medical center. I'll have committed treason twice over. You must live, eh'Nicodemus, to return to your people and to find those of yours who have broken the laws of your planet."

"Do you care?"

"Of human laws? Of course. The law is the law in whatever land it dwells. If your law has been broken and I have reason to know it, I am honor bound to see justice done." The gy' used his tail to wipe the sweat from Nick's brow. "So you see, it isn't just a silly old gy's lust for a young mind that makes me determined to save you. There are deeper issues involved."

Nick wanted to ask what those deeper issues might be, but his mind drifted as another wave of fever threatened. He could feel the cold edging into his bones, and his body started to helplessly shiver. The nightmares soon returned, and Nick moaned, wishing he could escape from them, from Gunera, from his very existence.

I'm going to die on gy'Bagrada's table, he told his mother, who stood beside him in the dream.

You should, she replied. *Death's as good an escape as any other.*

How can you say such a thing to your son?

I have no son! That horrid creature I belched from my body has abandoned me. No son of mine is he.

Mama, Nick pleaded, *it was you who sent me away, who wanted your son to be free.*

No mother wishes to be left to die alone and friendless. You were an evil child, an evil boy! I hate your very name.

Mama! Mama! Please don't leave me! Please don't tell me even you don't love me!

The sense of being manipulated tore Nick from the awful dream, and he screamed as he was lifted. gy'Bagrada was on Nick's left side, his tail holding Nick's body while Jason supported Nick's head with both hands. gy'Tikategra, with the help of two bah's, wrapped clear plastic around Nick's torso.

Nick blinked blearily. "Bubble wrap?"

"It will keep your ribs protected from additional blows," Jason explained. "It's the best these snakes could come up with. Apparently, the head snake has a lot of it lying around."

"He ships contraband," Nick mumbled. "Sells illegal crap back to those who try to smuggle it in."

Once the packing material was taped in place, the two carefully lowered Nick once more.

"Better?" asked gy'Bagrada.

"If I was a porcelain plate, I'd probably thank you."

The gy' belched. "You *are* a porcelain plate. A porcelain plate of great value that we don't wish broken further. Quickly!" gy'Bagrada said to his eh's. "Take eh'Nicodemus to my nest."

Immediately the two eh's advanced. One took Nick by the shoulders while the other grasped Nick's legs. Together the two lifted him while Jason held Nick's mouth shut so that he couldn't scream. Nick felt the uncoordinated movement of the three beings as they scurried him into gy'Bagrada's nest room. The group froze when the gy' trundled into the room on just his three feet. He threw himself into his nest then reached out with his tail.

"Pass him through, then place that one where not even the ghosts of Dakindil might find him!"

Nick felt the interchange of tails as he was swiftly drawn into the nest. He sensed more than he saw. The cocoon swallowed him up, then he was nestled into its fine feather down. He was still fighting a fever and lashed weakly, but gy'Bagrada had no problem holding him still. A hand placed over Nick's mouth muffled further screams.

"Three men have entered my residence," the gy' whispered. "They don't believe I'm sleeping, damn them! I trained my own men too well!"

Nick nodded. He could imagine the surprise on the part of gy'Bagrada's security forces should they discover that their leader had taken to his nest during a crisis. Such was not in character for gy'Bagrada. Nick froze when he heard movers whirring into the nestroom, and he felt gy'Bagrada's body tense against his back. The fingers involuntarily tightened over his mouth. Nick stifled a reaction to having his breathing cut off. The lights in the room began to glow.

With a grunt of anger, gy'Bagrada released Nick and crawled to the nest opening. His tail barb poked Nick hard in the breastbone, a clear indication for Nick to stay put and keep quiet.

"Have you lost your minds?" the gy' demanded as he trundled into the center of his nestroom, acting very much the disgruntled lord. Nick heard a familiar whap and knew that gy's tail had walloped one of his men.

"You ordered us to search the entire city," a soldier announced. "We've searched every residence except this one."

"You dare think I would hide a fugitive? In my own nestroom?" gy'Bagrada exploded.

"We're merely obeying *your* orders, esteemed gy'," another trooper replied.

The gy' trundled to his nest and sat down in the center of the opening, effectively denying his men access to it. Lying behind him in the depths of the nest, Nick tensed as he struggled to remain quiet. The shivers had returned, forcing Nick to bite his own fingers to keep from moaning. gy'Bagrada quietly circled his tail around Nick's neck and he suddenly realized he might die of asphyxiation if the gy' deemed it necessary. Shaking with cold, Nick felt the sweat pour off his face while the search continued. gy'Bagrada remained motionless. Finally, the sounds of movement settled.

"Leave this residence now," the gy' said to his men. "I'm going back to nest."

"Aren't you concerned about the fugitives?" asked one of the searchers.

"I am," snorted the gy', "but at this moment, I am beyond exhausted. Continue the search and find those fugitives. You have my permission to wake me when you do."

Nick heard muttering, but the words weren't audible. Clearly, gy'Bagrada's men found his behavior bizarre, but they had no excuse to search the depths of his nest. After a few more minutes of tense standoff, the gy's men finally relented, and Nick heard their movers heading for the door.

Acting on the pretense he had nothing to fear, gy'Bagrada climbed into the nest. The only way for the two to fit was if the gy' pressed against Nick's back, positioning his mouth in Nick's ear.

"You're enjoying this," Nick muttered.

The gy' chuckled as his short arms encircled Nick's shoulders. "Indeed. Rest now, eh'Nicodemus, while I think. My men are suspicious and will be watching this house. I have much to consider."

"What are you going to do with me? Do you still intend to smuggle me off-world?"

"Indeed. My staff has completed its study and determined that the mai' acted illegally in taking you prisoner and torturing you."

"But not in breaking the Protocols?" Nick asked.

"No, that lies within his purview. I can't say I disagree with his concept, but I question his ultimate conclusions. He makes a rather broad assumption that we'll simply overwhelm the Amaurau in a surprise move. The mai' ignores his own security briefings. The Amaurau have not been idle all these years, happily hiding behind humanity's skirts. While we've been developing the Gogarag stardrive, they've been working on biologicals."

"A fast way to spread disease," Nick murmured, contemplating what could happen if the Amaurau infected empire-traveling Gunera.

"We'd be injecting ourselves," gy'Bagrada growled. "Frightening thought. That's why I believe it's in the best interest of the empire to delay ratifying these new Accords. So, until the duly appointed Messenger of the humans can assure me that the Accords are legal, I must uphold the current Protocols." The gy's arms tightened around Nick, and his breath caressed Nick's ear. "You aren't in a position to assure the Accords are legal, are you, duly appointed Messenger?"

Even against the pain, Nick laughed. "No."

"Good. I assumed not. I'll file a protest stating that teg'Nicodemus Severin, Messenger of the Protocols, has attested in my presence that he cannot vouch for the legality of the document. That should give our esteemed mai' something to chew on while we ready your escape."

"Is that your intention?" Nick asked, still fearful that gy'Bagrada would take him for his own.

"After much consideration, my staff and I have concluded that we are within our rights to take possession of you against the orders of the mai'. We may legally return you to your rightful owners on Rhadamanthus. While I am, for personal reasons, reluctant to do this, I know you're in desperate need of medical care by your own physicians. To do otherwise would endanger you unnecessarily. It is my hope, beloved eh'Nicodemus, that you will look upon my gracious act and will be more forthcoming in our future engagements. I will so look forward to seeing you again, on your feet, with your mind at work."

Nick swallowed, hating that he was going to be beholden to the gy'. He was certain gy'Bagrada would exploit that debt to the best of his ability.

"I assume the day will come when you will demand repayment," Nick muttered.

The gy's tail barb gently touched Nick's face. "I will. You already know what I'll demand of you."

Encircled by the gy's arms and bound around the ribs in bubble wrap, Nick nevertheless managed a shudder. "We'll have to negotiate that demand."

"No negotiations. My price is set." The gy' gave him a gentle shake. "Try to rest, eh'Nicodemus. I need to think."

The gy' fell silent. Beyond the nest, the house also fell into tense, watchful waiting, all its inhabitants awake, alert, and nervous in the dark, ready for the ax to fall. Everyone knew the security service of which their lord was master had turned its baleful eye inward. Nick's fever overtook him yet again, and his mind drifted.

He woke to the sound of raised voices. A jolt of fear shot through his chest as he lay curled in a ball inside gy'Bagrada's nest while the agitated conversation continued in the room beyond. To Nick's dismay, the outline of a Gunera loomed in the opening, silhouetted by the faint light of dawn. Nick was pulled from the nest, neither gently nor particularly roughly, and deposited on the display table that had been his bed.

"Well, well, well. I must say I am surprised!"

The voice made Nick cringe. With a sinking sense of doom, Nick gazed at gy'Gravinda in all his finery. As their eyes met, Nick was sure his stomach had sunk to the floor. The ambassador, however, said nothing further to Nick but shot his fellow gy' a sly glance.

"I know you lust after humans and have a special desire for eh'Nicodemus, but don't you think stealing him from the mai' is going a little too far?" the ambassador asked.

gy'Bagrada jutted his tail directly in the air in indignation, and his air gills swept with frantic speed. "The one has nothing to do with the other."

"Humpff!" snorted the ambassador. "An awful lot of bother for one silly human." He glanced in annoyance at gy'Bagrada. "I hope you've checked every code and assured every document is in order. I don't like sticking out my tail like this."

gy'Bagrada issued an evil grin. "I devoted most of my staff to studying the legality of this endeavor, and I can assure you that all is in order as far as ownership of eh'Nicodemus and teg'Jason is concerned."

gy'Gravinda huffed. "I care nothing for teg'Jason. I'll see him off-world without a care. It's eh'Nicodemus who worries me. He's legally a citizen and vuh'Yguggli's slave, and I don't like crossing a man of his rank."

"We've hit a gray area in the law," gy'Bagrada said. "There's a section in the emigration statutes regarding the renouncement of citizenship, not that anyone has ever considered doing so. My staff believes eh'Nicodemus can renounce."

gy'Gravinda twitched his tail. "You'd best be right, gy'Bagrada! I'm not handing the mai' my tail to cut off so that you can lust after the vuh's property!"

"I'm taking all the risk."

"Using my name!" exclaimed gy'Gravinda.

"You'll be well paid," gy'Bagrada growled. "You're in no danger. There's only one authority under which such shipments fall. Mine. I assure you, there will be no investigation into why gy'Gravinda is shipping household goods to Hemera."

"Why must you use my name? Why can't you use your own?"

"At this moment, I am under suspicion from my own security forces. My people will be all over any shipment I attempt to send. No one, however, will suspect you. You, esteemed gy'," gy'Bagrada added with acid sarcasm, "are above reproach."

"I still don't know why I shouldn't call the mai', have you arrested, hand these creatures back to their rightful owners, and return happily to my nest!"

gy'Bagrada glared. "You have as much to lose as I do if the Protocols fall, gy'. You'll lose your position as ambassador. You'll lose your easy access to the shipping of contraband into human space. Don't look so shocked! Of course I know all about your little side business. Nothing leaves Gunera without my knowledge. I know you make a small fortune in your illicit spice trade."

gy'Gravinda stabbed hatefully at gy'Bagrada with his barb. "As if you don't sell illegal contraband back to those people who sought to export it!"

"You can lose the sense of outrage, gy'. I'm paying handsomely for the use of your bloody name."

gy'Gravinda snorted. "Damn right you are. There had best not be a single problem with an export seal or a tax stamp on any shipment of mine for the next ten years, or I'll be having a long conversation with the mai' about you."

"Try me!" shouted gy'Bagrada.

"Can we stop fighting?" Nick asked weakly. "The two of you are giving me a headache."

Nick's soft statement was so shocking to the two Guneri lords that they fell silent. They stared at Nick for a moment, each looking as chagrinned as a Gunera was capable of appearing.

gy'Bagrada lashed his tail in irritation, but he grudgingly agreed that the acrimony was pointless. "Were you able to get the supplies?" he asked.

gy'Gravinda issued a scathing look. "Of course. The containers are per specification. It took some doing finding the suits. I also filed the intent to ship. Are you sure you'll get the transships through to Eventide dockside?"

"Don't be insulting when we've just started working together. The paperwork will go through."

"Then let's finish this. You woke me out of a sound sleep!"

"I'm surprised you're aware of the fact," snorted gy'Bagrada. "It seems a sound sleep is your natural state of being!"

"Just stop!" Nick moaned. He pressed a hand to his forehead, wishing to end the pain.

Once again, the two lords fell silent and glared at Nick. They did, however, agree that the fighting was counterproductive.

"You understand, of course, that the plot will be useless if eh'Nicodemus dies on route," gy'Gravinda complained. "Have you given any thought to the fact that the human's condition is precarious?"

gy'Bagrada sneered. "While you have taken your blessed time about the containers, I've obtained appropriate stasis medication that should hold eh'Nicodemus to Eventide."

"I hope you purchased human compatible," grumbled gy'Gravinda.

"You must really think me a fool to issue such a statement," snapped gy'Bagrada.

A silence filled the room, broken only by Nick. "What are you going to do?" he asked.

gy'Bagrada beamed. "We can't book passage on a commercial flight, obviously. So we're sending you out standard freight."

Nick fell silent. He lay blinking at the two lords, thinking them both totally insane.

Jason must have figured out what the two conniving Gunera were planning because he dug through the containers and presented a pair of environment suits.

"Tell me they aren't sending us home as someone's set of fine china," he complained, looking to Nick.

"Apparently, they are."

The big man frowned. "This is going to be fun."

gy'Gravinda instructed Jason to change out of his clothing and don one of the environment suits as gy'Bagrada, along with a contingent of eh's, eased Nick into the second suit.

"How is this going to work?" Nick asked between painful breaths.

"We're going to place you in stasis," gy'Bagrada stated. "You'll sleep until you reach your destination."

A wave of panic washed through Nick. He and Jason would be helpless, unconscious until someone opened the crates. "Where will you be shipping us?" he demanded, trying to sit upright. The gy's tail wrapped across Nick's neck, shoving him flat while the eh's continued to gingerly maneuver his body into the suit. "*Who* are you shipping us to? You have to have a name, gy', or my office will reject the shipment!"

The gy' patted Nick's shoulder. "No worries, dear one. We're shipping you to yourself. Your name is on the receiving slips. I hope you'll remember to sign the receipt of goods when you awaken. We wouldn't want the esteemed Secretary of International Trade and Commerce breaking his own regulations, would we?"

"Wait. What?" Nick had barely managed to spout out the words before a helmet was placed over his head. He continued to protest even as the eh's set him in the shipping crate. He watched as a tube was hooked from the crate to his suit. The hiss of gasses followed. Nick tried to fight, to escape, but it was too late. A sedative in the gasses drove him down, down, down, into a deep slumber.

14

Nick floated on a cloud of light. His body wafted in the ethers, not a part of him in any pain. That blessed space was eternal, without time, without thought. He didn't care if he ever returned to consciousness. Yet with a crash, he found himself unpacked, the lid of his shipping crate torn open, immediately disconnecting his medicated atmosphere and jarring him awake. Through his Plexiglas helmet, he saw distorted faces hovering and hands reaching down to detach the helmet.

"Nick!" a familiar voice cried. "Good God, they weren't kidding!"

Nick blinked and found himself looking up at the shocked face of Corey Boyers. He took a deep and painful breath, a grim reminder of the injuries he'd sustained. Nick smiled but had neither the breath nor the wits to respond.

Jason appeared next to Corey. The man's dark visage was strained, a heavy frown between his brows.

"Are you still alive?" he asked.

"Possibly," Nick whispered. "I'm not sure."

Corey attempted to help Nick rise to a sitting position, but he was stopped by Jason.

"He's injured," Jason explained. "A bad wound in his left shoulder and a few broken ribs."

Corey frowned but then asked for a pallet runner. "Call for a medic!" he shouted.

When the pallet runner and a medic arrived, Corey grasped Nick's legs while Jason took his shoulders, and the two men lifted him onto the table of the pallet runner. Then they eased Nick out of the environment suit. Nick bit his lip, not wanting to scream in front of a dozen stoic dockworkers who dealt with discomfort on a daily basis. Once he was unpacked, the medic, who introduced himself as Dr. Tom Abrams and who looked as if he'd only recently completed his residency, ordered the bubble wrapping cut away.

"Damn, that was a clever way to get you out of Gunera!" Corey breathed as he watched the unpacking. "Half of the Rhadamanthan Commerce Department was suggesting ways to rescue you, but no one thought of shipping you in a packing crate."

"What are you doing here?" Nick asked, wincing as the wrapping was pulled from his back.

Corey squatted to face Nick. "I've been worried sick about you, buddy. As soon as your mission went to hell, Duncan contacted me. Since Gemini Space sits on the border, he hoped we could help, although none of my managers had any ideas. Then we received a dispatch to be on the watch for you. Sometime later, a packet arrived at Eventide dock listing you as the recipient of crates inbound from Gunera. My folks notified me, and I flew here to check out the contents. I had no idea I'd find you and Jason in them."

Nick looked beyond Corey's shoulder to see a dark, echoing space. In the shadows lurked stacks of packing crates and a pile of cordage. The space was frigid, and he longed for the protective comfort of the bubble wrapping.

"Where am I?"

"Like I said, Eventide transshipment dock. Gunera side." Corey turned to Dr. Abrams. "How is he?"

"Couple of broken ribs and bad lacerations," the medic replied. "Once we get him to the clinic, I can disinfect the wounds and do a closer assessment of the rib damage." Dr. Abrams snatched a shipping blanket from a nearby crate and tossed it over Nick to keep him warm. It smelled of mildew, but Nick didn't care.

"Let's go." Dr. Abrams gestured to the aide operating the pallet runner.

"I can walk," Nick complained, realizing they were threatening to ship him around the dock works like commercial cargo. "I refuse to be gy'Gravinda's household china for one minute longer."

Nick had barely risen onto shaky legs when an alarm throbbed through the station. While Jason kept Nick upright and Dr. Abrams searched his bag for pain medication, Corey rushed to one of the system monitors.

"You're not going to believe this, but three Guneri ships are approaching," he exclaimed. "They aren't scheduled."

"That explains the alarm. What kind of ships?" Jason asked grimly.

"Warrior class."

"This dock is unarmed," Dr. Abrams said, injecting Nick with a fentanyl derivative.

"I know that! It's my dock, remember?" Corey glanced at Nick. "They're after you, aren't they?"

"We can't let them take him back," Jason said, answering for Nick, who was already feeling the effects of the opioid.

"Why do they want Nick?" Corey asked.

"They want him to commit treason. Sign a new accord, ending the Protocols," Jason said. "He's refused."

Corey's eyes darted to Nick. "You refused the Guneri emperor?"

Nick issued a weak nod. His vision blurred, and his eyes insisted on closing. Jason gripped Nick's arms to keep him upright.

"What the hell do we do?" Corey asked no one in particular. "This dock wasn't designed for defense."

"Call for Alliance craft," Jason said. "Should be a carrier group in the vicinity. We keep one group in every sector."

"I'll call," Corey mumbled as he turned to his monitor. "I doubt they'll arrive in time."

As if to prove his point, a deep boom echoed through the dock. Even through the mist of painkillers, Nick sensed the metal hull straining.

"We're being fired on!" Corey exclaimed. "Damn them! Are they unhinged?"

"They're willing to face sanctions to get those accords signed," Jason growled.

"We're not talking sanctions; we're talking war!" Corey frantically vid-called the Alliance. "They're firing on an unarmed dock! My dad's going to flame Venus!" Another explosion shook the dock. Corey gripped the console and peered at the monitors, sweat beading on his brow. "What are we supposed to do? Send Nick back?"

"Are you insane?" Jason cuffed Corey. "We can't hand the Secretary of International Trade back to the Gunera, Mr. Boyers."

Nick frowned, trying to think through the mussiness as Corey stared blindly at Jason. Jason returned the stare and clenched a fist at the suddenly frozen corporate vice president.

"Is Duncan actually dead?" Nick managed.

"Yes," Corey replied with a strange flick of his eyes. "Heart attack. How did you know?"

"The Gunera killed him," Nick murmured, "with Amaurau poisons."

"No. Duncan had a heart attack."

"Murder," Nick insisted, slurring the word.

"We'll talk about it later. Assuming we survive," Corey said.

The dock was hit a third time.

"God!" Corey gasped as the floor bucked beneath his feet. He peered at the monitor. "We're getting a demand from the Gunera. *'Surrender illegal cargo shipped out of Gunera. Will board and take by force if necessary.'*"

"What? They didn't think your people would open the crates?" Jason asked. "They think you don't know what was inside?"

Corey flailed. "How do I know what they think? They're firing on an unarmed transshipment dock! Two bays have already blown. Jesus!" Corey glanced at the monitor with alarm. He opened a channel and began shouting orders. "Evacuate the inbound Guneri bays! Lock down the blast doors. What have we got outbound to Amaurau?"

Corey waited and listened while he received his report.

"Okay, I want as many people as possible on any freighter in working order. No! No! Evacuate everyone out of the Amaurau bays too. As soon as a section is cleared, launch and get those freighters out of here." He turned back to Dr. Abrams. "How's Nick looking?"

The physician stowed the empty syringe. "The narcotic should hold him. He won't feel much for the next several hours. The ribs should be treated with a fuser, but ultrasound fusion takes about twenty minutes per bone, so we're probably looking at two hours or more."

Corey shuddered as more explosions rattled the dock. "I don't think we have two hours."

"Then I'd suggest we run!" Jason growled.

Another deep boom hit the dock. Cargo tumbled. Jason's hand tightened on Nick's arm as they stumbled toward the exit. Nick staggered to keep pace with Jason, determined not to be a burden.

"The *Julius Summerton* just launched," Corey gasped as he listened to the cacophony of messages over the commlink.

"How many freighters were on the dock?" Jason asked.

"Three. Two more to launch, then the bulk of the staff should be safe … hopefully. I can't believe the Gunera would sick their warships on unarmed merchant vessels in human territory. Then again, I wouldn't have expected them to attack Eventide either."

"Where's the nearest freighter?" Jason asked. "We've got to get Nick off this thing."

"You can't send this man into space on a freighter!" Dr. Abrams exclaimed, panting as he raced with them toward the Amaurau side of the docks. "He needs to be treated in the clinic."

"There won't be a clinic in a few minutes, doc," Jason replied.

"I arrived here on a corporate jet," Corey puffed, hand pressed to his ear as he listened to an announcement that the second freighter had launched successfully.

Jason glanced at Nick for approval. "We're taking the jet. Now," he stated.

Alone in the huge corridors of the transshipment docks, while the alarms sounded and the automatic system relayed the number of bays that had been breached, the quartet raced as quickly as Nick's rubbery legs allowed. Corey appeared to be in shock. Dr. Abrams took the lead just as a new alarm sounded.

"A Guneri ship is attempting to dock without authorization," Corey stammered.

"Can they do that?" Jason asked.

"If they want to. There's nothing to stop them. We're the only ones left on Eventide."

"Goddammit," Jason said, continuing to run.

"It'll take them a while to track us down," Dr. Abrams gasped. "This dock is the size of a city."

"I'm not taking any chances," Jason insisted. They hit a long, open corridor, and Jason hoisted Nick onto his shoulder and broke into a full run.

They pelted through corridors and passages, dropped down via a lift to one of the lower levels that spat them out at a small airlock. Nick saw the tube that linked the corporate jet to the transshipment dock.

Jason shoved Corey ahead of him. "Tell the pilot to fire up! We're jetting out full burn the moment we're all inside."

Corey stumbled into the tube. Dr. Abrams dashed in next.

"Can you do this, sir?" Jason asked as he lowered Nick to the tube opening.

"I got this." Nick felt little except for occasional twinges of pain. He was more concerned about his vision and sense of balance, both of which were deteriorating. But he was damned if he would be the cause of the death of these men. He nodded, focused his full attention on maintaining his stability, and plunged into the tube. Fortunately, Nick could balance with his right hand. His left arm hung useless. Nick's shoulder wound had become inflamed, and his entire left arm was swollen. Nick recalled that the Gunera sometimes rubbed their tail barbs with poisonous sap. *The damned mai'Tegatriktrik's guards must have done just that,* he thought.

At the end of the tube, Nick stumbled into the jet's cabin, a space outfitted as an office rather than a transport. Corey stood and nervously fidgeted as Dr. Abrams pulled Nick inside. The medic unceremoniously dumped Nick onto a seat. At the same time, Jason arrived and slammed the door closed.

A lean pilot in a warship gray jumpsuit peered into the seating area. Jason glimpsed at a name patch that read *Carrigan*. "Is that everyone?"

"Yes," Jason said. "I hope you've readied us for liftoff."

"You might say that. Secure the hatch and buckle in," Carrigan ordered and vanished into the cockpit.

Corey threw himself behind a desk and fastened the harness. "Gotta be harnessed, or the G-forces will send you bounding into a wall ... or several," he explained. Already the small craft was rumbling as the pilot engaged the propulsion engines of *Far Horizons*.

Jason had just finished securing the hatch when Carrigan called out he was hitting burn. Nick heard mechanicals disconnecting. The small cabin gave a tremendous jolt, and the sound of tearing metal followed. The force of being pulled hard against his harness sent a shockwave of agony through Nick. The sudden acceleration threw Jason across the cabin, and he landed hard against the stern wall. Nick attempted to turn his head to see if Jason was unharmed, but the harness, the pull of acceleration, and his malaise prevented even that simple action. He gritted his teeth and hung on.

"We've got company!" complained Carrigan as he sent *Far Horizons* careening away from Eventide.

"How many?" Corey asked while struggling against the gravitational force to raise a tactical on the monitor embedded in the surface of his desk.

"Three," the pilot grunted. The vessel shifted as he sent it into a spin just as the Guneri ships opened fire.

"Take evasive maneuvers," Corey replied without looking up. He glanced across the cabin at Nick and shrugged.

"I ain't a fighter pilot!" Carrigan barked as he turned the ship hard to starboard. Nick's head snapped hard to the right. Jason was being tossed about like a ragdoll.

"They're insane," Corey complained as he sent multiple distress signals to all nearby coordinates. "This is an overt act of war!"

"The mai' is willing to risk war," Nick panted.

"What does the bastard want?"

"Me."

"Fuck that," Jason growled. The big man crawled to a seat near Nick and hauled himself into it. Jason harnessed in before wiping a hand over his dark brow; blood seeped beneath his fingernails.

An explosion rattled the small craft. "They're shooting just over our bow," Carrigan said. "Warning shots."

Jason leaned into the aisle. "Can you retaliate?"

"This is a corporate jet!" Carrigan exclaimed. "Hell no, I can't shoot back."

Explosions caused the jet to shudder. A starboard electrical panel exploded, and gold sparks cascaded through the cabin. Nick closed his eyes as random burning embers singed his skin.

"They're aiming for our engines," Carrigan said. "Another hit like that, and we'll be torn asunder."

"They won't destroy us," Nick said with a strange sense of calm that seemed unreal in the midst of such chaos. "They want me alive." He glanced at Corey's ashen face and then at Jason. "Maybe we'd better let them take me."

"Fuck no," Jason spat. "I didn't just go through hell to pull you out of Gunera only to toss you back."

Corey's gaze darted between the two men. He flinched when another explosion rocked the ship and a second panel ignited. The cabin filled with smoke. "Maybe Nick's right," he said, earning himself a glare from Jason. "They're going to blow us to hell otherwise."

"I am not turning my charge over to the enemy," Jason insisted.

To Nick's surprise, Jason's steely look didn't deter Corey.

"This isn't about you," Corey said. "We have to think about more than just Nick."

Jason clenched his fist. "Don't you even consider it!"

"Incoming!" Carrigan yelled.

Everyone flinched. Nick turned to the small porthole that gave a view of the stars. A huge gray shadow slid past them at very close range.

"It's ours," Dr. Abrams, nose plastered to an adjacent porthole, said in relief. "The *Waterford*. An Alliance destroyer."

Carrigan stabilized his flight path then jabbered with the Alliance ship, demanding protection. The Gunera weren't backing down. Within seconds, they fired on *Waterford*. The shockwaves rattled the jet.

"It's not over yet," Nick said.

Corey projected the tactical on the front wall of the cabin. Nick watched in growing horror as the three Guneri ships engaged the single, larger Alliance vessel.

"*Waterford* reports another three warships are en route," Corey said.

Corey knew the cavalry wouldn't arrive quickly enough. A strafing run caught the little craft across one of its struts and damaged a directional thruster.

"How important was that thruster?" Jason called to Carrigan.

"Not important at all. Unless you want to land."

Carrigan adjusted his pitch and sent *Far Horizons* in an arc, firing the side thrusters in an attempt to elude the Guneri ship and take shelter behind the *Waterford*.

The Gunera were making their move. The war Nick had worked his whole life to avoid began to unfold before his eyes. While *Far Horizons* sought cover, the Guneri ships fired on *Waterford*. The radio filled with distress cries as various stations on *Waterford* called for help. At the same time, *Waterford's* huge batteries opened fire and disintegrated two of the Gunera ships. The third avoided a direct hit, but a string of black holes bloomed along its side. The two vessels were so close. Debris spun off them in a mad dance. *Far Horizons* tried to avoid the cloud of death.

Debris pounded against *Far Horizons*. Nick winced at each sound. A long, screeching whine followed as something scraped along the hull. A second electrical panel exploded, sending sparks into the passenger cabin. Corey sat frozen with panic as, with a grunt, Jason unharnessed himself. He lunged to a door marked "utility cabinet" and withdrew a fire extinguisher. Another explosion pummeled the ship, and he was thrown down into the center of the cabin, losing his grip on the fire extinguisher, which rolled clumsily toward Nick.

With a groan, Nick reached down and grasped the object and doused the sparking panel.

Jason crawled to Nick and retrieved the extinguisher, and issued an appreciative nod before returning to his seat.

More explosions rocked the ship. Nick turned terrified eyes out the porthole to see the side of *Waterford* only meters away. Alarms on the control panel screamed of imminent impact, then *Far Horizons* shuddered with a heart-stopping crash as it skidded into the side of the huge warbird. The entire ship wracked, and the lights failed. Nick ducked at the sound of an explosion behind him as random metal shards shot past him. When Nick glanced through the porthole again, *Waterford* was growing ever distant as *Far Horizons* spun helplessly out of control.

Carrigan fought to stabilize the jet but failed miserably. The stars swung around them wildly as *Far Horizons* continued to tumble.

On the positive side, Nick thought, *we've tumbled our way out of the direct line of fire. Neither* Waterford *nor the Guneri ship, locked in battle, can chase us in free fall away from them.*

No one spoke while Carrigan attempted to reengage two of the damaged thrusters. Minutes became an hour, and still, they drifted aimlessly.

"This is ridiculous," Corey said. "We need to send a distress signal."

"Not happening," Jason said flatly.

"May I ask why?" Dr. Abrams inquired.

"It's highly likely there are more Guneri vessels lurking in the area just waiting to pounce," Jason explained. "We send a distress signal now, they'll be on us like fleas on an alley cat."

Jason helped Carrigan repair the wounded craft, but the worst damage was on the exterior, which they couldn't access. They worked in silent desperation, the cabin lit by dim red emergency lights. Even in the darkness, Nick could see the sweat beading Jason's brow. He knew their situation was beyond bad. The life-support system had been damaged, the cabin was growing cold, yet Jason was sweating.

Nick turned bleak eyes to his friend. "We aren't going to make it, are we?"

Jason grunted as he removed another panel and tried to make sense of the electronic spaghetti within. "Probably not."

Carrigan gave a sudden hoot. "We've got power to two of our thrusters."

"Does that get us out of trouble?" Corey asked.

The pilot cum technician sighed. "Means we can steer. Doesn't mean we've got life support. Without that, we'll freeze to death in a couple of hours."

"Thank you, Mr. Sunshine," Corey complained, staring morosely at his desktop.

A glance out the porthole revealed Carrigan had indeed stabilized the jet because the stars were no longer spinning, but he admitted he had virtually no control otherwise. The main engines were still down. All he had were maneuvering thrusters. Silence descended as the dire situation took root inside each individual psyche. The cabin smelled of burnt circuitry and human fear.

Another hour passed. Nick felt restless and decided he needed to act. He detached his harness and staggered to an empty chair alongside Corey. Nick fell with a groan next to his friend as he considered the information blinking on the desktop. Thoroughly annoyed with Corey, Nick spun the window around to face him and considered options.

"Can we send a distress via vmail?" he asked.

Carrigan shook his head. "We don't have a connection. We're moving out of radio range and on a dead run for nowhere."

Frowning, Nick flicked through the onboard databases. He found a star chart and stared at it with increasing depression. The Eventide dock works had been stationed at the very edge of human territory, in the middle of Lethe's Void. The supernova explosion that had created the nebula had obliterated everything in a ring around it, leaving it empty of habitable worlds. The *Far Horizons* was on a trajectory that would not pass a body of planetary size for three hundred years.

Nick persisted. His daily chore of handling shipping manifests meant he knew every rock and tiny outcropping where a wounded ship could make landfall. He flicked through the charts while wracking his brain for ideas.

"We're not on a dead run for nowhere," Nick said as he oriented the charts. "We're on a dead run for the Triangle."

"Ain't nothing in the Triangle," Corrigan complained. "It's just a cloud of dust left from Lethe's demise."

Nick flipped open another window in search of esoteric information. Fortunately, as he'd expected, the *Far Horizons* had been loaded with the standard pile of corporate software, including a generic encyclopedia. He rummaged through it, periodically blowing into clasped hands that grew increasingly numb from the cold. He looked up to see Corey, Tom, and Jason watching him as if wondering how Nick might magically save them all. Not knowing if he could, Nick turned back to the database. He searched in silence for another ten minutes until he found it.

"Deadwood," he said. The comment was received with blank stares. "It's an asteroid field. Nasty place. The original human colonists named it Deadwood because so many ships were destroyed exploring it."

"Sounds wonderful!" Corey exploded. "If we don't get shot by Gunera or die of hypothermia, we'll be smashed in an asteroid field. Thank you, Nick; great plan."

Nick scowled. "It's more than just an asteroid field. There's an Amaurau forward station located there."

Jason frowned. "Are you sure? I've never heard of an Amaurau base so close to human space."

Nick lifted his brows. "It's there. I've booked freight through it. Trust me, there's not an inhabited closet in the entire nebula I don't know about."

"Are you suggesting we ask for shelter from the Amaurau?" Dr. Abrams asked.

"I'm not suggesting anything. I'm merely pointing out we have a tiny chance to survive this flight, and it's located in Deadwood."

"If we survive the asteroids," Carrigan murmured. "And if the Amaurau don't atomize us."

Nick shrugged and gestured at the star charts. "There's nothing else around us. As you've said, we're on a dead run to nowhere."

His comment was met with silence. Returning to the cockpit, Carrigan set his coordinates for the deadly asteroid field known as Deadwood.

15

Jason found two blankets in a cabinet. He wrapped one around himself and Nick while Dr. Abrams and Corey shared the other. Together the four men huddled against each other for warmth as the cabin grew steadily colder. Even with the huge bulk of Jason's body next to him, Nick felt the ice gather around the tip of his nose and then his ears. He shivered in misery, ribs protesting every breath.

"We'll get out of this, sir," Jason said, sensing Nick's distress. "I've never lost a client."

"I guess I'm going to be your first," Nick replied.

Jason didn't answer.

Each man sat alone with his thoughts, waiting for the inevitable end to arrive. It took death ten hours to find them.

A shudder through the *Far Horizons* jerked Nick's thoughts out of the gloom into which they'd fallen. The jet had arrived in Deadwood. With his limited maneuverability, Carrigan strove to avoid the stones that caromed through that region of space. He evaded the biggest rocks, but many of the smaller ones hit the ship, echoing through the cabin. Nick winced at the sounds. A high grinding noise ensued as if the ship was being sandblasted. *Only a matter of time until the minor debris wears the ship to its nub,* Nick thought. He ducked his head and waited for the end.

"I'm getting a signal," Carrigan said. "Instruments can't read it, but it's strong."

"The Amaurau forward station," Nick answered.

"I'm following it in."

No one spoke as Carrigan adjusted his course to steer the little craft toward the source of the signal. Silence hung heavy as the sounds of destruction slowly rendered their tiny island of safety to shreds. A loud burst caused the lot of them to jump, and Carrigan murmured an apology. No one had the energy to chide him for his foolishness.

A new shudder overtook the ship. The tactical on the forward wall indicated a planetoid-sized asteroid coming into range. The *Far Horizons* was being tugged by gravitational tidal forces toward it.

"Brace for impact," Carrigan said. "This won't be pretty."

Jason slipped from beneath the blanket he shared with Nick, threw himself into a seat, and strapped in. Nick set himself in crash position, arms folded across his chest and head pressed to his knees. Closing his eyes, Nick started to pray.

This in itself was a cause of worry and confusion for Nick. His mother had taught him about the human gods, Jesus and Yahweh, and their strange coterie of serving men known as saints. Nick had never made sense of them and didn't think it appropriate to worship them. He better understood the pantheon of Guneri gods, from the mighty Jagjekcek, ruler of the skies, to the more down-to-earth Bibachek, the god of good fortune. But Nick didn't want to call on them either. That left his father. According to Guneri lore, one's ancestors were always listening, ready to aid their descendants in moments of crisis. Nick hadn't often consulted the elder Nicodemus. The man had seemed a giant in Nick's eyes. President. War hero. Anything but a father. But in those dark moments, with doom all but certain, he seemed the most logical deity to consult. Nick prayed to the elder Nicodemus for help and begged forgiveness for all the evil he'd brought to the world.

"Brace!" the pilot warned.

The *Far Horizons* hit the asteroid with a glancing blow before bounding upwards, the weak gravity unable to contain it. The sudden impact jerked Nick's body. He squeezed his eyes tight against the pain. The thrusters fought to retain control as the ship was flung into space only to be caught again by gravity. Down it came and impacted a second time. When an outcropping of rock caught its wing, the *Far Horizons* flipped and began to tumble. Nick was thrust against his harness as the ship went into a violent roll. Again and again, the little jet tumbled, metal squealing as it was torn away by rock. Nick was thrown forward, the safety harness gnawing at his ribs. His breath caught, and he whited out. The jet impacted a wall of rock and slammed to a stop.

All was silent.

Nick hung sidewise because the jet had come to rest at an angle. The emergency lights were dead; the cabin was black but for a faint gleam of starshine entering the portholes.

Jason groaned.

Dr. Abrams coughed.

Corey was silent.

Nick considered the view from the porthole. He saw a stark, dust-covered surface against a black, star-spangled sky. *No, not star-spangled,* he thought, *asteroid spangled.* Nick watched the various points of light shift in the darkness. There was no atmosphere out there, of that he was certain, and the cabin was now bitterly cold. Nick closed his eyes and awaited death's embrace.

The sound of an airlock opening awoke Nick from a daze, and he shifted painfully. The forward door opened. Nick winced, prepared to face a sudden vacuum, but whoever was moving outside had placed an access way against the door. A warm bloom of fresh air rushed into the jet's cabin and set the smoke dancing. Shadows moved through a gray veil. Nick blinked as a light flashed in his face. Several tall figures in environment suits emerged from the darkness. Their flashlights pierced the smoke like lasers, flicking left to right as they studied the tableau of injured humans.

Nick knew they were Amaurau.

One turned his light on Nick's face. "Who commanded this ship to come here?"

"I did." Even if he hadn't suggested coming to the asteroid, Nick still would have taken the blame. *We're here because of me,* he thought. *Corey is perhaps dead because of me.* "I brought us here."

"You're trespassing," the Amaurau stated.

"It was an accident," Nick insisted. "We didn't mean to land here. Well, we did, but we didn't have a choice."

"Alien species are not permitted in our territory."

"I know."

The Amaurau said nothing more. He stomped through the debris to reach Nick then waved a wand over him. After it beeped, the Amaurau stowed the wand in his belt and unhooked Nick's harness.

"Can you walk?" he demanded.

Nick painfully pulled himself out of his seat, staggering against the list of the floor. Through the confusion of flashing light, Nick saw Jason lying unconscious in the next seat. Corey's harness appeared to have failed, and he lay face down on the floor. Dr. Abrams was groggy but still restrained. He waved lightly in Nick's direction.

The Amaurau didn't permit Nick to aid his fellows. Two grasped him by the arm and dragged him to the door. Nick was thrust into a tubular access way and forced to walk. Gasping with each step, he lurched down the tube with an Amaurau escort on either side of him.

"Are you going to help the others?" Nick asked.

The Amaurau did not reply.

They soon reached the end of the access way and faced another airlock. Once opened, Nick was pushed into the cabin of a spacecraft.

The ship was nothing like any human or Guneri vessel he had ever seen. It was brightly lit and airy with ample headroom and was also strangely organic. Its seats grew out of the fuselage in smooth curving shapes. Control panels looked like seashells emerging from the walls. The lights and indicators were muted. The space exuded an eternal newness, right down to the pastel-colored floor that showed not a single scuff to mar its perfection.

Ignoring his gasps of pain, Nick's guards jerked his hands behind his back. He was handcuffed and thrust onto a seat that molded itself to Nick's shape. He felt as if the chair might swallow him as it settled around his form. Trapped, Nick watched another group of Amaurau in environment suits leave the craft via the access way, at which point the airlock was closed. Nick heard a suctioning sound, and the ship began to vibrate. A moment later, they were airborne.

"Wait!" Nick exclaimed. "What about the others? They're injured. They need help."

The cold, reflective face of a helmet turned toward Nick, but no one spoke. Nick stared back, trying to see a face beyond the glass, but it revealed nothing. *Maybe it's a machine,* he thought.

The small ship slipped through space, leaving Nick's companions and the damaged spacecraft behind.

"You can't leave them to die!" he insisted. "They were alive!"

Still, he received no answer.

Trapped within the strange seat, Nick collapsed against its softness and, in despair, realized he was again helpless. *Oh Bibachek, why have you so deserted me?* he wondered. *What have I done to deserve this misery?* He realized it would be unwise to speak his prayers aloud. *I don't dare worship a Guneri god while prisoner aboard an Amaurau ship,* Nick rationalized.

The journey was but a short hop across the asteroid. The ship had no windows, but its fluid surface functioned as a viewscreen that projected the space in which they traveled. The view was so lifelike Nick felt as though he was flying outside the ship of his own power. The grayish-white dust-covered ground passed beneath Nick's feet while overhead, the swirling asteroids danced. Forward motion slowed to a stop as the ship set down on a landing pad. Nick's seat firmed up and spat him onto his feet. Nick's guards also rose. Each took one arm and led Nick into the station of Deadwood.

Like the ship, the station was ablaze with light. The walls, floors, and ceiling all burned with an odd mix of pastel colors that united in an illumination like sunlight on steroids. Every thread in his guards' uniforms was visible. The light flowed, subtly changing colors so that the hallway seemed to undulate as they passed through.

The trek was strangely solitary. Although they passed numerous doors and passageways, no Amaurau was present. Nick hoped the walk would be short. His narcotics had worn off, and every step jarred his injuries. Each exhale was accompanied by a restrained moan. After a few minutes, the guards stopped at a door, unlocked it, shoved Nick into the small space beyond, and locked it again. Without a word, they departed.

Welcome to the Grand Republic of the Amaurau, Mr. Severin, Nick thought as he considered his new home. His hands were still bound behind his back, which he considered overkill. He had no idea how to free his hands or unlock the door. *Even if I could,* he thought, soberly, *I'd never escape the planetoid.*

The room was the size of a closet, brightly lit with a tall ceiling. The room was empty but for a molded object in the shape of a bed projecting from one wall. No chair, desk, sink, or commode; not even a lightbulb or a doorknob. Just a pastel-colored space of fluid plastic.

Exhausted and in pain, Nick accepted the only solace that cold space provided. He sank onto the protuberance and sought a position that didn't stress his ribs. Strangely, the modular surface sensed his discomfort because it adjusted to his shape. It even cradled his swelling left arm. There he was left to wait. And wait.

Had it been an hour, a day, a year? Nick had no way to measure the passage of time. The lights in his cell never flickered. He had no concept of day or night. Left to his thoughts, Nick was consumed in wondering what had happened to his compatriots. *Dead probably,* he thought. *Because of me.*

The door to his room opened suddenly, startling Nick out of his bleak thoughts. With a groan, Nick sat up to face the guards who came to rouse him. He had no doubt they were guards. Unlike the usual flowing attire he'd seen on Amaurau's ambassadors, these individuals were attired in tight-fitting uniforms. They wielded lyssestras strapped to bare forearms, as well as firearms holstered at the waist. Neither guard drew a weapon; Nick meekly complied with their order to accompany them.

Another long and painful walk followed. The trio passed several Amaurau in uniform, none of whom paid any mind to Nick, who felt as if he didn't exist as he marched between the two towering guards. He sensed he might die in that station. *Humanity,* he thought, *would never know what had become of their undersecretary and probably wouldn't care.*

He arrived at a large, circular room. The walls once again were projection surfaces, but instead of the stagnant view of the asteroid, a slowly shifting panorama of some alien world was displayed. Nick gazed at the imagery, a misty place of pastel rock and pink sky where thick green woods carpeted deep canyons while spires of weathered stone jutted toward the heavens and picked at the three crescent moons above. Nick assumed these were views of the Amaurau home world. He stood in awe at the sight of a forbidden land no human had ever before seen, not even in photos. *Too bad I'll never be able to tell anyone about it,* he thought.

Nick was shoved into the center of the room, a guard by his side. He swayed on his feet, lightheaded from hunger and thirst, woozy with pain and the aftereffects of narcotics. A door opened, and an Amaurau entered.

Nick blinked. "Sena Dessessah."

The comment earned Nick a blow between his shoulder blades.

"Have respect for Director Dessessah, prisoner," the guard scowled, hand still clenched in a fist.

Nick chose to translate Dessessah's title since *director* had no English equivalent. It meant leader or ruler or perhaps even lord. Nick had only encountered the word in language lessons he'd taken years earlier. He was stunned to find it applied to the woman he'd considered his college intern.

Dessessah strode into the room with long, regal steps. *She's changed,* Nick thought. Her head carriage was higher, and her stride crisp and professional. Instead of the fluid clothing of days past, she wore a fitted uniform. Her eyes had changed as well. On Rhadamanthus, those orbs had glowed with eager zeal. She'd possessed a childlike delight then. But now that joy was gone. This was a cold, angry Dessessah. She gazed at Nick with virulent distaste.

Knowing something profound had changed, Nick donned his own alter ego and gave the bow-cum-curtsy he'd been taught as Protocol Officer. The effort produced stabbing pain in his rib cage. The guards quickly pulled Nick upright.

"Have respect and stand still, prisoner," the guard growled, shaking Nick violently. Nick bit down on his tongue to keep from groaning.

Nick doubted it was worth mentioning that he was injured and in pain. He realized that he had no friends here, and he doubted empathy would follow if he spoke up.

"Nicodemus Severin," Dessessah spat, stopping inches from Nick. She stripped a lyssestra from an arm and tapped the long flexible plastic against her thigh in irritation. "I must say I am surprised."

Not nearly as much as I am, Nick thought.

"I as well, Sena. I can't imagine why a young student would be at a frontier station dressed in the garb of a general." The guard landed another blow, and Nick snapped forward so hard he bowed at the waist. Hissing in pain, Nick rose but refused to retract the rude remark.

Dessessah's eyes blazed. "You're hardly in a position to take umbrage with me. I could have you tossed outside with a flick of a finger."

Nick knew it was no idle threat. Without an environment suit, he'd be dead in seconds. *Might as well get some answers before I cash it in,* he thought.

"Why are you here?" he demanded.

Dessessah's hand twitched, and the lyssestra caught Nick across the cheek. It wasn't a hard blow, but it nonetheless stung.

"I'll ask the questions," she said, eyes scanning Nick's ashen face, his wild mop of hair, and the remains of his disheveled clothes. "What brought you to my doorstep, Severin? Not pleased with the damage you've done to your own world, you now come looking to damage mine?"

Nick shrugged. "Our ship was crippled. We had to land somewhere."

Dessessah snorted but said nothing.

"Where are my companions?" Nick asked. "They were injured. Please tell me they're okay."

"Do you really care?" Before Nick could respond, Dessessah flicked her wrist to silence him. "I don't think you considered their fate before directing your ship here. You were, no doubt, too intent on your own schemes."

"Our ship's life support had failed. This was the only place where I thought we could find help."

"Help? From the Amaurau?" She sniffed. "We don't accept alien visitors."

Nick felt suddenly cold. "Where are my friends?"

Dessessah narrowed her dark, birdlike eyes. "So, you care?" She grasped Nick's chin and turned his face upward to study it. Nick shuddered and jerked free. "They were alive last I heard of them."

"The last you heard of them?"

"I told you, we don't accept visitors." Dessessah stepped back. "They've been packed onto a drone freighter and shipped back to Earth. Assuming they survive the journey, they'll doubtless receive proper medical care from human physicians."

"*Assuming* ..." Nick's voice faded. "Jesus, you sent them off like a load of iron ore."

Dessessah lifted her brow. "We were more tolerant than we might have been. We could have killed them or left them to die. Instead, we shipped them home."

Nick's heart sank. He hadn't thought his dilemma could get any worse. "Thank you for that at least," he muttered.

Dessessah's gaze was stabbing and cold. "So, the pretext continues. You wish me to believe that you care for your fellow humans."

Nick gasped. "Of course I care! They're my friends."

"You have an odd way of showing friendship, Severin."

What does she mean? Nick wondered. *Have I offended her in some way? Done something during her stay at my apartment to earn such utter loathing? No. She'd been the treacherous one. She'd attacked me. Whatever game she's playing, I'm having none of it.*

Since he couldn't help Corey or Jason, Nick focused on his own survival. His eyes flicked over Dessessah. "So, you're a director. What do you direct?"

Her brows edged ever higher. "The Alien Intelligence Office."

Nick caught his breath. *Jesus!* "You're a spy?"

"I *gather intelligence* on our alien neighbors," she corrected.

"You have a strange way of gathering intelligence! Learning English from the lowly undersecretary of trade."

Dessessah immediately began speaking in English. "I speak your language quite well, thank you. I had no need of your tutoring."

Nick winced, stunned. The deception seemed endless. He stood, momentarily speechless, before gathering his wits together. The conversation had taken on a new importance.

"What in the name of Jagjekcek was that all about then?" Nick asked, also in English.

She lashed out with her lyssestra, and the plastic stick drew blood as it bit deep into Nick's cheek. "Don't swear in the name of your foul Guneri gods to me, Severin! I'll throw you outside and enjoy the pleasure of watching you asphyxiate if you raise such an oath in my presence again."

Nick snapped his mouth shut in impotent fury.

Her eyes flicked with disgust. "Although we always knew humans were consummate tricksters, you literally take my breath away. To think that I actually believed the wide-eyed innocence you portrayed on the beach."

"As if you're any different," Nick scoffed. "You played the ingénue quite well."

Her chin lifted. "I had hoped we'd found ourselves an ally. How sad to realize you're just like the rest of your vile species. Perhaps I should have killed you that day as you suggested." Dessessah's hands twisted the lyssestra as if she pondered using it. "I ignored the advice of my own staff and convinced them you deserved a chance to prove yourself. They wanted you dead."

Nick's eyes flashed with surprise. *So, the plan had been to kill me all along,* he thought. Nick looked nervously around the room as it occurred to him that he was now alone, a prisoner in the hands of an alien government he knew almost nothing about. An alien government that wanted him dead. And yet, he wasn't.

"What do you plan to do with me?"

Dessessah laughed. "I should kill you right where you stand." She glared as Nick raised his chin proudly. "But I won't. You're considered a traitor to your entire species, and a warrant for your arrest has been issued nebula wide."

Nick reeled at the verbal gut punch. *Why would my government have gone so far?* he wondered. *I'd done nothing except defend humanity. I nearly sacrificed my life for my accursed species.* He had to admit that, in fairness, no one on Earth or Rhadamanthus knew what had transpired in Gunera, the lengths he'd taken to keep the Balance. A sting of panic heated Nick's face. *Maybe my office knows. Maybe the higher-ups are part of the conspiracy and now fear my return. Because I'll reveal them for what they are— traitors. The new Protocol Officer, whoever he was, might even be one of the cabal. Dear God! How do I get out of this?*

"Humanity knows you betrayed your entire species by attempting to unilaterally overthrow the Balance Protocols and replace them with some new vile agreement with Gunera."

"I didn't sign," Nick muttered.

Dessessah ignored Nick's quiet statement. "They want your head. They blame you for the outbreak of hostilities with Gunera … as do we."

Nick's gaze jumped from its fixation on the floor. "How's the battle going?"

Dessessah flicked her long wrist negligently. "The Eventide shipping facility was obliterated. Seven human warships are currently engaging twenty-five Guneri ships in that area. I'm told the death toll is substantial. Congratulations, Severin, for bringing the Balance to its knees."

Nick snarled. "I never wanted the Balance to fall. As you so viciously pointed out that day on the beach, it's the only reason for my existence."

Dessessah sniffed. "Then it seems your raison d'être is at an end."

A fresh stab of panic shot through Nick as the reality of his dilemma sank in. He was bound and helpless, alone among a species that had little regard for his kind. Jason, the one individual who could confirm Nick's innocence, was either dead or beyond reach.

Nick straightened his shoulders, unwilling to surrender even in the face of his imminent demise. "Why bring me here? You could have left me to die on *Far Horizons*. Or shipped me home like unwanted laundry. Do you intend to kill me? Send my body back to Earth with a bow around my neck?"

Dessessah's laughter twittered through the room like a bird's warble. "I would so enjoy killing you, if only to soothe my wounded ego." She grasped Nick's chin a second time. "You're such a disappointment; I had much higher hopes." She twisted his face left and right as if trying to understand the man within. "I *should* kill you and send your rotting corpse to perdition. Leave your wretched people to wonder when you'll rise like a vengeful ghost to spite them. They deserve such a fate almost as much as you do. Alas, you're too valuable to kill."

"How am I of value?"

Dessessah smiled grimly, her fingers tracing along Nick's jaw with the same strange sensuality she'd exhibited on the beach. The touch sent a shiver of longing racing through Nick's body, and he trembled. *Once again,* Nick thought, *she can manipulate my emotions with just a touch.*

"As soon as I knew you would be visiting us, I contacted the Trade Commission on Rhadamanthus. They dearly want you back so they can charge you with treason. The Minister assured me they'll hold a fair and impartial trial followed by your prompt execution."

Nick's body jerked, and he knew the Sena felt it.

"We don't ordinarily perform executions," she said. "Capital punishment is a barbaric practice. But in this case, since they assured me you'll be given every opportunity to defend yourself, I see no reason to object."

"You're a vindictive bitch," Nick muttered.

Fingers tightened across Nick's jaw. "I am, indeed, Severin. I do not like being made the fool, and seldom does it occur."

"As you're the director of Alien Intelligence, I don't suppose it does." Nick wrenched his chin free. "How did you know I was aboard the jet?"

Dessessah turned her back and strolled away. "I've known exactly where you were every minute of every day since that afternoon on the beach. I believe I informed you of that fact."

Nick shuddered. "I remember. Assumed it was a threat."

"Not a threat," she chuckled and turned around. "Simply a statement of fact. I know you traveled to Gunera on the mai's personal yacht. I know you were entertained in the residence of vuh'Yguggli for two days before residing in the palace of the mai' for another two. You spent time with gy'Bagrada." She quirked a brow. "I assume during that idyllic period, you and the loathsome gy' consummated your tawdry little romance. One wonders, was it pleasurable, this cross-pollination of species?"

Nick glared at Dessessah in loathing. "I don't know how you know where I've been, but while you have the locations accurate, you don't have the facts behind them straight! I have not, nor will I ever, consummate a relationship with gy'Bagrada." Nick shook his head. "Although at this moment, I'm sad to say, he's probably the only soul in this entire universe I actually trust."

Dessessah twitched her lips. "How deeply you have fallen into the hands of your Guneri masters."

Nick debated telling Dessessah the events that had transpired on Gunera, but one glimpse at her face confirmed that he'd be wasting his breath. *She already tried and convicted me with not just my actions but with my words,* he thought. *I can't convince this conniving bitch of anything, but she's hardly in a position to claim the moral high ground.*

"How did you know where I was?"

Her smile became smug. "By your implants." At his look of surprise, she explained further. "The Gunera aren't the only ones who can read the transmissions, my dear. During our fateful afternoon at the beach, I had a receiver that I attuned to the transmission frequency. From then on, I could follow your implants wherever they went."

Nick thought back to that day. How she'd kept caressing his hand. How he'd thought it some sort of sexual advance. *Idiot, she was scanning my implants. Jesus! What a fucking idiot I am!*

"So this is the end," Dessessah sighed somewhat wistfully. Her eyes filled with an overwhelming sadness. "I had such hopes, Nicodemus Severin. Such hope." She narrowed her gaze. "You, sir, are a profound disappointment. Your father was a giant among humans, a man to inspire greatness in those around him. How far from the tree his seed fell. You are but a wretched shadow of that mighty man."

The words lanced Nick to the core, and he gasped, finding them more painful than his fractured ribs. He stood stricken, knowing

Dessessah spoke the truth, hating her for saying it, and hating himself for earning it. *Yes,* he thought, bleakly, as his guards pushed him from the room, *I'm indeed little more than a shadow of my father.*

"Get up, dog," a Gunera guard insisted. The loud voice roused Nick from his slumber.

He staggered from the bench that had been his bed. Groaning, a hand against his ribs, Nick stumbled forward. The guard spun Nick around and bound his hands behind his back. Nick hissed in pain. The barb wound in his shoulder had festered and now throbbed worse than his ribs. In misery, uncaring of his fate, Nick offered no resistance as he was hauled to a landing bay where a contingent of Amaurau, led by Dessessah, stood on one side. To Nick's surprise, a stoic group of humans in Alliance uniforms stood on the other.

At Dessessah's command, the guards escorted Nick to the side of the room where the Alliance group was gathered. An Alliance corporal stepped forward to take custody of Nick, eyeing him with a flash of anger.

"My brother is dead because of you, mister," the corporal spat. He slammed a fist into Nick's gut.

The pain that shot through Nick was so intense that he screamed and collapsed. He curled into a self-protective ball as waves of pain raced through him. Squeezing his eyes shut, Nick bit his tongue to prevent himself from screaming again.

Dimly through the pain, Nick heard Dessessah bark at the Alliance officers in English.

"Stand back!"

A scurry of movement followed, and Nick winced, fully expecting to be trampled. He opened his eyes to see an Amaurau lyssestra waving in front of his nose.

"We Amaurau don't abuse helpless prisoners," Dessessah stated.

The guards clustered around Dessessah, weapons at the ready. The human contingent retreated as a tense silence descended. Everyone seemed to be waiting for Nick to rise, but he was in no condition to acquiesce. Pain continued to radiate through Nick, and breathing was difficult.

The lyssestra next to his nose twitched.

"Get up, Severin," Dessessah ordered.

Nick ignored the order. *I'll be damned if I'm going to humiliate myself by trying to rise without the use of my hands and with my chest burning like fire,* he thought.

"Get up!" she barked, shifting a foot as if readying to kick him. "This is unseemly even for an ignoble traitor."

Still, Nick remained immobile.

Dessessah gestured to her guards, and two pairs of Amaurau hands pulled Nick onto his back before trying to lift him. The twisting motion sent stabs of pain through Nick's ribs, and he cried out involuntarily.

Dessessah immediately ordered her guards to stop as she glared down at him.

"This is more than I'd expect even from you," she snorted. Her eyes studied Nick's wan face and trembling body. Pinned by the obedient guards, Nick could only glare at her impotently.

"What's wrong with you?" she demanded.

"I was injured. In the crash," Nick grumbled. He'd already decided he wasn't going to beg for sympathy from the devious creature or bother to convince her of the truth.

She huffed and ordered the guards to lift him. Again Nick's ribs twisted, and he couldn't keep the sharp cry from escaping. Apparently the Amaurau were uncomfortable with causing another being pain because he was promptly released.

Dessessah grew bewildered. To Nick's surprise, she dropped on one knee beside him and lifted the tail of his tattered shirt. She caught her breath at the sight of the bruises. With a tug, Dessessah ripped the shirt in two, revealing Nick's battered stomach. He looked down and winced. The lower half of his rib cage was a massive purple bruise.

Dessessah's surprised eyes stared into his. "Why didn't you tell me about this? We aren't barbarians. We would have treated you."

Nick glowered, unwilling to surrender the last of his pride. "I don't trust you, Sena. Besides, it's nothing. A few broken ribs. Since I'm to be executed, what's it matter?"

"It matters to me," Dessessah huffed. "I'm not soulless. If humanity wishes to kill you, it's their affair. I would have seen to your injuries."

Nick gave the weakest of shrugs. "It doesn't matter now." He considered the humans who were waiting impatiently to take possession of him, aware that they had no interest in his physical well-being. "You'd best help me up. I need to go back with them."

The Sena's eyes narrowed while she studied Nick's face. "You understand they'll kill you."

Nick nodded. "Still, I have to return."

"Hoping to spin more treachery with your remaining minutes?"

Nick scoffed. He had no intention of telling Dessessah that he intended to save the Balance if at all possible. He had to find a human who would listen to him. Someone who could locate Jason and relay a message to President McAlastair on Earth. *Someone has to stop this war,* Nick reminded himself.

Conflict raged in Dessessah's dark eyes as they drilled into Nick's as if willing him to divulge his secrets. He glared back, refusing to submit. She frowned. Her gaze dropped to Nick's shoulder as his tattered shirt slowly slipped off, revealing the festering hole from the Guneri barb. Her fingers traced it lightly. Nick flinched as the angry skin burned even at that soft caress.

"This wound did not occur in any crash," she said.

"Yes, it did."

Dessessah's eyes narrowed. She poked the wound with a finger, and Nick hissed.

Her voice grew ominous, her expression stern. "I am Amaurau. The daughter of one who has fought the Gunera. I have seen wounds caused by a tail barb. A Gunera stabbed you. Why?"

Nick turned away.

Dessessah's hand caught his chin, forcing him to meet her stare. "Tell me, Severin." Her voice grew more strident. "Why would the Gunera stab their own man?"

When he didn't respond, her fingers tightened. "There's more here than meets the eye. Much more. War has come. Is that what you want? Humanity obliterated? Because that's what will happen. We and the Gunera will lunge at each other and annihilate you if you don't hold us back. Tell me, is that what you want?"

"I want you to send me back."

"Why?"

"To do what little I can to stop this insanity."

Dessessah rocked back on her heels, startled. Her fingers kneaded Nick's shoulder. As always, he found her touch both soothing and disturbing. He wished he could escape.

"What really happened in Gunera?" Her voice remained soft as she reverted to Amaurau. Her fingers cajoled and enticed, removing Nick's defenses. Resisting at first, he soon melted.

"They wanted me to sign those damned Accords," Nick finally whispered.

"And?"

"I refused."

Dessessah frowned. "You refused? I thought that was the purpose of your plot."

"*Their* plot," Nick insisted. At that moment, Nick wanted only to evade Dessessah's touch. But he was trapped. Not only by her grip on his shoulder or because his hands were bound. He was trapped because she could hold him, prisoner, with only two fingers.

"You're saying you weren't a party to that vile agreement?" She seemed astounded.

"Yes!" Nick threw his head back in frustration. "Lincoln Combs was supposed to sign the Accords. When you killed him, the Gunera needed a proxy. They tricked my government into sending me."

Dessessah's face pinched with confusion. "Did you know what was going to be asked of you?"

Nick rolled his eyes. "Of course not. I would never have agreed to go. Hell, I didn't agree to go at all. The State Department didn't give me a choice. Told me human factions wanted me dead. Told me *you* wanted me dead."

She reared back. "Some within my government did, but I did not. What gave your government cause to think that?"

"Your behavior," Nick snapped. "Forcing yourself into my apartment. Drugging me; asking questions."

Dessessah recoiled in surprise. "That day at the game with the animals? It wasn't I who drugged you. I was shocked when I saw you being led away."

Nick sighed. "I know that now, but my government still thinks otherwise."

"Why?"

"Because all I could remember about that encounter was you. What were you doing there?"

"When I saw you being taken, I flew after you. Your human captors had already drugged you by the time I caught up with them. I killed them to protect you."

"What? Why?"

Dessessah's eyes saddened. "I thought you were something that you're not." She hesitated then turned her attention to Nick's wound. "What happened to you on Gunera?" Again she fluttered her fingers across his shoulder. Again Nick felt himself melt.

"I was tortured for two days in the mai's dungeon," Nick sighed. He roused enough anger to counter her magic. "I was tortured, Sena! Beaten. My ribs, fractured. As well as a few other unpleasantries I'd rather not mention."

"They beat you into signing the agreement?"

"No! I still refused."

Dessessah's fingers traveled down Nick's chest, lightly touching the broken ribs and purple bruises. "You took this to save the Balance?"

"As I told you on the beach, I'd face torture for the Balance." Nick laughed bitterly. "How ironic. I had no idea what I was setting myself up for."

"My sources say you signed the agreement."

"Your sources are wrong. I didn't sign it, although, in the end, I agreed to." Dessessah stiffened, and Nick explained. "They tortured my mother, Sena. A poor, helpless, insane old woman!" Nick's eyes began to burn as tears traced down his cheeks. "They ripped out her eye right in front of me. I couldn't stand by and watch them remove her organs, one by one, until she was dead. I'm her son. I'm supposed to protect her. Instead, I've been a burden. Dear God, how I wish I'd never been born."

To his dismay, Nick couldn't stop crying. The Alliance crew, unable to discern Nick and Dessessah's conversation, stared at Nick in disgust. *Coward.* He could read it in their eyes, see it on their lips. Nick realized that to them, it appeared he was begging for his life.

Dessessah wiped away Nick's tears. "Don't do this," she whispered, her voice full of doubt. "I didn't know. However did you escape?"

Nick drew a shaking breath. "My bodyguard, Jason, and a dear friend took an incredible risk to get me out."

"What was gy'Bagrada's part in this?"

Nick laughed cynically. "eh'Kraghilg didn't know what else to do. He couldn't sneak me off the planet. The only person he thought capable of the task was gy'Bagrada. He knew how much the gy' … admired me."

"Lusted after you like a skeepak in heat," Dessessah muttered. "Disgusting."

Nick nodded. "It was. But eh'Kraghilg was right. gy'Bagrada was reluctant to turn me in. He convinced himself he had legal grounds to return me to human space instead."

"How?"

Nick laughed through his pain. "The only way he knew how. He shipped me, via commercial freight, to myself on the other side of the Gate."

"To the Eventide shipping docks," she finished. "Wounded like this?"

Nick nodded grimly. "I'll survive. I've made it this far."

Dessessah's hand returned to Nick's chest and lay atop his heart. Nick felt his pulse increase, although he didn't understand why. Dessessah's face had softened, and Nick sensed in her a growing despair.

"Ah, Nicodemus!" she moaned. "Why didn't you tell me this from the start?"

"You weren't in the mood to listen."

"True. I judged based on the facts I possessed." Dessessah blinked as if to clear her eyes. "I was wrong."

Nick shrugged. "It doesn't matter."

"It does!" she exclaimed. "I could have done something had you spoken sooner. But now, we have an agreement; the documents are signed. We've accepted humanity's payment for you. I must release you."

"Yes," Nick agreed. Although he knew the chances were bleak, he still had to return home. He had to stop a war.

Dessessah looked desperate. "They'll kill you! But the agreements … I can't withhold you."

Nick nodded. "Agreed. Help me up."

Her hands tightened. "They will kill you, Nicodemus!"

Nick nodded. "Yes." At her look of distress, he added, "It's okay, Sena. I'm prepared to die for the Balance if necessary. I have to return. I must convince Earth that war with the Gunera is insanity. That the Balance must remain. For your sake. For their sakes. Even for Gunera's sake."

Groaning, Nick fought to rise. Dessessah ordered her guards to assist him.

"What will you do?" Dessessah's eyes studied the humans who seemed prepared to execute Nick at any moment.

"I don't know. Something."

Her hand landed on his uninjured shoulder. "Perhaps we could delay. Give us time to consider options …"

"There are no options, Sena," Nick insisted. "Humans started this. Humans have to stop it. I have to stop it."

"Why you?"

"Because it's my job." Nick raised his chin, mustering his remaining courage. "I'm the Protocol Officer. It's my job to keep the peace or die trying."

Dismay marred Dessessah's delicate features. "I'll not see you again, will I?"

Nick shook his head. "I think not." He glanced at his fellow humans as they stepped forward to take possession. He bowed his head to Dessessah. "Farewell and safe landings," he said, the traditional Amaurau sendoff.

"I could not have been more wrong, Minister," Dessessah whispered in Nick's ear as the corporal, eyes still ablaze, took him. "I thought you a sad shadow of your father, but it is your father who would stand small covered in yours."

Startled, Nick's eyes held hers. "I am nothing like my father."

Dessessah smiled, and her fingers trailed away as their distance grew. "No, you're not. Your father was a great man who basked in the light of his greatness. You, Nicodemus, are a great man who hides his greatness in the darkness where no one but I will ever see it." To Nick's amazement, Dessessah bowed low. "I will honor your memory as I honor your father's. If there is aid I can give you, I will do so."

"If you mean that, defend the Balance," Nick said as he was dragged away.

Nick caught one last glimpse of Dessessah, who stood straight and proud with her guards at her side. He swore he saw tears in her eyes.

16

The hands that shoved Nick into the chair were rough, just as every touch he'd received upon his return to human space had been rough. Although his captors treated him humanely, Nick received only the bare necessities, and he existed in a cold and sterile world. Today was no different. His heart thrummed, and he felt a trail of sweat trickle between his shoulder blades as he settled behind the table alone. *No counsel,* he thought. *Just how legal will this trial be?*

It wasn't a trial, the Justice Department insisted. Rather, it was a military tribunal to determine if the most hated traitor in the Fortuna Nebula should stand trial in civil court or if the Alliance Fleet should handle the ugly mess. He should, they insisted, be relieved to face a closed hearing. The dust-up with the Gunera was becoming a full-blown war. Good men and women were dying because of him. Numerous people, most notably members of Humans First, wanted Nick's head. A public trial wasn't in his best interest, they reasoned.

In my best interest. Nick scowled to himself. *The hell. In their best interest.* Nick, with his Guneri-trained legalistic mind, knew the tribunal was anything but legal. Fleet wanted its pound of flesh for the pain the border war was causing. They intended to take it from him. Nick knew his sacrifice had been wasted. He could do nothing to stop the violence. Little he could do to even save himself.

Three somber-faced tribunal members, one male and two female, each attired in uniforms designating high rank, entered the room. A clerk settled at the end of the table to assure the proceedings were properly recorded. *If nothing else, this travesty is going to look legal,* Nick thought, watching the preparation for his order of execution to be completed. *Because that's what this was. A farce to hide the ugliness of betrayal. I'm the fall guy. Time to take the fall.*

The tribunal's leader, according to the nameplate at his seat, was Seamus Connolly, a hawk-faced general with blue eyes colder than the depths of the Rhadamanthan Sea.

"Let this tribunal come to order," Connolly stated with a gesture to the clerk to begin recording. "We're here on this third day of September in the year 2255 to determine the status of Nicodemus Severin the Second, Secretary of International Trade. The charge is high treason against the Western Alliance." Connolly's eyes glanced indifferently at Nick. "How do you plead, Mr. Severin?"

Nick immediately felt enraged. Still under the influence of narcotics to ease his physical pain, Nick knew he wasn't thinking clearly, but at that moment, he felt as though he had little to lose.

"I choose not to offer a plea because there's nothing to plead to," he snapped. Nick rubbed his hand across his ribs which still itched from a recent bone fusing procedure. "I refuse to accept this ... kangaroo court."

Connolly's eyes flickered as he jotted a note on his tablet. "Let the record state that the defendant pleads 'not guilty.'"

Nick glared at the panel. "Correction. Let the record state that the defendant refuses to issue a plea." He glanced over his shoulder at three armed soldiers and wondered how far he could push them before they'd react. "You seem to think I'm some provincial hack you can bully with this ridiculous farce. I'm not. I was raised on Gunera, the land that invented legal shenanigans. I demand a defense attorney. I also demand to know what happened to Jason McKittrick, Corey Boyers, and Thomas Abrams."

"You are in no position to make demands," one of the two female tribunal members snapped. She was older, with gray hair pulled in a severe bun at the nape of her neck. The name on her plaque read *Anna Beauregard.* "As for Mr. McKittrick, he's been suspended pending investigation of his activities."

Nick felt himself deflating. Although pleased to know that Jason was alive, assuming he wasn't being lied to, which, Nick realized, he had no way of knowing, he was still appalled to think Jason had been suspended for merely doing his job.

"He's a good man and a fine special agent," Nick insisted.

Connolly slammed his gavel on the table. "Be silent, sir. You're here to answer our questions. If you continue to disrupt the proceedings, I'll call a halt and move to findings."

Nick knew exactly what findings they were going to find. He fell silent.

"Are you an agent working at the behest of the government of Gunera?" Beauregard asked.

"No," Nick mumbled.

"Isn't it true you've maintained a romantic relationship with the head of the Guneri Secret Service?"

Nick half rose then sat down again. "Absolutely not."

Connolly referenced an accordion folder overflowing with papers. "According to reports, you and … how do you pronounce this … Guy Bagrada engaged in a romantic escapade at the signing ceremony of Protocol 10."

"The man felt me up," Nick growled. "I freed myself as soon as I could without blatantly insulting him."

"You weren't scheduled to attend the ceremony," Connolly continued. "Secretary Huntzinger took ill, leaving you to attend, isn't that right?"

"Yes."

Connolly raised his brows.

"gy'Bagrada told me he'd given Duncan food poisoning so he could see me," Nick admitted.

"Interesting."

Nick continued to wilt. *I can see where this supposed hearing is headed,* he thought. *They're laying out the reasons why I'm a traitor, and they don't care whether I answer or not. Nothing I say will make any difference. The verdict was decided long before I entered the room. Oh, Bibachek,* Nick prayed, *I don't have a chance, do I?*

Connolly sifted through his papers and placed one on the table between him and Nick. "This is a transcript of a message sent from the palace of the mai' to agents here on Rhadamanthus. Were you aware that certain humans have been providing unsanctioned information to the Gunera?"

The paper was too far away for Nick to read. His heart raced as he wondered what that vicious bit of white cellulose said. "I was not aware the Gunera have spies here," he said. "However, I'm also not surprised."

"Why not?"

Nick scowled. "Because where there are humans, there are people willing to do anything for a price, even betray their own government. Certainly the Gunera would be willing to pay for information the Alliance wouldn't provide through diplomatic channels."

"Are you one of those greedy *people willing to do anything for a price?*"

"No."

"Have you provided such backchannel information for money, Mr. Severin?"

"Absolutely not."

"Have you provided unsanctioned information without being paid?"

"No."

"You've not been tempted to aid the species that raised you by providing what you perhaps perceived as harmless information?"

Nick glared at his accuser. "I have not."

"Always stated the company line?" Connolly sneered.

Sitting forward in his chair, Nick stared his accuser in the eye. "I have always done my job to the best of my ability, within all laws and regulations of the Alliance, sir. Say what you will about my personality, my lack of manners, my horrible ability to bond with my own species. But I'll be damned if you'll impinge upon my professionalism, sir. I was a damned good undersecretary. I followed every minuscule regulation to the eyelash, and I'll stand up to anyone who dares state otherwise!"

The outburst took Connolly aback. The second female tribunal member, a woman with short black hair whose plaque read *Lai Chen*, smiled briefly.

"No need to be so defensive, Mr. Severin," she said. "Your reputation as a stickler for regulation precedes you."

Winded, Nick sat back, startled by his own vehemence. *Damned if you charlatans are going to take away the one and only talent I have,* he thought.

"It might be remarkable if being a legal stickler was not a Guneri habit," Connolly commented blandly.

Got me again, Nick sighed. *This son of a bitch is going to twist everything I say to his own purposes. Even my Guneri-style adherence to procedure is suddenly a condemnation, not a virtue.*

Connolly gestured to the paper that still rested in the center of the table. "Do you know who's been providing the Gunera with classified information?"

"No."

"Have you provided the Gunera with such information?"

"I've already answered you. No."

Connolly shifted more papers. "You exchange emails with Guy Bagrada on a daily basis, Mr. Severin."

Nick rolled his eyes. "Yes."

"What's the nature of that discourse?"

"I'm sure you can look it up," Nick growled. "I never made any attempt to hide my correspondence."

"Indulge me," Connolly said.

Nick shook his head in frustration. "The gy' likes to jerk my chain. He deliberately raises legal issues on a half-dozen transshipments every week for the sole purpose of getting my goat."

"Why would he do that?"

"Because he's a sick bastard."

Connolly twitched his lips. "You give the impression you don't like him."

"*Like him?* I can't stand him," Nick growled. "He's deliberately provocative."

"Why?"

"He says he likes locking horns with me."

Connolly drew a breath. "Is *locking horns* a Guneri mating ritual?"

Nick threw his hands in the air, earning a warning from one of the guards. "There's no *mating ritual*. There's no romance. gy'Bagrada fancies himself in love with me, so he provokes me to encourage conversation. I feel only revulsion for him."

Connolly nodded suspiciously then reviewed more documents. "According to the message sent from the mai' to his informants, you signed a new set of Protocols in Gunera."

"It's a lie."

Connolly slid a page across the table. Nick read it with a sinking heart.

> **To:** Antoine Hendrick
> **From:** gy'Dadamondi
> **Subject:** The Accords
>
> The new Accords have been signed by the Secretary of International Trade. They will arrive in a packet within 1 day. You are instructed to forward the document to the appropriate parties.

"It's a lie," Nick repeated, shoving the paper back toward Connolly. "I didn't sign."

"Can we assume that when the document arrives in London carried by Antoine Hendrick, you'll continue to deny having signed it?"

Nick gazed darkly at his accuser. "There is no document with my signature on it. If one appears in London, it's a forgery."

"The Gunera don't forge legal documents."

"No," Nick confessed, "they don't."

Connolly waved at the email. "Again, when the Accords arrive, they'll contain your signature."

"No."

"Both statements cannot be true, Mr. Severin. Either you signed the document, or the Gunera are willing to defy their own cultural traditions to deceive humanity. Which is it?"

Nick shook his head. "I don't know, but I didn't sign any document."

Connolly retrieved the email and shuffled through more documents.

"Why did you return to Alliance territory? You could have remained safe and warm in Gunera."

"No, I could not," Nick answered, feeling off balance by the changing direction of the interrogation.

"Are you not here so that you can foment rebellion? Plant additional misinformation to provoke a war?"

"No."

"You returned because you thought you could blithely resume selling classified information to the Gunera."

Nick glared. "I have never sold classified information."

"Alright, *give away* classified information."

"I've answered you twice. I've never provided information to the Gunera either for free or in exchange for payment, that I wasn't authorized to provide by my department."

"Then why did you return to Alliance territory?"

"I wanted to survive."

The inquisitor raised a brow. "Explain."

"I'd refused to sign those bloody Accords," Nick snarled. "The mai' was understandably upset. He tortured me. He tortured my mother."

"You signed under duress?" Chen interrupted.

Nick flailed his arms once more. "No! As I've already stated, numerous times, I did not sign the Accords." Nick rubbed his fingers over his temples. "I admit that after the Gunera began torturing my mother, I agreed to sign, but the opportunity never arrived. Jason McKittrick aided my escape. Ask him. He can confirm what I've told you."

"Mr. McKittrick is hardly a reliable reference," stated Beauregard. "He's currently imprisoned for treason."

"That's ridiculous!" Nick snapped. "He was once a personal bodyguard to the president."

"Yes, and frightening it is to learn that a man of his esteem is a traitor," Beauregard replied tartly. She raised a hand to stifle Nick's budding protest. "Save your breath, Mr. Severin. The evidence against Mr. McKittrick is overwhelming. We've obtained five years of his correspondence. He's been on the Amaurau payroll for at least that long."

Nick sunk further into his chair, winded. "Impossible."

Beauregard nodded. "When McKittrick arrived here from Amaurau territory along with your other co-conspirator, Mr. Boyers, we investigated them thoroughly. McKittrick had no authorization to accompany you to Gunera. He was, in fact, absent without leave from the Secret Service. Furthermore, he's been providing the Amaurau with information gleaned from meetings he's attended in the President's service. There's no debating facts, Mr. Severin. The man is a traitor."

"For the Amaurau?" Nick whispered. "I don't believe it!"

Beauregard's cold expression did not relent. "Believe it, Mr. Severin."

Stunned, Nick refused to comprehend the magnitude of the accusation. *Is she telling the truth? Was it even possible?* Nick stared blankly at the table, trying to run the scenarios, trying to understand the web of deceit that had allegedly been woven around him. *If true, then why hadn't Dessessah tossed Jason back to human space? Why hadn't she have slipped him in so he could retain his position? It doesn't make sense,* he concluded.

Nick's eyes focused on Beauregard. "I don't believe it. The Amaurau wouldn't send Jason back without a cover story."

"They probably concluded that their agent's cover was blown," Beauregard said, head shaking. "Do you think the Secret Service would fail to notice that an agent had fled to Gunera with the Undersecretary of International Trade? They noticed. It's what started the investigation into Mr. McKittrick. We knew he was giving information to the Amaurau long before his return through the Gate. We were pleasantly surprised to capture him without a fuss."

Once again, the gears of Nick's mind spun. *Why would Dessessah have thrown away a valuable asset? As a member of the president's security detail, Jason is a valuable asset. Why surrender him willingly? Unless his usefulness was at an end,* Nick thought. *Unless she knew Jason had been compromised. Perhaps tossing him back cleaned up another strand of the web she'd woven. Was all this merely an Amaurau scheme to drive its two enemies to war?*

"I didn't know," Nick insisted. "I didn't know."

"Please answer my question," Connelly rasped. "What did you intend to do when you returned?"

"As I've already explained, I intended to survive."

Connelly's blue eyes gleamed with disbelief.

"It's true!" Nick exclaimed. "The Gunera tried to torture me into signing the Accords. Jason helped me escape. All I wanted was to return home."

"To a species you admit you don't understand."

Nick nodded sadly. "Yes."

"Why?"

"Because you're all I have," Nick whispered.

Connelly grunted as he fiddled with various papers.

Beauregard took up the chase as the questions shifted direction once more. "Tell us, Mr. Severin. Are you an agent working on behalf of the Amaurau?"

"No. Don't be absurd."

Beauregard's dark eyes flickered. "We have information that states you have friends among the Amaurau. Among them, Lady Dessessah."

Nick flinched, already loathing the route the questioning was taking. "I would hardly call Sena Dessessah a friend."

"She lived with you for several days, didn't she?"

Nick's throat tightened as he sensed the noose being closed around him. It had been tied by the State Department earlier for fear the moment would arrive when Nick fell into the wrong hands and their plotting was revealed. Nick wondered if the tribunal was legitimately working from information the cabal had fed them or if they were part of the cabal itself.

"I was following orders," Nick said.

"Whose orders?"

"The State Department."

"A name, Mr. Severin."

"Duncan," Nick breathed. "Duncan Huntzinger told me he had orders from State. Sevay Ississita insisted that the Sena be tutored in English and our culture."

"Mr. Huntzinger told you this?"

"Yes."

Beauregard's face marginally warmed as she pretended to smile. "Would it surprise you to learn that Sena Dessessah speaks English?"

"No," Nick grumbled.

The woman's brow crept upward. "*No?* Didn't you just claim she'd been sent here to learn English?"

"That's what I was told. I thought she was a college student. She pretended she didn't understand a word of English." Nick rubbed his temple; his head throbbed. "I know better now."

"How's that, Mr. Severin?"

Nick gazed briefly at the ceiling, knowing his next words were simply more evidence against him. Nothing he might say could free himself from the grave that had been dug for him.

"How do you know Sena Dessessah speaks English?"

"She told me."

"When?"

"When she traded me back to you for concessions."

Beauregard tapped her computer screen, but Nick couldn't see the reason why. He leaned forward again. "I didn't know until that moment! I swear! She was an exceptional actress."

"One would expect nothing less from the head of Amaurau intelligence," Beauregard stated coldly. "I would hope she'd be a master of duplicity."

The way she spoke made Nick feel like a fool. "Yes, indeed she is."

"Especially those who are eager to be duped, isn't that right?"

Nick shrugged. "I don't know. I suppose."

"You suppose you were willing to be duped?"

"It appears that way, doesn't it?" he asked bitterly.

"It appears very damning," Beauregard replied. "Are you stating that you were unaware of Dessessah's role as head of the Amaurau Intelligence Service?"

Nick blinked at his accuser stupidly. His mind raced. *The division head? Not just a prominent director? Who, if anyone, had been telling me the truth? Not the Amaurau. Possibly not Duncan. Certainly not his superiors at the State Department. Perhaps the only people I can trust are gy'Bagrada and gy'Gravinda! How upside-down has the universe become?*

"Have you nothing to say?" Connolly demanded. "You've been cavorting with a known Amaurau spy and the head of their intelligence service. With no authorization, you traveled to Gunera, where you met with the emperor to discuss dissolving a union that has lasted for a century. Furthermore, your appearance on the Eventide docks has triggered armed combat with Gunera."

Nick gestured helplessly. *What can I say?* he thought. *It looks bad even to me.*

Connolly laced his fingers together. "My job is to determine how much damage you've done, Mr. Severin. How many secrets you provided to the Amaurau. Are you working for them? Or for the Gunera? Frankly, it's hard to say."

"I can't argue," Nick muttered. "I'm not even sure what side I'm on anymore."

Beauregard's ears pricked. "Are you saying you're willing to confess?"

Nick snorted. "No, because there's nothing for me to confess except for being the biggest damned fool in the nebula! I've been used, Ms. Beauregard. Well and thoroughly used."

"By whom?"

"By every goddamned person I've ever had the misfortune to meet."

Connelly grunted and flicked a hand dismissively. His patience appeared to be at an end.

Nick, however, intended to fight for his life or what remained of it. He was determined to stop the madness. *Someone has to stop it,* he thought.

Nick turned to Chen, who seemed undecided. He attempted to lock eyes with her. "I think we're all being used."

"How so?" asked Chen.

Nick tapped the table with a finger. "It's the Amaurau, Ms. Chen. I think this was an elaborate ploy to drive the Alliance and Gunera to war."

"Why would they do that?"

"Because they were going to pull out of the Alliance anyway. They weren't going to sign Protocol 10."

An icy silence descended.

Chen leaned forward. "How do you know that?"

Nick looked at the ceiling once more, knowing he was about to add another nail to his casket. "Ississita told me at the renewal ceremony."

"The Amaurau ambassador told you he was withdrawing from the Alliance?" Chen gasped.

Nick nodded unhappily.

"Did it not occur to you to inform your superiors when you learned of this news?" Connelly roared.

Nick flinched. "He didn't say it directly but only hinted it at. Now I realize that the hint meant he was setting the stage to withdraw."

"And force us into war with Gunera?" asked Chen, a steely tone to her voice.

"I believe so."

"How does that benefit the Amaurau?"

Nick rubbed his temples again. "They probably believe that we'll soften the Gunera up for them. A war between humans and Gunera only weakens both sides."

"You went to Gunera," Beauregard interjected, "to convince them we were leaving the Balance. Once the Gunera began nibbling on your line, you jerked it out from them, enraging them and bringing about the events at Eventide that are now culminating in war."

"No!" Nick insisted. "I didn't know. They used me!"

"Who? The Gunera? Or the Amaurau?"

Nick shook his head, bewildered. "I don't know. All I know is I wasn't a party to any of it. I was used." His eyes flashed around the table at the condemnation being heaped on him. "I knew I should never have gone to Gunera. I told Duncan I didn't want the assignment."

"Then why did you?" asked Chen.

"I was following orders."

"Whose orders?" demanded Beauregard. "Who arranged the mission? Who told you Mr. McKittrick had authority to travel to Gunera?"

Nick's mind flashed back to the briefing he'd received from the State Department team. He'd never learned their names but had blissfully trusted them as he'd trusted everyone, just as Duncan had warned him not to. He was too trusting, he realized. He'd gone on the mission because everyone had seemed so official. He hadn't asked any of the standard questions he should have asked. *Dear God,* Nick thought, *how could I have been so naïve? Had Duncan known the office on Rhadamanthus was being used?* Nick winced as he considered the brilliance of the conspiracy. *Dump everything on the distant office of Rhadamanthus. Leave the provincial hicks to take the fall if everything went to hell. Leave a trail of breadcrumbs leading right to Nick Severin's door.*

"Who arranged your mission?" Connolly pressed.

"The State Department," Nick whispered. "I didn't get a name."

Connolly snorted. "Protecting your superiors might seem noble, but you're only making things difficult. Give me names, Mr. Severin. If you cooperate, we might be able to work something out."

"Have you not been paying attention? I have no names to give!" Nick snarled. "I took my orders from my direct supervisor, Duncan Huntzinger."

"Who is, rather conveniently, dead."

Nick nodded glumly, beginning to wonder if Duncan had been killed by humans. The past week was spreading out before him as a vibrant quilt of lies and deception. All designed to send him to Gunera to commit treason and protect the orchestraters of the affair. Conspirators whose names remained unknown to him.

Except one.

"Johans Sprouse."

"Excuse me?"

"Johans Sprouse. His name appeared on the email messages between gy'Dadamondi and Earth."

Connolly sat back in his chair, looking stunned. "That's a hell of a name to throw out! The Undersecretary to Millingham? Are you sure?"

Nick shrugged. "Sprouse's name was on the mai's emails. Millingham's name was listed as well."

"Bullshit," Connolly swore. "Millingham is as staunch a humanist as they come."

"That's what Jason McKittrick said." Nick focused on the table surface. He no longer had the strength to face his accusers. "Both names were on the emails. I don't know if either man actually authored the messages. Perhaps they were falsified to fool me. Or maybe they were real. Right now, I don't know who or what to trust."

Silence met Nick's words. He awaited the verdict, already knowing what it would be. *Not that it matters,* he thought. Whether he'd been an agent of the Amaurau or a fool they'd duped, Nick's actions had been contrary to the interests of the Alliance. He was a traitor in action if not in intent and would, like Joseph Bruce Ismay, Alfred Dreyfus, Gaëtan Dugas, and countless others before him, take the fall while those who'd orchestrated the crime escaped unscathed.

The thought galled him. *No,* he silently declared, *I'm not going to fall on my sword. I'll fight to see that those responsible pay for their crimes. I've a duty, damn it! A duty to the Protocols. To defend them. And I will, to my last breath.*

Connolly cleared his throat. "Mr. Severin, unless you can offer proof of your accusations against Mr. Sprouse and Mr. Millingham, I believe this hearing is over."

Nick desperately gazed around the room as his mind reeled. *How can I prove my innocence? How I convince them that I'd been sent to Gunera on someone's orders? I've only Duncan's word and that strange meeting with the three unnamed individuals I'd never seen before or since. Members of the cabal, probably.*

Nick's eyes narrowed as he focused on the clerk shifting files on her tablet. *The computer,* he thought. *My God, could it be so simple?*

"May I use your computer?" he asked.

Connolly blinked. "Excuse me?"

"You asked for proof of my allegations. If you'll allow me access to a computer, perhaps I can fulfill that request."

The suggestion stunned his accusers.

"He has a right to defend himself," Chen whispered.

"This is preposterous," Connolly replied as Beauregard nodded in agreement.

"I agree. But if we're going to continue this farce of a tribunal, we can't exactly deny the accused access to documentation that might exonerate him."

Begrudgingly, Connolly and Beauregard agreed.

"Attendant," Connolly said, "obtain a tablet for the accused."

Minutes later, his request having been granted, Nick attempted to log in to his accounts. His email and State Department accounts were locked. *But not the trade databases,* he thought with grim amusement. *No one ever thought those damned databases held anything of value.* Nick, however, knew they held the universe in their depths. His fingers flew across the screen, running queries, seeking answers. It took several minutes before he found what he was seeking: manifests for August 27, the date of his journey to Gunera. Nick drew up his itinerary. He retrieved the booking information entered by the travel office for the Trade Commission on Rhadamanthus. Approval: Duncan Huntzinger.

Nick spun the tablet around. "The authorization for my trip to Gunera shows that it was approved by Duncan Huntzinger."

Connolly barely glanced at the tablet. "You're an expert on those databases. You could have inserted that data."

Nick grinned. "I am an expert. It's unfortunate that whoever dreamed up this plot to frame me forgot that fact." Nick's fingers tapped again and brought up the little-known tables that resided behind the itinerary data. He spun the tablet around again and stabbed it with a finger. "That, sir, is the addressing behind the booking. It was booked on Duncan Huntzinger's office computer on Rhadamanthus, using his personal security code, which I don't know."

"Can you prove that?" Chen asked.

Nick tapped again. "The approval took place July 25 at 2005 hours. If you check with the news bureaus, you'll discover that at 20:05 or thereabouts, I was saving the life of gy'Gravinda at the renewal ceremony. I couldn't possibly have inserted that record."

"Perhaps not. But you could have done so after the fact," Connolly insisted.

Nick snorted. "You obviously don't understand our security system. Approvals require not only a password but also retinal and DNA scans. Only Duncan could have entered the approval."

Nick's words stunned the tribunal. Chen asked the clerk to search on the night of the renewal ceremony. The woman responded that the attack on gy'Gravinda had taken place at 20:09 and lasted until 20:26, during which time the undersecretary was in full view of the gathering. Nick nodded with a grunt of approval, trying his best not to say *I told you so*.

"All right," Connolly conceded. "Fair enough. Your trip was approved by Huntzinger. Perhaps you duped him."

Nick started searching again now as much for his own information as for the tribunal's. He wanted to know what had happened to him and who had set him up so thoroughly. He would take the bastards down or die trying. Nick attempted to burrow into the transactions beyond the travel approval but could not pass the security walls, which meant that he couldn't determine the source of Duncan's orders. Those who'd issued the orders had covered their tracks too well. Frustrated and frightened that he couldn't click his way to freedom, Nick sat with his mind blank as his fingers moved aimlessly, giving the appearance that he was actively searching. Random clicking took Nick back to the travel itinerary. The image on the screen stopped him cold.

"My God!" Nick's gaze froze on the data. "It's not there."

"*What's* not there?"

"My return booking." Nick scrambled, trying to find a reservation for his return through the Gate. Not during that week or the week after that. Nick found no evidence he or Jason were ever expected to return to human space. "They sent us there on a one-way ticket."

Connolly snatched the tablet. "What?"

"Duncan sent me to Gunera, knowing full well I wasn't coming back!" Nick sat back in his chair, stunned. "Why would he do that?"

Connolly frowned. "Why indeed?"

Nick gazed at Connolly for a moment, unsure if his attempt to defend himself was working. Nick's hands, almost of their own accord, scrambled for the computer once more. "There has to be another booking. Someone must have deleted it after Duncan made it."

He frantically searched the databases. Nothing. His heart lay like lead in his chest. He'd been betrayed. By humanity. By Jason. By the Amaurau. By everyone.

"I've been used," he muttered, aware that he was probably beginning to sound like a broken recording, and shoved the computer back at Connolly. "Well and thoroughly used."

Connolly was studying the computer. "So it seems," he murmured.

"Are you in this, too?" Nick asked bitterly of the tribunal. "Are you here to fool me in the final act? Convince me to walk to my own execution?"

Beauregard's face flushed. "I can assure you, Mr. Severin, that we take our duty to the Alliance quite seriously. We are not *in* on anything."

"Why this tribunal then?" Nick asked. "Who called for it? Who's pulling *your* strings?"

Connolly's head jerked. "No one's pulling our strings. We received our orders directly from General Karageorges, commander of the Alliance Third Fleet. He's the most trustworthy and ethical human in the entire nebula."

"In fairness to Mr. Severin, it appears he has valid reason to distrust us," Chen commented thoughtfully. "You've raised serious accusations against highly placed people—Huntzinger, Sprouse, even Secretary Millingham. I, for one, cannot take those accusations lightly in view of the evidence of this travel itinerary." She whispered something to the clerk who jotted a note. "I want to know who ordered your travel to Gunera. I also want to understand Jason McKittrick's role in this debacle."

"Thank you," Nick murmured.

Connolly was neatening his stack of papers. He seemed bewildered. "I believe we're finished for now, Mr. Severin. You're excused."

"Um, what happens now?" Nick asked as he rose at the behest of his three armed guards.

"We'll review the evidence and determine our findings," Connolly said unhelpfully. "Thank you for your time in this matter."

"Like I had a choice," Nick grumbled as he was led away.

—

The Justice Department probably doesn't know what to do with me, Nick thought as he prowled the floor of his cell. The room appeared to be an abandoned workplace, consisting of an office desk and chair. The desktop was empty but for a TV remote and pair of dead flies in a pencil tray that included a handful of paperclips. A decrepit chair squeaked of rusty joints, so he paced.

The TV was wall mounted. Nick grabbed the remote and channel surfed. He stopped at the Rhadamanthan News Network but immediately regretted the decision. RNN was reporting live from a skirmish near the Gate where two carrier groups were engaged against a host of Guneri craft. The Alliance was holding its ground. A bubbly female correspondent aboard the destroyer *Fortitude* was explaining how battery crews loaded iridium torpedoes. The image of the reporter trying but failing to mask a growing fear disturbed Nick. He knew that one well-placed shot by the Gunera could atomize *Fortitude* and its occupants on global television.

And I'd be to blame, he thought.

A shiver surged through Nick as he paced. He lamented switching on the TV, yet like a child picking at a scab, he felt powerless to stop. He paced, listening as the reporter described the carnage. Five dock works had been destroyed; over five thousand souls lost. Three freighters bound for Amaurau had been hit, resulting in ninety-eight fatalities. *All my responsibility,* he thought. *Their blood is on my hands.* Nick clenched his arms around his chest as if he might contain his inner pain if he gripped hard enough.

"We're going to interrupt you for a moment, Shelley," the RNN news anchor, a perky brunette named Rochelle Hudson, announced, "with breaking news from Rhadamanthus City."

"RNN has learned that accused traitor, Nicodemus Severin, has been brought before a military tribunal to determine his fitness to stand trial." Nick winced at the image of his own face emblazoned across the large screen. "The tribunal had issued a formal statement," Hudson continued. "Joining me now is RNN's legal expert, Carl Zucker."

"Astounding news today, Rochelle, as we've learned that the military tribunal, in a unanimous decision, has failed to indict Nicodemus Severin."

"What the hell?" Nick raged. "Thanks for letting *me* know, Connolly!"

"What can we expect next?" Hudson announced, her cherry smile ever present.

"Severin made several serious and potentially incriminating allegations. He'll likely continue to be held pending an investigation of those allegations. In all likelihood, Severin will be seeking a plea deal."

"Carl, what do we know about these allegations made by Severin?"

"Rochelle, according to Severin, he was merely a patsy. The real conspirators consisted of a group of anti-government subversives and Severin, who, as you know, is the son of a former president of Hemera, had been pulled into the fray. As I said, it's likely Severin will cop a deal to save his life by selling out his fellow conspirators. Specifically, who those conspirators are remains classified pending further investigation."

Nick wilted into the squeaky chair, placed his arms atop the desk, and dropped his head forward. *Praise Bibacheck I've no family to mortify*, he thought. *Only Duncan would have cared; thankfully, he'll never know the humiliation heaped upon the man he'd raised as a son.* Nick muted the TV as the news anchor launched into a sidebar honoring the fallen, leaving Nick to wallow in the misery of his own creation.

Hours of isolation passed. Nick felt hungry and needed a bathroom break when the door to his room swung open and a guard appeared, accompanied by a tall man dressed in civilian attire. The two men were engaged in a heated discussion. Nick didn't recognize the stern-faced stranger, nor could he read the ID badge clipped to the man's jacket pocket. Nick rose as the men entered the room.

"Mr. Severin, my name is Barnabas Pintero. I am the aide to Senator McCoy. It's a pleasure to meet you." Pintero extended a hand in greeting.

Frowning, Nick accepted the handshake.

Pintero placed a hand on Nick's shoulder. "Let's get you out of here."

Startled, Nick allowed the senator's aide to escort him quickly down the hallway. His eyes darting, Nick said nothing as he rushed alongside his unexpected savior. Pintero looked nervous, and he moved with ever-increasing speed until he and Nick were nearly running.

"I get the impression this isn't exactly kosher," Nick grumbled.

Pintero hauled Nick down a quiet hallway that led away from the main corridor. "Let's just say we want you out of here before the authorization credentials I presented have been thoroughly reviewed."

Pintero inserted his badge into a reader then pushed open a door that led outside to a clutch of trash dumpsters. *Fitting,* Nick thought as he raced past them. *Let's toss Severin out with the trash.* They had just darted around the hulking dumpsters when the alarm blared.

Pintero kept running.

The duo circled around toward the back of the building, where a black limousine pulled up alongside them.

No sooner had the vehicle stopped before Pintero shoved Nick inside. "They've noted discrepancies with your paperwork. Best check into that when you get the chance," Pintero said. He slammed the door, and the limo sped away.

Panting, Nick twisted on the fine leather seat to find Alessandra McCoy next to him. Stunned, Nick blinked at Alessandra. Feeling self-conscious about his appearance, Nick quickly swept the hair out of his face and wiped the sweat from his forehead with his shirt sleeve. He hated that he was hot, rumpled, and in need of a comb as he faced the woman who had played a role in his rescue. Dressed in a tailored red jacket and a pencil skirt that revealed a good length of thigh, Nick's gaze, as always, froze on Alessandra. For a moment, Nick's troubles vanished, and his primal instincts began to get the better of him. He longed to stroke Alessandra's shapely thighs. Squelching the raging thoughts, Nick laced his fingers together, swallowed hard, and breathed slowly.

"Nick!" Alessandra gave his arm a squeeze. "Thank God you're okay! I'd heard you'd been beaten up in the crash. Nice to know it wasn't as bad as it sounded."

The greeting took Nick aback. No mention that he was under suspicion of treason, that she'd used her considerable influence to spring him, that life as he knew it was over. He decided to follow Alessandra's lead and pretend his plight wasn't as desperate as it seemed.

"It's good to see you too, Sandra."

Her lovely eyes studied him. "Is it true what I heard? Were you injured?"

Nick nodded. "Damaged a few ribs, but they've been fused. I'll be fine in a couple of days." Not wanting to admit that he'd nearly succumbed to torture, Nick decided not to explain how his ribs had been broken.

Alessandra smiled warmly. "Good. I'm glad. You had us worried."

"*Us?*"

"Corey, Jordan, and me," she said, surprised. "Who else?"

"How is Corey? The last I saw, he'd been injured in the crash, but no one would tell me if he'd survived."

"You can decide for yourself when you see him. He was knocked around a bit, but you know how thick his skull is." She tittered uncharacteristically at her own joke.

"Yeah," Nick agreed, feeling a sudden unease. Something didn't feel right. Alessandra was acting as if nothing was wrong. But the world was wrong. Everything about *him* was wrong. To pretend otherwise was insane.

"No permanent damage then?" he asked.

"No. His beautiful face will shine on." She grinned.

Nick nodded. "Good to hear. I was worried. The Amaurau weren't gentle with him."

Alessandra's brow puckered. "*The Amaurau?* What do the Amaurau have to do with this?"

Nick scowled. "They saved us, Sandra."

"Saved who?"

"Everyone aboard *Far Horizons*. We crashed." He said this pointedly as if she lacked the intelligence to understand.

Alessandra cocked her head. "I know you crashed. Plowed into the Greentree dock works. The lot of you were lucky you survived." She eyed Nick nervously. "You do remember crashing into the dock works, right?"

Nick started to refute but hesitated. He had no idea why Corey had lied, but Nick decided it best not to counter those lies until he understood the reasons behind them. Perhaps Corey had developed amnesia or a similar condition that affected his memory.

"Any word on Jason McKittrick?" Nick asked. Nick desperately needed to find the man who held in his hands not only Nick's future but perhaps the future of the Alliance.

"Your bodyguard?" At Nick's nod, Alessandra shrugged. "I don't know. He disappeared."

"*Disappeared?*"

"That's what I heard. He refused treatment on Greentree, and that was the last anyone saw of him."

Again Nick felt his heart fall. He had to find Jason. Only Jason could attest to what had transpired in Gunera. Nick considered the limousine, which was inching through evening traffic. "You've got resources. You have to find him."

Alessandra shrugged. "I can ask. Why do I need to find him?"

"He can verify my story. I'm not a traitor, Sandra," he insisted. "I'm not."

She smiled and innocently patted Nick's knee. "Of course you aren't. We'll get it all straightened out."

Nick's heart quickened. "Will you be charged for helping me?" He gestured behind them. "Breaking me out of there? You didn't have the authority, did you?"

Alessandra laughed. "No! But when do I ever ask for permission to do anything?"

"You could be arrested!"

The beautiful woman hushed Nick. "Relax. I haven't done anything that Daddy can't resolve. I called in a couple of favors and promised some people access to him. He'll be furious, but he'll do it for his little girl." She smiled sweetly and batted her beautiful brown eyes. *She's always been able to manipulate others like puppets,* Nick thought. *A fringe benefit to being rich, beautiful, and a senator's daughter. No wonder Senator McCoy is putty in his daughter's hands.*

Nick glanced out the window. They'd entered the jungles outside the capitol, and night was falling. The limo's headlights cut a murky swathe through the humid air, revealing a one-lane road unknown to Nick. The road twisted through the darkness.

"Where are we going?"

Alessandra patted his knee once more. "Somewhere safe. Relax."

Easier said than done, Nick thought. Nick's nerves remained a jangled mess following his flight from the Justice Department and the thought that he was an escaped fugitive. His body shivered even in the warmth of the tropical night. He clasped his hands to avoid revealing his nervousness. The journey continued silently for another twenty minutes until the limo slowed. Nick looked out the windscreen at an iron gate bathed in the glow of the vehicle's headlights. The limo driver said, "We're here," into his phone, and the gates swung open.

They crawled along a winding drive that passed through a landscaped garden that was largely lost in the darkness. Nick noted garden lights and sparkling fountains, and he imagined life must be a paradise for its inhabitants. The drive ended in front of an imposing house, the Chateau McCoy. Although Corey and Jordan had spoken of it, Nick had never been to Alessandra's home. That exclusion had always stung, and Nick wondered why he'd not been invited prior to today.

The large, Baroque building bearing a hint of old-European grandeur was graced by a half-circular portico that prevented arriving dignitaries from having to endure the area's daily rain showers. Lights glowed warmly from diamond-paned windows, and gaslights burned at intervals along the gravel drive. *Every inch of this place screams of more money than I've ever touched in my life,* Nick thought. *Old money.* He could smell it even from the confines of the car.

As soon as the limousine stopped, its massive front doors opened, spilling a welcoming glow onto the marble pavers of the portico. The driver opened Alessandra's door, and she stepped out, followed by Nick. In the distance, a familiar silhouette loomed beneath golden lights.

"Corey!" Nick exclaimed. He walked toward and flung his arms around his longtime friend.

Uncomfortably, the young executive issued a pat. "Good to see you too, Nick. Um, you can let go now."

Nick staggered backward, surprised by the formal tone in Corey's voice. It then occurred to Nick that, once again, he'd failed to follow standard human operating procedures. This was neither the time nor place for warm embraces.

"Sorry," Nick mumbled. "I'm just glad to see you're okay."

"I know." Corey issued a trademarked ten-megawatt smile as he studied his friend. "I appreciate the sentiment, just not the execution." Corey turned to Alessandra and nodded. "No problems breaking him out, I take it?"

Alessandra gave a grand bow with a sweep of her hand. "Please, sir, don't insult my abilities. Pintero could charm the Devil into leaving Hell. Charming the Justice Department into letting Nick go without realizing it was far easier."

"It sounds like all hell's breaking loose," Corey said. He stepped aside as Alessandra wafted into her magnificent home. "RNN says the Gunera just took out the *Josef Rostov* destroyer. All hands lost."

Alessandra gasped, and Nick stumbled as Corey read from his phone. "'Experts fear a full border collapse is imminent unless the Alliance can move reinforcements from the Amaurau side of the nebula. The Amaurau issued a statement requesting a conference with the Secretary of International Trade. Specifically, they are demanding to speak with Nick Severin.'" Corey's eyes darted uncomfortably between Alessandra and Nick.

"How would the Amaurau know Nick was named Secretary *pro tem?*" Alessandra demanded. She turned accusing eyes on Nick.

The coldness of Alessandra's gaze stabbed Nick; he felt his heart skip a beat. *Even Alessandra doubts me,* he thought. *Whatever. I'm not going to answer her until I know where I stand. Until then, what little I know is off-limits.*

Corey continued chattering as the trio walked into the house. "'General Karageorges was quoted as saying he "doesn't want to reduce our forces on the Amaurau side."' He seems to think they're getting ready to act."

"Not surprising," Alessandra said. "It's the worst-case scenario we've all feared since day one."

"So we just allow the Gunera to take the Gate?" Nick demanded.

Corey rounded on him. "Unless someone can wave a magic wand and bring resources from Earth, we may have no choice. If we don't withdraw and defend what we can, Rhadamanthus could fall."

"Are people starting to panic?" Alessandra asked.

"Probably, but no one's bolting just yet." Corey glanced at Nick. "Your unauthorized exit is hitting the headlines. The police are on the lookout for you. So far, they're not labeling you a fugitive, but they're sure eager to have you back."

Nick swallowed. "I'm not surprised. Not with the Amaurau demanding to see me."

"The news is hinting you've got secret information about subversives," Corey added over his shoulder as he walked ahead of the group. "When I heard the case they have against you, I thought for sure you were going down. Then suddenly, there's news you're cutting a deal. What did you offer, Nick?"

Once again, Nick felt a frisson of unease. Although he trusted his two friends implicitly, he'd been deceived by too many people to blunder in wide-eyed wonder any longer.

"Nothing, because I haven't anything *to* offer. I'm guilty of treason. What more is there to say?" Nick asked, effectively killing the conversation.

The house is certainly grand, Nick thought. He'd always known Alessandra was wealthy—she oozed grace, charm, and money from every pore. But he'd had no idea the senator was this wealthy. The entrance hall was three stories high, the heavily paneled walls decorated with medieval armor and hundreds of banners. Priceless works by Degas, Van Gogh, Metzkel, Kelley, and others graced the walls. The floors were covered in marble mined from the Holden Crater on Mars; the fixtures were Zenith crystal.

Alessandra touched Nick's shoulder as they reached the base of a majestic staircase. "You look exhausted, Nick. What can we do for you?"

Nick felt lost. He considered himself a fugitive from justice, regardless of what the authorities were saying. He suspected the only reason Connolly hadn't issued a warrant for his arrest was because of the Amaurau's meeting request. The Justice Department couldn't present a criminal to the Amaurau as their ambassador. Furthermore, if Dessessah refused to admit she spoke English, no one on Rhadamanthus could replace Nick at the meeting.

Deciding he needed to bolster himself for what was forthcoming, Nick murmured, "I could use some food."

Corey flicked his eyes over Nick's rumpled appearance. "Why don't we find you a guest room? You can clean up. Sandra, order some food from the kitchen and have it brought up."

Nick noticed Alessandra's startled glance, but she immediately masked her uneasiness with a breezy smile. "Sure. Good idea." She pecked a kiss on Nick's cheek then headed for the back of the house.

Corey, acting as if he owned the house, led Nick up a curving stairway. Numerous coats of armor decorated the landing. Nick trailed his hands across the cold metal as he walked by.

"I had no idea you lived like this," he murmured.

Two steps above him, Corey darted a glance over his shoulder. "I don't, Nick. This is Senator McCoy's house, remember? You've been to my place a couple of times."

Nick recalled Corey's house, a sprawling rancher buried in thick jungle close to the city. Although a fraction of the size of the McCoy estate, it was a palace compared to Nick's tiny apartment.

"Why do you bother with me?" Nick asked as he stepped past Corey into an elegantly appointed bedroom. Like the rest of the house, it possessed a medieval air with a mahogany four-poster bed and a seventeenth-century suit of armor in the corner. Nick wondered if Alessandra's father had cornered the market on medieval armor.

As Corey flicked on the lights, he glanced at Nick with annoyance. "Why would you ask something like that, Nick? We're friends, aren't we?"

"Are we?"

The question stopped Corey cold and his handsome face puckered. "Look, I know it's been tough, but seriously. What's wrong with you?"

"What isn't?" Nick's shoulders sagged as he looked around the beautiful space. It occurred to Nick that the bedroom was larger than his entire apartment and the value of its furnishings far surpassed everything he owned. "Everything about me is wrong, Corey. Everything. I don't belong here, in this house. On Rhadamanthus. I don't belong in your circle of friends. Why are we friends?"

Corey's face twitched into a frown before his brilliant ten-megawatt smile resurfaced. He gave Nick a gentle cuff. "Because I like you, Nick. Isn't that enough?"

"Right now, I'm not sure."

Corey stared blankly. He seemed at a loss until his face softened. "It's okay. I get it. You've been through hell and back. You're not thinking straight. Get some rest; we can talk in the morning."

Nick stood between Corey and the door, blocking his friend from leaving. "I'd like to talk now if you don't mind." He realized his voice was getting sharp. It was a tone he'd never used with Corey. Corey's face became wary, and he took a step backward. "Why did you befriend me, Corey? Why did Jordan and Sandra? Did Duncan con you into it? The State Department? Were the three of you ordered to pretend to like me?"

Corey scowled. "No one ordered me to do anything, Nick. As far as I know, the same is true for Jordan and Sandra." He raised his hands and looked around the room. "There's no conspiracy here. It's just you, me, Sandra, and a house full of servants. There's no need to be paranoid."

Nick glared, feeling as if Corey was dancing around the truth. "I was conned into going to Gunera, Corey. My mom was brutalized before my eyes. I was tortured and almost killed. Then, when I finally make it home, I'm arrested for treason. At this moment, I'm not even sure I trust myself."

Nick's outburst seemed to ease Corey's tension, and he tried to smile.

"Yeah, I get why you're freaked," Corey said, running a hand through his hair. "I promise there's nothing going on here. I can't speak for Sandra, but I'm your friend whether you want me or not." He gave Nick a gentle shake. "Get some rest. You really need it."

Corey withdrew slowly as if Nick might suddenly lash out at him. "Goodnight, Corey," he said, feeling utter exhaustion stealing over him. *Maybe I am paranoid,* he thought as he watched Corey exit the room and close the door. *Maybe I'm becoming completely unhinged.*

Nick sank onto the bed and rubbed his face with his palms. He'd never understood his relationship with Corey, Jordan, or Alessandra. Nor could he imagine why three vibrant, important people would befriend him. He didn't understand human interrelationships and thought that, perhaps, he was being too hard on himself and on them. At the same time, he questioned their motives. When he'd first passed through the Gate at eighteen years of age, he struggled to speak English and hadn't comprehended anything related to humans or human culture. He was a public embarrassment the first time Duncan took him to a restaurant. And while he'd learned much over the years, Nick knew he wasn't an easy man to like. His words and demeanor were sometimes off-putting, his behavior occasionally bizarre, and he still lusted after women publicly despite knowing better. Why did his friends give a damn about him?

Feeling utterly alone, questioning every aspect of his life, Nick curled in a ball, still fully dressed atop the bed, and fell asleep.

Nick awoke disoriented. The lights were still burning, but a silence hung over the world that indicated the hour was late. At first, he wondered what had woken him, but then his stomach grumbled.

Remembering Alessandra had mentioned ordering food, Nick looked in his room and outside the door but found no tray. *Perhaps,* he thought, *they hadn't wanted to disturb me.*

He lay on his back staring at the ceiling, wondering what now would become of his life, if indeed he still had one. His mind replayed his testimony at the tribunal, pondering if he'd convinced anyone of his innocence. He suspected he'd swayed Chen. She'd understood what he was trying to say about the travel itinerary. *I'd been sent, damn it!* he thought, echoing his testimony. *I hadn't volunteered. And someone had known I wasn't coming back because they hadn't bothered to book a return flight.*

The thought stung as no other. Nick wondered if Duncan had simply overlooked it. He'd been under tremendous pressure with countless issues on his mind. The insignificant details of Nick's travel might not have registered. *And yet …* Nick thought.

He sat up, swung his legs over the side of the bed, and scratched his brow. Something wasn't right. He'd missed it during the stress of the trial, but now his mind niggled him. Something else was wrong with the itinerary. Nick strained to remember the details. A flight to the dock works with a transfer to a Guneri vessel. No mention of Jason McKittrick, but that wasn't surprising. Jason's travel would have been handled by his own office. Nick focused his mind's eye on Duncan's electronic approvals. Nothing odd about them either. Standard procedure. An electronic signature and date.

The date.

Nick's mind froze, unwilling to go where his intellect said he must. Directly to the heart of the conspiracy. It had been staring him in the face the whole time. The date of Duncan's approval. Independence Day. A full two weeks before the supposed attempt on mai'Tegatriktrik's life. Duncan had approved Nick's travel to Gunera before the reason for the travel had been conceived.

Dear God, Nick thought. *The man I'd thought of as a father was my betrayer.*

For long minutes Nick's mind refused to move beyond the realization that he'd been deceived and betrayed by Duncan Huntzinger. He sat staring blindly at the beautiful room, unseeing, unable to process anything but the date printed on the travel document. For ten minutes, Nick totally shut down.

Why? his brain screamed at him. *Why did Duncan betray me?*

I need answers, and I need them now, Nick thought, a*nd I'm going to get them from Corey and Alessandra in whatever bed they're sharing.*

He slid to the door and poked his head out, but only a dim hallway met his eyes. A light burned near the stairs, but otherwise, the hall drowsed in darkness. Every door was closed.

Quietly slipping into the hallway, Nick moved quickly toward the stairs. He studied his floor and the one below. The house appeared to be asleep. *This is going to be a long search,* he realized. *Let's try door number one.*

A darkened bedchamber met his eyes. Empty. Unused for a while, judging by the faint odor of dust. Same for the next four rooms he searched. As he progressed down the hallway, Nick felt his gut tightening. He told himself he was prepared for the vision of his two friends in bed together. They had to be lovers, he concluded. It only made sense. Corey had been too comfortable moving through the house. It was obvious to Nick that he'd been here many times.

He checked every room on the second level but did not find his prey. *Maybe I'm wrong,* he thought, not daring to hope.

On soft toes, Nick headed down the stairwell, straining his ears for any sound. He stopped when he reached the main hall, wondering if his friends might be in the kitchens. Perhaps he hadn't slept as long as he'd thought, and they were preparing food for him. He hoped the truth was that simple.

He chose a hall that led toward the back of the house. Midway through, he froze at the sound of male voices arguing. Nick doubted servants would be up at that hour, and he couldn't imagine Corey yelling at a servant or a servant yelling back at him.

The voices led Nick to a series of drawing rooms and an ajar door. The voices were clearer now. Nick recognized both, but they weren't the voices he'd been expecting.

"This is going beyond anything I ever agreed to," Corey said insistently. "I mean, for God's sake, you wanted me to pretend to like the man. I've done that. I've feigned friendship for ten years. That's quite long enough."

"We've got to return him to Gunera. Don't you understand how important that is? We're looking at total war, damn it!"

The words pierced Nick's heart, not only because of their severity but because of the man who spoke them. Duncan Huntzinger.

"I get it, Huntzinger!" Corey shouted. "Believe me, I do! You have no idea how hard it was for Dad to hold his tongue while the Gunera ransacked Eventide. But he did it. For the sake of the plan. For the Accords. But Christ, do you really expect me to mail Nick back to the Gunera?"

Nick felt as though he were entombed in ice. Even if the forces of hell descended on him at that moment, Nick couldn't have moved to save himself. He stood frozen and listened as the two men he'd trusted the most in life tossed away what little remained.

"I expect you to do whatever it takes to seal the deal with mai'Tegatriktrik," Duncan insisted. "We've gone too far. It's going to unravel unless we give the mai' something."

"How will returning Nick save the Accords?"

"The damned mai' wants him back! The snakes require the Accords to be legal, and they'll only be legal if Nick signs them. You have to understand Guneri thinking, Corey. They don't budge when it comes to their legal system. Jesus, it would all have been so much easier if Nick had just signed the damned parchment in the first place!"

"That was your first mistake," Corey growled. "Expecting Mister No-Nonsense to sign a document he knew was bogus. What the hell were you thinking?"

"I was thinking Combs would handle the bloody mess! Jackass, getting himself killed. Goddamned Amaurau interfering."

"Well, when they took him out, *you* should have gone!" Corey insisted. "Made up some excuse. Or just went AWOL. I told you Nick wouldn't sign. I told you!"

"I honestly thought we'd arranged things with the mai' well enough that Nick couldn't wriggle out of it. With me supposedly dead, Nick named secretary, and Sprouse ordering it, Severin should have signed. Damned fool!" Duncan leaned back in his recliner.

"Now we've got the Amaurau on our asses!"

Nick heard Corey's footsteps stride toward the door, but then they faded again. "They're demanding to see him as Protocol Officer. They're refusing to take Les as a substitute."

"What are those damned birds up to?"

"I don't know! But obviously, they're up to something. They had Nick for two days. Who knows what he told them! Who knows what they're thinking."

"I doubt he means much to them. They sold him back to us after all."

"Have you considered maybe they didn't sell him back? Maybe they *sent* him back. Maybe he told them everything, including the truth about us."

"He doesn't know anything."

"You can't be sure. The birds sent him back to blow the whole thing open. And he was about to do it. That damned tribunal is investigating his allegations. Jesus. We're just lucky Sandra got him out before he started singing like a bird."

"He can still take the fall," Duncan said. At that moment, Nick felt as though his heart had stopped. "He looks damned guilty, going fugitive. We'll package him up and ship him to the mai'. That'll keep his highness happy and put the kibosh on whatever the Amaurau are brewing. The Justice Department will have no choice but to declare Nick a traitor and disregard anything he previously told them. We'll have it all, just as I promised."

"How does that get us the Golgarag stardrive?"

"The mai' will complete the deal. If there's one thing the Gunera are good at, it's keeping agreements."

"What about the war?"

Duncan seemed unflapped by the question. "Once the mai' has his concessions, he'll settle down. vuh'Yguggli will have the damned stud he wants. We'll no longer police the universe. All will be right with the world."

"And the Amaurau?"

"Fuck the Amaurau," Duncan growled. "You'll have your money. I'll have mine. We can go wherever we damned well please, and the Amaurau can rot in hell."

"Aren't you bothered by what you're doing to Nick?"

"Yes, aren't you?" Nick asked, pushing the door fully open. His heart raced though he felt icy cold with sweat. His life was over. It had ended the moment he realized he'd been used by everyone, from his friends to his supervisor. *There's no one,* Nick thought, *not a single soul in the universe, who hasn't been using me from the start.*

Duncan bucked backward in his recliner while Corey spun around with a drawn breath. *At least Corey has the decency to look embarrassed,* Nick thought, *though Duncan looks cucumber cool.*

"Hi, Nick," Duncan said nonchalantly. "Glad you could join the conversation. We weren't expecting you, but your presence is certainly welcome."

"How so?" Nick demanded. He remained standing just inside the doorway, rage burning through every sinew.

Duncan waved negligently. "Since I assume you were listening, you know your immediate future determines the course of not only your own life, but ours and that of every man, woman, and child in the nebula."

Nick raised his eyebrows. His anger was so hot it was eclipsing his ability to feel any other emotion, especially betrayal.

"That sounds a bit melodramatic, don't you think?" Nick asked. He took two surprisingly steady steps into the room and only stopped when, equally calmly, Duncan drew a pistol from his belt. "It sounds like you have everything worked out. You ship me back to Gunera, and the mai' forces me to sign his Accords. You get the stardrive and money. vuh'Yguggli gets his breeding farm. The minor annoyance of people dying at the border goes away. Life returns to normal for everyone. Voila! The only person who pays is me." Nick paused to feign his admiration. "It's brilliant when you think about it. I'm impressed."

Corey's eyes darted between Nick and Duncan.

Duncan smiled benignly. "Thank you, Nico. I certainly think so, although I'm surprised to hear you say it."

"Why? You've obviously convinced yourself that it's all to the good for everyone, including me."

Duncan leaned forward, both his hands clutching the pistol. "It *is* for everyone's good. Don't you understand? The Balance has to end."

"Why?" Nick eyed the weapon, calculating his odds of successfully seizing it. He'd never fired a gun before, but he also knew Duncan was no marksman either. Nick also realized Duncan was older, slower, and perhaps not quite as determined as he was years ago.

"I knew you'd never understand," Duncan sighed. "That's why I didn't bring you into the fold."

"*The fold?*"

"Humans First," Corey murmured. He'd remained frozen several feet away, eyeing the firearm nervously.

Good old Corey, Nick thought derisively. *A coward to the bitter end.*

"I didn't see the point," Duncan said. "Given you were raised by the Gunera." He lifted his hand to forestall Nick's protest. "I know you hate the bloody reptiles as much as we do, but our reasons are different. I hate them because of the position their goddamned quarrel with the Amaurau placed us in. You have to understand, Nico, the Balance couldn't exist forever. Eventually, one of them would make a move, and we'd be casualties of the crossfire."

"Your solution was to unilaterally and single-handedly unwind the Balance," Nick scoffed. "Makes perfect sense."

"It does," Duncan protested as he rose to stand. "By unwinding it, *we* set the terms of its demise. *We* decide when it all goes to hell rather than waiting for the snakes or the birds to spring it on us. *We* make the decision. *We c*all the shots."

"Handing over our freedom to the Gunera," Nick asserted, disgust in his voice.

"We're *allying* ourselves with the Gunera, Nico," Duncan insisted. "We get out of the way, and the Gunera wipe the Amaurau from the nebula. Afterward, it's just them and us. Peaceful allies."

Agitated, Nick raked his fingers through his hair.

"Are you really that fucking stupid?" Nick asked. "You really believe the Gunera will become peaceful allies once the Amaurau are annihilated? The mai' isn't an idiot, Duncan. He'll betray our 'alliance' the minute the Amaurau are history. Why do you think vuh'Yguggli is contemplating his human breeding program? You're prepared to allow them to breed humans? You think humanity is gonna be okay with that? Blessed Jagjekcek, you're insane."

Duncan's face hardened. His fingers tightened on the pistol. "It won't matter to me, Nico. I'll be well compensated and can go where I like; the further away, the better. I'll never have to deal with the snakes or birds again."

"Ultimately, this is about your retirement?" Nick snapped. "Jesus. I'm glad my well-being ranks so high on your list of priorities."

Duncan glared. "Just stop, Nico. Don't act as if you're a victim. We both know you don't belong here. Lord knows I tried to humanize you. Ten years of my life spent trying to make you into a human to no avail. I knew it was a lost cause several years ago when I literally had to buy you a few friends."

Nick winced. His pained eyes darted to Corey, whose face smacked of shame as he looked away.

"Yes," Duncan growled. "I also bought your sex partners to keep you from going off the deep end and raping half the women in this city. I swore an oath to your father to take care of you, and I did my best. But of course it wasn't enough, Nico. You arrived too badly damaged." Duncan hesitated, and Nick thought he saw genuine pain in his blue eyes. "Would life on Gunera be so bad? You belong there. You're one of them more than you're one of us."

Nick stared hard at Duncan. "I'll be enslaved again and used to breed more slaves. You call that a life?"

"At least there you'll fit in," Duncan insisted.

"I won't even dignify that comment with a response."

"If you're expecting an apology, look elsewhere," Duncan huffed. "I took a bullet for you and for humanity as a whole. This is the only remaining option. It's better for everyone."

"It's better for you," Nick retorted. "You're selling humanity to buy comfort in your old age. To hell with the consequences. I'm sure you'll sleep well at night with a clean conscience."

Duncan appeared to be taken aback by the comment, which was exactly what Nick had intended. He wasn't about to submit meekly to the fate planned out for him. He knew at that moment he would resist it until his last breath. Not for himself but for the Balance and all it represented.

Duncan scoffed as he raised the pistol.

"You're not going to kill me," Nick said.

"No, but I can sure as hell shoot to wound," Duncan said. "Corey, find something to bind Nico with. Can't have him wandering around unsupervised; he might hurt himself."

Corey jumped at the terse command then looked around helplessly.

"Over there," Duncan said, turning his head to point at the curtain pulls.

Nick lunged, hands stretched for the pistol. He connected with Duncan's wrists. The older man reacted surprisingly quickly, drawing his arms upward. Nick managed to grasp only a shirt sleeve, but it was enough. His fingers dug into the cotton and he pulled, forcing Duncan's arms down. The gun discharged, propelling a bullet into the nearby sofa. Corey yelped and dropped to the floor. Nick threw himself bodily into Duncan, hoping his greater muscle mass would win against the older man's larger, heavier frame. Instead, Duncan held his ground, and the two men collided, each grappling for the firearm. Duncan's fingers flinched on the trigger, and the pistol discharged a second time, shattering a glass door that led to the gardens. Corey pressed himself into the carpet.

Duncan cocked his arm and slammed an elbow into Nick's face. The blow split Nick's upper lip open and knocked him backward, giving Duncan room to take aim at his former protegee. Nick's hands tightened, arms stiffening, to keep the pistol away from his face. He lunged forward, his forehead connecting with Duncan's temple, stunning them both. They staggered apart.

Nick quickly recovered and struck out with his foot, kicking Duncan in the shins. The man howled and swung at Nick with the pistol. It hit Nick in the cheek, and he nearly went down. Duncan took aim again. Nick twisted barely in time to avoid a shot that would have torn through his right bicep. His eyes spangled at the repercussion.

"Get the damned cords!" Duncan grunted as he attempted to kick Nick into submission. "The mai' needs him alive."

Corey scrambled to his feet. Nick knew that he didn't have a chance against both men without a plan.

He gave Duncan a chance to kick him a second time, but as he did, he tangled his leg into Duncan's, and the older man tumbled. Nick landed a strong kick to the stomach and leaped for freedom. He jumped over Duncan, lunged for the French doors, slammed his body directly through the glass, and ran. He dashed across the terrace and leaped over a low wall at its end. Nick hit a slope covered with recently watered plants and lost his balance. He slid downward, coming to rest in a pile on grass clippings at the base of the hill.

He turned and spotted Corey and Duncan above him, silhouetted by house lights. Wasting no time, Nick jumped up and continued to run. He dashed through the garden and heard a gunshot. He felt a sharp blow on the back of the head. It sent him flailing, and he landed face first on a gravel path where he lay stunned and unable to move.

Nick's vision failed, but the sound of heavy footsteps grew closer by the second. His instincts screamed. *Get up—run. They're coming for you.* He could hear distant grunting as they skidded closer. *Run, goddammit! Run!* Nick's mind shrieked, but his body refused to move. Even his eyes refused to open. The gravel felt cool against his face.

The world around him felt like snapshots from an antique Polaroid he'd once seen in a museum.

A cry of alarm.

Corey's voice.

The discharge of a firearm.

Screaming.

Scuffling.

Nick's lungs burned for oxygen, but nothing seemed to clear his throat. He tried to roll over but couldn't. The darkness hit him like a wall.

It seemed to last an eternity.

Nick's eyes opened.

A blurry world presented itself to him as he tried to blink away the tears from his eyes. After what felt like eons of frozen darkness, Nick's mind leaped at the ability to move his muscles. He felt sensation in his arms, but he couldn't move them. He could twitch his biceps. He felt fabric against his skin. Although his legs wouldn't move, he could still wiggle his toes. He could feel the rise and fall of his chest and the steady beat of his heart. *Praise Bibachek!* he thought. *Perhaps the nightmare is over.*

Nick turned his head at a sound to his left. His eyes focused on the smiling face of Jason McKittrick.

Nick's eyes widened, and he struggled to form words. His mouth resisted until a burble of sounds that were incomprehensible even to him tumbled out.

"Take it easy," Jason insisted. "Gonna take a while for everything to come back online."

"Thought. You. Dead." Nick managed, with extreme concentration.

The big man's body shook as he chuckled. He was seated in a chair next to Nick's bed, elbows on his knees, palms rubbing together. "No, sir. Not dead yet." He tilted his head to study Nick's face. He nodded approvingly and then slid back the bedsheet before sliding a hand along the length of Nick's right arm.

"Can you feel that?"

Nick nodded.

Jason grasped one of Nick's fingers and pinched it. "Which finger did I pinch?"

"One ... I'd use ..." The words started to form easier now.

Jason laughed. "Good, sir. I'll look forward to seeing you flipping me the bird." His huge hands passed along Nick's legs and feet. He gave the soles a tickle, and Nick jerked. He still wasn't able to move his legs, but he certainly could feel them. "Good. Sensation seems to be returning to the feet." He grinned, white teeth shining in his dark face.

"How long ... have I been ... asleep?" Nick asked.

"A ... while," Jason answered cryptically.

"Why can't ... I move?" Now that he was awake, Nick felt an urge to jump, run, and dance.

"You're restrained," Jason said. "We didn't want you leaping out of bed the moment you awoke. You'd likely injure yourself."

"*We?*"

"The docs, sir."

Nick fidgeted with his tongue, gaining greater speech control with each passing moment. He studied the sterile room—unadorned white walls, nondescript cabinets. The door to the room wasn't a door at all but rather an opening with brilliant iridescent light that was painful to look at. It was strangely empty for a hospital room.

"What happened?"

Jason grunted and sat down again. "Well, sir. That's a tough story." The big man glanced around as if debating what to say. "Today is March 12, 2256. You've been in a vegetative state for six months. Those weasels at State convinced pretty much God and country that you're to blame for the war."

Nick frowned. "Where am I? Why are you here?" His eyes narrowed in suspicion. He'd learned to trust no one. "You're more traitor than I."

Jason nodded and glanced down at his clasped hands. "Yep. I deserve that one. Been working with the Amaurau for five years." His dark eyes met Nick's, demanding the helpless man stay with him. "I've never done anything to endanger humans or the Balance, sir. I provided innocent information to the Amaurau when I felt it necessary."

Nick twitched his lips. "You're rationalizing."

Jason nodded and smiled. "Yes, sir, I am. Leave it to you to catch me in the details. Glad to see you're coming around."

Nick considered the room. "What is this place? What happened to me?"

"You were shot in the head. The bullet passed right through you, left to right, severing your upper brain from the lower. You'd have died, but your buddy Jordan Nash filed suit. Demanded you be provided all the medical assistance any human deserved as their right. Paid for your care in a long-term hospital. You own that man your life."

Nick's eyes flickered. While he hated to question Jordan's loyalty, it was necessary. Jordan was but another member of Humans First, another supposed friend Duncan had purchased.

Jason continued. "Nash got you the best care available. The finest neurosurgeons in the nebula sewed your brain back together."

"Why would Jordan do that?"

"Because he cares. He's a good man." The Jamaican's green eyes widened. "I get it. You think he's one of *them*. Nope. Not a member of Humans First and not in league with Huntzinger."

Nick was desperate to believe Jason but unsure if he should. "Are you certain?"

Jason smiled. "Positive. He was enraged to learn what those bastards had done. How they'd used you. I swear, half the reason he donated his personal fortune to bring you back to life was to shove a functioning Nick Severin down their throats."

Nick smiled weakly. "I'll have to thank him."

Jason nodded. "You will, sir. According to the docs, you're going to be fine. The neural fusions are taking nicely. You should be walking in a day or two."

Just as Nick began to feel at ease, he tensed again. "How did you get here? You were arrested."

Jason shrugged. "A bit of legal wrangling. I'm free but still under indictment. Have to face all that in the days ahead. But I wanted to be here when they brought you out of stasis. I figured you deserved to see a familiar face after the hell you've been through. Besides," he gave Nick a gentle shake, "you damned-near ruined my perfect record. I've never lost a client, sir. I'm damned grateful you weren't my first."

Nick laughed softly.

Jason tucked a blanket around Nick's shoulders. "Get some rest, sir. You'll need your strength once they get you moving. Physical therapy can be a bitch."

Nick wanted to thank Jason, but he felt exhausted. He managed to wave a hand before fading back to sleep.

When Nick awoke, Jason was no longer in the room. In his place stood a somber-faced woman wearing a nurse's uniform. Her blonde hair was bound in a tight bun, and her pinched face showed little emotion. Adding to her detached appearance was the pair of dark sunglasses that covered her eyes. Her feigned smile was as tight as her bun.

"Now that you're finally awake, I have a few tests to perform," she said emotionlessly.

"What kind of tests? Who are you?"

Ignoring his questions, the nurse began checking Nick's neurologic responses in a coldly clinical fashion. A pupil light reflex test was followed by an auditory evaluation and a deep-tendon reflex which she administered by jabbing a needle into Nick's skin. Her smile widened, and it occurred to Nick that she seemed to enjoy causing him pain.

"Please remove the restraints," Nick said.

Although he couldn't see her eyes, Nick sensed the woman's anger. "You don't give the orders here, Mr. Severin." To prove her point, she stabbed him in the base of his right foot. She made several notations on a tablet. "Peripheral motor skills acceptable," she said.

"Damn you," Nick growled.

The nurse set the tablet on the bed and pursed her lips. "Do you really want to go running around?" she asked. Nick nodded. "So be it. With any luck, you'll fall down a flight of stairs and crack your head open. It would serve you right."

"I'm not a traitor," Nick complained.

The nurse snorted under her breath.

"Go fuck yourself, lady."

Raw hatred twisted across the clinician's face. "There isn't enough money in the nebula for this job!" she growled. "To hell with all of you."

Without another word, the nurse ruthlessly unlatched the restraints on Nick's arms and legs. Desperate to move, Nick flexed his limbs. The hateful caregiver muttered something snide under her breath and then made a swift exit.

What the hell was that about? Nick wondered in stunned silence. *Granted, everyone probably believes the stories Duncan is telling about me, but I'd expect a bit less judgmental condemnation from a medical professional.* As Nick worked his muscles, he felt uneasy about this strange facility and the even stranger nurse. *Damned if something isn't very wrong.*

Confident that he could control the movement of his body, Nick cautiously sat upright. He drew his knees into his chest and huddled with both arms around his legs, studying his surroundings. The sterile room stared back at him blankly. No windows. No framed artwork or photography. Not even an anatomy chart to explain the many ways trans fats could be lethal. It was unlike any hospital room he'd ever seen.

Determined to stand, Nick swung his legs over the side of the bed and gingerly placed his bare feet on the floor. The coldness of tile penetrated his soles. He'd been wardrobed in scrub pants but nothing more. He shivered and felt faint. Nick clutched onto the bed railing until the sensation dissipated. He started to take a step forward. *Jason had been right,* he thought. *My first adventure walking will probably find me kissing the floor.*

Nick frowned. There were no sensors strapped to his body. No equipment monitored his respiration and heartbeat. The room lacked any medical equipment at all. Was his medical team extremely confident of his recovery? Or so sure he was a traitor they didn't care? Nick didn't know whether to feel relieved, concerned, or insulted.

Nick took a few cautious steps. At first, his legs seemed reluctant to listen, so he slowed his pace. He shuddered, fearing that his legs weren't actually attached to him. Suddenly, his body began to obey Nick's mind. He walked slowly across the small room until he reached the wall. His palm splayed against its cool smooth surface. *Strange surface, strange room,* he thought.

Nick felt his heartbeat accelerate. *Glad to know it still responds to fright,* he thought, although he wished he had no reason to be afraid. *Where am I?* His eyes darted to the mass of white light that was the doorway to his room. To view it brought pain to his eyes. He demanded to know why.

With one hand braced against the wall for support, Nick minced toward the doorway. When he reached it, the light was even more blinding than it had appeared from the opposite side of the room. His eyes filled with tears, and he blinked and squinted. He sensed movement. Fearfully he dashed forward into the room beyond, arms raised to defend himself against whatever might be coming at him. A cry of alarm followed. Still blinded, Nick floundered into a surface that felt like a desk. He fell against it, arms extended to break his fall. Objects caught in the path of his flailing arms shot to the floor. A pair of hands tried to grab Nick, but he struck them away in terror.

This is no hospital! Nick thought. *Jesus! What has Duncan done to me now?* Panic-stricken, Nick whirled around, trying to see into the blinding space. *It has to be vuh'Yguggli's farm,* he thought. *The vision of Jason had been either a dream or a drug-induced hallucination. They're readying me for the vuh's vile farm.*

More hands tried to grasp at Nick, but he lashed out wildly. Something fell to the floor and shattered. He heard a scream. Voices shouted. He blinked, desperate to see.

A stern voice spoke sharply. "Stop before you kill yourself."

The voice sounded familiar, and he tried to place a face to it.

"I can't see!" he wailed.

More hands grappled him. They caught his arms and pinned them behind his back. His shoulders were restrained as well. The hold was neither brutal nor gentle. Nick struggled against the implacable restraint, but he realized he wasn't being forced around. He was merely held as he expended what little energy his body possessed. The struggle ended with Nick feeling totally exhausted.

"It's all right. No one is going to hurt you. The light is too strong for your eyes. You should have let us prepare you."

Nick blinked uncontrollably; his eyes continued to be awash with tears.

"Close your eyes. You won't be able to see no matter how hard you try."

"Why not?" Nick demanded.

"If you value your eyesight at all, you'll keep them closed." Nick reluctantly nodded, and his companion grunted in approval. "Give me your hand."

He reached out blindly and found his fingers laced with another's. Those who had been restraining Nick ceased their hold on his body.

"Come with me."

The hand guided Nick along. He walked, clutching the hand, the only solid object in a frightening ethereal world.

"Is this Gunera?" *The blinding light must be the Guneri sun gleaming on the white walls of Imperial City,* Nick thought.

The question was answered with a deep chuckle. "No, this isn't Gunera. Keep walking. Not much longer now."

"Where are we going?"

"Only to the counselor's office."

Nick frowned. It was the sort of statement a schoolteacher would make of a recalcitrant pupil. "I don't think I want to go there."

Again his guide chuckled. "No matter. We're here."

The guide eased Nick to a chair

"Keep your hands over your eyes. I've sent for a screen."

Nick frowned at the cryptic comment. *Why would I want a screen?* But he didn't argue. He sat quietly with his palms to his eyes, listening for sounds that might provide clues about his location. He heard only the gentle whoosh of an office building ventilation unit, the murmur of distant voices, the bells from some sort of mechanical system, the tapping of fingers on computer equipment. *How have I gone from a hospital room to an office building?*

Nick heard footsteps as someone entered the room and stood beside him. "Lower your hands but keep your eyes closed," the voice commanded.

Nick did as ordered. A blindfold was tied around his head. Panicked, he tried to remove it, but a pair of hands prevented the action.

"Relax, Severin," the voice stated. "You should be able to open your eyes now."

Fearful of what he might see but also curious, Nick did as instructed. His blindfold was a bit of gauze fabric that eased the glare against his pupils. Although the world was fuzzy, Nick could tell he was in an office. A desk stood in front of him, and windows glared beyond. A shape moved between the desk and the window before sitting down.

"Better?"

Nick looked around. Two individuals flanked him. He had to look a long way up to see their faces. They were Amaurau in military attire, rifles on their backs, lyssestra strapped to their arms. Their black eyes gazed at him emotionlessly.

Squinting against the glare, Nick could finally identify the man seated behind the desk.

"Ambassador Ississita."

"Welcome to the Grand Republic of the Amaurau, Sevay." Ississita spread his hands in greeting.

Nick might have jumped up, but his guards placed their hands on his shoulders in warning. He considered removing his blindfold.

"I don't suggest it," Ississita said. "Our sunlight is too strong for your retinas. You'll just blind yourself if you remove the screen. You've been without any vision at all for more than six months, Sevay. Asking your eyes to see in our light is asking too much."

"What am I doing here?" Nick asked, panic swelling in his chest. "Dear Jagjekcek! What do you want with me now?"

Ississita's face hardened. "Do not swear in the name of your Guneri gods here," he said. "If you must swear to mythical creatures, let them be of human origin."

Nick wasn't in the mood for cultural niceties, not after everything he'd been through of late. "Fuck that, Ississita! Tell me what I'm doing here!" He leaped to his feet, but he immediately regretted the impulse as pain shot to his head. "Dear God! Amaurau! Why did you bring me here?"

"To save your life," stated Ississita in that ever calm manner Nick recalled from the Independence Day party.

"Why would you want to do a thing like that?"

Ississita's head tilted. "Is your life not worth saving?"

"No."

"*No?*" Ississita sounded amused.

"Certainly not to my own people."

Ississista gestured to the chair. "Sit, Sevay. Sit before you fall over."

Grudgingly, because he knew Ississista was right, Nick sank into the chair. The guards made no move to restrain him. Nick supposed he looked pathetically weak and not worth the effort.

"I'm sitting," he growled. "Why am I here?"

His brusqueness didn't rattle the alien's composure. Ississita continued to smile as he accepted a teacup from an aide. "As I said, you were brought here to save your life, Sevay." The smile remained even as he sipped his drink. "To answer your first question, you're here because you are valuable to us."

Although it was the answer Nick had expected to hear, it still shot a wave of panic through his body. *Jesus! Still more people using me,* Nick thought. *When will it ever end?*

"Whatever you want of me, I won't do it."

Ississita lifted his brow quizzically. "You're so certain we want something of you." When Nick offered no reply, Ississita set down his cup and clasped his long fingers together. "Of course you're right. We do want something of you, but it's probably not what you're thinking. Have you nothing to say?"

"Why would I? I'm your prisoner, aren't I?"

Ississita laughed quietly. "You are not." He gestured lightly. "You're free to go whenever you wish."

"You'll kill me."

Ississita's smile faded. "I'm not a barbarian, Sevay. You may go."

Nick rose to his feet on unsteady legs. Although he sensed his guards unholstering their rifles, he lurched toward the desk anyway. But it was the windows, not Ississita, that interested him. He longed to see what no other human had ever beheld: the world of the Amaurau.

Even through the thin gauze covering his eyes, Nick immediately recognized it as the landscape he'd seen at the forward station. A blinding pink sky arced overhead adorned by the three crescent moons. On the near horizon, a huge ship blasted off, engines burning white against the brilliant pink. Smaller ships, which Nick assumed were likely transports and personal craft, plied the air currents. Among those were even smaller objects which he initially thought were large birds. *Not birds,* Nick thought, *the Amaurau. The Amaurau in flight.*

Nick held his breath as he watched them soar. They didn't exactly fly but rather glided.

Which only makes sense, Nick thought as he considered the topography. The landscape was a Karst plain. Pink spires of rock jutted into the air, some thin and delicate like needles of stone, others more massive like the high rises of Rhadamanthus City. They rose out of a sea of green, a forest as great as the jungles of Rhadamanthus. The vista was an endless march of forest punctuated only by the spires of stone. Why the Amaurau evolved, flight suddenly made sense to Nick. They simply, he realized, launched themselves from their fortresses of natural stone and glided from one tower to another. *It's alien; it's breathtaking; it's anything but home,* Nick thought, staring in awe.

He turned toward Ississita.

"Where do you expect me to go?" he asked. He couldn't escape the tower, let alone the planet or the Grand Republic.

Ississita gestured. "You may return to human space if you wish, though that's probably not your best option at the moment. Or you may return to your masters in Gunera. You may remain here in Amaurau if you dare. Or you may take the easy way out and kill yourself." Nick flinched. "Are those not your options?"

"I suppose they are. I didn't expect them to be stated so baldly." Nick's eyes narrowed. "What would you do if I demanded to be returned to human space?"

"I would try to talk you out of it. There's still a death warrant waiting for you."

Nick flinched again, bothered by the ambassador's candor. "If I choose Gunera?"

Ississita sighed and rubbed a finger across his temple. "I'd order a freighter to haul you to a forward station. Couldn't drop you off like ordinary freight at a dock works because the humans would kill you. I'd be forced to invent some ridiculous story about misplaced freight for the Trade Commission and have the Gunera pick you up. It would be most tedious."

Frustrated and feeling shaky, Nick returned to his chair.

"If I chose suicide?"

"Obviously, I would mourn the loss of you."

To Nick's amazement, Ississita pealed the lyssestra from his arm and laid it on the desk between them. He said nothing. Nick eyed the deadly weapon but made no attempt to retrieve it.

"Is that really what you want?" he demanded. "Did you really drag me halfway across the nebula and unscramble my brains merely to see me take my own life? Is this some sort of Amaurau honor ritual?"

Ississita laughed. "How I wish it were, Sevay! You've been a royal pain from the onset. I should have killed you in the garden."

Nick lifted his chin, fighting down the fresh rush of fear that burned through his chest. "You've been the instigator from the start," he growled. "All of this. From the day you crashed the Independence Day party."

"I can assure you," Ississita said, his smile ever present, "it was well before that, Sevay. I became involved when I learned Sevay Lincoln was working to break the alliance."

"When you learned …" Nick murmured. He wished the gauze didn't cover his eyes so that Ississita could read the rage burning in them. "You're not actually an ambassador, are you?"

Ississita waved his hands in a grand gesture. "I am not. I'm an agent in the employ of the Alien Intelligence Office. It's my job to know when aliens are plotting against us."

Nick felt his heart sink. "How did you find out?"

"I have spies, of course."

"Jason McKittrick." Nick wasn't sure why knowing that hurt so badly, but it did. Right to his soul. *Even damned Jason lied to me.*

Ississita bowed his head but said nothing.

"You son of a bitch."

The outburst earned him yet another of Ississita's smiles. "I'm not sure how my relation to a wolf creature of Earth has any bearing on this discussion, but for your sake, I'll accept that it does."

"Jason was in on this from the start."

Ississita waved but said nothing.

"Jordan?" Nick asked bitterly, determined to get the very last name sorted out. *There's no one else in the universe who could be out to betray me,* Nick thought. "What was Jordan's piece in the game?"

Ississita's head tilted. "Jordan Nash had no part to play, save to deliver you into our hands at the end."

"I don't understand."

Ississita leaned forward. "I was sent to Rhadamanthus to kill you, Sevay. The plan was as simple as that. Sevay Jordan had no part in it. Not on our side, at least."

"You just admitted he handed me over to you," Nick protested.

"Because the poor man had no other option." Ississita settled back in his chair again, aware that the brilliant windows behind him were blinding Nick. "The brain damage you sustained was beyond what human medicine could correct. You could be kept alive with machines, but the neurological damage could not be undone. Sevay Jordan arranged for your long-term storage where you would have survived for a few years, but he did not want that to be your end. We offered him a solution."

"I'm sure you're going to explain it to me."

Ississita fiddled with the lyssestra that still lay on the desk. "Sevay Jason informed us that you had been totally paralyzed. After we arranged Jason's release from the military police, we asked him to contact Sevay Jordan and offer our help." Ississita picked up the lyssestra and waved it in the air. "While the Gunera have been busy building faster starships and the Alliance has been reaping unparalleled revenue through its taxation of the universe, we Amaurau have not been idle. We have been focusing the energy we once wasted on warfare toward bettering our society. We've made huge strides in our study of neurology, among other medical fronts. We knew we could fabricate replacements to the damaged neural networks in your brain."

"And Jordan accepted the offer?"

"Of course. As I said, he had little choice. Humans couldn't save you, but we could. We agreed to hire a human nurse to attend to you and concurrently brought Sevay Jason here to watch over you."

"Why not Jordan?" Nick asked.

Ississita issued another grand gesture. "We don't allow alien visitors. It was enough that we allowed the nurse's presence. Not that she was happy about the assignment. Sevay Jordan spent a fortune to convince her, though it didn't really seem to matter."

Nick grunted at the understatement. *No wonder she was so rude,* he thought, *and so anxious to run for her life.*

"We considered the nurse and Sevay Jason to be adequate to your needs."

"Why Jason?"

"We wanted him here to aid in your mental stabilization when you were revived. We feared you might lose your mind if you awoke to find yourself surrounded only by Amaurau."

Nick nodded in agreement. "I'd likely have jumped out of my skin."

His fingers brushed the gauze blind. Although he was beginning to realize a handful of people actually cared about his well-being, he still felt horribly alone, appallingly small, and utterly helpless.

Nearly blind.

A million miles from home.

Homeless.

A traitor who could never return to Rhadamanthus and who would never voluntarily return to Gunera.

That leaves the Amaurau, Nick thought. *The people who'd been using me from the start and who are still playing games. Still in need of their little human piece. Lord only knows what they'll want of me now.*

"What will you do with me?" he demanded. "Obviously, you think I'm still useful." Nick lifted his chin. "You should have left me to die. I won't help you."

"No?"

Nick shook his head. "No."

"Not even after we saved your life?"

"For your own purposes, not for mine." Nick tried to glare at the shadow between Ississita and the windows. "I won't help you, Sevay. I refuse. Whatever you want, you can go to hell."

Ississita again fiddled with the lyssestra. "I don't want anything, Sevay. I'd be more than happy to send you to your final rest. But that isn't my prerogative. I'll let you give your answer to those who actually care."

Those who care, Nick thought. *Harsh words.* "They'll receive the same answer."

Ississita grunted and rose. He moved to the door, murmured to someone outside the room, and returned to Nick's side.

"Close your eyes, Sevay," he commanded.

Knowing he was in no position to argue, Nick obeyed while Ississita removed the gauze covering his eyes. It was immediately replaced with a fully light-proof blind.

"Why?" Nick asked as the blind was tied firmly, plunging him into darkness.

"Since you're determined to shove our compassion in our faces, you'll need to do it with someone who cares. Far be it from me to save you from your foolishness. I'll escort you, but your eyes must be protected from our sunlight. I'm afraid, Sevay, you'll just have to trust me."

Although Nick wanted to say he'd never trust another soul, he knew he'd be wasting his breath. Ississita's cold expression indicated he didn't care. He aided Nick to his feet, after which his long, delicate fingers gripped Nick's forearm. He led Nick unhurriedly from the room. The pace had to be agonizingly slow for an Amaurau. Not only was Nick one-half Ississita's height, he was still unsure of his legs' stability and totally blind. Only once did he try to lift the blindfold. The blaze of sunlight was so intense that Nick screamed. He quickly replaced the blindfold and made no further attempts to remove it. Helpless, he stumbled at Ississita's side while the stoic Amaurau remained silent.

The walk seemed endless. Nick panted from the exertion. He'd been immobilized for six months, Ississita had said, while they knitted his brain back together. Although they had performed therapy to limit muscle atrophy, Nick realized that nothing could replicate his full body weight moving in a walk. *No wonder I feel as weak as a child,* he thought. When he stumbled, Ississita grasped Nick firmly to keep him upright.

As they walked, Nick heard whispers from the Amaurau they passed. The sight of a half-naked, barefoot, and blinded human drew startled comments that Nick tried to ignore. He didn't want to hear one more species excoriating his name. But they didn't. Instead, he heard *Severin* whispered with something akin to wonder. Nick flinched when someone touched him, and he cowered against Ississita's slim body. Ississita, however, paid no attention. He simply walked on, keeping Nick on his feet.

Nick was staggering with exhaustion and clutching Ississita's feathered arm when the Amaurau finally stopped. Ississita shoved him down, and Nick dropped onto a hard, stony surface.

Quicker than Nick could blink, Ississita whisked off the blind and replaced it with gauze. Through the mesh, Nick watched Ississita approach a series of glaring windows that darkened at his touch.

"Remain here," Ississita commanded. "Your new owners will arrive shortly to collect you."

"*New owners?*" Nick asked.

Ississita laughed. "You were property in Gunera, were you not? You bear the implants of property which we can read just like the Gunera. If you leave this place, we'll track you down. You've enemies enough in this universe, Sevay. I'd suggest you make nice with the handful of people you haven't offended."

Laughing, Ississita swept from the room.

Nick stood in thoughtful silence as he gazed out the polarized windows at the alien landscape. He'd been waiting for hours. The limited patrol of his prison told him it was an apartment with a kitchen, a living room, an office, and a bedroom. Not much different from a human residence. Yet, it was also thoroughly alien. The dining table rose to his shoulders, and the chairs were barstools on steroids. The furniture in the sitting area was tall and uncomfortable. The place was utterly silent. Not a hint of speech came through the thick wooden door, nor did he hear the sound of mechanicals turning on and off.

Nick suspected its owner was a high-status individual. The furnishings seemed luxurious–damask fabrics on the upholstered pieces, and fine carving on the wooden ones. The dining table possessed incredible grace with its thick piece of glass atop arching metal legs. A delicate silver light fixture stood in its center. To keep warm, Nick nabbed a plush, soft, and silky throw he'd found near the fireplace. Like everything else, it screamed status.

Nick stiffened when the door opened. He turned to see Dessessah enter. Nodding, she peeled off her lyssestra and dropped them on a table, followed by her necklace of grenade stones. She murmured something about changing clothes and disappeared into the back room, leaving Nick with her weaponry. Not that she needed to worry. He couldn't use them. He knew he wouldn't survive two steps outside Dessessah's door. He was her prisoner whether she locked the door or not.

She returned several minutes later wearing a flowing dress with a halter neckline that left her downy back and feathered arms bare. Nick gazed at an exposed area of her chest, although her figure was birdlike. Silver bracelets clicked from her wrists; long, dangling earrings brushed her shoulders.

"Welcome to my home," she said. Her dark eyes flicked over him, noting his blindfold. "Ah, pardon. Ississita did warn me." Preening her long head feathers with her fingers, she swept to the windows and darkened them further.

When she returned, she deftly removed the blindfold.

"Much better," she said. "Are you hungry?"

What a banal question to ask, he thought. *Like I'm merely a guest dropping in for a visit.*

"I suppose."

She nodded and drifted into the kitchen. Nick remained next to the windows. A few minutes later, Dessessah reappeared carrying a basket which she set on the high table. From it, she withdrew objects required for an Amaurau-style meal. She set the table with long, narrow spoons, pointed sticks, and small bowls of colorful enamelware, several of which she filled with a red liquid. Once finished, she gestured to the table.

"Dinner is served, Minister."

"I'm no longer the Minister." Nick didn't know what sort of game Dessessah was playing, but he didn't intend to indulge her.

"Dinner is served, Sevay Nicodemus," she corrected. Her voice was soft, cajoling.

Nick shivered as the sound trilled across his nerves. He detested her strange ability to make him shiver.

"Don't try to seduce me," he growled. "I'm done being used."

She smiled. "You're a liar. We Amaurau have long known that if we modulate our voices just so, it causes a certain resonance in the bones of the human ear, providing pleasure. I could reduce you to a helpless pile of quivering flesh were I to press hard enough."

Nick flinched, stunned to know she'd been playing him from the start. "Then you admit that you manipulated my mind, brainwashed me."

Dessessah laughed. "Of course! I admit it. I've used the ability as necessary." She tilted her head. "I never used it to brainwash you, however. Only to convince you of the sincerity of my words or to comfort you." Nick scowled. "On the night we met, you were in tremendous pain. I used my voice to soothe you to sleep."

Nick well remembered that night. How his headache had been intolerable and how she'd entered his room upon hearing him tossing. He'd thought she'd seduced him with her fingers. Now he knew it had been her voice.

"Don't use it on me anymore! I resent it."

"As you wish." She gestured to the table. "Please sit down. You haven't eaten in some hours, and humans, like Amaurau, become cranky when they're hungry."

"I'm not cranky!"

Dessessah's smile deepened. "Of course not."

Nick felt his stomach rumble. "I suppose I might be hungry. And cranky."

Reluctantly, he considered the chairs. They were too tall for a human, and he had to climb into one like a toddler scaling a jungle gym. He sat with his legs swinging, feeling like a child. Dessessah sat in an adjacent chair and offered him food from the bowls.

The Amaurau diet was not much different from a human diet, although they preferred their food unprocessed with few sauces or spices. It was plain, simple, organic fare. Nick selected a number of vegetables and various seeds. The red liquid, Dessessah explained, was fermented berry juice. Nick sipped cautiously.

"I assume you're my new owner."

Dessessah turned her head, a delicate fragrance wafting at the shift of her long head feathers. *Perfume?* Nick wondered.

"Why do you think I own you?" Her eyes sparkled as she sipped the juice.

"Ississita mentioned it."

She chuckled a soft birdlike sound. "It's a lovely thought. I rather like it. Owning you." She smiled slyly but sobered upon seeing Nick's incensed expression. "Ississita is playing with you. I own you no more than any other Amaurau could own you. We don't own people, Sevay. The concept is a Guneri one."

Nick eyed her suspiciously. "Then why am I here?"

Dessessah set down her enameled bowl. "Because a man of my acquaintance wanted to meet you. I promised him if I had the chance, I would bring you here. The severity of your injuries made taking you possible, so I snatched you." She tilted her head. "It was to your benefit, wasn't it?"

"Considering if you hadn't, I'd presently be in a vegetative state, yes," Nick admitted reluctantly. "So it was your idea to bring me here, not Ississita's?"

She warbled a laugh. "Ississita would slit your throat before he'd offer you hospitality. He's old-school in that regard. Give him time, Sevay Nicodemus. Work on him with your quirky charm like you do all who know you. I'm sure you'll sway him in the end."

Nick snorted. "If I'm so charming, why does the entire universe want me dead?"

"The entire universe doesn't want you dead," Dessessah insisted. "On the contrary, most of the universe wants you alive, well, and in their possession." When she saw his look of disgust, she gave his arm a poke. "I'll admit the Western Alliance takes a dim view of you, but that's only because a handful of malcontents have slandered your name. However, mai'Tegatriktrik would trade an estate to have you back; vuh'Yguggli would sell his tail. I can only imagine what gy'Bagrada would be willing to yield to possess your title."

"Yeah, I'm well-loved in Gunera," Nick grumbled.

"Some in Amaurau love you as well."

Nick jerked. "That's not funny, or remotely true."

Dessessah sipped while her dark eyes flicked over Nick. "It's true, Sevay. I told you an Amaurau wanted to see you. Expressly asked if I could obtain travel visas for you. Fortunately, I was successful."

Nick's eyes narrowed. "What Amaurau? Why?"

She didn't answer. Instead, she traced her fingers across the smooth surface of the tabletop, which acted as a computer console. With it, she could control the visuals on a wall doubled as a projection screen. A photograph of two Amaurau appeared. Nick could tell the one on the left was female by its smaller size and the quality of the feathers. She was older. The feathers around her eyes and mouth were turning white against the backdrop of soft tan. The male was taller and darker, his feathers a warm brown, but he, too, showed signs of age. The female wore civilian dress while the male wore some sort of body armor, although his feathered arms were bare.

"I don't know them," Nick stated.

Dessessah extended a long finger. "His name is Tisstrisha. He was elected Grand Chairman of the Central Committee an unprecedented eight times. Many thought he would serve for the rest of his life, but he stepped down several years ago for health reasons."

Nick considered the photo. Although he knew little about the structure of the Amaurau government, he suspected the title of grand chairman equated to something like president. Neither the photo nor the knowledge that this was a powerful individual held any meaning for Nick; he waited for Dessessah to explain.

"Among my people, Tisstrisha is considered a hero, a living legend," Dessessah explained in a soft, reverent voice. "He served well as chairman, and no one wanted him to step down, but his age is beginning to wear on him. He lives now in constant pain." She gestured to the body armor. "He must wear that special appliance to aid in walking, otherwise he would be bedbound."

"Not a pleasant situation," Nick commented dryly.

"Certainly not for an Amaurau," she agreed. "He's used to the armor now and has worn it for most of his life."

"Where's this story going?"

Dessessah sighed. Her face showed both love and distress. "Before he was elected chairman, he was a member of our diplomatic corps on the Guneri side. The choice was a brave one. While most Amaurau could tolerate some interaction with humans, very few will deal with Gunera. Tisstrisha did so as a young man."

Nick lifted a brow but said nothing.

"That position nearly destroyed his life," Dessessah said. "He was sent to Gunera to deal with the vuh'Gragalag uprising. I'm sure you've heard of that, Sevay."

Nick nodded. "vuh'Gragalag killed my father. Enslaved my mother."

"Enslaved *you,*" she added gently. Her right hand rested atop Nick's left. Nick considered withdrawing his hand but didn't.

"The vuh' tortured Tisstrisha," Dessessah whispered. "Broke his back. Nearly killed him." Her eyes sought Nick's. "Do you know why he survived that horror?"

Frowning, Nick shook his head.

"Tisstrisha survived because the human President of Hemera, Nicodemus Severin, ordered a lightning raid on the compound where he was being held. Humans freed him, Sevay. Your father freed him."

Nick considered what he'd read of the uprising. He vaguely remembered the story of the Amaurau ambassador his father had rescued. He'd never given any thought to what might have happened to that individual. His eyes studied the projection and the image of the Amaurau his father had saved at the cost of his own life.

"What does he want of me?"

The fingers on his hand tightened. "He always wanted to thank your father. He knew the raid had been impossibly dangerous and was only undertaken to rescue him. He knew the risks your father took and was sickened when he learned Severin died in his place." She gave Nick's hand a tug to draw his eyes back to her. "He wants to thank the son since he can't thank the father."

"You brought me the whole way to Amaurau for that?" Nick exclaimed.

Dessessah's brows arched. "You sound annoyed."

Nick gasped in frustration. "Not that I'm complaining, Sena, but sainted Bibachek, that was a lot of work to help an old man express his thanks."

She laughed. "He's not just an old man. He's a hero. A legend. All of Amaurau worships him." She smiled tenderly, her hand still gripping Nick's. "He's also my father."

Nick caught his breath.

Dessessah's fingers caressed the back of his hand. "Your father saved his life and made my life possible. *Of course* I'd bring you here if I found the means. How could I allow the son of such a man to die in misery and disgrace when I possessed the ability to stop it? How could I, knowing all that you personally conceded to save the Balance? How could I, Sevay?"

"I don't know what to say." Nick blinked rapidly.

"Say nothing," she said. "You will meet with Tisstrisha and allow him to thank you for the sake of your father. I know you'll do it with grace."

"Grace!" Nick grunted. "I am anything but graceful, Sena."

"My name is Dessessah," she said. "I ask that you use it. You're like family to us—my father, my mother, and me." She nodded at the picture. "They're anxious to meet you. For a man raised by the Gunera, you have such a lovely charm. My parents will adore you."

Nick eyed her dubiously. He felt at a loss for words.

"Forgive the impertinence, but I will ask," she pressed. "Permit my father to call you *Nicodemus*. Sevay would seem so formal to him."

Nick shook his head to clear his thoughts. "Sure. You both can. I don't generally stand on ceremony. The name is Nick, by the way. No one calls me Nicodemus."

"Victory for the people," she said, surprising him by remembering the translation. "Such a fitting name for both you and your father."

Nick felt his budding joy ebb away. "No, it's not. I've been a disaster to my people." Feeling annoyed with himself and what he considered his many failings, Nick slid off the tall chair and stormed away.

"How have you been a disaster to your people?" she asked.

Nick threw his arms wide. "Look at what I've done! My people are at war with the Gunera. They're dying because of me."

Nick stopped near the windows and stared blindly at the beautiful scene through the heavily polarized glass. He heard movement behind him but didn't turn. He shivered when Dessessah wrapped her long arms around him and pressed her chest into his back.

"You did everything you could, Nicodemus," she whispered, resting her chin on the top of his head. "You did far more than anyone had any right to ask of you. More than I ever dreamed when I realized the danger we'd placed you in."

"Danger? What are you talking about?"

"The destruction of the *Death's Festival* placed you in mortal danger."

Nick felt himself tense and knew she must have felt it too. "You ordered its destruction?"

Dessessah's chin shifted as she nodded. "Yes. When I learned of the plot Humans First was brewing from Jason McKittrick."

Nick sighed despondently. "I won't claim I'm happy that a man so close to the President is an Amaurau agent."

"I wouldn't describe him as an agent," Dessessah said. "He's been a source of information for us, nothing more." At his snort, she gave him a gentle shake. "He's not an agent, Nick." Her voice sounded amused as she spoke his name. "Some years ago, he was aboard a transport that ran into mechanical difficulties. Its life support had failed. The ship drifted into Amaurau space and was rescued by our border patrol. Jason was the sole survivor aboard. The patrol returned him to a transshipment dock. As a sign of gratitude, he promised to provide us with information as he unearthed it. Understand, Nick, he was never an agent. He never accepted commands from us. He merely forwarded information that he thought might be of value to us, but nothing that could lead to human harm. That's all. Jason informed us, and his own superiors, of the Humans First plot. Unfortunately, it appears those self-same superiors were members of Humans First; they ignored him."

"How did you do it? You must have used human forces. No Amaurau ship could have gone that far and back without being caught. Jason must have given you resources to annihilate that ship."

Dessessah shook her head. "I swear he did nothing. The decision, planning, and attack were all handled by Amaurau forces. It was not an easy decision for us because it meant that we would assassinate a human of high status within the boundaries of human space. Earth is our ally, and the action we were contemplating frightened us all. If we were caught, the Balance would have ended at that moment, and with us to blame."

"How did you do it?"

Her arms tightened around him. "We gambled. Nowhere along the *Death's Festival's* flight path would it cross close enough to our republic for us to launch an attack. We equipped a small transport ship with large-capacity fuel tanks, packed it with explosives, and removed its transponders and flagging. One of our pilots volunteered to navigate it straight into the *Death's Festival.*"

"A kamikaze," Nick breathed. "No wonder I couldn't make sense of it. I never thought the assailant would plan a one-way trip."

"The plan worked," Dessessah said quietly. "Lissansaht will be remembered for her bravery."

Nick stood in silent memorial to that lost pilot whose sacrifice had not saved the Balance, only staved off the unwinding a month or two. He closed his eyes and whispered a prayer, hoping the loving arms of human or Guneri gods would find her since she hadn't any gods of her own.

Nick reopened his eyes and frowned. "You knew humans were plotting to end the Protocols. Why didn't you protest? Demand retributions? It's what the Gunera would have done."

The arms tightened again. "The Central Committee met in heated discussion. Many felt we should allow the evil to run its course. Others suggested we start the war on our terms. Fortunately, saner minds prevailed. We decided to maintain the Balance. However, we knew the treachery wouldn't stop with Lincoln Combs. The mai' would try again, and we knew whom he'd approach next."

"Me," Nick whispered.

Again her chin nodded against Nick's hair. "Yes. We assumed he'd come for you, so the committee made the decision to eliminate you."

Nick flinched.

She gave him another squeeze. "I fought with the committee for hours, trying to convince them the son of President Severin wouldn't allow himself to be used by the Gunera. Unfortunately, the committee refused to listen. It felt your upbringing offset any ties of blood to your father. Hence the vote to assassinate you." She rubbed her cheek in Nick's hair, sensing his increasing distress. "I did, however, convince the committee members to allow you a chance to save your own life."

"How so?"

"The committee agreed to permit me to accompany the mission. En route, we were stunned to discover your appearance at the renewal ceremony. We assumed we would arrive on Rhadamanthus after the ceremony and deal with you at that time. However, we were monitoring Alliance news transmissions and saw the altercation between you and the assassin sent to kill gy'Gravinda. We assumed you'd gone to the ceremony intending to take up where Combs left off. We knew we had to act."

"That's why you appeared so suddenly."

"Yes," Dessessah said. "We hadn't planned it. But Ississita was determined to stop you. Your defense of gy'Gravinda convinced him you were already a part of the plot. He felt we had to kill you that very night. So we landed and then crashed the party."

Nick groaned. "How is it, then, that I'm still alive?"

"The agreement that I made with the committee was specific. Your fate was in Ississita's hands. He was determined to eliminate you, but he agreed to first question you. If you were to convince him of your honesty, he would, in return, withdraw the assassination order."

Nick tilted his head to look at Dessessah's frame as she towered over him. "Again, how is it that I'm still alive?"

"Because we took a walk in the garden," she chuckled. "Ississita lured you out there to kill you."

Nick shuddered, and Dessessah's comforting arms tightened around him once again. "I felt it," he murmured. "I sensed my life was in terrible danger that night, but I felt powerless to do anything. God, I was terrified of that fountain."

She laughed. "With good reason. He would have used it to end your life."

"Why didn't he?"

"Because you answered his question."

"What question?"

"How you personally felt about the Amaurau leaving the Balance. You said it would be devastating. You told him the Balance was a sad, tilting affair, built on uncertain ground, but that it was all we had. You told him you would defend it with your life, if necessary."

"I meant it."

Dessessah adjusted her face, and Nick thought maybe she kissed his hair. "I know. Your response convinced Ississita that I'd been right—a Severin wouldn't destroy the Balance."

"So he spared me."

"Yes. He didn't even tell me his decision. I only knew when he walked away, leaving me there."

"Why did he leave you behind?"

"To protect you."

"From what?"

Her laugh warbled in his ear. "We knew the Gunera would still come for you. I wasn't joking when I told you that day on the beach that your life was in danger, that you were the weapon we couldn't allow the Gunera to possess."

"I thought you were threatening to kill me."

"No. I was promising to protect you. I ran my scanner over your location implants so that no matter where you went for the rest of your life, I would know where you were." Her hands caressed his tattoos. "And I will, Nick. You will never again be alone. I will always know where you are."

Nick caught his breath at the soft words and the gentle caress. She'd moderated her tone, and as it fluted signals along his nerves, he shivered but with pleasure. *Someone,* he thought, *actually cares about me. Me. Nick. Not the president's son, or a useful slave, or a talented interpreter. Just me.*

"I'm not sure how I feel about you following me wherever I go," he murmured.

She chuckled, her breath causing his hair to flicker and tickle him. "You have no choice, Nick Severin. I have your signals. Forevermore I will know if your heart is racing or calm, if your blood boils or runs cool. I have taken the burden of your life in my hands. I will not hold it lightly."

It was a hell of a thing, Nick realized, knowing the Amaurau had followed every move he'd made since that day on the beach. They'd been watching him from the very beginning.

Nick pulled himself away from her embrace and marched across the room. The revealing conversation was disturbing. He couldn't believe the extent to which he'd been used. He stopped near the fireplace and rubbed his face with his palms. "If all this time you'd been assigned to protect me, why did you leave me when I went to Gunera?"

She spread her arms, feathers fanning wide. "What else could I do? Demand your superiors to rescind the order? Drug you myself and take you prisoner?" She hesitated at that thought, and a soft smile crossed her lips. "Perhaps I should have. It would have saved a lot of pain. Unfortunately, you weigh too much for me to carry you off."

Nick waved a hand at his surroundings. "It seems you've carried me off this time."

"I had help."

Realization dawned. "You sent Jason to guard me."

Dessessah nodded. "It was the only option I had. He understood the importance of keeping you safe and volunteered for the mission."

"He wasn't joking when he said he didn't have permission to leave his post?"

"No. He was absent without leave. Unfortunately, it blew his cover, but he felt strongly about going. Like me, he values the legacy of the Severin family; he also refused to see you harmed."

"He was certainly dedicated to the job." Nick recalled that the big man had never left his side.

She smiled. "Indeed. He swore he'd never leave you, and I don't think he did."

"No."

"I couldn't contact him, so during your travel to Gunera, the only information I could access was provided by your location implants. I was, frankly, shocked when you spent two days in the palace of the mai' then another two being hosted by gy'Bagrada."

Nick threw his hands in the air. "The mai' was holding me captive in his dungeons where he tortured me … and my mother."

"I know that now, but I didn't then."

"So now you believe me?"

"I believed you the moment I saw that barb wound in your shoulder. I could imagine no reason why the Gunera would stab you except to demand your compliance." She blinked unhappily. "I'm sorry for distrusting you. I couldn't trust my own instincts when my intelligence indicated you'd signed the new Accords and spent time with the mai' and the gy'."

"As a prisoner," Nick complained.

Her fingertips touched his face. "Forgive me. But yes, I thought you'd deceived me. When you arrived at the forward station, I was certain I'd been made a thorough fool. I would have killed you on sight, except I knew a death sentence awaited you on Rhadamanthus. Thus, I decided to reap value for my troubles by trading you back. As soon as I saw your wound, I realized I'd made a terrible mistake." She tilted her head. "Why did you lie about it? You could have admitted that you'd been tortured. I would have believed you."

"I didn't know if I could trust you," Nick said. "At that point, I didn't know if I could trust anyone. I was so damned angry at you. There was no way I was going to plead for my life. Besides, I knew I had to return to Rhadamanthus."

"Even though I told you about the death sentence."

Nick shrugged. "I had to try to save the Balance, Dessessah. I had to."

She smiled and cupped her long fingers under his chin. "It was a brave thing to do. Incredibly stupid, but incredibly brave."

She drifted toward the windows, appearing deep in thought.

Nick gazed bleakly around the room. "All right, so I'm here. I'll accept the grateful thanks of your father on behalf of my father. What happens to me afterward?"

Dessessah turned. "That's for you to decide. My only desire in bringing you here was to see my father's dream fulfilled. Beyond that," her free hand drifted in the air, "there's no plan. Concepts and ideas, yes, but no plan."

Nick looked her in the eyes, seeing only concern for him in their depths. "What do you suggest I do?"

Dessessah pursed her lips while considering the question. "It seems you have three choices. You can return to your people to face whatever justice they will demand, although I don't suggest it. The members of Humans First have covered their tracks and placed the scuffle with Gunera at your doorstep."

Nick groaned.

"Your second choice is to return to Gunera."

Nick muttered, "Gunera."

"It is the only other home you know," she said pragmatically. "And I believe the mai', vuh'Yguggli, and gy'Bagrada each desire to possess your title."

"My title."

"Yes. We'll sell you to the party of your choice and demand all legal titling be done prior to handing you over. You'll be guaranteed to remain the property of the party you select. I would suggest the mai'. I suspect imperial enslavement would confer the highest standard of living. Although suffering as the lover of gy'Bagrada might have its allure if you wish a life of leisure."

"And a daily trip to the 'special room,'" Nick snapped. "No thank you."

Dessessah didn't ask what he meant by the remark; he could see by the twitch of her lips that she understood. "As I said, it's your choice."

"I'd take the mai' if that's the only choice I have."

Dessessah looked down at her hands as she rubbed her fingers together. "There is a third choice. You could return to humanity as Protocol Officer."

Nick grunted. "No chance, Dessessah. My brethren will kill me the moment they get their hands on me."

"Not if you return as Protocol Officer."

Nick guffawed. "As if that's gonna happen!"

Dessessah lifted her brows. "You assume I mean the *human* Protocol Officer. What if, instead, you returned as Protocol Officer to the Amaurau?"

Nick blinked. "What did you say?"

"You will return as the Amaurau Protocol Officer."

Nick stared at her, still unsure if he'd heard her correctly.

She poked him. "Go as our officer, as our ambassador to humanity." She could tell he was still struggling to grasp the concept. "The General Committee has already discussed it, and everyone agrees you would make a splendid officer. You speak fluent Gunera. You understand humans at a level well beyond us. And no one knows the Protocols like you do."

"Amaurau hate humans."

Dessessah laughed. "Not true. Some of us find you annoying. Some find you greedy. But most of us appreciate that you've thrown yourselves into the breach between the Gunera and us and have paid a high price in doing so."

"Ississita doesn't like me."

"Ississita is an ass."

Nick's lips twitched, surprised by her bluntness.

She grinned. "It's true. He's old school and old money. Dreams of the grand-old days when we ruled ourselves without the interference of humans. He doesn't dislike you personally, Nick. He dislikes your entire species. As I mentioned, if you work on him with your particular charm, I think you'll win him over."

Nick folded his arms and grunted. "Somehow, I'm finding that hard to believe. I also can't believe the Amaurau would accept a human as their ambassador. No one would ever trust me."

Dessessah's hands gripped his arms, and she gave him a gentle shake. "A few wouldn't, but most would. Your name was revered long before you ever rose to prominence. And now, with the news of what you've done for the Balance, even old cushions like Ississita grudgingly agree you are worthy of our trust." She tilted her head and smiled. "You're becoming a legend, Nick. The son who rose above the father."

Nick shook his head. "No."

"Yes."

He sighed. Rubbed his temples with his palms. "I don't know what to do. I'm lost, Dessessah. You can't believe that I belong here. I'd be the only human for a million miles among a species I know almost nothing about. A race that hasn't a clue about what it means to be human. Hell! I can't even open my eyes outside your door! Where do I belong, Dessessah? Where have I ever belonged?"

The emotional plea caused her to blink, and Nick realized he'd brought her to tears. She wiped them quickly away, then walked toward the windows and adjusted the polarization to allow more light to enter. "You're at a strange place in your life. You, alone, may choose where you go."

"It's not much of a choice."

She gestured out the window. "Do you know why Amaurau fly?" she asked.

Nick shook his head, not understanding the sudden change in topic. "Because it's easier than walking?"

She laughed. "That's certainly true. But there's a more important reason. You see how this continent is built, its topography."

"Yes. We call it a Karst. Heavily eroded rock. It makes the spires."

Dessessah nodded. "Did you notice the forests that carpet the canyons?"

Nick nodded, wondering where she was wandering now.

"Carnivores live in the forests. They love to eat Amaurau."

Nick opened his hands, palms out. "And?"

"They aren't intelligent even though they're quite smart. They infest the forests so the forests are unsafe for Amaurau to walk in. That's why we evolved to glide. Our ancestors took refuge on the spires. To form communities, we needed to soar. To hunt, we learned to glide. To land is to be eaten."

"I'm not sure I understand how this relates to my fate," Nick murmured.

She raised her brows. "Why do you suppose those carnivores exist?"

"To eat Amaurau?"

She laughed. "They eat anything they can catch. We just happen to be one of the larger prey available on the planet. No, they exist because we haven't killed them."

Nick frowned. "I don't understand."

"If this was Earth, and Amaurau were humans, do you think carnivores would lurk at our feet?"

Nick considered the question and shook his head. "No."

"Why not?"

"Humans would have hunted them to extinction."

"Because?"

"They were a threat to humans' survival."

"And humans don't allow threats to survive."

"A few would be allowed to remain," Nick reasoned. "Kept in zoos for study and entertainment."

Dessessah stood at the windows in silence.

"I don't understand what you're trying to tell me!" Nick protested.

Dessessah pointed out the window. "Those carnivores are there because we haven't killed them. Because we live within the environment we've been given. Only humans rewrite their worlds, decide which creatures live and which creatures die. Only humans take entire planets and make them into their own world's image. You, Nick, are human."

Nick lifted a brow. "I think we've established that."

She spread her hands. "You must follow your species' destiny. You must carve out your own world. Don't allow the universe to make *you* suit *it*."

Nick considered her earnest expression, then the world beyond her shoulder. In typical Amaurau fashion, he realized, she'd made him think.

"Consider it," she said. "In the meantime, meet my father. Listen to what he has to say. Then make your decision." She ran a fingertip down the bridge of his nose then sauntered away to clear up dinner.

Nick collapsed onto the stone ledge of the hearth. *Damn,* he thought, *I'll never get ahead of her.*

Nick twitched uncomfortably as the sewing continued. He'd been trapped in a chair for almost an hour as three Amaurau stylists wove threads adroitly through his hair. One by one, the long, dark feathers were attached until his head was covered. They weren't a perfect match because Nick's hair was darker than Amaurau feathers. The closest match of feathers, chocolate brown, was offered by Tisstrisha. The poor man was now bald and enjoying every minute of it.

"I'll fledge new feathers in a month," he insisted. "For now, I'm proud to donate all I possess so that our young Protocol Officer is adequately feathered."

When Nick stood, the feathers just brushed the ground. The sensation was strange but tolerable. Dessessah was insistent he was Amaurau now. As such, he needed to look the part.

Along with the bizarre headdress, he was clothed in flowing Amaurau robes tailored to fit his diminutive size. He even wore a strand of explosive beads around his neck (though he patently refused to adorn earrings).

Dessessah approached him, bearing two lyssestra. She measured them against his forearms, but his limbs were too short for the traditional weapons.

"I'm afraid I'm going without them," he said.

"No Amaurau travels without his lyssestra," she stated. "That includes you, Sevay Nick." She rapped him playfully with one of the sticks while considering her options.

She called for a knife, and Nick chuckled at the thought that she'd chop the things off to fit him. She set the lyssestra on the floor and knelt beside him. Without warning, she slit open Nick's trousers from hip to knee.

"Dessessah!" he protested. "What are you doing?"

"An Amaurau never travels without his lyssestra," she repeated. She pressed a lyssestra to his bare skin along the muscle of his thigh. It stuck there of its own accord.

Nick fought to keep from dancing away from her as her fingers pressed the second weapon to his skin. The intimate touch of her hands was startling.

"Much better," she commented as she rose to survey her results. "Your thigh bone is the perfect length."

Nick fluttered the trousers uncomfortably. "It's a bit airy for my taste."

She grinned. "Unfortunate but necessary, Sevay. You'll wear your lyssestra whenever you leave Amaurau. We'll have you fitted with trousers that feature custom-made slits as soon as possible."

"Dessessah!" Nick protested. He felt ridiculous walking about with his legs exposed. As he fiddled with the trousers, he realized he'd need to be careful when sitting down to avoid any unnecessary exposures of flesh.

"No complaints, Sevay," she commanded. "You cannot wear them any other way."

"Can't we cut them down?" he protested. "I'm sure they'd look better on my arms."

"No. I like the slits." She grinned. "Your legs are handsome, Sevay. The sight of them will drive gy'Bagrada wild."

Nick rolled his eyes heavenward. "Dear God!"

She stood him at arm's length to study the effect. Nick was sure he looked ridiculous. A human could never look like an Amaurau, but he knew that wasn't really the purpose. Dessessah was determined to make a statement to the Alliance that Nick was valued by the Amaurau people and that he'd be defended should anyone act against him. The feathers and lyssestra were merely the Amaurau marking their territory.

"Okay, I'm ready," Nick announced.

His heart thrummed in his chest, knowing what he was about to face. While Dessessah had confidence in him, Nick felt less self-assured. Nevertheless, he'd made his commitment to the Amaurau Protocol Officer. *There's no going back,* he thought.

The new Amaurau delegation had landed on Rhadamanthus and taken up residence in a mansion not far from the Capitol building. The diplomatic corps of Rhadamanthus had been taken completely by surprise at the sudden appearance of fifty Amaurau demanding permanent accommodation on the planet (as per Protocol A6 subsection 2.a[1] paragraph 95) and had scrambled to rent the mansion from its out-of-town owner. Immediately thereafter, the Amaurau landed, shocking the city to its core. The news media flocked to the mansion to obtain photos and interviews, but the reclusive aliens remained true to their nature and stayed out of sight. Dessessah was taking no chances. She wanted the element of surprise firmly in her grip.

Nick moved with his corps through the hallways of the capitol building toward the assembly hall where nervous members of the

Western Alliance awaited the arrival of their uncertain allies. With war still raging on the border shared with Gunera, the humans had no choice but to accept the Amaurau with decorum even though every man, woman, and child on the planet was terrified by what the sudden appearance of the aliens portended. The news media filled the hallways, recording video of the tall, stoic aliens as they strode swiftly toward the assembly hall. Because Nick was shorter than the Amaurau entourage, he was well concealed in their midst. No one was aware that a human strode within the Amaurau contingent.

When they reached the assembly hall, President de Walt hurried forward to welcome the group. At her side strode Duncan Huntzinger, the only human left in the nebula who spoke the difficult Amaurau tongue. Ississita stood at the vanguard of the Amaurau faction. He bowed to de Walt but gazed scornfully at Huntzinger.

"Welcome, Ambassador," de Walt gushed while Duncan translated at her side. "While we're surprised at your sudden appearance, the Western Alliance is happy to see you." She paused to give Duncan time to translate. Ississita continued to stare at him without a word. "We've been understandably nervous about your government's take on the situation," de Walt continued.

Ississita quirked his lips. "President de Walt, your welcome is gracious. The Grand Republic of the Amaurau assures you of its continued friendship with the Western Alliance."

The relief was so obvious on de Walt's dark visage that even as he peered between his bodyguards, Nick could see a visible change in her complexion. She'd been terrified, he realized, waiting for the Amaurau ax to fall.

"You're most kind, Ambassador," de Walt said, attempting a curtsy.

"I'm afraid I must correct you, Sena," Ississita intoned. "You are much in error."

De Walt's eyes flicked toward Duncan, and Nick could read the question she couldn't voice. Duncan's face was white with strain as he gave the slightest shake of his head.

"My apologies, Ambassador," de Walt stammered. "How might I have offended you?"

A dark chuckle escaped Ississita's lips. His was a low, haunting sound that could cause anyone in earshot to shiver. Ississita could disconcert an enemy with just a laugh. "You haven't offended me. Not yet."

De Walt stiffened. "I don't understand, Ambassador."

"That's precisely my point. I am *not* the Ambassador. I was merely sent to hand the baton of my office to the new Ambassador."

"*The new Ambassador?*" de Walt spluttered.

Ississita grinned as he stepped aside, revealing Nick, who stood behind his flank. "Sena de Walt, I am pleased to introduce Sevay Nicodemus, the new Protocol Officer for the Amaurau. Sevay Nicodemus has graciously agreed to take the office."

De Walt's complexion faded as Duncan stifled a choke. Nick thought his former boss might faint. Nick stepped forward and gave the bow-cum-curtsy required of his office. "Madame President," he said in English. "It's an honor to be working with you again."

Audible gasps echoed throughout the human delegation all the way to the press corps. Nearly a minute of astonished silence elapsed before members of the media resumed the task of recording the historic event.

"You're the ... Amaurau Protocol Officer?" de Walt garbled. "I don't understand."

Nick wore a placid smile, recalling the weeks of painful training in Amaurau mannerisms he'd endured. "Since humanity saw fit to toss me aside, the Grand Republic of the Amaurau elected to snare a *human* resource that was no longer wanted."

"I still don't understand," de Walt stammered again.

Nick bobbed his head. "Madame President, would you not agree that I *am* the foremost authority on the Protocols?"

De Walt stood blinking at Nick in complete bemusement until her diplomatic training took hold. She smiled grimly. "Yes. Why are the Amaurau here? What do they want?"

Nick's smile deepened, but it wasn't pretty. "They wish to begin discussions that will result in the signing of Amaurau Protocol 10."

De Walt's eyes darted among the alien delegation. "Protocol 10 is still more than four years away."

Nick nodded. "It's going to take that long."

The President's mouth hung agape until she recalled that the press corps was broadcasting the event live. She snapped her mouth shut and, with a taut smile, gestured to Duncan. "I believe, Secretary Huntzinger, that would be your area of expertise. I'll leave you to it."

Without another word, she bobbed something vaguely resembling a curtsy to the Amaurau delegation and scuttled to escape the assembly hall, leaving a dumbfounded Duncan Huntzinger to deal with the mess.

Duncan's blue eyes burned with fury. "Don't think you're going to get away with whatever game you're playing, Nico," he hissed.

Nick raised a finger. "Careful, Duncan. The Amaurau are more fluent in English than you're aware."

Duncan's lips pressed tight as he studied the crowd of well-armed Amaurau warriors that surrounded his erstwhile undersecretary.

"Is this serious?" he demanded.

Nick gestured to his new assistant, Jashassha, an eager young soldier bursting to kill his first alien. The Amaurau youth stripped off his lyssestra with smooth grace, set a dart to it, and flicked it to readiness onto his shoulder. Duncan's face blanched.

Nick's smile never wavered. "So, Secretary Huntzinger," he said, "shall we begin our negotiations? I sincerely hope you're prepared; they're going to be very expensive."

MEL LEE NEWMIN

Science fiction and fantasy author Mel Lee Newmin is a native of Lancaster, PA, home of the Amish and not much else. Following a career in corporate accounting, Mel began a new profession as a fiction author. Mel's short stories can be found in numerous publications including *Ligurian Magazine*, *On the Premises*, *Sixfold*, *Full Metal Horror*, and *Rapture*. Mel's 2021 science fiction novel, *Noman's Land*, is available from Clarendon House.

Mel chronicles the exploits of Baltimore-based vampire hunter and detective, Niles Gule, in a weekly web series available at newminworlds.wordpress.com and vampiresofbaltimore.wordpress.com. Visit to learn more about Niles as well as Mel's other projects.

In addition to writing, Mel paints, serves as a library bookstore volunteer, and mentors other aspiring writers. Mel still calls Lancaster home, along with Jojo and Lizzy, the incorrigible corgis.

Made in the USA
Middletown, DE
26 August 2022